BLUE MOON

Ruby Bateman works at the prestigious Warnes Hotel on Worthing seafront. She enjoys her job and the camaraderie with the girls at the hotel, but she also loves a day off. On an outing to the Sussex Downs, Ruby meets handsome photographer Jim Searle and instantly falls for him. The only cloud to overshadow her otherwise perfect trip is the dark mood of her father when she returns home. Ruby dreams of a life outside of the seaside town with Jim, but it falls to her to hold the Batemans together. However, a long-buried family secret may just undo all her hard work.

BLUE MOON

BLUE MOON

by

Pam Weaver

Magna Large Print Books
Long Preston, North Yorkshire,
BD23 4ND, England.

British Library Cataloguing in Publication Data.

Weaver, Pam
    Blue moon.

    A catalogue record of this book is
    available from the British Library

    ISBN   978-0-7505-4264-7

First published in Great Britain in 2015 by Pan Books
an imprint of Pan Macmillan,
a division of Macmillan Publishers Limited

Copyright © Pam Weaver 2015

Cover illustration © Gordon Crabb by arrangement with
Alison Eldred

Published in Large Print 2016 by arrangement with
Macmillan Publishers, trading as Pan Macmillan Publishers Ltd.

Magna Large Print is an imprint of Library Magna Books Ltd.

Printed and bound in Great Britain by
T.J. (International) Ltd., Cornwall, PL28 8RW

To Mark and Heather Weaver –
the best brother and sister-in-law a girl could have

CHAPTER 1

Ruby Bateman glanced up at the clock in the corridor. The slow tick-tock reassured her that although time was passing, she was doing well. She was still ahead of herself and could probably get away a little earlier than she had anticipated. She pushed the heavy linen trolley towards the next room. Only three more to go. She knocked gently on the door and listened.

At the other end of the corridor Winifred Moore, the florist, looked up and waved shyly. A homely woman, she was working with a large vase of unruly gladioli on the table at the top of the stairs, her Sussex trug full of beautiful blooms at her feet on one side, with a galvanized bucket with the dead blooms on the other side. Ruby returned her smile and knocked again.

As chambermaid at the prestigious Warnes Hotel on Worthing seafront, Ruby had to follow the strict protocol that Mrs Fosdyke, the housekeeper, had drummed into her from the moment she'd arrived. She and Edith Parsons were responsible for the whole of this floor. Edith worked in rooms 20–29, while Ruby cleaned rooms 30–40. They were supposed to work quietly and quickly and, as far as possible, to be so unobtrusive as to be invisible. Because of that, they must never go into the rooms if the guests were still there.

'You are servants of the hotel,' Mrs Fosdyke told

them on the day they'd arrived, 'and, as such, you must always be polite to the guests, but never treat them in a familiar manner. Remember that the guests who stay at Warnes are a better class of people.'

If, by any chance, a guest returned to the room before they had finished cleaning, Mrs Fosdyke went on to say that they should extradite themselves discreetly and come back later. They were on no account allowed to speak, unless they were spoken to, and must certainly never indulge in friendly conversation. That might have been the rule, but of course Ruby didn't always stick to it.

At seventeen, she was an attractive girl with short, dark hair and large brown eyes. She had been born and brought up in Worthing, a town that, although often overshadowed by its larger and flashier neighbour Brighton, had a secret charm all of its own. She lived only a short walk from the hotel with her mother and father, her younger sister May and her older brother Percy. Family life was not always easy. Her father and brother were fishermen and there was always a risk, where the sea was concerned, but Ruby loved where she lived. Even though it was by the seaside, Worthing remained rustic and unspoiled. There were a few tourist attractions: the Dome cinema, the pier, and Ruby loved walking along Marine Parade. If she took a bus, within minutes she could be on the Sussex Downs or in one of the small villages on the outskirts of the town. But most of all, she loved people. In fact she often struck up a conversation with a guest. Some were fascinating, like the very old lady (at least seventy) who had come to Warnes for a few days, before travelling back to her home in Monte Carlo. During the several days the lady had stayed at Warnes they'd talked about her career on the stage, and Ruby had got on so famously with her that Mrs Walter de Frece had given her a signed copy of her auto-biography. It wasn't until she saw the title, *Recollections of Vesta Tilly*, that she realized who she'd been talking to. And then there was the butterfly man, who'd spent the whole of last summer going out in his motor car to collect specimens from the South Downs. It broke Ruby's heart to see them all quite dead and pinned in his cases, but he was fascinating all the same.

The hotel didn't have any interesting guests at the moment. She'd chatted with Dr Palmer in room 31, a studious and serious man. She had discovered that he had recently retired from some big hospital in London (she'd forgotten the name) and that he was in town to give a series of lectures about the events unfolding in Germany. She had wanted to ask him what he thought about Herr Hitler, but then she'd heard Mrs Fosdyke in the corridor and had made her excuses to leave the room before she got caught.

Ruby knocked on the door of number 38 for a second time and, when there was no answer, she went in. The room was tidier than most, but the bed was unmade.

She picked up a discarded bath towel and threw it by the door, ready to push it into the laundry bag on the end of her trolley when she left the room. She moved around quickly and quietly, working methodically so that she didn't miss

13

anything. She made up the bed with clean linen. At Warnes – being a more upmarket hotel – every bed was changed daily.

Stuffing the soiled bedclothes and the towel into the laundry sack, Ruby reached for the bathroom cleaner. The guests at the other end of the corridor shared a bathroom, but here, in the rooms with a sea view, they had their own. She rubbed gumption onto the enamel sink and cleaned the tide-mark left on the bath. Next she polished the taps and replaced the towels with snowy-white replicas. The toilet bowl got the same treatment, and then she mopped the linoleum floor, being careful to reach into every corner, and not forgetting the area behind the S-bend. Mrs Fosdyke would check every room, and woe betide any girl if she found so much as a speck of dust or a stray hair in the bathroom. The bedroom itself had a thorough clean and, as soon as she'd finished with the Vactric vacuum cleaner, Ruby got ready to move on to the last two bedrooms.

She'd only seen the guests who occupied these two rooms a couple of times. He was small with round-rimmed specs, and Ruby guessed that he was a learned man, because he always seemed to have his nose in a book. He said little, barely even acknowledging her existence. He was staying in the hotel with his daughter, who had the adjoining room. She was a pale girl with dark circles under her grey eyes and an anxious expression. She was about the same age as Ruby, and although she was staying in the best hotel in Worthing, she seemed a little distracted. Ruby had bobbed a curtsey a couple of times when they'd bumped into each other in the corridor, but hadn't spoken to her.

As soon as she was satisfied with her work, Ruby took one final look around the room and was content to close the door. Another glance at the clock at the end of the long corridor told her that she was still in good time.

She had come in early today. Her normal day began at six, but because her neighbours on Newlands Road were going on an outing later on – something she herself had instigated – Ruby had come in half an hour earlier. Of course she couldn't clean the rooms then, but she could make a start on other cleaning duties, such as the lounge and the front hall and the steps. It was a nail-biting experience asking the housekeeper if she could change her hours. Mrs Fosdyke wasn't known for her generosity, being a notoriously mean-spirited woman, and Ruby knew she was quite capable of refusing to let her go, just for the sake of being unkind.

'Mrs Fosdyke,' Ruby had begun nervously, 'my neighbours are going on a bit of an outing. We're planning a charity concert for the Dispensary for Sick Animals of the Poor.' Her heart sank as she watched Mrs Fosdyke's lips purse together in a firm line. She was going to say no, wasn't she...? And Ruby had been so looking forward to it. She knew that the Dispensary for Sick Animals of the Poor, a local charity, was a cause very dear to the management at Warnes. Spearheaded by a woman in the town, it existed to help people who couldn't afford to take their pets to a vet for treatment. There had been regular dances in the hotel to help raise funds. 'I'll come in early and do all my work,' Ruby had promised.

'And who will turn the beds down?' Mrs Fosdyke said, in an accusatory tone.

Ruby didn't give up. 'Edith says she wouldn't mind doing my rooms as well.'

'Parsons seems to be taking on rather a lot, doesn't she?' Mrs Fosdyke sniffed.

'She says she doesn't mind,' Ruby said feebly.

Mrs Fosdyke held her gaze for several seconds. 'Very well, but you are not to skimp on anything, Bateman,' she said firmly. 'I shall be on your trail before you go.'

Edith's reaction, when Ruby told her what had happened, was more strident. 'Miserable old bugger!'

Ruby glanced around nervously. 'You'd better not let her hear you calling her that,' she chuckled.

Ruby had now reached room 40 and knocked on the door. The corridor was empty. Winnie had gone – presumably up to the next floor. She saw to the flowers every other day and it took her all morning. There was no answer, so Ruby went in. The room was a tip, and her heart sank. It was going to take some time to tidy all this. It looked as if the guest had thrown the whole of her wardrobe on the floor. A half-packed case lay on the bed. Ruby tripped over a shoe as she walked in, and found its match on the dressing table. She began picking up dresses and putting them on the hangers in the wardrobe. The shoes went into a shoe rack. It was only as she reached the bed that Ruby noticed the blood. At first she struggled to comprehend what she was seeing. Had the guest started her monthlies in bed? She had come across that sort of thing before; not very pleasant, and embarrassing if she was in the room with the guest at any time, but an unavoidable fact of life. Yet something told her this was different. This was something more.

She heard a small moan coming from the direction of the bathroom and her heart immediately went into overdrive. 'Who is there?'

There was no answer, but she heard a distinct intake of breath. Ruby picked up her feather duster and walked towards the door. Quite what she was going to do with the feather duster, she didn't know, but the long handle felt like something she could use to defend herself, if necessary. Her heart was going like the clappers. Cautiously she pushed open the bathroom door and gasped.

There was blood everywhere. The pale-faced girl was on the floor. She was leaning against the bath, with her legs drawn up under her. Her feet were bloodied and her nightgown was saturated at the edge. The toilet seat was smeared with blood, and a small rivulet was running down the outside of the bowl. As Ruby came into the room, the girl looked up. Her face was ashen and tearstained. It was immediately clear what had happened. The girl had had a miscarriage and was in shock. Ruby grabbed the towel from the rail and draped it over her shivering body.

'I was trying to get away,' she whispered, 'but it was all too quick.'

'It's all right, Miss,' Ruby said gently. 'You sit tight, and I'll go down to reception and ask for an ambulance.'

17

'No!' The girl snatched her arm. Her eyes were wide with panic. 'Please don't do that. My father ... he doesn't know about the baby... If an ambulance came – oh, please, no one must know.'

Ruby frowned. Didn't the girl understand the seriousness of the matter? 'But, Miss, you've lost a lot of blood.'

'I'm fine,' the girl insisted. 'Just help me up and I'll be all right.' She tried to stand but, as she moved, a pain in her stomach bent her double.

'I can't leave you like this, Miss,' said Ruby.

'No, please, you mustn't,' the girl said again. 'If I'm found out, I shall be ruined.'

Ruby bit her lip anxiously. The girl wasn't wearing a ring. Her naked fingers told Ruby that she wasn't married. By losing the baby she had been spared the shame of telling her father that she was pregnant, but now, by another cruel twist of fate, he was going to find out anyway, when he saw the ambulance coming to take her to hospital. They might be living in a more enlightened age than their mothers had but, even though this was the 1930s, having a baby outside marriage was still taboo.

'If you could just help me get cleaned up,' the girl went on, 'I can pretend nothing has happened.'

Ruby looked at the beads of perspiration forming on her top lip, and at her face, which was still deathly white. She shook her head. As much as she wanted to help, she couldn't take that sort of responsibility. Supposing the girl died? 'I can't, Miss. I'm sorry.'

The girl was distraught. 'It's not fair,' she began

18

to wail. 'It's not bloody fair.'

It was at that moment that Ruby thought of Dr Palmer. He didn't always go out straight away. With a bit of luck, he might still be in his room. He would know what to do. She was sure he would help. 'One of the other guests is a doctor,' she said quickly. 'If you let me help you into bed, I'll go and get him. I'm sure he will be discreet.'

The girl looked as if she was going to pass out as Ruby hauled her to her feet. She helped her to the bed, pulling the towel from her shoulders and placing it over the already soiled sheet before the girl lay down. 'What's your name, Miss?'

'Imogen,' said the girl weakly. 'Imogen Russell.'

Stopping only long enough to wash her hands, Ruby ran along the corridor to Dr Palmer's room and knocked on the door. To her immense relief he was still there. He looked up in mild surprise when Ruby walked in. As she quickly explained that the guest in room 40 had apparently had a miscarriage, he didn't hesitate. Seconds later they were on their way back to Imogen's room. Ruby showed him in, then made as if to go.

'Stay here,' he said gruffly as he walked to the bed. 'I may need you.'

While he examined Imogen, Ruby busied herself in the bathroom. It gave her time for her racing heart to slow and, besides, it was going to take some time to get it back up to Freda Fosdyke's standards.

Tears pricked her own eyes as she heard Imogen begging the doctor not to tell anyone. 'You have to go to hospital,' he said. 'You may need a blood transfusion.'

'But I don't want my father to know,' she choked again.

Their voices dropped, and Ruby pushed the bathroom door to and got on with her work. Of course Imogen had been a silly girl, giving herself before she was married, but she was right: life was unfair. When a young man sowed his wild oats, everyone nudged one another and said, 'Boys will be boys.' But for every lad having his bit of fun, there had to be a girl doing the same, and yet, if she was caught out, she would be called a loose woman or, worse still, a slut.

A few minutes later Dr Palmer put his head around the door. 'She has to go to hospital,' he said. 'We cannot avoid it. However, I'm going to arrange for a taxi to come to the back of the hotel. If you can help Miss Russell to get herself cleaned up and dressed, we'll try and get her down the servants' staircase.'

'Yes, of course,' said Ruby.

'For the purposes of discretion, we'll let it be known that Miss Russell has appendicitis,' he went on. 'That it will explain the haste and the hospitalization. I trust that we can rely on you not to gossip about this?'

'Absolutely, sir,' said Ruby.

They managed to do it with military precision. By the time Dr Palmer had come back to say the taxi was waiting outside, Ruby had helped Miss Russell to get washed and dressed. In fact, luck was on their side, because they managed to get her out of the hotel without seeing another living soul. Back in the bedroom, Ruby rinsed some of the blood on the sheet under the tap. If the

20

laundry questioned it, she would say that the guest must have done it herself. It took some while to do the room and, just as she'd finished, she had a nasty moment when Imogen's father knocked on the door, looking for his daughter.

'She's not here, sir,' said Ruby innocently. Should she tell him his daughter was in hospital? Then, to her immense relief, she heard Dr Palmer's voice in the corridor. 'Ah, Mr Russell? May I have a word...'

Her work done at last, Ruby hurried to put everything away.

'You still here?' asked Edith, when Ruby appeared by the broom cupboard.

'You won't believe the morning I've had,' Ruby began.

'Oh?' Edith was all ears.

Ruby hesitated. Much as she wanted to tell Edith all about Miss Russell, she had promised to keep it a secret. 'Every room was a tip,' she said quickly, 'and it took me ages to clean one of the bathrooms.'

'Tell me about it,' said Edith. She was picking off the fluff from one of the long brooms. 'That Mr Herbert kept hanging around, and I couldn't get started in his room for ages. Here, leave that – I'll tidy it up for you. You go, or you'll miss the coach.'

'Are you sure?' said Ruby, rinsing her dustpan under the tap.

'Go on,' said Edith, taking the pan from her. 'Hurry up.'

'Thanks, Edith. You're a pal.'

Ruby changed out of her uniform – a grey belted dress with a starched white collar – in the staff cloakroom and made her way back to the servants' staircase. Edith was right. She was going to have to hurry if she was going to make it to the coach.

'And where do you think you're going?'

As soon as Ruby heard Mrs Fosdyke's acid tones, she froze and her heart sank. She had hoped she could slip away without being seen. Ruby turned with a smile – not too bright, or it would have been deemed insolent. 'It's my afternoon off, Mrs Fosdyke,' she said. 'It's the day of the outing.'

Mrs Fosdyke's lip set in a thin red line and her expression hardened.

'I did ask you, Mrs Fosdyke,' Ruby protested mildly.

'Is all your work done?'

'Yes, Mrs Fosdyke.'

'Are the bins emptied? Is the broom cupboard tidy?'

'Yes, Mrs Fosdyke.' Ruby bit her bottom lip and, clenching and unclenching her fists, prayed inwardly: *Please don't let her make me go back. I'm late already.*

'Come with me,' the older woman snapped.

Reluctantly Ruby followed her back upstairs, her angry thoughts hitting Mrs Fosdyke's back like arrows. Why did she always have to spoil things? Ruby had asked weeks ago for this time off. In fact Mrs Fosdyke had agreed to it, and had put it on the staff roster herself. All the girls working at Warnes Hotel dreaded the housekeeper who was strict and critical, and Ruby had never once heard her compliment any of the staff on their work. Instead she towered over them, like a glowering vulture ready to pounce on its prey. No matter how hard they worked, she seemed to take great delight in demoralizing all the chambermaids. For two pins Ruby would have told her where to stick her job and would have walked out, but times were hard and getting another job wasn't always easy.

As she trailed behind her, Ruby held her breath. Mrs Fosdyke's favourite trick was to make a girl tidy her locker room, after she'd stripped the locker and tipped everything into a big pile in the middle of the room. If she did that today, Ruby would have no chance of making it to the coach in time.

On the landing Mrs Fosdyke opened the linen cupboard, as if she was expecting it to be untidy, but every towel was neatly folded in exactly the same way, so that the edges were level. You could have laid a ruler against them and every towel would have touched it. Ruby watched the house-keeper running her hands over the sheets. Beside them, the pillowcases were in matching pairs, ready to take down at a moment's notice. Everything looked perfect, but Ruby could hardly breathe. If Mrs Fosdyke decided something wasn't to her liking, she'd pull everything out onto the landing floor and Ruby could kiss the trip good-bye. It would take at least an hour to put everything back the way it was. To her great relief Mrs Fosdyke closed the linen cupboard, but then headed for the broom cupboard. Miserably, Ruby followed.

As they walked round the corner, Mrs Fosdyke

had just gone past one of the doors leading to a guest room when Edith came out, carrying a tray of dirty cups.

'Blimey, Roob,' she blurted out, 'you're cutting it a bit fine, aren't you?'

Ruby flashed her eyes, in the hope that Edith wouldn't say too much, but she didn't seem to notice.

'Give my love to your mum when you see her. Tell her I hope she'll soon be better...' The words died on her lips as she finally understood Ruby's frantic eye movements and realized that Mrs Fosdyke was in the corridor as well.

'Don't stand there gawping, Parsons,' Mrs Fosdyke snapped, as Edith turned round. 'I'm sure you have work to do.'

'Yes, Mrs Fosdyke,' said Edith, giving her a little bob before she fled.

They'd reached the broom cupboard and Mrs Fosdyke threw open the door. It was tidy enough to be a showroom: polishes on the top shelf, labels facing to the front; dusters neatly folded on the lower shelf; the dustpans washed and spic and span, and lined up along one wall with the matching brushes dangling from hooks above them. The vacuum machines were at the back of the cupboard, and the floor cloths were draped over mirror-clean galvanized buckets. The floor was spotless and, as Ruby's mother would have said, you could eat your dinner on it.

'Very well,' Mrs Fosdyke said, surveying the room, 'you may go, Miss Bateman.'

'Yes, Mrs Fosdyke,' Ruby breathed. 'Thank you, Mrs Fosdyke.' As she hurried away, the dreaded

24

voice called after her, 'Walk, Miss Bateman. Walk.'

Ruby slowed her pace to a sedate walk until she was halfway down the stairs, where she broke into a frantic run, at the same time muttering, 'Miserable dried-up old prune.'

Outside in the street the bright September sunshine hit her like a wall. The Indian summer of 1933, which had brought many day-trippers to Worthing, was a welcome end to the season. It was still so hot that few promenaders were out and about along Marine Parade. The odd one or two sat on deckchairs in the Steyne, a pretty shaded area that overlooked the seafront. Her brother Percy, a bit of a history buff, once told her that the name Steyne meant 'stony field' and that, in Victorian times, local fishermen mended their nets there; and before that it had been the garden of a big house – all of which were long gone. The many fishing families who worked along the shores of Worthing had, since its heyday, been reduced to a few diehards, and now mended their nets on the beach or in their own back gardens.

Ruby was glad she had chosen to wear her coolest dress, a pretty blue-and-pink cotton frock with a V-neck and a large blue bow across the chest. Gathered at the waist and tied with a blue sash and bow at the back, it had small cap sleeves, which flapped cool air onto her arms as she ran. She carried a side-fastening white clutch bag, and had matching shoes with straps across her feet. She wore no cardigan – something that she already regretted because, when the sun went down, she might be cold; but there was no time to go home for it now. Her short dark hair was, as her mother would say, as straight as a yard of pump water, but suited the new bob style very well. The other chambermaids in Warnes told her that, with her big sultry eyes, she looked just like the American movie star Louise Brooks, so Ruby didn't complain.

She had to run the length of the town to where she was supposed to meet the coach, and she was hot and out of breath long before she got there.

As she turned the corner, Cousin Lily's shrill voice rang out, 'She's here!'

And May, Ruby's seven-year-old sister, pretty as a picture in her blue-and-white gingham dress and with a blue bow in her light-brown hair, ran up the road to meet her. 'I was scared you weren't coming.'

Ruby gave her a quick hug. 'Of course I'm coming.'

'Did you really think we would go without our Ruby?' Cousin Lily laughed.

Ruby smiled and put her arm around May's shoulders. She could put all the horrors and frustration of today behind her and relax now. She was going to have a lovely afternoon.

As they made their way to the coach, to the sound of cheering, an ambulance went by, its bells clanging. Ruby's thoughts went immediately to Imogen Russell. That poor girl was still living her nightmare, but at least Ruby could console herself that she had done her best to help her keep her secret.

'Nice to see you, Ruby,' Albert Longman said, as she climbed on board the coach. He grinned and ran his tongue over his slightly protruding teeth. Although twenty-nine and reasonable-looking, he was still single and, according to some, looking for a wife. He worked for the local paper, the *Worthing Gazette,* as the reporter who covered local events, but he also wrote the occasional feature. 'You're looking very pretty today.'

Ruby gave him a polite nod, but tried not to encourage him. He was all right, and he always made a point of chatting to her, but she wasn't interested in him – not in that way anyway. He was too old!

Her father was sitting in the seat behind the driver and, as she walked past, he stepped out of his seat to let May have the window seat, blocking the gangway in the process. Taking his watch out of his waistcoat pocket, he stared at Ruby. 'You're late,' he began gruffly.

'Sorry, Father,' said Ruby.

'Can I sit with Ruby for a bit?' May asked.

Their father looked crestfallen. 'Don't you want to sit with your old pa?'

'I do,' said May, 'but I'd like to talk to Ruby as well.'

Nelson Bateman threw himself sulkily into his seat, and May skipped off down the aisle without a care in the world. Ruby was concerned to see her father's flushed and angry face and felt sorry for him. He adored May, and she knew he would have taken her thoughtlessness very personally. She bent to kiss his cheek as she went by, but he quite deliberately turned his head. Embarrassed, Ruby lowered her eyes. It hurt when he shunned her, and yet there was always that urge to try and get him to show some affection towards her. He never had, but she found herself falling into the same trap again and again. She tried hard not to be jealous of her little sister, but Ruby was no plaster saint, and it was a struggle. *Get a grip,* she told herself angrily. *You should have known he wouldn't let you kiss him. Why would he?* She had never even seen him kiss her mother. It wasn't his way, although he had plenty of kisses for May. According to her mother, it was the war that had changed him, although Ruby had no idea why. She had been born in 1916, a couple of years before it ended. May had come along seven years later. Nelson never talked about his experiences; few ex-soldiers did, although everyone knew that places like the Somme had been hell on earth. Her mother and Aunt Vinny (short for Virginia) always said it was best not to think about the bad things, for what good would it do? What was done was done; better to forget it and get on with life. As a result, theirs was a household where everyone, except May, tiptoed around their father, afraid of his sudden mood swings and of upsetting him. But if it was difficult for Ruby and her mother, it was even worse for their brother Percy.

Ruby made her way to the back of the coach, where her mother was sitting.

'Glad you could make it, Ruby love,' Bea smiled as her daughter came closer and kissed her cheek.

Bea Bateman looked older than her forty-two years. A constant nagging illness had worn her down. Every winter she would succumb to one cold after another, and when her chest was bad even breathing became difficult. Ruby was heart-

28

ened to see that she was looking much better today and that she was wearing a new dress, an attractive peach-coloured two-piece with buttons down the front and a small belt at the waist. The white collar on the neckline was scalloped, as were the cuffs on her sleeves. Her skirt was straight with side-pleats, and she wore white peep-toed shoes. There was a bit of colour in her cheeks and she'd done something different to her hair.

'You look really lovely,' Ruby smiled.

Bea smoothed down her dress. 'I've been saving up for ages to get this dress.'

'The colour suits you,' said Ruby, 'and I love your hair.'

Bea patted her curls. 'I tried finger-waving it,' she whispered confidentially, then added anxiously, 'You don't think I'm too old for it, do you?'

'No, Mum,' Ruby smiled. 'I think you look fantastic.'

Ruby settled down. She was really looking forward to this afternoon and, after her fraught morning, it was good to be with the family. When the coach moved off, it was pleasant to feel the breeze playing with her hair through the open window, and it cooled her down. As May struggled to sit on her big sister's lap, Bea handed her daughter a sandwich.

'Ooh, thanks, Mum,' said Ruby. 'I had to go without lunch, to get away this early.' True to her word, she didn't say anything about Imogen Russell.

'Did Mrs Fosdyke make trouble?' asked Bea.

Ruby nodded. The ham-and-tomato sandwich was delicious. 'For an awful minute,' she said, as

29

she pushed a stray crumb back into her mouth with her finger, 'I thought she was going to make sure I was too late for the coach.'

Bea shook her head in disgust.

'Why would she want to do that?' May wondered.

'Some people enjoy being unkind,' her mother said simply.

Ruby glanced around. 'Where's Percy?' There seemed to be no sign of her brother.

'He and Jim Searle have gone ahead on their bicycles,' said her mother. 'They took a few others in tow as well.'

'He'd better lay off the parsnip wine when he gets there, if he wants to get home safely,' Ruby chuckled.

'I don't think he'd get drunk, with your father around,' said Bea.

'You know Percy,' Ruby laughed, as she helped herself to another sandwich. 'He'd do anything for devilment.'

The coach was one of the old Fairway Coaches. The company had been bought out by Southdown the year before, and some of the old stock sold off. Cecil Turner had snapped up this one, and used it mainly for works outings and day-trips. The coaches were in good nick but rather old-fashioned, so Cecil's prices were dirt cheap. Ruby and her neighbours and friends could never have afforded to book the trip otherwise. They were going to drive around on a kind of mystery tour and then, after tea in the High Salvington tea rooms, some of them would take part in a small concert. They had managed to sell about forty-eight tickets, and all proceeds would go to the Dispensary for Sick Animals of the Poor.

They had just reached Broadwater bridge when the driver suddenly braked. A few people cried out in shocked surprise, and everybody stopped talking as he sounded the horn.

'What the hell do they think they're doing?' his angry voice rang out.

They had encountered a crowd of young men marching down the middle of the street. Ruby hazarded a guess that there were about fifteen of them. Dressed entirely in black, they were clean-shaven and had smart Brylcreemed hair. Their leader, a fresh-faced man of about twenty, carried a Union Jack on a long pole. They had attracted a crowd of angry onlookers, mostly men of the same age, and fists were flying. Everyone was jostling and pushing as the crowd shouted slogans like 'Mosley out!' and 'Hitler means war', whilst a few marchers had lunged into the crowd and begun hitting back.

Ruby frowned. What on earth was happening? Suddenly, the man with the flag on a pole swung it at the hecklers like a weapon, and an angry shout went up. Some ducked to miss the pole, but a couple of them were hit and fell backwards. It was then that she could see two more of the men in black shirts laying into someone who had been knocked to the ground.

'I don't like it,' May whispered, with a frightened expression on her face.

'Don't worry,' said Ruby. 'It's all right. They can't get in here.'

'I'm going back to Pa,' said May.

31

When she'd gone, Ruby turned to her mother. 'Who are they?'

'They look like Mosley's Blackshirts,' somebody further down the coach said and, at the same moment, one of the men banged ferociously on the side of the coach with a silver-topped stick. After that, it seemed like all hell broke loose. Ruby drew in her breath as she saw the man who had been knocked to the ground struggle to his feet. It was Dr Palmer. His face was bloodied and his suit was covered in dust. His glasses were hanging from one ear only, and he took out a large hand-kerchief and pressed it to a bleeding cut on his head.

The coach still hadn't moved. Ruby flew down to the front. 'Cecil, we have to help that man,' she cried. 'I know him. He's a doctor.'

'Sit down, girl,' growled her father as she drew level with him. 'Don't interfere.'

'It's best to do as your father says,' said Albert with a smile.

Ruby frowned. She might have been surprised by his remark, but her concern for Dr Palmer was so strong that she wasn't listening. She had to do something. Pulling the door open, she leaned out as far as she dared. 'Dr Palmer! Dr Palmer, over here, quick. You'll be safe in here.'

Cecil Turner stopped the engine. 'Ruby, get back inside,' he said anxiously. 'Let me. It's no place for a girl.'

'Ruby!' barked her father.

Moments before Cecil pulled her back into the coach, Dr Palmer looked up and saw Ruby. He headed towards her, but then someone bumped

32

into him and he almost fell over again. He was clearly very dazed. Although the fighting was getting worse, it was spilling away from the coach, so Albert Longman pushed past Ruby and went outside. He and Cecil got Dr Palmer inside, and the door closed just as the first police whistle sounded.

'Ooh, Albert,' said one of the girls further down the coach, 'you were amazing.'

'You're ever so brave,' said another.

Albert's chest swelled and, basking in the glow of his success, he wet his fingers in his mouth and, pressing his hair down at the front, grinned at Ruby. He seemed oblivious of the other girls' giggles.

Two of the other passengers, who were sitting together at the front, helped Dr Palmer into a seat and produced a mug of tea from a flask. He was clearly very shaken.

Cecil jumped into the driver's seat and cursed out loud. 'Looks like we'd better get out of here,' he shouted as he put the engine into gear. 'If the police come aboard to ask questions, we'll be here all day; 'ang on to yer 'ats, folks.'

The vehicle lurched forward, but then a boy brandishing a toy gun appeared in front of the windscreen and Cecil jammed on the brakes again. 'Bloody 'ell.'

The boy was shouting, 'Bang-bang!' Nelson yelled at him and the boy stuck out his tongue. Nelson jumped to his feet. 'Cheeky young tyke,' he shouted, shaking his fist angrily.

'Let it go, Nelson,' said Cecil. The fight was on the move again, and the weight of the bodies outside buffeted the coach.

Ruby's father ignored him and climbing down the step, attempted to open the door. It wasn't a wise move. The coach jerked and Nelson fell sideways, hitting his head on the rail. Quick as a flash, Albert and one of the other passengers dashed to his aid and then, with one hand on the horn, Cecil finally managed to get away from the melee outside.

Nelson moaned as Albert held a handkerchief to his nose.

'What on earth did you think you were doing, Nelson?' Cecil cried, as he kept an eye on the road.

'No boy his age sticks his tongue out at me like that,' Nelson countered angrily. 'What he needs is a damned good hiding.'

'Oh, come on. He was just a lad having a bit of fun,' said Cecil. 'I'll admit he was a bit daft, getting in front of the coach like that, but no harm done.'

Nelson grunted.

'Keep your hair on, Nelson,' said Cecil good-naturedly. 'You were young yourself once.'

Bea had come to the front of the coach to help her husband, but he knocked her hand away. 'Don't fuss, woman.'

Dr Palmer's attitude was totally different. He knew that he'd been rescued, and wasted no time in telling everybody how wonderful they were. It had obviously been quite a shock to get beaten up, and Ruby could see that his hands were still trembling.

'I'm afraid we can't take you back to Warnes, sir,' she said, 'but would you like us to put you down somewhere? You could get a bus back to town, or maybe a train?'

Dr Palmer dabbed his sore cheek. A livid bruise was forming. 'Where are you all going?'

Ruby explained about the mystery tour and the concert.

'You're welcome to tag along too,' said Cecil over his shoulder. He was coming up to Offington crossroads, the events at the bridge being far behind them now.

'Then I shall elect to do just that,' said Dr Palmer, closing his eyes and relaxing against the headrest, 'if you don't mind. I think I should enjoy a ride around the countryside.'

Ruby was still concerned. He was no spring chicken and he had had a nasty experience. She glanced anxiously at the people gathered around them. 'Do you think he's all right?' she whispered.

'The old boy does look a bit pale,' Cousin Lily whispered.

'The old boy is perfectly fine,' said Dr Palmer, without opening his eyes. 'A little tired, that's all. Let him rest for a while and he'll soon bounce back.'

The passengers melted away, but Ruby and Bea lingered with him a little longer. Ruby was pleased to see that the rise and fall of his chest had calmed and the colour was returning to his face, but the bruise on his cheek was quite pronounced and his bottom lip was swollen.

'Would you like to sit in my seat?' said Albert.

Dr Palmer opened his eyes 'Still here, Miss Bateman?'

Ruby took in her breath. 'How did you know

my name?' she blurted out.

'It's hard to ignore Mrs Fosdyke barking her orders,' he said, resettling himself more comfortably in his seat. 'Bit of a dragon, isn't she?'

Ruby grinned. 'It's not for me to say, sir.'

'Then take it from me,' said Dr Palmer, closing his eyes again, 'she is. Now, run along and let me rest. I'll be fine.'

As Ruby and Bea made their way back to their seats, friends and neighbours alike asked, 'Is he all right?' as they walked past. Her mother said, 'Yes, thank you,' but Ruby had a sneaky feeling, that they weren't asking about her father.

Once the coach had got under way, everyone's relief was palpable, but the incident had them talking for quite a while.

'I honestly thought they were all coming inside, when Mr Bateman opened the door.'

'Fancy beating up a doctor, for goodness' sake. Whatever next?'

'From what I could see, they weren't doing anything except marching down the street with a flag. It was the rest of those hooligans who were causing trouble.'

'My cousin went to a BUF meeting once. He saw Mosley himself.'

'Well, I for one don't want to hear him. Looks like they're nothing but trouble, to me.'

'What does BUF stand for?'

'British Union of Fascists.'

At the front of the coach, Albert Longman leaned over the back of his seat. 'Are you sure you're all right, Mr Bateman? That was quite a whack you got.'

'I'm fine,' said Nelson as he dabbed his sore nose. 'It's my own fault, for having such high standards.'

Albert grunted in a sign of appreciation.

Nelson gave him the handkerchief back. Holding it between his thumb and forefinger, Albert was unsure what to do with it.

The coach journeyed on and everyone settled down. Bea leaned towards her daughter. 'Who is that man you pulled onto the bus?'

'One of the guests at Warnes,' said Ruby. 'He's very nice.'

'I hope you're not getting yourself too involved,' Bea remarked cautiously.

'Mum!' said Ruby. 'He's old enough to be my grandfather!' She paused. 'Father didn't upset you too much?'

Bea sighed and shook her head. 'I was only trying to help him.'

'I know.' Ruby squeezed her hand. 'I'm surprised he came. He doesn't much like family outings.'

'May persuaded him,' said Bea. 'That girl could persuade the Pope to join the Baptists.'

Ruby giggled.

Her mother had made a joke of it, but Ruby could see she was still upset. She kept hold of Bea's hand and they spent a few minutes wrapped in a companionable silence.

Outside the window the pretty Sussex countryside sped by. From Crockhurst Hill they motored on to Arundel, and then they were on their way to Bury Hill, but Ruby's thoughts were miles away. She was remembering the way Dr Palmer had helped Miss Imogen. Not many men of his age would have been so sensitive to her predicament. He hadn't judged her, and he'd done his best to help her keep her secret. That's why it was so hard to understand why he'd been treated so badly by the Blackshirts. Why on earth would anyone want to beat up a nice man like that?

CHAPTER 2

Cousin Lily, who had been chatting to some of their friends and neighbours, made her way to the back of the coach and sat next to Ruby. She was a pretty blonde, and petite. Ruby admired her lightweight pale-lemon lawn dress with tiny white dots all over it. As she moved, it flowed around her body, showing every contour.

'I've just got engaged,' she announced as she sat down beside them.

'What – again?' The words slipped out of Ruby's mouth before she'd had time to think.

'Well, it is a whole month since I broke off with Tommy Dixon,' said Lily indignantly. She held out her left hand for them to admire her ring.

This was Lily's third engagement in two years. As soon as she'd left school, she'd got herself engaged to William Warner, breaking it off almost as soon as she'd put on the diamond solitaire he'd given her. Ruby felt sorry for him. She knew it had taken William the best part of a whole year to save up for the ring, but as soon as his mother found out what he'd done, the engagement was off.

Tommy Dixon hadn't fared much better, either. He and Lily had been stepping out for about three months when he'd given her a pretty ring with a diamond cluster and a small emerald at the centre. The engagement had lasted barely a month. Ruby had been sad to see Tommy go. He was a nice man. And now here Lily was with another ring: a minuscule ruby inside a diamond-shaped setting.

'Lucky girl,' said Ruby. 'What's his name?'

'Hubert Periwinkle,' said Lily. She glanced round as Ruby and her mother struggled not to laugh. 'I know, I know,' said Lily. 'It's a ghastly name, isn't it? Mrs Lily Periwinkle ... ugh!' She held her hand up to the light. 'Nice ring, though.'

'So when is the wedding?' said Bea pointedly.

'I haven't decided yet,' said Lily firmly.

It was pleasant driving around the Sussex lanes. After Bury Hill they took in the villages of Fittleworth and Storrington, before returning to Findon and High Salvington mill. Ruby was always interested in her surroundings. She hadn't been far in her life – to Eastbourne once when she was a small child, and to Chichester on the bus a few times – but she longed to travel and see something of the world. Her passion was kindled when she found a magazine in the rubbish bin in one of the rooms she cleaned. Ruby smuggled it home (she felt sure if she'd asked Mrs Fosdyke if she could have it, the woman would have said no) and, curling up beside the fire in the late evening, devoured its pages. Under a picture of a boy with several huge bunches of green bananas on his bicycle there was an article about Uganda. It made Ruby long to see the Bujagali Falls and to eat beans, rice and vegetables with the locals.

As the coach climbed the hill away from the Gallops, Ruby made her way down to the front to see Dr Palmer. Happily, he was looking a lot better and was sitting up talking to Albert and her father.

'We're about to stop at the mill, sir,' she said. 'How are you feeling?'

'Much better, thank you, Miss Bateman,' the doctor smiled. 'In fact I've had a wonderful afternoon.' He patted the seat beside him and Ruby lowered herself down.

'We shall be having tea when we get there,' she said. 'You are welcome to join us, sir.'

'And would I be right in guessing that, if I say yes, you will be giving up your own tea, Miss Bateman?' His merry eyes twinkled as he saw her discomfort and he chuckled. 'You have a big heart, Miss Bateman,' he said, patting her hand. 'Don't let anyone shrink it.'

'Here we are, folks,' Cecil called and the coach pulled up. Built in 1750, the old timber round-house underneath the mill had been replaced at the turn of the century and tea rooms installed. The mill itself, which was said to be the last working post-mill in Worthing, had been going for 150 years. Cecil stepped down and threw open the door of the coach. 'Toilets over there to the left,' he pointed.

Just as Ruby had feared, Albert was waiting for her when she got off the coach but, stepping to one side, she managed to put Cecil and her father between them. As the passengers made their way out of the coach, the children ran across the grass to let off steam, whooping and shouting as they went. The tea that had been laid on for them looked absolutely delicious. Ruby's mouth watered as she gazed at the Sussex lardy Johns, scones and jam, Sussex plum heavies and the Victoria sponge that graced the snow-white tablecloth next to the rows of cups and saucers. By the time they sat down, Cecil Turner had already asked the caterers to lay on an extra tea so that Dr Palmer could join them. Ruby heaved a sigh of relief. There was no need for her to go without.

Everyone was seated at small tables, so Bea, Ruby and Cousin Lily stayed together. Vinny Cutler, Lily's mother, was still working at the laundry. May sat at a special table reserved for the children, where they had jelly and cake and drank lemonade. Nelson and Dr Palmer sat with some of the men, who had cracked open a beer barrel rather than drink tea.

Ruby's brother, Percy, and his friend Jim had already arrived on their bicycles by the time the coach got there. 'You took your time,' Percy grinned when he saw Ruby coming towards him. 'We've already been up here for hours.'

'We saw the Blackshirts,' said May, running by. 'They made the coach stop, and our Ruby rescued a doctor from the hotel.'

Jim frowned. 'Why would the Blackshirts want to stop the coach?' he asked. Tall and fair with powerfully built shoulders, he was by far the best-looking man there. 'And what doctor?'

'They were fighting with some local lads,' said Ruby. 'I think it was mainly because they were trying to take away their flag.'

41

She didn't notice her father coming up behind her. 'I've heard about them – the Blackshirts. They're a bad lot,' said Nelson. 'Troublemakers, the lot of them.'

'They were only trying to get their flag back,' Ruby insisted.

'And I'm telling you: they were up to no good,' said Nelson, raising his voice. 'What they all need is a good hiding.'

'My father seems to think a good hiding will solve all the world's ills,' Percy laughed, embarrassed. Nelson glowered.

'I've been talking to that doctor fellow, and he agrees with me.' Nelson was already in a belligerent mood. It seemed that he and his son couldn't say two words without getting angry these days. 'Why do you think they beat him up?' Nelson said, wagging his finger in his son's face. 'Because he tells the truth about them – that's why.'

'All the Blackshirts I've met spend their time putting on football matches and boxing competitions,' said Percy, his eyes flashing. 'What's wrong with that?'

'Mosley and his cronies want to take over the whole country,' Nelson insisted. 'We've always done things a certain way; we've done them that way for the last thousand years, and his lot want to change everything. My mates died at Ypres to stop people like him.'

Percy rolled his eyes. 'Here we go again.'

'Percy,' Ruby cautioned softly. Her father looked as if he was going to blow a fuse. She sighed inwardly. Why did Percy always have to antagonize him?

'I'm afraid your father is right, young man,' said Dr Palmer, coming up behind him before Nelson could retaliate. 'Mosley's message sounds all well and good, but I'm afraid there's a hidden agenda. He's looking for a one-party dictatorship.'

Nelson nodded with an 'I-told-you-so' expression. Percy looked a little disconcerted. 'This is Dr Palmer,' said Ruby. 'He is one of the guests at Warnes Hotel. Dr Palmer, this is my brother, Percy Bateman.'

The two men shook hands. 'No disrespect, sir,' said Percy, 'but I think you are wrong. What this country needs is strong leadership...'

Ruby moved away and left them to it. She refused to allow the men to spoil her one day out by talking politics, so she went to join her mother and Cousin Lily.

'Oh, dear. You look as if you've lost a pound and found sixpence,' said Bea as her daughter came up to her. She was relaxing in a deckchair that someone had put on the grass outside the tea rooms.

'Father and Percy are arguing about politics,' said Ruby, flinging herself onto a wooden chair. 'Honestly, I could bang their heads together. Where's May?'

'Playing Hide-and-Seek with the other children,' said Bea. 'Lily's going to buy an ice cream. Want one?'

'Yes, please.' Ruby spread her legs and fanned her skirt to try and get cool. The sun was warm on her face, and the gentle breeze toyed with the hem. She kicked off her shoes. This was so relaxing. She closed her eyes and made herself think of nice things.

A few minutes later Cousin Lily appeared with two ice creams. 'Here, have one of these and forget your troubles,' she smiled.

'What about you?' said Ruby, sitting up to take it.

'I'll get one in a minute,' she said. 'There's plenty there.'

'Thanks,' said Ruby. 'That's very kind of you. How's the job going, Lily?'

Lily was working in service to an old woman who lived in Richmond Road.

Lily sighed. 'The old lady is moving to her nephew's home in Yorkshire.'

'Yorkshire!' cried Bea. 'My goodness, that's a long way away.'

'Oh, I'm not going with her,' said Lily, 'but the family have assured me that they haven't sacked me. It's just that they have their own servants.'

'What on earth will you do?' said Ruby.

'Her nephew says he'll give me a good reference,' said Lily.

'That's something, I suppose,' Bea conceded.

'Why are they taking her to Yorkshire?' asked Ruby.

'Didn't you know?' said Lily. 'She had a stroke. She can't talk any more.'

As Cousin Lily hurried off to get another ice cream, Bea sighed. 'You know why she gave her ice cream to you, don't you?'

'No?' Ruby followed the jerk of her mother's head. 'Ah,' she said. 'I see what you mean. The ice-cream vendor is quite good-looking, isn't he?' And they both laughed.

Albert Longman wasn't with the rest of the

men. He was showing the children some magic tricks. On her way to buy another ice cream, Lily stopped to watch him make a queen of hearts appear in someone's pocket, and May was thrilled when he found a sixpence behind her ear. Everyone stared wide-eyed as he made a furry mouse disappear from his hat, even though they'd all seen him putting it there. The children spent several minutes looking for it, to no avail. It wasn't until one heard the mouse calling from under the wood-pile that they found it.

'He's awfully good with children,' Bea remarked, but Ruby only made a non-committal remark. She didn't want her mother getting any ideas about Albert Longman.

After she'd finished her ice cream, Ruby went back to the men and, unbelievably, they were still arguing.

'Speaking personally,' said Jim Searle, 'I've never had any problem in getting a job around here.'

'People may be affluent down here in the south,' said Dr Palmer, 'but you mark my words, up north it's a totally different story.'

'We've all seen what that Muzzaleni fellow's done to his country,' said Nelson. 'If this Mosley is anything like him, God help us.'

'I think you'll find that Mussolini has made a big difference in Italy,' said Percy, enunciating the Italian leader's name in such a way that everyone would know his father hadn't got it quite right. 'For a start, he's making it far more productive.'

'What you may not know, young man, is that already the secret police are carting people off for no good reason,' said Dr Palmer.

'What would the likes of Percy know about it anyway?' Nelson said dismissively.

Percy's eyes flashed. 'Quite a bit, as a matter of fact,' he said.

'Percy, please,' Ruby interjected, 'please let's not fight.'

'You keep out of this, Ruby,' her father said.

'She's right, Mr Bateman,' said Dr Palmer. 'I shouldn't have started this discussion now. This isn't the time or the place. Miss Bateman, I apologize. I'll say no more.'

'Don't mind her,' said Nelson.

'I would hate to spoil such a lovely day,' Dr Palmer insisted. 'You should feel very proud of your daughter, Mr Bateman. Organizing such a wonderful outing is no mean feat.'

'What – Ruby?' Nelson made no attempt to hide the disbelief in his voice. 'She couldn't organize a bun fight in a baker's shop.'

'Didn't you know, Uncle Nelson?' said Lily, coming to join them and slipping her arm through Ruby's. 'All this was Cousin Ruby's idea. Isn't she clever?'

'It's Cecil's coach...' Nelson began.

'But it was Ruby who drummed up the support,' said Lily.

Ruby blushed. 'I couldn't have done it without Cecil's help,' she said quickly.

Clearly annoyed, Nelson Bateman picked up his jacket from the back of a chair. 'You finished those nets yet, boy?'

Percy bristled. Ruby knew he hated being called 'boy', especially in company. 'Not yet.'

46

'Thought not,' said Nelson. 'Can't trust you to do a damned thing, can I?'

'We're not going out tomorrow, are we?' said Percy. 'I'll do them first thing Monday morning.'

'Nets should be mended straight away,' said Nelson pedantically.

'How about we all go for a walk?' Jim suggested. 'It's lovely up on the hill and there's quite a good view.'

'The concert will be starting soon,' said Cousin Lily, fluttering her eyelids at Albert, who was busy packing away his playing cards and the mouse into a small leather suitcase.

'I heard someone say it'll be at least another twenty minutes,' Jim insisted. 'It won't take us long to walk up Honeysuckle Lane. You will excuse us, won't you, Mr Bateman, Dr Palmer?'

'It'll be a lot better than listening to his drivel,' said Percy, and his father glared.

Lily grabbed Jim's arm and they started walking.

'Would you like my arm?' Albert asked Ruby.

'Thank you, but I'm walking with my brother,' said Ruby, pulling Percy away. They set off. 'You really shouldn't antagonize Father,' she scolded him, once they were out of earshot.

'He drives me mad,' said Percy. 'He always has to be right, and everybody else's opinions count for nothing.'

'You're right,' said Ruby, 'but just ignore it.'

'I can't, Ruby,' said Percy. 'I've got to leave this place. I can't stand being with him a moment longer than I have to.'

'But where will you go?'

'I don't know – anywhere.'

47

'It's not easy to get a job,' said Ruby, 'and Father's counting on you to keep the fishing boat in the family.'

'I hate fishing,' said Percy. 'I don't want to be forced to do something I hate for the rest of my life, and certainly not with the old man.'

'Oh, Percy... You know what he'll say.'

'I'm sorry, Ruby,' he said, 'but just because four generations of Batemans have fished, it's no reason for me to mess up my life. I can't even stand the smell of fish.'

'When will you go?' she asked.

'As soon as I've saved up a bit of money,' said Percy. 'He leads me a dog's life, and I've had enough.'

Ruby squeezed his arm. She knew how he felt. He'd told her often enough, and their father's belligerent attitude didn't help. Yes, it was a shame, but Percy was right: he deserved to live his own life.

They soon reached the lane. High Salvington itself was part of the South Downs, and the views from the top were indeed lovely. The hill had always been an area of quiet natural beauty, but since the early 1920s a great many large detached houses had been built on the slopes leading to the top, and now this was a much-desired spot. Dr Palmer was right when he said there was little sign of poverty in this area. Only people with plenty of money could afford to live up here. Ruby couldn't actually see the houses at the summit, but she couldn't help feeling that they had changed this tranquil spot for good.

She glanced back and, to her amazement, saw

her father striding away from them all down the hill. 'Father's walking home!' she gasped.

'Good riddance,' said Percy.

'But what about May?' cried Ruby.

'It's about time May understood what Father is really like,' said Percy.

'Oh, she'll be so disappointed,' said Ruby.

'She'll get over it,' said Percy flatly.

Albert was back. 'Would you care to walk further down the meadow?'

'No, thanks,' said Ruby cheerfully. 'You go ahead. I prefer to be on my own.'

Albert pushed his hands into his pockets and set off sulkily down the hill.

The meadow at the top of the lane was full of wild flowers. Ruby marvelled at the way the colours always seemed to blend together. The lady's bed-straw and the scentless mayweed, which looked like the kind of yellow and white daisies you'd find in any cottage garden, danced in the grass along-side the gentle violet of the field scabious and the more vibrant common knapweed. It was so lovely and peaceful. Why couldn't life always be like this? If she wasn't dodging Mrs Fosdyke, she was trying to keep the peace between Percy and Father. Life was like a war zone, even without Mosley and Mussolini and their cronies stirring up dissention everywhere.

Further down the meadow, Percy had run ahead of her and was trying to put a handful of grass down Cousin Lily's back. She ran off screaming in delight. She might be getting engaged every five minutes, but Ruby couldn't imagine Lily as a married woman. Ruby herself didn't join in with the fun and games. Instead, she stood with her arms folded and enjoyed the view.

Jim came and stood beside her, and they watched a skylark soaring high in the air to hover above the grass.

'Look at that,' she whispered, without turning her head to look at him.

'I wish I had my camera with me,' said Jim. The skylark, singing its heart out, plunged a few feet and rose again. 'Beautiful.'

She became aware that they were alone and, even more disconcertingly, Jim wasn't watching the bird; he was looking at her. 'You look so attractive, with the wind playing with your hair like that. I'd like to take a picture of you sometime.'

Ruby felt herself blush. 'Oh, go on with you, James Searle,' she said, pushing his arm playfully.

'I mean it,' he said. 'You're very photogenic.'

She turned away and the skylark dived down, probably having spotted some insects to eat. Ruby could feel herself becoming self-conscious. Jim was so handsome. When they were at school, all the girls liked him. Of course he was a couple of years above her year, and he'd never even looked at her. His name had been linked to Martha Greenway, and there was talk that perhaps they might marry.

The silence between them was becoming so awkward that Ruby felt the need to say something. 'I heard that you're working at Warwick Studios,' she said. 'How are you getting on with your photo-graphy?'

'I'm really enjoying it,' he said, his enthusiasm

shining through. 'I'm learning all about the business, and I'm being stretched all the time.'

'So what comes next? Have you got any ambitions?'

'Not sure,' he said. 'I'd rather like to be a newspaper photographer. There's always good money to be made for on-the-spot pictures.'

'So you're driven by money,' she teased.

'Absolutely not,' said Jim, suddenly serious. 'I just want to be at the forefront of what's going on.'

'I'm sorry,' said Ruby, blushing. 'That must have sounded rather rude. I didn't mean it to. No offence.'

'None taken,' Jim smiled. 'What about you? I heard that you went to work in Warnes Hotel. What's it like?'

'Very strict,' said Ruby, 'but I know I'm getting a good training and, if I ever wanted a reference, there's none better than a good one from Warnes.'

'And do you have ambitions?'

'Well, that's a first,' Ruby chuckled, 'someone asking me if I have ambitions.'

'Why not?' said Jim.

'I know what I've got to do and what's expected of me, but I've never even dared to think what I'd *like* to do,' said Ruby.

'Now's your chance,' Jim smiled. 'What do you enjoy?'

'Being with people, I suppose,' she said. 'I'm not supposed to talk to them, but I enjoy hearing what the guests have been up to. You meet such interesting people.'

'Would you like to travel?'

'That's hardly likely to happen to someone like me,' said Ruby wistfully.

'But if you could...?'

'I'd like to speak another language,' she said, her eyes bright with excitement. 'I love it when the foreign guests talk to each other. I try to imagine what they are saying.'

'Who is this beautiful chambermaid?' said Jim, making his voice sound like a foreigner speaking bad English.

'Oh, I'm sure they'd never say that,' Ruby laughed.

'Have you ever thought of trying the WEA?' he asked.

'Whatever's that?' cried Ruby.

'The Workers' Educational Association,' said Jim. 'They do classes for working-class people.' He paused. 'They're not very expensive.'

Ruby pulled the corners of her mouth down and shook her head. 'Never heard of them.'

There was a short pause and then he said, 'You know, I think every one of us gets at least one chance in life to change direction. It happened, for me, when I was watching Mr Hayward taking some pictures of the pier.'

'I remember Percy telling me the story,' Ruby smiled. 'He asked you if you wanted to look into the viewfinder.'

Jim nodded. 'I was fascinated right from the word go. I was just a kid, but Mr Hayward told me if I still felt the same about photography when I left school, I should come to his studios.'

'And you did?' said Ruby.

'I nearly didn't,' said Jim. 'The people in the

Home wanted me to be a nurseryman. They even had a job lined up for me, in the glasshouses along the Littlehampton Road.'

'Yes, of course,' said Ruby. For a moment she had quite forgotten that Jim was an orphan and was brought up in a children's home. 'I'm sorry. I didn't mean to remind you.'

'Don't be,' said Jim. 'It's life.'

'Were they upset that you didn't want to work in the glasshouses?'

'For a while,' said Jim, 'but then they could see that a love of the camera was in my blood.'

'Making choices is fine for a boy,' said Ruby. 'Girls don't have that luxury. Girls are expected to get married. They won't have a lot of time for anything else, once children come along.'

'One day you will get your chance to follow your dreams,' said Jim. 'Just be sure of what you want, and don't let anything get in the way.'

'You sound like one of those agony aunts in magazines,' Ruby chuckled.

They stood quietly side-by-side, and Ruby began to think of other things. Was Jim still stepping out with Martha? The last she'd heard, Martha had got a well-paid job with a titled family and was saving hard, because she and Jim were practically engaged. She chewed the inside of her mouth anxiously. In the end she had to ask him. 'How is Martha? Does she still write to you?' But as soon as the words were out of her mouth, Ruby could have kicked herself. Why did she have to bring up Martha Greenway?

'She's fine,' said Jim. 'She's coming back to Worthing in a couple of months.'

53

'It'll be good to see her again,' said Ruby. As a matter of fact she didn't really care one way or the other, but it was something to say. Although she had nothing against Martha, she and Martha Greenway had never been the best of pals.

'I guess so,' said Jim with a shrug.

His remark puzzled Ruby. He'd made it sound as if he wasn't bothered if he never saw Martha again.

There was a shout, and they knew it was time to go back to the tea rooms. Ruby shivered and rubbed her bare arms.

'Cold?' asked Jim.

'It is a bit chilly,' she conceded. He took off his coat and threw it over her shoulders. 'Thank you,' she whispered.

'You're welcome,' he said

As they walked back to the mill, Ruby pulled the sleeves around her. Jim's coat was lovely and warm, and it smelled of him.

CHAPTER 3

The little concert was a great success and everyone agreed that it had been a lovely day. With the proceeds from the raffle as well, they had raised £4 19s. 6d. Of course May had been disappointed that her father wasn't there to hear her sing her solo, but the encouragement and praise she got from everyone else more than made up for it. On the way home she fell asleep on Bea's lap on the coach, and Albert Longman carried her back into the cottage, almost falling over a suitcase left by the front door. Ruby carried it into the scullery and put her sister to bed. By the time she'd done all that, Albert had gone and she was ready for bed herself. She had to be up at five the next day to make sure she was at the hotel by six. It wouldn't do to upset Mrs Fosdyke.

Ruby began her new day at Warnes Hotel by cleaning the front step as usual, followed by the dining room and the hallway. After using the Vactric, she had to dust every piece of furniture, straighten every cushion and, in the winter, lay the fires. Now that it was summer, she had to dust around the big flower arrangement in the hearth and pick up any cigarette ends that the guests had thrown into the empty grate. As she worked, a couple of flowers fell out of the vase. Winnie, the florist, wasn't due in that day, so Ruby stuffed them back as best she could. She was sure Winnie would have made a much better job of it, but it was the best she could do.

Ruby enjoyed this part of her work the most, because she wasn't alone. The other cleaners and chambermaids joined in and they all worked together. Few people were up at that time of the morning. Breakfast wasn't until eight-thirty, unless a guest specifically asked for an earlier one, so even the kitchen staff didn't appear much before seven. As part of her privileged position, Mrs Fosdyke didn't come on duty until eight forty-five, so the girls could chat as they worked. There was too much to do to indulge in frivolity, and Ruby kept them in line, but at least they could catch up with everybody's news.

Most girls were about Ruby's age, although Phyllis Dawson had been in the hotel for more than twenty years. They called her a 'simple girl' because there were things she couldn't understand and she got very upset if she was told off, but Phyllis had a sweet nature. She liked working with Ruby, so she stuck close.

Edith Parsons came from the area of Worthing called Heene, where she lived with her widowed mother and three siblings. A rather plain girl with dowdy clothes, Edith was a little older than Ruby and she had already had a hard life. Her father had died of tuberculosis about a year ago and, young as she was, Edith was the main breadwinner in the house. Her mother took in washing and cleaned at the local public baths to make ends meet, but Ruby knew Edith had little time for fun.

Doris Fox was by far the prettiest of the chambermaids. At nineteen, she had blonde hair and blue eyes and a fashionably slim figure, perfect for the long-line dresses so favoured at the moment. She was stepping out with a taxi driver she'd met at one of the dances at the Assembly Hall, and Ruby felt it wouldn't be long before she left to get married. Unemployment wasn't as bad in Worthing as it was in other parts of the country, but no self-respecting hotel employed young married women. A woman's place was in the home, especially once children came along; and besides, there were plenty of single young women who would jump at the chance to work for a prestigious employer like the Warnes Hotel.

'So come on, Ruby,' said Doris. 'Tell us all about yesterday.'

Ruby made sure they were all doing specific jobs, and then Doris, Edith and Phyllis were all ears as she told them about her rescue of Dr Palmer, and about the concert they'd all enjoyed on the hill.

'We began with a couple of old Sussex songs,' she said. '"Sussex Won't be Druv" and "Sussex by the Sea".'

'I like that one,' said Phyllis, and immediately started humming the tune.

'Everyone was touched by May's sweet solo,' Ruby went on. 'I saw several people wiping away a tear or two as she sang and, when she'd finished, the applause went on for a very long time.'

'Aaah,' sighed Doris. 'I wish I'd been there.'

'Nice doing things as a family,' said Edith wistfully.

Embarrassed, Ruby turned her head. She had deliberately left out the bit about the row with Percy, and her father stalking off in a huff, but then some things were best left private. She was now on her hands and knees, dusting the ornamental legs of an Indian-style table. Once it was dusted, she put a little polish on a cloth and gave the legs a shine. She loved the smell of lavender and took pride in her work.

'I suppose your brother went up on his bicycle?' said Doris.

'He did,' said Ruby. 'Quite a few of the cycling club went with him.' She named a few names, including that of Jim Searle.

'Oooh,' said Edith. 'Did Martha come as well?'

With a little stab of jealousy, Ruby shook her head.

Doris pulled the corners of her mouth down. 'So did Dr Palmer stay to the bitter end?' she asked.

Ruby nodded. 'I was quite surprised,' she said. 'I mean, the singing wasn't the sort of quality he must be used to.'

'But he enjoyed it,' said Doris.

'Actually, he was quite generous in his praise.'

'How did he get home?' Doris was putting a vase of limp flowers onto a trolley, ready to push it into the outside kitchen. 'You never brought him back here in the coach, did you?'

'We did,' said Ruby. 'Right to the door.'

'Blimey,' said Doris. 'Talk about lowering the tone. A coach outside Warnes Hotel. Whatever next?'

The four of them laughed, although Ruby had a sneaky feeling that Phyllis didn't really understand why.

They heard pots and pans clanging in the kitchen and knew that the chef must have arrived and that breakfast was on its way. Before long, a delicious smell of bacon filtered through, and it was time to move into other areas of the hotel. They wheeled the flowers into the outside kitchen and laid the table in the staffroom. Breakfast for them would come much later, between nine and ten, and would have to be taken in haste, and in shifts. No guest had to be kept waiting, so their needs came first. Ruby was grateful for her meals. Some were much better than she could expect at home, but she often ate cold bacon and congealed eggs because she had been delayed in coming to the table.

She had lunch at the hotel as well. Once her shift was done, she came back to the staffroom to eat pie and vegetables or fish or, best of all, her firm favourite of chicken stew. Apart from the occasional broiler, the chances of eating chicken at home were slim, except maybe at Christmas. With a few hours off in the afternoon, Ruby would be back at five for a cup of tea and a piece of cake, before she had to turn the beds down while the guests were eating dinner.

Cleaning the bedrooms passed without incident today, which was just as well because Ruby was tired from the day before. She had barely started on her plate of beef stew and dumplings when Mrs Fosdyke burst through the door.

'Mr Payne wants to see you, Bateman,' she blurted out. 'In his office – now!'

The Warnes family might own the hotel, but Mr Payne was the manager. A strictly no-nonsense man, a stickler for punctuality and strong on personal hygiene, he had only been seen once by Ruby in passing, but she'd heard about his reputation. Until now, she had never once spoken to him or been to his office.

Ruby's knees buckled. A summons from Mr Payne meant only one thing: the sack. But what had she done? She glanced around helplessly, but the other chambermaids avoided her eyes.

'I'll keep your dinner warm,' said Phyllis, putting a clean plate over the top of Ruby's meal.

'Come along, Bateman,' Mrs Fosdyke snapped. 'Mr Payne doesn't want to be kept waiting all day.'

It had been another warm day, so Nelson was preparing his boat and the driftnet, ready to set off in the early evening, an ideal time to catch mackerel. The net itself would drift with the current and form a curtain underwater; and the fish, going into the net, would be trapped by their gills. Nelson always did well, catching everything from herrings to pilchards, sprats and sea bass, as well as mackerel. Although the waters around Worthing had been depleted since the halcyon days of the Victorian era, he made a decent living. He knew exactly where to find a shoal congregating in the upper water offshore, which was fast-flowing and where the gulls often dived down. He planned to stop his boat and drift through it. If finding mackerel there was a problem, he could move on to Goring, where there was a good chance of finding some flounders or plaice, both of which were popular with the locals. At this time of year the sea yielded up her plenty, and he was doing all right.

A shadow fell over him, blocking the sunlight. 'Oh, so you decided to turn up after all,' he said sarcastically. He looked up to see not his son Percy, as he was expecting, but Albert Longman, dressed in what looked like his Sunday best.

He frowned. 'What are you doing on the beach dressed like that?'

'I've come straight from work,' said Albert. 'I wanted to ask you something.'

Albert lived with his mother north of the railway line somewhere near St Dunstan's Road. He'd met Percy through the social club, although he and Percy had never been great friends. At nearly

60

thirty, Albert was unattached. He was dark-haired and had a rather large nose and narrow eyes. He had high cheekbones and wore his hair short, cut in an old-fashioned pudding-basin style. Being a reporter, he was – in Nelson's opinion – a bit of a big-head. Nelson's lip curled as Albert took off his trilby and coughed into his fist.

'Well?'

'I've come to ask your permission to step out with your daughter, Mr Bateman,' he said, licking his fingers and pressing down his hair at the front.

Nelson snorted. 'Good God!'

'I've got a good job,' Albert went on, 'and...'

Nelson's eyebrows shot up. 'You want to marry Ruby? Whatever for?'

Albert's expression darkened. 'What do you mean: whatever for? Why would you say that? She's your daughter.'

'But you've got the pick of the town,' said Nelson, recovering quickly. 'There isn't a girl in Worthing who wouldn't give her right arm to marry you.'

Albert tilted his head and smiled. 'That's true, but I want Ruby,' he said. Nelson hesitated, so he added, 'I may only be at the *Gazette* right now, but I have good prospects. I also have an inheritance from my grandfather.'

'An inheritance?' said Nelson.

'A small cottage,' replied Albert. 'They say it's perfect for a young married couple.'

'And where might that be?' said Nelson.

'Hastings.'

Nelson tidied up the already-tidy nets, to give

61

himself a chance to think. Hastings was nearly fifty miles away. If Ruby went to live that far away, it would be difficult for her to get home that often and, once she had children... He smiled to himself.

'All right.' He swung his legs over the side of the boat and stood on the beach. 'I'll say yes, but I won't have any of my family bringing trouble home.'

'I won't touch her until the day we wed,' said Albert quickly.

The two men each held the other's gaze, then Nelson shook Albert firmly by the hand. It was a little damp.

'Thank you, Mr Bateman. You won't regret it.'

As the two men parted, Nelson couldn't believe what had just happened. What a turn-up for the books. Ha! Albert would make Ruby the perfect husband. He watched his future son-in-law struggling over the pebble beach and chuckled to himself. He leaned over the boat and put in the dhan flag he used as a marker when putting out the nets. He might not have got rid of Percy, but it looked like the girl would soon be off his hands. His duty as a father was almost done.

'What have you been up to, Bateman?' Mrs Fosdyke hissed as they headed for the lift.

'Nothing, Mrs Fosdyke,' Ruby protested.

'Well, it must be something,' the housekeeper insisted. She pressed the button for the top floor. 'I make an exception, to give you a special day off, and this is how you repay me. In all my years working in this hotel, no member of my staff has ever been summoned to Mr Payne's office.'

The lift doors opened and the startled lift operator, an ex-soldier called Scotty, stepped back nervously. Mrs Fosdyke and Ruby walked in.

'The manager's office,' Mrs Fosdyke snapped.

Scotty glanced sideways at Ruby, but she averted his gaze and stared down at her shoes. As the lift ascended, she was racking her brains to work out what she had done wrong. What could possibly be so bad that she should be sent for by Mr Payne? Had someone seen her helping Miss Russell down the back stairs? Or into the taxi? There was nothing left in the room to indicate that she'd been taken ill, for Ruby had cleaned it thoroughly. In fact the whole plan seemed to have been executed perfectly. So what had gone wrong? Had Miss Russell's father found out, and complained that Ruby should have told him? Ruby's head ached with the thought of it. She should never have gone for Dr Palmer. She should have ignored Miss Russell's pleas and sent for the hotel doctor. If this was the reason why Mr Payne had sent for her, there was little point trying to explain. Miss Russell was guilty of fornication, and Ruby had aided and abetted her in covering up her sin. They would think Miss Russell had got what she deserved if it came out, it would be a public scandal, and the management of the hotel would need a scapegoat. She didn't need three guesses as to who that might be.

Ruby's heart was thumping. They rode to the top floor in silence. The doors opened and Mrs Fosdyke sailed into the corridor. As Ruby followed meekly behind, she glanced back and Scotty gave her a sympathetic thumbs-up sign. The doors closed behind her and he was gone.

Outside the office door Mrs Fosdyke looked Ruby up and down. 'Smooth down that apron,' she commanded, 'and put that stray bit of hair back under your cap.'

Miserably Ruby complied with her wishes.

Mrs Fosdyke cleared her throat, pulled back her shoulders and gave the heavy wooden door a sharp rap.

'Come,' said a voice on the other side.

When Mrs Fosdyke opened the door and marched in, Ruby wondered if it would be better simply to run away. If they sacked her, she'd be without a reference. She'd never get another job. Not a decent one anyway. Father would never let her hear the end of it. Her eyes were already smarting with unshed tears.

The room itself was quite dark, even though it had a large window overlooking the Steyne. At least, she supposed it was the Steyne. A large tree waved its uppermost branches just beyond the windowpane. The walls were panelled with dark wood. Mr Payne, a pale, bald-headed man, clean-shaven but with thick-rimmed glasses, sat behind a huge desk that almost engulfed him. As they walked in, he put his elbows on the leather top and pressed the tips of his fingers together.

'This is Bateman,' said Mrs Fosdyke. 'You sent for her, sir.'

'Yes, yes, I did,' said Mr Payne. The sound of his voice was quite a surprise to Ruby. For someone reputed to be so fearsome, she had expected a large, booming voice, but it was thin and high-

64

pitched, almost squeaky. 'Step forward, girl. Let me have a look at you.'

Trembling, Ruby stood with her head bowed in front of the desk.

'Is this the girl?' Mr Payne asked, and for the first time Ruby became aware that someone else was in the room.

'It certainly is.'

Ruby turned her head to see Dr Palmer sitting in a high-backed wing chair beside her. 'Oh, sir!' she gasped.

'Speak when you are spoken to, Bateman,' Mrs Fosdyke snapped.

Ruby's mind was in a whirl. Why was Dr Palmer complaining about her? She couldn't think of a single thing she might have done to upset him – unless, of course, it was because they had brought the coach to the front door of Warnes. Had Mr Payne found out and complained? Was Dr Palmer blaming her? The driver had only been trying to help. Or maybe it was nothing to do with the trip itself. Was Dr Palmer annoyed because Father and Percy had got into a heated argument with him?

'I'm sorry if I upset you in any way, sir,' she said, ignoring Mrs Fosdyke's instructions and addressing Dr Palmer. And, turning to Mr Payne, she added, 'I had no intention of damaging the hotel's reputation, sir.'

Beside her, Mrs Fosdyke tutted and sighed.

'Damaging the hotel's reputation?' repeated Mr Payne. 'Why, my dear girl, it's quite the contrary.'

'Indeed,' said Dr Palmer. 'I have told Mr Payne of the great service you did me yesterday, and what a credit you are to Warnes Hotel. In fact, he agrees with me that you should be rewarded, Miss Bateman.'

Ruby was conscious that her mouth was gaping.

Mr Payne stood up. 'Permit me to shake your hand, Miss Bateman,' he said. 'I only wish we had more conscientious girls like you working in the hotel. Dr Palmer has explained to me that had you and your friends not plucked him from that scurrilous mob, he might not have survived beyond yesterday afternoon.'

With that, Mr Payne shook Ruby's hand warmly and then handed her an envelope. 'Mrs Fosdyke, give this girl the rest of the day off, and inform the wages department that she is to have an extra two shillings and sixpence in her wage packet.'

'This week, sir?' Mrs Fosdyke asked stiffly.

'This and every week,' said Mr Payne.

As Ruby gasped in surprise, Dr Palmer gave her a wink.

CHAPTER 4

Nelson was still by his locker checking his nets and lines. He was a meticulous fisherman, always up to date with his cleaning and making sure that his equipment was in top-notch condition. He heard a footfall on the stones and looked up. Linton Carver, although well dressed, was a pathetic shadow of his former self. Unable to function properly since he was gassed during the Great War, he lived in the old village of Heene to the west of

Worthing. However, everyone agreed that Linton was a lot luckier than the other poor sods at Ypres, who'd died a terrible death in those trenches, gasping for breath and in agony. He might have trouble breathing sometimes, but at least he was alive, with his own private income and a home of his own. Like Nelson, he never spoke of his experiences in France, but today something was clearly troubling him.

'Somebody's been asking questions,' he said bluntly.

Nelson looked round crossly. 'What do you mean: somebody's been asking questions?' he snapped. 'What questions? Who?'

'I dunno who,' said Linton. 'I couldn't see her face, but two women on the bus were talking about Victor.'

Nelson froze. 'Why bring him up, after all this time?'

'Search me,' cried Linton. He flopped onto the stones and, picking one up, threw it as hard as he could. It fell short of the water by several feet, and his breathing became bad. 'What are we going to do, Nelson? If this ever gets out...'

'Keep your voice down,' Nelson hissed. 'Nothing is going to get out.'

'You sure about that?'

'Course I am,' Nelson snapped.

'I'm not,' said Linton. 'You see, I think it's more than what happened in that barn. There's my uncle Jack Harris, remember?'

'Jack Harris!' Nelson scoffed.

'And the others,' said Linton.

'What others?'

67

'You're forgetting Chipper Norton,' Linton went on miserably.

'For God's sake!' said Nelson. 'Look, Jack's death was an accident, and Chipper Norton never could hold his liquor. What's the matter with you? Pull yourself together, will you? You're getting yourself all worked up over a couple of gossips on a bus.'

'I suppose you're right,' Linton agreed sulkily.

'Of course I'm right,' said Nelson tetchily. 'Forget about it. Just keep your head down and your trap shut.'

Linton nodded miserably. 'If only we could turn the clock back...'

'I don't want to hear it, man,' Nelson hissed. 'Get a grip, will you?'

Linton stayed where he was, staring glumly out to sea, but the silence between them was hardly companionable. After some time Nelson slammed the lid of his locker shut and trudged back up the beach.

It wasn't until she had changed into her own clothes and was ready to go that Ruby opened the white envelope. She lowered herself onto the only chair in the staff changing room and her mouth dropped open. She was quite alone and, apart from Mrs Fosdyke herself, no one knew she had been given the rest of the day off. That and a pay rise were, in Ruby's mind, reward enough. In fact she didn't even deserve that accolade. She'd only done what any other decent person would have done in the circumstances, and if the boot had been on the other foot, she hoped that Dr Palmer would have rescued her from the mob. If that had been the case, there would have been no reward. Her position was such that she would only be able to give him her heartfelt thanks. But here she was, staring at a five-pound note. Ruby had never seen one before – at least not close up. She'd sometimes seen them peeping out of a wallet when she was cleaning someone's room, but she'd never owned one of her own. She took it out and smoothed it out on her lap. It was flimsy and white, and she read the words carefully:

I promise to pay the Bearer on Demand
the Sum of Five Pounds
1930 July 12 London 12 July 1930
For the Govr. and Comp^a. of the
Bank of England.

And it was signed: *B. G. Catterns, Chief Cashier.*
Five pounds. *Five pounds!* She'd never had so much money in her life before. Five pounds was three weeks' wages all in one go. What she could buy with five pounds. She could have a party and invite everybody she knew. She could buy brand-new clothes instead of second-hand ones. She and her mother got their dresses from the DeLux Dress agency and they were good-quality, but they were still someone else's hand-me-downs. She could take a trip to London and see some of the sights people talked about: Trafalgar Square and Buckingham Palace ... or perhaps the Tower of London. Ruby enjoyed a delicious little shudder as she imagined herself walking around the same cold rooms where poor Anne Boleyn had waited

69

for her execution on the orders of King Henry VIII. What she could do with five pounds!

As she put it back into the envelope, Jim's voice came back to her mind: *'every one of us gets at least one chance in life to change direction...'* Was this her moment? Yes, she could do all the things she'd imagined, but they would be over in a trice. All she would have to show for it would be a lovely memory, or a pretty dress that would eventually wear out, or she would grow bored with it.

Five pounds wouldn't necessarily change her whole life, but it could be the start of something that might make a difference. *'Just be sure of what you want, and don't let anything get in the way.'* That's what Jim had advised, but right now she couldn't make up her mind what she wanted. She carefully put the note back in the envelope, and put the envelope in her bag. Just then, the door burst open and Edith stood in front of her.

'Oh, Ruby,' she cried, looking her up and down, 'I am so sorry.' She put her arms around a startled Ruby and pulled her close. 'I can't believe this has happened. How awful for you. But you mustn't worry too much. I'm sure you'll get another job straight away.' When she let go and stepped back, Ruby could see that Edith had tears in her eyes.

'Hang on a minute,' Ruby laughed. 'I haven't been sacked.'

'You haven't?' said Edith. 'But I thought the fact that you've got your coat on...'

'I've been given the rest of the day off, for saving Dr Palmer.'

Edith stared at her for a second and then beamed. 'You jammy dog!' she said, giving Ruby a playful slap on her arm. 'That's two days running.'

Embarrassed, Ruby avoided her eye.

'Oh, go on,' said Edith. 'Enjoy yourself. Next week it'll be my turn to save some poor old boy and, when I do it, I won't stop at a measly half a day off. I shall insist that he marry me and, when I've got all his money, I'll divorce him and marry the handsome chauffeur.'

The two friends laughed and, arm-in-arm, Edith escorted Ruby to the door.

As she strolled towards the beach on her own, Ruby felt a twinge of guilt that she hadn't told Edith everything. She sat on the stones. She loved this place, with its pretty pier jutting out to sea. It had been put up in Victorian times and visitors were charged tuppence to walk along the boards from the kiosk at the entrance. The fee allowed people to listen to the orchestra, which played between spring and autumn in the Southern Pavilion. The other pavilion, on the shore side of the pier, had variety shows. There was also a souvenir shop next door. Ruby loved it all. She loved the Dome cinema opposite, the Punch-and-Judy on the beach and the deckchairs you could hire. She loved to see the tourists strolling along the promenade and to hear the cry of the gulls.

The Lyons ice-cream boy went by calling, 'Stop me and buy one...' and she smiled to herself. The ice creams were loaded into a big box on the front of his tricycle, and the slogan on his crossbar also said: *Stop me and buy one.* The sun was still warm and bathers splashed in the sea. The tide was coming in now, and she knew that on the beach at East Worthing her father would be preparing the

71

boat ready for fishing. She sighed and wondered what he would say when she told him she'd been given five pounds. For a moment or two she fantasized that he would smile and tell her it was wonderful. He would give her a bear hug and kiss her roughly on the forehead, in the same way he kissed May, and then he would grab her hands and they would dance around the kitchen, laughing and crying at the same time.

A gull landed a few feet in front of her and regarded her with its cold eye. That's when Ruby came down to earth. Her father wouldn't be pleased about the money, would he? He'd probably stare at her like that gull, with its cold and untrusting eye, and question her honesty. And, even if he did believe her story, it wouldn't occur to him that she might want to do something with the money herself. She could just hear him making his own plans for a new bit of fishing gear or a couple of new lobster pots.

'Well, you're not having it,' she said crossly. 'It's *my* money.'

Until she was sure what she wanted to do, she wouldn't tell anyone about the five pounds. She would put the money somewhere safe – somewhere nobody could touch it – and then make up her mind. The sun came out from under a cloud and warmed her face. Ruby stood up and brushed the back of her dress down. She would go straight into town and open a Post Office savings account.

Back home, Ruby pulled the suitcase out of the scullery, where she'd left it the night before. It felt quite heavy; she was disappointed. Obviously not much had been taken out yet, and she'd thought it would be really helpful. She'd been reading an article in one of the magazines left behind by a guest. In America, the Depression had bitten deep. Years of drought and deep ploughing had created 'black blizzards' as the soil, now with the consistency of dust, was carried away by the wind. The people were starving, and yet the article spoke of their resilience and how they helped each other by sharing their skills instead of paying money for services. The idea had created a strong sense of community, and it struck a chord with Ruby. The people in her own street were all going through some sort of hardship, to a lesser or greater degree. She knew, for instance, that Tilly Morgan's girls – a couple of years younger than May – wore dresses that were far too small, and yet when her mother had offered Tilly a couple of May's old dresses that were in perfectly good nick, Mrs Morgan had refused them. 'Thank you very much, but I don't take charity,' Tilly had said stiffly.

At the time Ruby had thought it just plain stupid but, on reflection, perhaps her stubborn pride was all Tilly Morgan had left. There had to be a way of sharing things that didn't allow pride to get in the way. It was when she saw her mother and Aunt Vinny swapping a couple of cardigans that she had the idea.

Bea gave her the old suitcase from under the bed, and Ruby put some of May's old dresses inside. She herself had bought a frock from the second-hand shop, but when she'd got it home, she didn't like it. That went in too; and Aunt Vinny contributed a few things, including some of Cousin Lily's casts-offs. With a little room left in the suitcase, Ruby set out for her neighbour's house.

'We've been passing this suitcase around the neighbours,' she'd told Thelma Brown, her first choice to try out the new scheme. 'The idea is that you see if you'd like something from it, and put something that you don't want in the suitcase, to replace it.'

Thelma had looked a little sceptical until she opened the case.

'Of course, it goes without saying that whatever you put in,' Ruby went on, as Thelma held up one of Aunt Vinny's blouses to the light, 'should be clean and usable, but it doesn't matter how many things you take out, so long as you put something back in.'

Thelma looked up. 'I'm not sure if this will fit.'

'Try it on,' said Ruby. 'In fact,' she added, as if she'd only just thought of the idea, 'why don't you keep the case for a day or two, and then pass it on to someone else. Tilly Morgan perhaps.'

'I will,' said Thelma, 'and then I'll bring it back to yours.'

That was a week ago, and now the suitcase was back. She undid the fasteners and lifted the lid. May's dresses had gone, but some smaller clothes were in their place. There was a man's pullover and a couple of skirts she didn't recognize, but there was also a blouse she was sure she'd seen Norah Granger wearing on the day of the outing, when she'd helped Dr Palmer onto the coach.

Ruby tugged at the pretty scarf, which had come from Cousin Lily. She had really liked it when she'd put it into the suitcase, but nobody had taken it out. When she'd put in the dress that she'd bought at the second-hand shop, she hadn't taken anything for herself, so Ruby took it for herself now. With the scarf around her neck, she closed the case. It was time to pass it on to Florrie Dart.

'What do you mean, you were given half a day off?' Her father was incredulous. 'What – just for pulling that old man into the coach?'

'And another two and sixpence in my wage packet,' said Ruby.

Her mother gave her a hug. 'Oh, Ruby, that's wonderful. Well done.'

Percy clapped her on the shoulder. 'Good on you, Sis,' he grinned. 'Do that a few more times and you'll be a rich woman.'

May stayed where she was, with her elbows on the table and her head resting on her left hand. 'Will you buy me some sweeties when you get paid?'

They had just eaten their tea. When Ruby got back from Florrie's place, she had gone straight up to the room she shared with May. She'd put her Post Office book in the wardrobe, right at the back, in an old handbag she never used. It was her secret. She wasn't going to tell anyone about it; but, after their meal, she had to explain why she wasn't going back to Warnes to turn the beds down.

Her father stood up and, for one glorious moment, Ruby actually thought he was going to give her a hug, but instead he went to the hearth and picked up his fisherman's boots. Sitting back in his chair, he pulled them on.

'What gets me,' he began, 'is that you didn't even do it yourself. It was Cecil and Albert Longman who did all the work. Where's their reward then, eh?'

'Couldn't you – just for once – say something nice to Ruby?' Percy demanded.

'It's all right for you, swanning around with your extra two and sixpence and a half-day off,' said Nelson, ignoring his son, 'but some of us work hard for a living.'

'I work hard too, Father,' Ruby bristled.

Her father grunted. 'Coming, boy?'

'Trust you to go spoiling things,' said Percy. 'You miserable old devil.'

Their father leapt to his feet, his eyes blazing and his arm raised.

'Don't you dare lay a hand on me,' said Percy coldly. 'Hit me and it'll be the last thing you do.'

'You should learn some respect,' Nelson spat. He began to unbuckle his trouser belt. In an attitude of defiance, Percy stood slowly to his feet, his eyes fixed on his father's face.

Ruby pulled on her brother's arm to stop him. 'Percy, don't.'

'Respect is something you earn,' Percy retorted.

'Nelson, please,' cried Bea, standing between them.

'If he hits me again, Mother, I swear I'll walk out of that door and never come back.'

'Don't tempt me,' said Nelson, lowering his arm. 'Get your boots on. The tide is on the turn.' He looked away and the atmosphere in the room became less charged.

Reluctantly Percy went to get his boots. Nelson swung round and looked at Ruby. 'And you can give that two and sixpence to your mother,' he said. 'It's about time you paid your way in this house.'

Ruby's face flushed.

'Be fair, Nelson,' said Bea. 'It's Ruby's money. If she hadn't seen Dr Palmer and made Cecil stop the coach, nobody would have been any the wiser.'

'Did anyone ask your opinion?' Nelson demanded. Bea cowered. 'No. Then keep your nose out of it.'

Deflated and miserable, Ruby sat back down at the table. Avoiding her daughter's eye, Bea busied herself by stacking the dishes, ready to wash up.

'By the way,' Nelson said to Ruby, 'Albert Longman stopped by to see me about you.'

Ruby frowned. 'Albert Longman?'

'It seems he's sweet on you,' said her father. He laughed sardonically. 'Although what he sees in you, I can't imagine. Your hair is as straight as a die and you've got no shape, but there it is. There's none so blind, as they say, and he wants to court you.'

'Albert Longman?' said Ruby again.

'That's what I said, cloth ears,' Nelson snapped. 'Anyway, I told him it was all right.'

'But I'm not in the least bit interested in Albert Longman,' Ruby cried. The thought of it filled her with horror, and she could feel tears pricking the backs of her eyes. 'I've never thought of him in that way. I don't even like him.'

'Well, you must have encouraged him some-

77

how, or he wouldn't have asked me,' said Nelson. 'Anyway he's coming round Sunday. Come and kiss your pa, May darlin'.'

'Father, he's years older than me,' Ruby insisted. 'I don't want to be married to an old man.'

May climbed down from the table and Nelson picked her up. 'Be a good girl for Pa, won't you?' he said, kissing her cheek and ignoring Ruby.

'I will,' said May and wriggled down. Stopping only to ruffle her hair, Nelson walked out of the room.

'Father!' cried Ruby.

Percy turned to follow him, but then turned back to kiss his mother and sister.

'Good fishing,' said Ruby, giving him a sad smile.

'Well done, Sis,' he said, lowering his voice. 'Whatever they gave you, you deserve it.'

'But I don't deserve Albert flippin' Longman.'

'You coming, boy?' their father shouted from the street. 'We haven't got all day.'

Percy patted her shoulder. 'You're right. You definitely don't deserve Albert Longman.' And they both grinned.

CHAPTER 5

The next few days were difficult for Ruby. Nothing was said, but it was clear that the events in Mr Payne's office had for some reason annoyed Mrs Fosdyke. From her demeanour when she'd summoned her, Ruby guessed that Mrs Fosdyke had expected her to get a reprimand, or the sack. She had been as surprised as Ruby herself when she got an accolade and a reward. Ruby did her work efficiently, as usual, but the housekeeper followed close behind her, complaining about trivial things. 'Those towels aren't straight, Bateman.' 'Bateman, the curtains in room 34 weren't pulled back far enough.' 'You've forgotten to put a serving spoon on the staff table again, and where's the soap for the sink in room 38?' The final straw came when Ruby returned to her perfect linen cupboard to put in some clean sheets.

'Morning, Ruby,' Winnie, the florist, called cheerfully as she walked by.

'Good morning,' Ruby smiled. For some reason she'd difficulty in getting the linen-cupboard door open and, when she finally did, she discovered that Mrs Fosdyke had pulled everything from the shelves onto the floor. Her heart sank and tears sprang to her eyes. She was going off-duty in ten minutes, and refolding and stacking everything into neat piles would take at least an hour.

'Oh, dear,' said Winnie sympathetically. 'That's a shame. I'd offer to help but...'

'Blimey, Roob,' said Edith, coming up behind her. 'What has the old witch done now?'

'I wondered what Mrs Fosdyke was doing,' said Winnie. 'That was a bit unkind, wasn't it?'

'I really wish I hadn't been given that extra half-day off,' said Ruby miserably. 'She's made my life hell ever since.'

'Don't let the bugger get you down,' said Edith. 'She likes to see she's upset you. Don't give her the satisfaction.' She bent to pick up some pillow-cases. 'Come on, let's get started.'

'Well, I'll leave you to it,' said Winnie, collecting her things and going upstairs. 'I've only got a couple more vases to do, and then I'll come and help.'

'That's all right, Mrs Moore,' said Edith. 'Ruby and I'll get it done in no time.'

'You don't have to stay either, Edith,' said Ruby, blowing her nose. 'Why should you give up your afternoon as well?'

'Because you're my pal,' said Edith, 'and besides, with two of us on the job, we'll get it done in no time.'

Ruby could have hugged her.

'You'll never guess,' said Edith.

'What?'

'I've got a gentleman caller.'

Ruby's eyebrows shot up.

'Don't look so surprised,' beamed Edith.

'I – I'm not,' said Ruby, slightly flustered. 'It's just that you used such an old-fashioned expression.' She hoped Edith believed her. She didn't want to hurt her feelings, for the world. 'Who is he? Do we know him?'

'His name is Bernard Gressenhall,' said Edith, 'and he works at Potter & Bailey in Montague Street – on the bacon counter.'

The people who worked at Potter & Bailey wore long aprons over their clothes, so it was hard try-ing to recall any distinguishing features. However, Ruby did vaguely remember a rather jolly man with dark hair who worked on the bacon counter.

'He's ever so nice,' Edith went on. 'He's got a

80

brother in the army, and his dad works on the railway. We're off to the pictures on my day off.'

'Good for you,' smiled Ruby. 'I wish there was someone I was keen on. Though there is someone interested in me, it seems,' she said.

'Oh?'

'Apparently,' Ruby said confidentially, leaning closer, 'Albert Longman asked my father if he could court me.'

'Oh, Ruby,' cried Edith. 'He's such a bloomin' bighead.' They were folding sheets as a team, and the cupboard was quickly taking shape. They heard a rustle behind them and froze, thinking it was Mrs Fosdyke, but it was only Winnie Moore coming back downstairs. 'Oh, you gave us a scare,' said Edith.

'Sorry, dear,' she said. 'Can I give you a hand?'

'We've nearly finished,' said Ruby, 'but thanks for offering.'

'I'll leave you to it then,' said Winnie with a nod.

Edith waited until she was out of earshot and then said, 'You don't like Albert Longman, do you?'

'No, I don't. He may be good with children – that's what they all say – but he's old. He's boring.'

'All right, keep your hair on,' Edith laughed. 'Do you fancy a stroll when we've finished this? There's hardly time for me to get back home, before I have to come back to turn the beds down.'

'Yes,' said Ruby, 'why not? I might even treat you to an ice cream, if you like.'

'Oooh, thanks, Roob,' said Edith.

The weather was quite good as they came down the staff stairs, but when they stepped into the

81

street there was an acrid smell in the air.

Edith took a deep breath. 'Whatever's that?'

'It smells like a fire,' said Ruby, and at almost the same moment a fire engine came hurtling out of High Street and into the Steyne, its bell clanging. People were running along Marine Parade, but it wasn't until they turned the corner that they saw the heavy pall of dark-grey smoke.

'The pier!' cried Ruby. 'The pier is on fire.'

They hurried along the road, hardly able to believe their own eyes. Hundreds of holidaymakers, some still in their bathing costumes and others with wet towels over their mouths, had formed a human chain and were struggling to salvage articles from the Southern Pavilion. As they broke into a run along Marine Parade, a group of men were trundling a grand piano along the walkway, and by the time they got onto the pier themselves, they were met by people carrying plush seats, tables and chairs. It was obvious that the people of Worthing were anxious to save whatever they could from the inferno.

Ruby was so upset she could have cried. The lovely pier, where she'd walked as a child, was going up in smoke. Where would the men who fished off the end go now? Where would the Waverley paddle steamer dock if the pier was gone? Who would want to come to Worthing if there was no pier?

The firemen had rolled out a hose, but some well-meaning civilians had accidentally knocked one of the joins apart before the water could reach the seat of the fire.

'Look out!' someone cried, as another man reversed a car onto what remained of the walkway. Ruby and Edith helped the rescuers load it up with bits of furniture and anything else they could lay their hands on. It was imperative to take it to the shore, and safety. Another human chain, from the iron steps to the water's edge, was passing buckets of sea water up and was dousing the decking. Dodging a photographer who was taking pictures, Ruby and Edith decided they could be of more help by joining them.

Fit young men then began attacking the wooden planks halfway along the pier.

'What on earth are they doing?' Ruby cried, dismayed. 'Why are they pulling it apart?'

'To try and stop the flames from taking the whole thing,' said a man with a handkerchief on his head, knotted at each corner. 'I'd help them too, if it weren't for me bad back.'

Some men had picks and some had crowbars, whilst others prised the planks away with whatever they could find. They were doing quite well until a man stepped back, not realizing that the decking behind him had already been removed. There was a terrified scream, and seconds later he hit the water some fifteen feet below. By some miracle he missed the girders on the way down and wasn't hurt. Ruby was relieved to see him being picked up by the coxswain of the Worthing Inshore Rescue boat, who was patrolling the area in the sea around the pier.

Underneath them, and a little further along, a fireman had attached a workman's ladder to one of the steel girders and began aiming the hose at the underside.

'The fire's running along the bottom,' said Edith anxiously. 'Let's hope it doesn't get all the way to shore and burn the pavilion at the other end.'

Then they heard the sound of breaking glass. It sounded like machine-gun fire. 'Get back! Everybody get back,' shouted a fireman. 'It's too late. We haven't got a bloody chance.'

The smoke cleared for a second, and Ruby saw about fifty people running from the flames. They'd been caught out unawares as the cafe began to burn. A waitress came by in tears and was met by a man who pulled her into his arms.

'I've lost all our lovely wedding photos,' she wept. 'I brought them to show the girls at work.'

'Don't worry about it, darling,' said the man.

'We didn't even know it was on fire, until Mrs Tull saw the flames coming through the store-room door,' the girl sobbed.

'Never mind,' said the man, putting his arm around her and drawing her away. 'At least you're safe and sound. That's all that matters.'

The firemen had attached their hose to the only hydrant, which was 500 yards away from the seat of the fire. Ruby shielded her eyes from the smoke. It was beginning to catch in her throat, making her want to cough. Like the others, she was forced to pull back. Tears pricked her eyes. It seemed crazy that a structure overhanging the sea might be lost forever, for lack of water to put the flames out. Her chin was quivering. It felt as if an old friend was dying. How could this possibly have happened? And in broad daylight as well.

'Here, somebody take this.' A woman was pushing a charity box into her hands. She was covered in sooty marks and was perspiring profusely. Her dress, was dirty and torn. 'Keep it safe for me, luv.' She turned back and began picking her way along the pier.

'Where are you going?' Ruby cried after her.

'I've left my handbag on the seat,' the woman called.

'You can't go back,' Ruby shouted after her. 'It's too dangerous.'

'I must. It's got everything in it.'

She didn't get very far. A fireman sent her back in floods of tears, protesting loudly that she *had* to return. Eventually her friends came for her and she disappeared into the crowd.

Judging by the lack of sound from the collection box the woman had given her, there wasn't a lot inside it. Ruby looked round for a policeman. Once she and Edith had surrendered the box to a passing constable, they joined with others in moving the stacked deckchairs, in case the fire engulfed them as well. By now all the flames had given way to thick black smoke. The restaurant was completely engulfed, and the choking fumes lay along the pier like a shroud. After only about thirty minutes of chaos and controlled panic, it was all over, and the lovely pavilion was nothing but a charred ruin. Ruby and Edith stood with the others on the beach in a shared sad silence.

'Hello, Ruby.'

Her heart leapt as soon as she heard his voice. She knew who it was, without turning round. Jim Searle looked as handsome as ever. She hadn't realized he was the photographer taking pictures when she and Edith had rushed past him.

'I thought it was you,' he said, 'but I wasn't sure until I saw you handing in that box. That was amazing, what you did.'

'What – handing in a charity box?' said Edith incredulously.

'No, trying to save the pier.' Jim came closer. 'I've taken some pictures of you. I hope you don't mind.'

Ruby felt her face colour. 'Why on earth would you do that? I must look a dreadful sight.' She ran her fingers through her untidy hair.

'I will admit that you've got a smudge on your nose,' said Jim, taking out his handkerchief. 'But I thought you looked lovely. Here, allow me.'

As he gently rubbed her nose with the handkerchief, Ruby could hardly breathe. Surely he could hear her heart pounding in her chest. It was thudding so hard that she was scared it would jump out.

'Did you get some good pictures of the fire?' she asked, her voice an octave too high.

He nodded. 'Alan did too.'

'Alan?'

'Alan Duncan,' he smiled. 'He works for the *Worthing Herald*.'

'Which means you're worried that his pictures will be in all the local papers, and not yours?' said Ruby.

Jim smiled ruefully. 'Never mind. I've got some good ones to show my grandchildren.'

Ruby frowned. 'There's more than one paper in this country,' she said. 'The *Herald* and the *Gazette* might be spoken for, but what about the *Daily*

86

Sketch or the *News Chronicle?* I bet the London newspapers would give their eye-teeth for some good pictures.'

For a second Jim looked startled by her outburst.

'Get on the phone,' she cried.

Jim put his hands up in surrender. 'You're right. I will.'

'We'd better be getting back, Roob,' said Edith, looking down at her sooty hands. 'We've only got an hour to get cleaned up.'

'Come back to the studio,' said Jim. 'You can have a wash and brush-up, and I'll make you both a nice cup of tea.'

Ruby hesitated.

'Then you can make sure that I phone,' he grinned.

She lowered her eyes, blushed and smiled.

Warwick Studios wasn't far from Warnes Hotel. It was a little untidy, but contained just about everything you might need as a background for a photograph. Ruby spotted some lovely drapes, and a maidenhair fern in a large jardinière. There were several chairs of different shapes and sizes: you could sit in a Windsor chair, a chair with a padded seat or a burgundy-coloured chesterfield. One wall was panelled and another had floral wallpaper. Although the windows had something over them to mute the light, she could see that it was all spotlessly clean.

Jim took them through to the back rooms. 'There's a sink and a toilet to the left,' he told Edith as he handed her a towel. As she left, he showed Ruby to a chair.

'So this is where you work,' she said.

He nodded. 'The darkroom is through the back door,' he said, lighting the gas under the kettle. 'My boss is out today. He's working with a client in Ashington. I'm usually the general dogsbody, but occasionally I get to be on the right side of the camera.'

'Like today,' said Ruby.

'Like today,' he nodded.

The kettle had just boiled when Edith came back. She handed Ruby the towel, and Ruby took her turn in the washroom. When she'd finished, her clothes still smelled of smoke, but she couldn't do anything about that. Having combed her hair, using the comb in her handbag, Ruby came back to find Jim and Edith enjoying a lively conversation.

'Edith has just been telling me about your windfall,' said Jim.

For a second Ruby almost panicked. How on earth did Edith know about the five pounds? Had somebody told her what was in the envelope? Did Mrs Fosdyke know? And who else knew?

'An extra two and sixpence a week,' Jim teased. 'Ruby Bateman, you're a rich woman.'

'She said she was going to buy me an ice cream,' said Edith.

'Oh, Edith!' cried Ruby, 'I'm so sorry. What with the pier catching fire, I clean forgot.'

'Don't be daft,' said Edith. 'I was only teasing.'

'I think we all deserve an ice cream,' said Jim. 'If you girls are free next Monday afternoon, I'll buy you one.'

'You're on,' said Edith and, glancing up at the clock, she added, 'Come on, Roob. We'd better go.'

'And I've got an appointment with the telephone,' smiled Jim.

No one would have noticed her, a nondescript woman of a certain age. She shivered as she waited by the crossing for the gates to open again. She wasn't cold, for the evenings were still warm for the time of year and she wore a coat, but she shivered as she stared across the railway line to the houses beyond and remembered the awful disappointment. Was it only a year since she'd stopped going to see Mrs Knight? She'd turned up on the doorstep religiously every month for the past ... she didn't know how many years. Ten? Twelve? And every time she'd crossed the threshold she'd gone with renewed hope, only to have it dashed again and again. It was strange, really. Mrs Knight had such a reputation for success.

They were a select few, all hand-picked and personally invited. They would file in one by one, not talking; that would disturb the atmosphere. She didn't mind that. She was used to keeping herself to herself. She never even told anyone why she was there. Mr Knight stood in the doorway, taking five bob from each person. He did it discreetly and it had to be the right money. No change given. Mrs Knight didn't do it for the money, but everyone has expenses.

Of course she was no fool. She knew that, since the Great War, spiritualists had mushroomed all over the place. Most were charlatans who were in it to fleece vulnerable people who were looking to make sense of terrible events. That's why she'd refused to talk about her husband. She'd decided that she would know it was him, if he used her pet name when she made contact. No one else knew it, because it was an intimate, secret name.

The room was hot and stuffy in winter with the fire on, and the curtains were always drawn. They would wait at the table in silence until Mrs Knight came and then they would turn all the lights out. Mrs Knight would close her eyes and put her head back, saying, 'Come. We are all assembled and we welcome you. Speak, spirit, for we are all listening…'

As the train thundered by, it brought her back to the here and now and she shivered again. A second or two later the great gates began to make their jerky way back across the line, as Johnny Morgan in the signal box turned the wheel. As they clanged shut together, she trudged her way home, being careful not to cast a glance at the Knights' house. They'd be in there now: a new group, all hoping to hear from some long-lost loved one. The last time she'd waited in that stuffy room, the evening was what Mrs Knight would have called a resounding success. There had been a message from June's dearly departed mother, and another from the son of a man who was there for the first time. The hour had been charged with so much emotion and tears that she was positive it would be the night that her dearest would speak too. But no … before long Mrs Knight slumped exhausted in her chair, and it was over.

That was a year ago. She'd stopped going then.

90

It didn't matter, though. He was talking to her now, which was why she was hurrying to get home. She could never be sure when it would happen, but tonight might be the night.

CHAPTER 6

For the next few days, Ruby was walking on air.

She knew she should be feeling depressed. Worthing's lovely pier was a heap of acrid-smelling charcoal and, because the middle of the walkway had been pulled up, there was no chance of taking a stroll to the end. Although they had saved half of it, the ticket kiosk was closed and barriers had been erected.

She should, by rights, be miserable about work as well. Mrs Fosdyke's vendetta against her seemed as bad as ever. Ruby had hoped that by now she would have run out of steam, but oh, no; Mrs Fosdyke hadn't pulled the linen cupboard apart again, but there was a permanent scowl on her face and whenever she spoke it was only to criticize. Ruby toyed with the idea of giving notice, but she had only been in the job for less than a year and her father would go mad if she walked out. Having consistently refused to allow her to train at anything, he'd been the one who'd found the position in the first place. She'd argued, complained and sulked for ages, but he wouldn't back down. There would be hell to pay if she defied him again. And besides, if she gave in her notice, although Mr Payne might give her a good reference, Mrs Fosdyke certainly wouldn't.

Then there was Albert Longman. She really should be concerned about him. He had turned up the same day as the pier went up in smoke. She had only just got in, after turning down the beds, so her mother had answered the door, and by the time Ruby went to see him, Albert was licking his fingers and plastering down his hair again – it was a habit of his that really irritated her.

'Hello, Ruby,' he said as she peered round the door. She didn't invite him in. 'I asked your father, and he said it would be all right for you to step out with me.'

Ruby swallowed hard. 'I'm sorry, Albert,' she said, politely but firmly. 'I'm afraid I'm not really interested in courting yet. I'm only seventeen, and I think that's far too young.' For the past few nights she had lain in bed for ages trying to think of something she could say, if Albert came calling. It had to be something that would give him the message, and yet not upset him too much. This was far and away the kindest thing she could come up with.

He looked slightly surprised, then recovered himself quickly. 'But you will go out with me when you're older?'

'Oh, my goodness, Albert,' she said, alarmed that he hadn't taken the hint. 'I haven't a clue how I'll feel when I'm older. Um...' She was panicking now. Did that sound as if she wouldn't mind if he came calling again?

Her mother came to the door again and opened

it a little wider. 'Is everything all right?'

Ruby was flustered. 'I – I think it best if you look elsewhere, Albert.'

'Look elsewhere for what?' said Bea.

Albert took a backward step. 'Oh, I understand your little game,' he said, tapping the side of his nose.

Why did he do that? Every now and then she wondered: what did that mean?

The other thing that made her unhappy was the situation at home. Since the day of the coach outing, her father had become silent. She didn't know which was more vexing: his constant rants or the silent treatment. Whenever he was in the room, everyone behaved as if they were treading on eggshells, and even Percy looked uncomfortable. May didn't seem to notice anything of course, but then her father treated her in a totally different way to the rest of the family. It cut Ruby to the quick to hear him call May his 'sweet poppet' and 'darling girl' as he cuddled her on his knee. She couldn't ever remember having a hug from him, not even as a small child. In fact it wasn't until May came along that Ruby realized fathers cuddled their children.

All of these things should have made her life an absolute misery, but they didn't. Why? Because she was seeing Jim on Monday afternoon. She thought about him all the time. At night she lay in her bed, trying to imagine his powerful arms around her, his warm, sweet breath on her face, and his lips gently pressing hers. Somewhere deep inside her she discovered feelings she never knew she had. They were delicious and scary, all at the same time. Sometimes, when she'd been thinking about him for a long time, she felt a muscle between her legs expanding and her panties would get damp. Ruby longed to talk to someone about it, but it seemed too personal, too rude, maybe even naughty. What was happening to her? Was she being wicked in some way? Did anyone else feel like this? She also felt guilty. Jim belonged to Martha. That's what everybody said. What was she doing, flirting with someone else's boyfriend? Why, Jim and Martha were practically engaged. What would people say if they could read her mind?

There were three of them on the boat: Nelson, Percy and Albert Longman. Albert had told them that he'd never been out on a boat before, but when his editor had sent him out to go and find some local people to interview, his first thought was of Mr Bateman.

'Let me come fishing with you,' he'd asked Nelson. 'I'd like to understand what you do.'

Nelson looked at Albert as if he'd swallowed a fish-bone, and sniffed. It was obvious that he didn't want some novice on his boat, but Albert could be very persuasive, and the promise of a couple of pints in the Anchor did the trick.

The *Saucy Sarah* was an open boat with a Marston Seagull motor – something that Nelson had apparently bought the previous year. He proudly told Albert that he was one of the first Sussex fishermen to have one.

His favoured way of fishing was with a trammel net. 'It's made up of three layers of net,' he told a bemused Albert. 'A fine mesh sandwiched between two layers of larger mesh. They're attached to a floated headline and weighted, so that all three hang vertically in the water.'

Albert wrote it all down in his little notebook and, under supervision, drew a diagram. Once they'd set out to sea, the three of them said little. It didn't take long before Albert said that he was feeling queasy. Percy and his father simply did what they always did, following a skill that had been passed down from generation to generation. After a while Percy threw the dhan flag overboard and, as the boat moved through the water, he paid out the rope until it reached the anchor attachment. After that, Percy dropped the anchor and began running out the nets.

'Don't the fish just swim through the net?' asked Albert.

Nelson looked at him as if he was an idiot.

'They get caught by the gills,' said Percy, 'or else they get trapped by the inner net, which becomes like a bag around them.'

Albert changed his position, in the vain hope that he might feel better with the wind in his face, although it messed up his hair and made the bit in the front stand up on end.

'Did you talk to Ruby?' Nelson asked. He spoke in low tones, even though Percy was busy at the other end of the boat and wouldn't hear over the sound of the engine. He was busy keeping an eye out for the end of the net, so that he could drop the second anchor and the dhan flag.

'I think she's playing a game with me,' said Albert. 'Her mother interrupted us, and I think she might have felt shy. She said she's too young.'

'Poppycock,' said Nelson. 'She's seventeen. She's old enough.'

'I know that,' said Albert.

'Then be firm with her, man,' said Nelson, making his hand into a fist. 'Show her what's what.'

'I can't make her like me,' Albert protested.

'Don't be daft,' said Nelson. 'Good-looking fella like you could charm the knickers off a nun.'

Albert blinked. 'She already knows I have good prospects,' he went on. 'I earn a good wage. I could look after her.'

'Course you can,' said Nelson, giving him a hearty slap on the back.

'Has she got somebody else?' Albert asked anxiously.

'Ruby?' said Nelson. 'Good God, no.'

Albert turned his head with a sigh. 'When are we going back?' he said feebly. 'I don't feel too well.'

'Ha!' Nelson laughed. 'Got a few hours on the water yet, Albert,' he said.

The days seemed to crawl by, but then at last it was Monday. The weather wasn't as good as it had been. In fact it was deteriorating all the time. The skies were leaden and the wind was cold. Never had a morning seemed so long. Ruby had brought her best dress with her and, as soon as their shift was done, she got ready in the staff cloakroom. It was a pity about the weather; her coat was a bit frayed at the cuffs, and she would have looked a lot better without it. But, looking out of the window, she had no choice, for autumn had arrived. Edith didn't bother to change out of her uniform, but Ruby made no comment.

As they walked to the Stanhoe, the place along the seafront where they'd arranged to meet Jim, the wind snatching at their coats and their hair being blown all over the place, Ruby was suddenly seized by a terrifying thought. Supposing he had changed his mind? What if he wasn't there? Or, worse still, what if he wanted to be with Edith and not her? Ruby couldn't bear the thought of playing gooseberry. She was a bag of nerves when they arrived, and her thoughts were blanking out Edith's constant chatter.

She needn't have worried. Jim was leaning with one foot up against the wall.

'There you are!' he cried. 'Not really ice-cream weather, but if you still want...'

'I'm sorry, Jim,' said Edith, 'but I'm afraid I can't stay.'

'Edith!' cried Ruby.

'I have to get home. My mother is expecting me,' said Edith, her eyes wide. 'But don't let me spoil it for you two. Have a nice time.' And with that, she was gone.

'I hope you're not thinking of walking out on me as well,' said Jim good-naturedly.

'Oh no,' said Ruby, a little quicker than she would have planned.

'Good,' he smiled. 'So what's it to be, ice cream or tea and cake?'

'Tea and cake,' said Ruby with a small shiver.

They walked to the nearest tea rooms. The Pantry was a popular haunt of day-trippers and locals alike. The pretty embroidered tablecloths and

matching chair cushions created a cosy atmosphere. The waitress showed them to a window seat
and Jim placed their order. Ruby could see from
the menu that it would cost him two shillings and
tuppence ... each! Gosh.

They chatted about nothing in particular: difficult clients at the studios; Mrs Fosdyke at
Warnes; and, of course, the pier.

'Do you think they'll rebuild it or just pull it
down?' asked Ruby.

'They've already started up a fund to help get
the rebuilding started,' said Jim. 'We've got a box
in the studios. They'll be insured anyway.'

'Worthing isn't Worthing without its pier,' said
Ruby sagely.

'By the way,' said Jim, as Ruby poured the tea,
'I think I may have found you someone who can
teach you another language.'

Her eyes grew wide with excitement. 'Really?'

'He's a lodger in the same digs as I have,' he
said. 'A refugee, actually. He's Jewish and has just
escaped from Germany. He could teach you
some German. Would that do?'

'I should say so!' said Ruby.

Jim looked thoughtful. 'He's had a rotten time
of it lately. Things are getting pretty difficult for
them over there.'

'I remember Dr Palmer talking about that,' said
Ruby. 'The shift of power – or something like that.
He was very concerned about the new leadership.'

'I'm not in the least bit political,' said Jim, 'but,
according to Isaac, Chancellor Hitler has some
dangerous ideas.'

'Isaac?'

'Isaac Kaufman, my German friend and fellow lodger,' said Jim. 'He's had to flee for his life.'

'What does he do?'

'In his own country he was a cobbler,' said Jim, 'but at the moment he's working for Worthing's Parks and Gardens. At least he feels safe now.'

She nodded.

'I told him about you,' Jim went on, 'and he said he would be happy to teach you.'

'Then I'd be happy to meet your lodger,' said Ruby, wiping the corners of her mouth after a delicious piece of sponge cake, 'but I'd prefer it if someone else was with me.'

'Of course,' said Jim. 'If I can't be with you, you could always meet in the library.'

'You have to be quiet in the library,' Ruby grinned. When they had finished their tea, Jim suggested a short stroll on the beach. They lingered for a while by the charred remains of the pier, before moving on. Ruby had to be back on duty in time to turn the beds down.

'Ruby, can I see you again?' he asked as they arrived at the staff entrance at Warnes.

'I should like that,' she smiled.

'How about a bike ride?' he said. 'Do you have a bike?'

'I do,' she said, 'but I'm not as fit as you and Percy.'

'That's all right,' he said. 'I know a lovely tea room in Ferring. A bike ride and a cup of tea: does that sound all right?'

'Heavenly,' she said.

'Hello, you two,' said Edith coming up behind them. 'Did you have a nice time?'

'Yes, lovely,' said Ruby.

Jim tipped his hat. 'Thank you for an enjoyable afternoon.'

'Thank you too,' said Ruby, but he was already striding away.

CHAPTER 7

Another magazine! Ruby felt like Christmas had come early when she found it under the bed. It looked so interesting that she had to stop herself reading it there and then.

She had spent a very confused hour and a half in the hotel while she turned the beds down. She really liked Jim, but he hadn't even mentioned Martha, even though everybody knew they were stepping out together. She felt excited at the thought of being with him, but guilty at the same time. She wasn't the sort of girl who got mixed up with someone else's beau, and yet she really, really liked Jim. If only Edith hadn't interrupted them, she might have been brave enough to bring up the subject; but in her heart of hearts she knew she wouldn't. When she was with Jim, everything else went out of the window.

It didn't take her long to realize that Edith had never intended to come along with them that day. How sweet of her to leave them together, but she didn't want Edith getting big ideas. For that reason Ruby was cagey about their meeting. Yes, she had enjoyed herself. Yes, Jim was a lovely

you ask your friend Isaac if he will teach me to speak German, tell him I can pay him now.'

Jim raised an eyebrow, so Ruby told him about the five-pound reward that she'd saved.

'That's amazing,' he said. 'Isaac arrived in this country with only the clothes he stood up in. I think anything you can afford to give him will make him very happy.'

'You don't think I'm selfish, keeping the money to myself?' she asked. 'My family know nothing about it.'

'Absolutely not!' said Jim. 'I think it's a brilliant idea, and who knows where it might lead you in the future.'

As they parted, they agreed that she should meet Isaac on Monday, her day off.

The next evening, when she came out of Warnes, Ruby was surprised to see her brother Percy waiting for her. She was immediately anxious. 'Has something happened to Mother?'

'No, she's fine.'

'Then why are you here?'

'I'm leaving, Sis,' he said, as she slipped her arm through his and they set off for home. 'I meant what I said the other night. I can't stay in the same house as him a minute longer.'

Her heart sank. 'What's he said now?'

'Nothing out of the ordinary,' said Percy.

'Then why do you have to go? Something must have happened.'

'I found out something about him,' said Percy, 'and before you ask me, it's better that you don't know.'

'Oh, Percy,' she protested. 'You can't say something like that and just leave it there. It must be something bad. Tell me.'

'I can't, Sis,' he said. 'It's nothing for you to worry about, but I can't bear to be in the same house as him a minute longer. I've nearly saved enough, and then I'm off.'

It was frustrating, but she knew Percy well enough to realize that if he said something, he would stick by it. She didn't want him to leave, as she knew she would miss her brother. 'But what about the fishing? You know Father wants to carry on the family tradition. And what about Mother?'

'You know perfectly well I don't give a damn about the fishing,' he said vehemently. 'Look, I am sorry about Mother. I'll try and send money, but if I go, there'll be fewer rows for her to cope with anyway.'

'Oh, Percy, what will you do?' cried Ruby. 'You get so passionate about things that you forget everything else. You must have some sort of a plan?'

'No... I don't know.'

'Then stay a little longer until you do.'

'Ruby, I can't live with him.'

'Can't you think about it for a while? Stay until after Christmas, and if you still feel the same...'

'A pal of mine has promised me a long-distance driving job,' he said. 'Next year everybody will have to take a driving test before they can drive on their own. That costs money, so I want to get in before you need it.'

'What does Father say about all this?'

'He doesn't know yet,' said Percy. 'I've still got

to pluck up the courage to tell the old bugger.'

They had reached the Quashettes, a network of brick passages that ran from High Street to the railway and the tunnel at Ivy Arch. 'You really mean it, don't you?' Ruby stopped and hugged her brother. 'Oh, Percy, I shall miss you,' she sighed.

'You must get away from him too, Ruby. Don't end up like Mother. Don't let him crush your spirit.'

'You're the second person who's said that,' she said, remembering that Dr Palmer had said something similar on High Salvington, 'but I can't leave Mother.'

'Then find yourself a husband, and take her with you,' said Percy, 'but for God's sake don't marry Albert Longman. I'll never forgive you if you do that.'

'Not much danger of that,' she said with a hollow laugh. They linked arms again and walked on. 'When you go,' she said, suddenly stopping, 'you will keep in touch, won't you?'

'I'll do my best,' said Percy.

It was hard having to wait until she saw Jim again. She wanted to talk to somebody about Percy, but she didn't want to tell her mother or the girls at work. Time seemed to crawl and yet, apart from worrying about her brother, Ruby was happy. She still felt a bit guilty about Martha, but it wasn't as if Jim had asked her to be his girl or anything, was it? They'd shared a bike ride and she was going to meet his fellow lodger – that was all.

Monday turned out to be another lovely day,

although it was obvious that the sun was beginning to lose its strength. Last week the temperatures had still been in the 70–75°F bracket, but now it was more like 65–68°F, still balmy, but with the offshore breeze it was definitely cardigan weather. Ruby dressed with care, choosing a pretty cerise dress with white cuffs and collar. Everyone told her the pink colour suited her dark hair and complexion, and it was a flattering style.

Jim met her at 2 p.m. He was waiting by the Dome, and as she approached he pushed his hat back from his forehead in an attractive way. His eyes creased as he smiled that wonderful wide smile of his. 'Ruby!' he cried. 'You came.'

'Of course I did,' she said, wondering why he should doubt her. 'I promised, didn't I? I'd never let you down.'

'I'm glad,' he said, falling into step beside her, 'and Isaac is very excited.'

They walked side-by-side, not quite touching, but Ruby was very aware of his presence.

'So what have you been doing since we last met?' he asked.

There was little to relate. The routine at Warnes never changed, and things had gone on as usual, with the cleaning taking up the lion's share of her time. At home in the afternoon she'd done her share of the ironing and cleaning the brass for her mother, and on Sunday afternoon she'd taken May to Sunday school. Father and Percy had had a spat or two, but she didn't mention that. Ruby had been carefully taught that you didn't air your dirty washing in public, as her mother would say. What happened in the family was meant to stay in the family.

Since they'd last met, Ruby had spent a lot of time thinking about Jim, but of course she didn't tell him that, either. She had thought about Isaac quite a bit too, and she wondered if she would master learning German, so she told Jim that.

'What about you?' she asked as they reached the other end of town and were heading towards Rowlands Road. 'What have you been doing?'

'The old man let me photograph a wedding on Saturday,' he said. 'Miss Cheryl Warner married Mr Lawrence Pye at Holy Trinity in Shelley Road.'

Ruby started giggling.

'It was quite a swanky affair,' said Jim, pretending to be offended. 'Luckily I got everything in order.'

'I'm sure you did,' Ruby laughed.

'Then what's so funny?'

'The bride's new name,' said Ruby, by now almost helpless.

Jim frowned.

'If she's Mrs Cheryl Pye, I wonder if they'll call her "Cherry Pye"?'

'I never noticed that before,' he said, and they both laughed.

They arrived at the house in a side-street off Rowlands Road, where Jim lived. It was part of a terrace that had seen better days. The paint was flaking and the brown front door was cracked and the wood starved. A short wall separated the house and road, and a few bedraggled weeds waved their heads in a tiny flower bed. When Jim opened the front door with his key, a stale smell crept out of the house and a woman came out of

107

a room at the back. She was quite old, fifty at least. A lit cigarette hung from her bottom lip. It appeared to be permanently stuck there because, whenever she spoke, it went up and down with her mouth. The smoke was going into her eyes and, because of that, she had one eye partially closed most of the time.

'Mrs Grimes, this is Miss Bateman,' said Jim.

'Miss Bateman,' said the woman with a polite nod.

'Miss Bateman has come to see Isaac.'

'Show her into the dining room,' said Mrs Grimes and added, as a word of caution, 'I don't allow any young women upstairs. This is a re-spectable establishment.'

Jim opened the door and Ruby stepped into a clean but rather cluttered dining room. The four small tables and chairs, and the wall with a cabinet containing trinkets and souvenirs, seemed to fill every corner. China dogs with 'A present from Weymouth' on them competed with lighthouses filled with coloured sand, and with dolls of all shapes and sizes. Several pictures hung from the picture rail, but these were mostly dull landscapes showing long-horned Highland cattle standing around.

On the other side of the room was a small dresser with a drawer, and two cupboards made of heavy wood. Ruby lowered herself onto the edge of a chair, careful not to disturb the knives and forks laid for tea.

Jim disappeared and came back with a small man, aged about twenty-five to thirty, wearing a shabby suit and a shirt with frayed cuffs. He

108

shook her hand warmly.

Isaac repeated some of the things Jim had already told her, about being a cobbler back in Germany and how the new chancellor's policies had made life increasingly difficult. Since his wife and child had tragically died, and his sister-in-law was missing, presumed dead, he had no family, so he'd decided to come to Britain while he still could. He was matter-of-fact about the details of his enforced exile and admitted that he had been unable to find work using his skills. He now worked for Worthing Parks and Gardens, and walked to their big nursery in the Durrington area every day. 'I enjoy to work the flowers,' he told her. 'It is good in the open air. Healthy, *ja?*' He beamed and thumped his chest, but Ruby could see the heartache behind his smile.

With the nights beginning to draw in, there was no hope of doing lessons outside, so it was agreed that they would meet in Mrs Grimes's dining room, twice a week for one hour. Mrs Grimes wanted two bob a week, starting with a month's payment in advance. Ruby had come prepared and handed over eight shillings. Isaac said he would do the lessons for nothing, but Ruby insisted on giving him two pounds to start with, which they agreed would cover the first six weeks of lessons. She didn't want to embarrass him, but in his present predicament, a few extra shillings might be helpful. 'I'm not sure if I'll be clever enough,' she explained cautiously. 'I have a little money saved, so I need to find out before the money runs out.'

'Then we must work very hard,' Isaac said.

They shook hands again and Jim walked Ruby home.

'How's Martha?' she blurted out during a lull in the conversation. There, she'd said it at last. She waited with bated breath. How much did he care about Martha, and where was she?

'I don't understand why you keep asking me about her,' Jim said, with a puzzled expression.

'One of the other girls told me you were stepping out with her,' said Ruby.

Jim threw back his head and laughed. 'I have never stepped out with anyone,' he chuckled. Then, suddenly looking very serious, he added, 'But while we're on the subject, if I was tempted to ask you to step out with me, what would you say, Ruby Bateman?'

Ruby's heartbeat quickened and she felt herself blushing like mad. She was grateful that it was getting dark or Jim might have seen her face. 'If you did ask me to step out, James Searle,' she said, willing her voice not to give away her excitement, 'I would tell you I would think about it.'

'I sort of expected you to say that,' he said. 'You're an astute woman, Ruby. I would expect nothing less.'

Jokingly Ruby wet her eyebrow with her finger and grinned. What did 'astute' mean? She might try and look it up in the dictionary in the hotel, if she got half a chance.

Because the two of them dawdled so much, it took them three times as long as it normally did to get home. By the time they had arrived, Ruby had agreed to meet Jim again on Friday to go to the pictures, although neither of them had a clue what was showing.

'I'll meet you outside Warnes on Friday then,' he said, as Ruby stepped inside the gate and onto the postage-stamp-sized garden. 'We can decide then.'

'All right,' she said.

Jim lifted his hat. 'Night then, Ruby.'

'See you Friday,' she returned and, with a warm, excited glow inside, she went into the house.

When she got home the next day, the meal was Ruby's favourite: cottage pie with cabbage. She helped her mother dish it up, and everybody sat down. May was at Brownies and Tilly Morgan was bringing her home. Bea saved her a plate of food and put it over a pan of boiling water to keep hot. Their father said little except 'Pass the salt' and 'Where's the HP?'

Ruby knew Percy planned to make his announcement tonight, and the anticipation of what might happen when their father discovered he was leaving made her nervous. She dropped her fork twice.

'What's the matter with you?' Nelson said gruffly, the second time it happened.

'Nothing,' said Ruby, keeping her eyes on her plate.

'Been out with the nitwit yet?'

Ruby looked up. 'What nitwit?'

'Albert Longman, of course,' said Nelson. 'Him who wants to court you.'

'No.'

'Why not?'

'I told you, I don't want to step out with Albert Longman.'

'Why not?' her father challenged. 'He's got a cottage for you to live in and all.'

Ruby looked around the table helplessly. 'Father, I'm too young to be courting,' she said. 'I don't want to settle down with anyone.' In her head she was thinking, *Except perhaps with Jim Searle, but nobody else.*

'Huh,' said her father. 'You might live to regret that, my girl. You won't get a better offer, and I can't afford to keep you for the rest of your life.'

'If he's so wonderful, why do you call him such horrible names?' snapped Ruby, suddenly finding the courage to speak out. She stared at her father defiantly. 'You never have a good word to say about him.'

'Then I reckon you two are perfectly suited,' said Nelson, leaning forward with a jut of his chin.

Ruby returned to her meal, although she had lost her appetite. She should answer back, but what was the point? He'd said enough for one night, and she didn't want to give him the satisfaction of letting him see her upset.

Nelson threw his knife and fork onto the table-cloth and picked up his plate to lick the gravy, and then, sitting back in his chair, he belched. 'Where's the tea, woman?' A rancid smell filled the air and Ruby knew he'd farted as well.

'Oh, sorry,' said Bea, starting to get up.

'I'll do it, Mum,' said Ruby.

Her disgust for her father meant she was glad to get out of the room and away from him. Out in the scullery she splashed her face with cold water and filled the kettle. Forcing herself to calm down, she waited a second or, two before she came back into the room to put the kettle on. Why did he say such terrible things? He never had a good word to say about her. When she'd left school, the headmistress had told Ruby she would make a good secretary, but when she'd told her father that, he'd poured scorn on the idea. 'We're working-class people,' he'd said. 'I'll get you a job.' So she'd skivvied for a couple of people and had ended up in Warnes. Oh, it was all right as far as jobs went, but at times she felt frustrated. She was capable of doing so much more than making beds, but she dared not question her father's decision. What had she ever done to him to make him so spiteful? She should pluck up the courage to ask him outright, but she was too scared. Unlike Percy, who had suffered all his life from their father's belt. Nelson had never laid a finger on her, but his vicious tongue left her wounded for days. She hated herself for being such a coward. *Don't be such a twit*, she told herself crossly; *words are just words*. The old children's rhyme came to mind: *Sticks and stones may break my bones, but words can never hurt me...* It wasn't true, of course. Sticks and stones might bruise the skin, but words went a lot deeper; words could destroy your soul.

She could hear Percy's voice as she walked back into the room to make the tea. Her father was on his feet.

'What do you mean, you're leaving?' he shouted. 'You can't walk out on a hundred and fifty years of

113

fishing in this family.'

'Just watch me,' said Percy. 'I hate everything about it. I hate the sea and I hate being in that damned boat with you. I hate always being on the sharp end of your tongue too. I won't put up with it for a second longer. When was the last time you said "Thank you" for anything?'

'Oh, poor little lamb has his nose out of joint,' said Nelson sarcastically. Then, changing his tone of voice, he added harshly, 'Well, beggars can't be choosers in this life, boy. You're not going to sit around here all day on your lazy fat arse, doing nothing. You're coming out on the boat with me.'

'I'll come tonight, but that's the last time,' said Percy. 'After that I've got a job driving long-distance lorries.'

For a moment Nelson seemed totally winded and sat down heavily. Ruby put the tea on the table in front of him and he rounded on her. 'I suppose you knew all about this and didn't bother to tell me,' he cried. 'I wouldn't be surprised if you didn't put him up to it, in the first place.'

'I didn't,' she protested.

'I told Ruby and Mother a couple of days ago,' said Percy, 'but I told them not to say anything. I knew the way you would react. Don't worry, I'll pay my way.'

'You won't be living in this house, that's for sure,' said Nelson.

Bea put her hand to her mouth. 'But, Nelson, Percy said he'd go out with you for one more night,' she said nervously.

'He's not staying under my roof a second

114

longer,' Nelson shouted. 'If you're going, you can go now.'

'Father,' Ruby began, 'if you would just see reason—'

'See reason?' her father bellowed. He took a swipe at her, but instead knocked the tea flying. Bea jumped up to stem the ensuing flood, but it was too late. The two men stared at each other, with Nelson pointing to the door. 'Get out!'

'Well, if that's how you feel,' said Percy, getting to his feet.

'No, Percy, please,' cried Bea. 'Nelson, you can't...'

'It's all right, Mother,' said Percy in a kindly tone. 'This day has been a long time coming, and it's fine by me.'

The door burst open and May ran into her father's arms. She looked so sweet in her Brownie uniform and, oblivious to the atmosphere in the room, she prattled away, full of the lovely evening she'd just had. 'I practised my Brownie promise,' she said, 'and Brown Owl said I was the best. "I promise to do my best, to do my duty to God and the King and to help other people every day, especially those at home."'

'Bravo!' cried Nelson. 'There's my clever girl.'

Percy turned away and went upstairs. Bea and Ruby turned to follow, but even though he was distracted by May, Nelson spotted them. 'Leave him,' he hissed. 'And get this mess cleared up, woman.'

Miserably, the two women did as he told them. A little later Percy came back downstairs with a suitcase.

'Bye, Mother.'

'Where are you going?' May wanted to know.

'He's going on holiday,' said Nelson.

'Oooh,' said May, 'can I come too?'

'You wouldn't want to leave your poor old pa, would you?' said Nelson.

Bea looked broken-hearted as she hugged her son.

'I'll write,' Percy said, but they both knew he wasn't much of a letter-writer.

'Where will you stay?' asked Ruby, holding out her arms as well.

'That's enough of that nonsense,' said Nelson, getting to his feet. 'Time this child went to bed and, unlike some around here, I've got a living to make.' With that, he pushed himself between Percy and Ruby and held the door open until his son had gone. Then he slammed the door and, turning the key in the lock, went into the scullery to change into his work things.

CHAPTER 8

Ruby woke with a start.

In her dream, she was sailing around the burning pier in a boat with a Union Jack flag. Jim Searle was right behind her, banging the sides of the boat with a silver-topped cane. As the dream faded, she realized that she had woken up because someone was hammering on the front door. She flung back the covers and swung her legs over the edge of the bed, shuddering as she felt the cold floor under her feet. She stood up, her heart already pounding. Her sister May, beside her in the double bed, stirred sleepily.

The banging got louder.

'What's that?' May sat up. Her voice was apprehensive.

'Somebody at the door,' said Ruby, scratching her tousled hair. A flash of lightning lit up the room; the weather outside was wild. Ruby snatched her dressing gown from the bedpost. Whoever was at the door was determined no one should sleep. Something must be terribly wrong. 'Don't worry. I'm going.'

Stupid thing to say. She was already frantic with worry herself. She raced barefoot downstairs. The blood beat in her head and her hands trembled as she struck a match and lit the gas lamp on the wall. As the light grew stronger, the shadows fled, but the chill morning air cut like a knife through her nightdress as she drew her dressing gown around her and tied the cord. The banging had woken her mother in the back room. Ruby heard her cough.

Downstairs at last, she pulled open the front door and the cold morning rushed in uninvited. Albert Longman stood on the empty street, his hand raised to bang on the door again. His hair was all over the place and his grey eyes were as wild as the wind. She stared at him crossly. 'What on earth do you think you are doing?' she demanded. 'It's the middle of the night.'

'It's your father,' he blurted out.

Ruby's blood ran cold.

117

'They found your father's boat,' Albert blundered on. 'It was empty. He must have gone overboard...'

She heard a far-away boom and another flash lit up the sky.

'That'll be the maroon for the Shoreham lifeboat,' said Albert as they both turned to look. 'One of the other fishermen ran to the telephone by the pavilion to get help. I came here to tell you.'

For a second Ruby couldn't speak. She found it hard to take in what he was saying. 'I don't understand,' she said. 'What were you doing with Father?'

'I wasn't in the boat with him,' said Albert, 'but I've been writing an article about local fishermen. Ruby, this is wasting precious time. Have you any idea what time he went fishing?' Albert ploughed on. 'That boat could have drifted for miles.'

'Who is it?' her mother called.

Ruby shook herself. 'What about Percy? Was he with my father?'

'Percy? I don't know,' Albert shrugged. He ran his fingers through his hair. 'I only turned up as the boats were coming in. No one mentioned Percy. What time is it now?'

Ruby glanced at the clock on the mantelpiece. 'Nearly five,' she said and, for the first time, she realized that it was raining hard and that Albert was getting soaked. 'Come in, Albert.'

He shook his head. 'I'm very wet.'

'Ruby?' Her mother was on the stair, her voice cracked and breathless. 'What's happened? Who's there?'

118

'It's about Mr Bateman, Mrs Bateman,' said Albert. 'Some fishermen found his boat with nobody in it. They've brought it up on the beach, but there was no sign of Nelson.'

They heard Bea draw in her breath.

'You never know,' Albert added quickly, 'he could have swum ashore or something.'

'You say the boat is on the beach?' said Ruby, springing into life.

'I'm on my way back there,' said Albert.

'Wait for me,' Ruby cried as she raced back up the stairs, passing her mother on the way.

'Where are you going?' Bea asked after her receding back.

'I need to see his boat for myself,' Ruby said. Part of her knew it was ridiculous and there was little point in going, but the other part of her felt that if she didn't see the evidence with her own eyes, she would never believe it. Albert wouldn't have come all the way here to tell a lie, but he was no fisherman and he could easily have made a ghastly mistake.

Back in her bedroom, May was sitting up yawning. Ruby threw off her nightdress and pulled on some warm clothes.

'Where are you going?' May asked.

'I just have to pop out for a bit,' said Ruby. 'You lie down and go back to sleep. I'll be back in no time.'

'Who was banging on the door?'

'Albert Longman.'

May grinned. 'Is he here to ask you out?'

'Something like that,' said Ruby, pulling up her stocking.

119

'Father said you two suited each other,' May yawned. 'He said you were both a couple of numb-skulls.'

Ruby faltered, bristling with anger.

'What does "numbskull" mean?' said May.

'I'll tell you later,' said Ruby, recovering herself and pushing her feet into her shoes. 'Now, go back to sleep, there's a good girl.'

May yawned again and then lay back and rolled onto her side. Ruby stopped only long enough to pull the covers right over her shoulders and then dashed downstairs. Albert was still by the door, with a large puddle of water forming by his feet. Pulling on her coat and a scarf, Ruby kissed her mother's cheek. 'Try not to worry. I'll be back as soon as I can.'

Bea had a handkerchief to her mouth. 'Oh, Ruby, that water will be so cold.'

'Don't give up on him yet,' Ruby said. 'And don't forget, he's got Percy to help him.'

Her mother leaned heavily on the banister. 'Percy was there too?'

Ruby could have bitten off her tongue. Of course Percy wasn't there; she had quite forgotten about the events of last night. 'Oh no,' she said, remembering something odd that she had seen last night, 'but we can't be absolutely sure, can we? He did tell Father he would do one more night.'

'Please God,' said Bea, 'Percy wasn't there.' Her shoulders drooped and it seemed to Ruby that she'd just aged ten years.

Ruby swallowed hard. Her mother was no fool; she knew all too well that the weather was really bad. It was a wonder she didn't say something

120

like, 'Listen to that wind howling, Ruby. The boat is seaworthy, but your father is not as strong as he used to be...' But neither of them wanted to put anything into words. It was as if voicing it out loud might make their worst nightmares come true. So Ruby looked at her mother's anxious face and did what she always did at such times. Lighting her own face with a bright smile, she said, 'It'll be fine. You know Father. He's as tough as old boots.'

As Ruby ran after Albert to the beach, her mind was in a whirl. What if the empty boat *was* her father's? What if he was badly hurt? What if he was lost at sea? And should the worst come to the worst, what would become of *them*?

Over the years her mother had made a decent home for the family, but without the income from her father's fishing, how would they survive? This couldn't be happening... He had to be safe.

The Great War had interrupted their lives because, right from the start, Nelson had joined Kitchener's Army. Wounded, he was still in hospital at around the time Ruby had been born. Of course she was far too young to remember anything of it, but her mother had told her it had taken her father a long time to recover. In the years before May was born, Nelson had taken them all along the coast to Eastbourne and Hastings in search of work, but Bea had hated it. When they came back to Worthing, Nelson had taken over his father's boat and later on, when Grandfather died, the cottage too. That was the one good thing, if this terrible nightmare turned out to be true. They owned the cottage so at least they would always have a roof over their heads. Things were much better now, although in the winter – in keeping with a lot of other families in the country – they spent all their waking hours in one room to save fuel.

The real problem had nothing to do with their daily struggle with life. There was something fundamentally wrong with their family. The row Percy had had with her father the night before had been the worst yet. Plenty of things had been said, but Ruby wasn't stupid. There were many more things left unsaid. Why was her father so hard on Percy? It seemed that no matter how hard Percy tried to please Nelson, he could never measure up. Come to that, her own relationship with her father wasn't much better. He ignored her nearly all the time and, when he did speak to her, he always seemed to preface everything with a cutting re-mark. She could never understand why she made him so angry. And then there was their mother. She was his wife, but Nelson hardly had a good word to say about her, either. It was as if she didn't exist, except when they were in bed. Ruby would often hear them talking in angry whispers, through the thin walls that separated their two bedrooms. Her father continually demanded 'his rights' and, although she didn't understand exactly what was going on, his determined voice and her mother's pleas made whatever they were doing sound very one-sided, and at times very rough. 'Shame,' she had heard her father say once, 'don't talk to me of shame. Your shame is much greater...' and her mother had burst into tears. What sort of a marriage was that? The only person in the family that her father had any time for was May.

As she and Albert came out of the Quashettes, she began telling herself that when it came to making choices, Nelson Bateman was a sensible man. He was also by nature a careful man. The only reason he had decided to go fishing on such a stormy night was because he was angry.

Walking straight down High Street and on to the Steyne, Ruby was desperate to make sense of everything, but she couldn't. Percy should be here. Where was Percy anyway? After the row last night, Percy had left with a suitcase, but some time later, when she was getting ready for bed, Ruby had heard a footfall outside her bedroom window. When she'd lifted the curtain, she'd seen Percy scooting along the street. He had obviously come back to the house for something, but what? At the time she'd wondered vaguely what he was up to, but what struck her as really odd was the way he was walking. He kept dodging into dark doorways and looking back over his shoulder, as if he didn't want anyone to see him. At the end of the road he turned and patted his head, then ran off into the night.

At last they arrived on the beach, where a group of fishermen were standing around her father's empty boat. Albert was right. Everything was gone: his fishing gear, the nets and his marker flags ... everything.

'Any sign of him?' she asked. The men couldn't meet her eyes as they shook their heads. The wind whipped her hair and the rain soaked her clothes. 'Was my brother Percy with him when he set off?'

'He was on his own,' said Bluey. 'He was cursing Percy to the skies for leaving him in the lurch.'

Ruby heaved a sigh of relief.

Amazingly, Albert seemed more concerned that he'd got a quote for his newspaper than with taking part in the search for her father. Ruby quickly found out that although some fishermen were out looking for Nelson, the rest of them considered it too dangerous. 'If he's to be found,' Silas Reed said sagely, 'lifeboat'll find 'un.'

She stayed with the fishermen for a while, but then decided there was nothing she could do by hanging around the beach. Besides, she was soaking wet and freezing cold. If she caught pneumonia, she wouldn't be much use to anyone.

'I'll take you back,' said Albert.

'No!' said Ruby. Then, seeing his crestfallen expression, she added, 'Thanks, Albert, but I need to be on my own.'

Miserably she retraced her steps. Back home, as she peeled off her wet things, her mother was silent when Ruby told her that it was true: Father was missing. Bea didn't react at all. Ruby supposed it was the shock. As the dawn broke, they sat together drinking hot, sweet tea until it was time for Ruby to leave for work.

As she set off for Warnes, the sky was still a strange colour. Ruby shivered, but not from the cold. There was something eerie and strange about the day, yet as she reached Steyne Gardens and shielded her eyes to look out to sea, there was no sign of the lifeboat. *Oh, God,* she prayed inwardly for the umpteenth time, *please bring Father and Percy home safely.*

She changed into her apron, ready to start work in the big dining room. There were several pairs of wet shoes in the staffroom. Clearly Mrs Fosdyke, Winnie and Edith had got very wet coming to work and must have brought extra pairs of shoes to wear on duty. Ruby only owned one pair of shoes, so she had no choice but to work in her wet ones.

'How did you get on with Jim?' said Edith, coming up behind her. She began to move the shoes nearer the radiator and to stuff them with old newspapers to help them dry out.

'Um?' Ruby was miles away.

'Jim Searle,' said Edith. 'When are you seeing him again?'

Jim ... she'd forgotten all about him for a moment.

'I wanted to ask you last night,' Edith ploughed on, 'but your brother whisked you away, when we came off-duty.'

At the mention of Percy's name, Ruby felt her eyes smart. If Edith said much more, she'd start to howl and that wouldn't do. She took the Vactric out of the cupboard and plugged it in. Was it really only yesterday when she'd last seen Jim? After all that had happened since then, it seemed like a lifetime ago.

'Are you all right, Roob?' Edith asked anxiously. 'You're very quiet.'

'Not really,' said Ruby miserably. 'My father is missing at sea.'

Edith and the other girls were wonderful. They

125

were not only sympathetic, but also kept an eye on Ruby and covered her back by picking up on the things she'd missed. Winnie gave her a sympathetic wave in the corridor. 'I heard about your poor father,' she said. 'If there is anything I can do...'

Ruby thanked her and, somehow or other, she got through the shift. Because no one had been sent to fetch her, she felt a little better by the time she was ready to go home. If anything was really wrong, surely someone would have come to the hotel. Oddly enough, Mrs Fosdyke didn't check up on anybody that day. Edith said it was because she and Mr Payne were planning the mayor's forthcoming banquet, but one of the other girls said Mrs Fosdyke had taken the rest of the day off. Whatever the reason, Ruby was glad.

'Do you want me to come home with you, Roob?' Edith asked as they walked down the stairs. She had the newspaper that Ruby had used to stuff the shoes with in her hand, ready to throw it in the bin downstairs.

'Thanks, Edith,' said Ruby, 'but I'll be fine.'

Edith lobbed the newspaper into the bin and wiped her hands down her coat. 'Ugh,' she said, 'there was something gritty all over that.'

Ruby walked home with a leaden heart, consumed with the desire to be back at home and in the know, but dreading it at the same time. As she turned the corner into Newlands Road, a few of their neighbours were gathered in the street. She waved as she walked towards them, but no one returned her greeting. Instead the small group of women huddled closer together, whispering and secretive. Then Albert Longman came out of the front door, looking very smart in a dark suit with a black tie. A sliver of fear gripped at Ruby's throat.

'I'm so sorry, Ruby,' he was saying as he shook his head.

'Father?' she asked.

Albert nodded. 'I'm sorry for your loss.'

The other neighbours echoed his sentiments. 'Deepest condolences.' 'So sorry, Ruby.' 'If there is anything we can do...'

Ruby stared at them all in shocked surprise. Then she felt angry. It seemed they all knew what had happened to her father, but not one person had thought to come to Warnes and fetch her!

'They found his body along the coast, dear,' said Mrs Marley, their next-door neighbour. Her voice was barely above a whisper. 'He's...' She glanced around at the others. 'Oh, Ruby, he's been drowned. Drown-ded dead.'

Ruby didn't respond, but pushed open the door and went inside. 'Mother?'

Bea was sitting bolt upright in the chair by the empty fireside, her face completely expressionless. Ruby touched her hand; it was icy cold. She knelt in front of her and laid her head in Bea's lap. After a couple of minutes, her mother placed her hand on Ruby's head, but then she gripped the arms of her chair as her body juddered. Ruby stayed perfectly still. She knew Bea was a proud woman and wouldn't want anyone making a fuss about her grief. Neither of them spoke. Someone – Ruby supposed it was Albert – had closed the door to give them some privacy.

'Has Percy come back, Mother?' she asked eventually.

Bea shook her head. 'They say your father was fishing on his own,' she said, still stroking Ruby's head in her lap. 'But of course we knew that, didn't we?'

Ruby nodded, but the relief she felt in knowing that Percy wasn't drowned at sea was enormous. It washed over her in waves, but then she felt terrible again. Shouldn't she feel some sort of grief for her father?

'We should get news to him,' said Bea.

'But we don't know where Percy is,' said Ruby. 'Have they any idea what happened?'

Bea blew her nose. 'No. Nobody can understand why he didn't shout out.'

'Who would have heard him, over the sound of the storm?' asked Ruby.

'The weather only got worse later on,' her mother went on. 'There were other boats nearby. They launched the lifeboat, but it was too late.'

Albert put his head back round the door. 'I'll get over to the doctor's surgery now, Mrs Bateman, if that's all right. We'll bring Mr Bateman back home as soon as possible. No need for you to worry about young May. Susan Marley says she'll keep her at her place for a bit.'

'Thank you, Albert,' said Bea.

He smiled at Ruby, but she looked away quickly. It was kind of him to help, but she was determined not to encourage him. She stood up. The thing Susan Marley had, said was going round and round her head: *They found his body ... he's been drown-ded.* But the whole time she'd sat with her head in her mother's lap, Ruby hadn't shed a single tear for her father. She'd wanted to. It was the right thing to do when somebody died, but she couldn't. She guessed it must be because she was in shock. Her father wasn't easy to live with, but she wouldn't have wished him harm. Now that she was on her feet and could see her mother's face, she was slightly surprised. Bea's eyes were tearless as well, but she looked different. She seemed so alive ... almost elated. She gave her daughter a thin smile. 'He's not coming back, Ruby,' she said, pressing her handkerchief over her mouth. Her body juddered again and Ruby realized that her mother wasn't grief-stricken at all; she was struggling not to laugh.

Later that evening when Ruby got back from turning the beds down, May was still staying with Susan Marley and her father's body was in the front parlour.

'I've told Warnes what's happened,' said Ruby. 'They'll give me the day off for Father's funeral.'

'Is that all?' her mother complained.

'I can't make too much fuss, Mother,' said Ruby. 'You know Mrs Fosdyke, and how she's always on at me. If I make too much of a fuss, she's just as likely to give me the sack. It may not pay much, but with things the way they are, we can't afford for me to lose this job.'

Her mother nodded. 'You're right. Do you want to see him?'

They never used the front room, but Bea kept all her nice things in there. Nelson was lying in a plain coffin perched on the table. He looked peaceful, but there was an ugly gash on the side of his head. When Ruby looked up at her mother, Bea said, 'They say he must have bashed his head when he fell in.'

Someone had dressed him in his best suit. He didn't look like her father at all. His mouth should be snarling, and he should have angry spittle on his lips. But, for all his faults, the enormity of what had happened was beginning to dawn on Ruby and she was starting to worry. If the family was to survive, she would have to work out a way of keeping them all together. Everyone needed an anchor and, from now on, that's what she would have to be. She'd keep her job – and get another one, if necessary. Her mother was in no fit state to do anything except take care of May.

The steady stream of people coming to pay their respects began. They were mostly other fishermen, for Nelson had few personal friends. Ruby was kept busy making endless cups of tea, and by the time they'd all gone she was exhausted. She was just about to lock up and go to bed when there was a soft tap on the front door. She opened it crossly, wondering who on earth would come at this time of night. It was Jim. Her heart lurched with joy, and for the first time since Albert had knocked on the door early that morning with the news that her father's empty boat had been found, tears sprang to her eyes.

'Ruby, I've only just heard,' he said. 'I am so sorry.' He grasped her hands in his.

'Come in,' she said.

'It's late,' he said, shaking his head. 'I just wanted you to know I'm here for you.'

'Thank you for coming,' she said, her voice thick with emotion.

'You must be tired,' he said, touching the side of her face gently. 'I'll come back tomorrow. Let me know if there is anything I can do to help.'

He leaned towards her and his lips brushed hers. Ruby closed her eyes.

Jim closed the door himself. She stood looking at the wood and still feeling the warmth of his hand so tenderly on her cheek. *Oh, Jim...*

Turning out the gas light, she made her way wearily up to bed. Somehow – now that Jim knew what she was going through – the terrible events of the day didn't seem quite so insurmountable.

When Ruby got back from her morning shift the next day, the coxswain of the lifeboat was at the house. He told them they couldn't bury Nelson until there had been an inquest. For the first time, Bea began to cry.

'H'everyone concerned with your father's death will be called to give h'evidence before the coroner,' Coxswain Taylor said, adding an 'h' before every word that began with a vowel, in his usual pompous manner. To emphasize the point, he'd threaded his thumbs through the braces of his thick canvas trousers. 'H'and his verdict will determine if Nelson was unlawfully killed or if he suffered a h'accident or...' he sniffed in an exaggerated fashion, '...or if the said party committed suicide.'

Bea and Ruby looked at each other, aghast.

'Nelson wasn't the sort of man to take his own life,' Bea protested angrily.

131

Ruby chewed her bottom lip anxiously. After everything else, she couldn't face that. A verdict of suicide would mean that her father couldn't have a Christian burial, and that seemed especially cruel for her mother.

'And a member h'of the family should be present at the h'inquest,' Coxswain Taylor went on.

'No.' Bea pressed her handkerchief to her mouth. 'I can't go!'

'I'll go, Mother.'

'With h'all due respect, madam,' said the coxswain, 'you will have to give h'evidence.'

Bea looked up at her daughter helplessly.

'It'll be fine,' Ruby said, grasping her mother's hands. 'We'll do it together.'

When the coxswain had gone, Rea pointed to a paper bag on the table.

'What's that?' Ruby asked.

'The things they took from Nelson's pockets,' said Bea.

Ruby's first reaction was: *what a small bag.* It had contained everything on his body when he'd been found. She watched her mother tip the contents onto the kitchen table and run her fingers through them: a crumpled handkerchief, his penknife, four shillings and eightpence in coins, Nelson's lucky rabbit's foot, won at a fairground when he was a boy, and a bullet.

'Is that real?' Ruby asked anxiously. 'Why on earth was he walking around with a bullet in his pocket?'

'It's not real,' said her mother, picking it up and looking closely. 'It's hollow. Something's been etched onto the side.'

They peered at the lettering, but it didn't make sense: *Victory*.

'Must be something from the war,' said Ruby. 'Perhaps it was to remind him.'

'I doubt it,' said her mother. 'He never talked about the war.'

Ruby took the bullet from her mother's hand and held it up to the light. 'Maybe it was a near-miss.'

Bea shrugged and Ruby put everything back into the bag. By the time she'd finished, her mother was reaching up for the tin on the mantelpiece. She tipped the contents onto the kitchen table and some coins rolled out. 'The first thing we have to do,' she said, 'is find the money to bury him.'

'Oh, Mother,' said Ruby, 'don't worry about that now.'

'I need to do this, Ruby.'

With a sigh, Ruby nodded.

'Doesn't look much,' said Ruby, as she helped her mother stack the money into neat rows.

'Two pounds, seven shillings and fourpence,' said Bea. 'And he had an insurance policy, which will give us about five pounds.'

'How much does a funeral cost?' asked Ruby.

'Susan Marley says it cost twelve pounds eighteen shillings and sixpence to bury her old mum,' said Bea, 'so we need at least another five pounds.'

'Where are we likely to get that kind of money?' said Ruby gloomily, remembering the money she had once had in her Post Office book. She would have to tell her mother about the five-pound reward she had received from Dr Palmer, but there was less than three pounds left. If only she hadn't been so eager to pay Isaac up front for all those German lessons.

CHAPTER 9

The next couple of days passed in a haze of work and keeping vigil over Nelson's body. Everyone at Warnes was sympathetic, and nobody asked Ruby too many questions. It was as if they thought she wouldn't be able to hold it together, if they probed too much. In fact she was numb.

Ruby didn't like the idea of sitting with a dead person, especially in the dead of night, but she soon got used to it. Susan Marley had organized a few of the neighbours to sit with Nelson during the day, and Winnie Moore offered to come one night; but in the main it was left to Ruby and Bea to take turns. Cousin Lily offered to sit, but had to be carried from the room in a dead faint after she claimed she saw his chest moving.

Jim Searle had come back the following afternoon and promised to go with Bea and Ruby to the inquest, which was to be held in the old Town Hall on Monday, October 2nd. It would be held a week and a day after Nelson had died.

'Albert Longman has already offered,' said Bea, who was sat at the kitchen table.

'I'd prefer to go with Jim,' Ruby insisted and, to her great relief, her mother agreed. In the meantime, Albert called every day to see if there was anything they needed.

Bea made small talk with Jim when he visited, asking him about his family.

'I was an orphan,' he smiled matter-of-factly. 'I was brought up in a children's home.'

'How awful,' cried Bea.

'It wasn't too bad,' he said. 'I got on all right and, when you don't know any different, you think that's the way it is. No one had any great expectations of us, so I suppose that's what has given me a determination to prove myself.'

'And you've done very well for yourself,' Bea smiled.

She got up from the table and went into the parlour room, where Aunt Vinny was sitting with the body. Ruby watched her mother go and sighed.

'She's taking it very well,' said Jim.

Ruby nodded. She wanted to say *too well*. Her mother was acting like a bird that had been set free – one that was still waiting inside the cage, until it was the right time to fly away. 'So it would seem,' she said. 'I keep wondering if it hasn't really hit her yet. I'm afraid she might collapse later on.'

Jim nodded sagely. 'How is May taking it?'

'There's another strange thing,' said Ruby. 'She and my father were very close, but May seems to have taken it all in her stride. She cried a bit the first night, but since then she's been fine.'

'Where is she?'

'Susan Marley, next door, has been looking after her for us,' said Ruby. 'Quite frankly, I don't know what I would have done without her.'

Jim rose to his feet. 'Well, if you are sure there

is nothing more I can do,' he smiled, 'I'll see you in time for the inquest. What time is it?'

'Ten-thirty at the Town Hall,' said Ruby. 'Mrs Fosdyke is letting me go at nine-thirty, so Mother is going to wait for me, and then we can go from here.'

Jim nodded and, picking up his hat, headed for the door. Ruby went with him and, as he left, he turned and brushed her cheek with his lips. 'Bye then, Ruby,' he said softly. 'See you tomorrow.'

Ruby closed the door and, leaning her head against the wood, smiled dreamily. Despite all her worries at the moment, Jim was the one ray of sunshine in her life.

Dr Rex Quinn called the dogs and they bounded out of the sea. He loved this time of day. It was early morning and the weather was crisp and fresh. The clouds had formed ripples in the sky – a kind of reflection of the ridges formed on the sand when the tide was out. It was quiet too. The only sound came from a lone gull standing on one of the groynes jutting out to sea. He called the dogs again and they trudged up the beach to the shore. A ten-minute brisk walk and he would be home again.

His small cottage was perfect for his needs, and he was reasonably happy with his life. He'd become used to living here, and this uncomplicated existence was better than he had ever expected. He still had scars but, unlike a scar on the skin, they were hidden in his heart and only occasionally caused him pain. He had once thought he would never recover, but they say time is a great healer; in his case, time wasn't the physician, but it did put distance between him and the rawness.

Rex turned the hose on the dogs and, once they had shaken themselves, he towelled them down. The salt water irritated Harvey's skin and, not to be outdone, Maisie wanted her share of the fun. Their tongues lolled and their eyes were bright as he rubbed their backs.

Pulling the morning paper from the letter box, he and the dogs went inside. The light level was low in the kitchen, but he didn't turn up the gas. Instead he cooked a couple of rashers of bacon for himself while he fed the dogs. They ate noisily and quickly, and had already flopped to the floor to doze by the time he was ready to eat.

Rex took his meal into the lean-to, an all-glass room that he had erected on the side of the house, just off the sitting room. It wasn't heated, but he liked the feeling of being out of doors and, under the glass roof, he had the best of both worlds: an open heaven, with protection from the elements. The dogs followed him and positioned themselves at either end of the room.

He poured himself some tea and shook the paper open. In France the Cherbourg-to-Paris express had been derailed and had gone over a precipice. Among the thirty-seven dead was a local man, Christopher Jackson, a schoolteacher and a man who had been highly decorated in the Great War. His wife, Esme, was among the eighty or so injured.

Herr Hitler was threatening to pull Germany out of the League of Nations, prompting several columns' warning of the dire consequences; and, by contrast, a revolutionary concept in mass catering was announced, as the Lyons organization opened a new style of restaurant which they called the 'London Corner House'.

Rex was just about to turn the page when a short paragraph in the 'Stop Press' section caught his eye. A fisherman had drowned at Worthing. It only took a second to read it and, as he did so, he stopped eating, his fork halfway to his mouth. *'The inquest will be held tomorrow on the death of Nelson Eldon Bateman…'* Harvey sensed something was wrong and sat up.

Rex began to eat quickly. He could hardly believe what he was seeing. The day he had thought about for so long had come at last. There was so much to do. His mind raced ahead. Where was the railway timetable? And his suitcase? Luckily he was already on annual leave, but he'd have to find someone to look after the dogs. It was time to make the final move. He had to settle this thing once and for all.

'My God, Bea,' said Susan Marley, pushing a wisp of grey hair back into her bun, 'it's in the paper!'

Bea turned her head away. Ruby got up and shut the front-room door when she heard Susan and May come in. When Nelson's death happened, she and her mother had decided that, to save distress, they would simply tell May that Nelson had gone to see Jesus. May let her mother kiss her now, and then she ran to Ruby.

'Hello, sweetheart. Are you being a good girl for Auntie Susan?' Susan Marley was no relation, but every child in the street called grown-ups

'Auntie this' and 'Uncle that'.

May nodded. 'I got all my spellings right at school.'

'Good for you,' said Ruby.

Susan Marley was spreading a newspaper over the table and, sure enough, there in column five on the front page was a short piece headed *'Drowning at Worthing'*:

The inquest will be held tomorrow on the death of Nelson Eldon Bateman of Newlands Road, who drowned in the waters off Worthing and Littlehampton. Mr Bateman, 49, leaves a widow and three children.

'I've never known anybody who had their name in the paper before,' said Susan.

'Neither have I,' said Bea drily.

Although, in May of that year, the new Town Hall had been opened by the stuttering Prince George, with a lavish ceremony including military processions and fireworks, some public meetings were still being held in the old Town Hall. The familiar building at the crossroads between Chapel Road and South Street stood facing the sea. It had stood guard over the town since Victorian times, and had been the place where people gathered spontaneously in times of trouble and to celebrate coronations and victories in battle. The new Town Hall might have won accolades and prizes, but to the people of Worthing the old Town Hall seemed like a trusted friend.

Jim was waiting when Ruby dashed in from Warnes to change into a long-sleeved black dress, which ended just below her knee. On top she wore a dark-grey coat and a black hat with a tipped brim. Bea was in what would be her funeral outfit: a calf-length black pleated dress with a wide band across the hips. Jim helped her into her black coat with a fur collar and she put on a close-fitting hat with a long black veil. Jim wore a black tie with his only suit.

When they walked up the steps of the Town Hall and in through the front door, they were shown into a room to the left. The chairs were set out in rows, facing a put-up table with a single chair behind it. The usher indicated that the two women should occupy the front-row seats. As she sat down, Bea took a handkerchief from her handbag and scrunched it into her hand in case she needed it, and then pulled the edge of her veil over her face. Ruby took the opportunity to look round every time the doors opened, to acknowledge the friends and neighbours who had turned out. Aunt Vinny had come along with Cousin Lily. The only notable absentee was Susan Marley, who was looking after May. Ruby recognized the faces, although she didn't know all the names of the local fishermen from the area around the Steyne; and the coxswain of the lifeboat was there, as well as a couple of policemen. When Albert Longman came into the room he seemed slightly put out to see Ruby sitting with Jim. He glared at Ruby and didn't respond to her apologetic smile.

At ten-thirty the clock on the front of the old Town Hall struck the half-hour and the coroner walked into the room. He was a nondescript man in a grey suit with grey hair and a grey expression, and began the proceedings by explaining that his name was Dr Thomas Fox-Drayton.

'A coroner's court is held,' he went on, 'when a death is sudden, unnatural or violent. I shall be considering all the evidence concerning the death at a later date. We have met today for the death to be recorded and we shall reconvene at a later date to be decided, when all necessary investigations have been completed. Has the deceased been formally identified?'

One of the policemen rose. 'Yes, sir. The deceased has been formally identified as Nelson Eldon Bateman.'

'In that case,' said the coroner, 'the death of Nelson Eldon Bateman is duly recorded, and permission is hereby given for the burial of the said Nelson Eldon Bateman.' He looked directly at Bea before adding, 'May I offer you my most sincere condolences, Mrs Bateman. This court is adjourned until Thursday November the twenty-third.' And with that, he stood up, gathered his papers and left.

There was a buzz of conversation as people stood up to leave, but they waited for Bea and Ruby to go first. Outside, Jim offered to take them to a tea room, but Bea was anxious to get back home, so they hurried off.

Back home, Ruby put the kettle on. 'I thought they were going to do it all there and then,' she said, doing her best to hide her disappointment.

'The police have to gather all the evidence,' said Jim.

'But we know how he died,' said Bea. 'He drowned.'

141

'The coroner will want to know what he was doing,' said Jim. 'If anyone actually saw what happened; if he could have been saved, if a different course of action had been taken – all that sort of thing. It takes time to gather all that information.'

'But we can go ahead and have the funeral,' said Ruby, pulling off her hat.

'That's right,' Jim nodded. 'Do you know a funeral director?'

'We've got a policy with the Co-op,' said Bea. 'I've already been to see them.'

'It's all set for Monday,' said Ruby.

'I should like to come, if I may,' said Jim. 'I didn't know Mr Bateman too well, but I should like to pay my respects anyway.'

'Thank you,' said Bea. 'The only person we haven't told is Percy. I don't suppose you know where he is?'

Jim shook his head. 'But I may be able to find out.'

'Would you?' said Bea. 'It doesn't seem right that he's not here.'

For a while, the people who had been at the inquest congregated on the Town Hall steps. Few of them talked about Nelson. They were more interested in the topics of the day: the disastrous fire on the pier; the bad weather and its effect on fishing; and Watkins, the boot-maker in Chesswood Road, who was no good at mending shoes any more, but still charged the earth to do it. Cousin Lily sashayed down the steps, trying to look every inch the film star, and was gratified to turn at least a couple of heads. She had already

142

kissed her mother goodbye in the courtroom. Aunt Vinny was anxious to get back to the laundry where she worked.

As Lily turned the corner to get back to her employer's in Richmond Road, she was accosted by a man she'd never seen before. 'Excuse me, Miss.'

He was ordinary-looking, wearing a smart brown suit, and he carried a trilby hat, which he lifted as he spoke. Lily looked him up and down. He was old – at least forty-five – but he was clean-shaven and smelled vaguely of some sort of toilet water. He might have been a perfect stranger, but she wasn't afraid or concerned. He seemed a respectable person.

'Am I right in thinking you are a relative of Mrs Bateman?'

'She's my auntie,' said Lily, lowering her eyes and reaching for her handkerchief. 'It's so awful what's happened. I can hardly believe it.'

The man nodded. 'I am very sorry for your loss.' He hesitated. 'I wonder,' he began again, 'would you do me the great kindness of delivering a letter to the widow?'

'A letter?' said Lily, suddenly curious.

'I would go myself,' he said, 'but I have no wish to intrude.'

'Yes, of course,' said Lily. 'I have to go back to my work right now. My employer only gave me an hour off, but I can take it around this evening, if you like.'

'That would be perfect,' said the man. He reached into his breast pocket and drew out an envelope. It was fairly flat except for one corner

143

and, when she took it, Lily could feel something slightly bulky inside. She looked up curiously.

'I hope I can trust you,' said the man.

'Oh, absolutely,' said Lily with a smile. 'Aunt Bea shall have it tonight.'

He nodded and tipped his hat again. 'Much obliged,' he said, making as if to leave, but then he turned back. 'Tell me, who was that young woman with Bea?'

'Her daughter,' said Lily. 'My cousin Ruby.'

'Her daughter,' the man repeated. 'How old is she?'

'Same age as me,' said Lily. 'Seventeen.'

'I see,' he smiled.

'When I see Aunt Bea, who shall I say gave me this letter?'

'She'll know,' he smiled.

CHAPTER 10

The headquarters of the British Union of Fascists was in Warwick Street. Jim had no desire to go there, but he had a sneaky feeling that someone in this place might know Percy's whereabouts. Percy wasn't a political person, but following Nelson's undisguised disapproval of the movement, Jim knew that he harboured desires to join up, just to spite his father.

Jim climbed the steps and opened the door. The receptionist, a rather severe-looking woman with a tight bun, greeted him warmly. At first she obviously thought he wanted to become a member, but when he explained why he had come, he was asked to take a seat. A picture of Sir Oswald Mosley dressed in a military-style uniform dominated the wall opposite. The office was a hive of activity. While he waited, several young men came in, asking to be recruited. Each one was sent down a corridor and Jim didn't see them again.

Presently an older man came to see him. Dressed entirely in black, with a shirt that buttoned on the shoulder rather than at the neck, the man shook his hand.

'Drayton,' he said stiffly. 'Lemuel Drayton. What can I do for you?'

'James Searle,' said Jim. 'I'm trying to trace a friend of mine, Percy Bateman.'

'Oh yes?' When Jim said Percy's name there wasn't even a flicker of recognition on Drayton's face.

'I think he may have joined the BUF,' Jim ploughed on. 'He certainly talked about it.'

Drayton drew in his breath noisily. 'Anyone coming to us comes of his own free will,' he said stiffly. 'This is a free country, and a man can make his own choices.' He moved his head slightly, and Jim noticed two thickset men coming towards him.

'I haven't come here to complain,' said Jim.

'Then what have you come for?' said Drayton in a prickly tone. The heavies stood either side of him now. They said nothing, but their presence was threatening enough.

'I don't know if you've heard about the fisherman who drowned a few days ago?' said Jim,

145

eyeing the other two men nervously.

'What of it?' said Drayton. 'It has nothing to do with us.'

'The man was Percy's father,' said Jim. 'If Percy is here, he needs to be informed.'

The three men deflated. Drayton frowned. 'A rum do,' he said, jerking his head again. The other two men stepped back and stood to attention by the wall, their hands clasped together in front of them, staring somewhere in the middle distance.

'Is he here?' Jim asked again.

'No.'

'But he is a member?' said Jim.

'I can't tell you that,' said Drayton.

'But surely...' Jim began again.

'I'll inform the recruiting officer, but the said party might not want to have contact with his family,' said Drayton. 'Come back tomorrow.'

'But under the circumstances...' Jim started.

'Tomorrow,' said Drayton, and with that he and his heavies walked away.

Ruby woke up to the sound of someone moving around. She raised her head from the pillow and saw a light on under her mother's bedroom door. May was still sleeping soundly, so she slipped out of bed and, pulling an old cardigan around her shoulders, padded quietly to her mother's room.

'Are you all right, Mum?' she said softly as she tapped on the door. 'Can I come in?'

'Yes.'

The room was in chaos. Her mother, dressed only in her nightie, had an overflowing suitcase on the bed and was busy stuffing her father's things into a pillowcase.

'Can't this wait until morning, Mum? It's the middle of the night.'

Her mother looked at her with wild eyes. 'I can't sleep with it in the same room. I want him gone. I can't bear him in my life a second longer.' She sat on the edge of the bed and put her head in her hands.

For a second Ruby didn't know what to do. She knew Bea had led a dog's life, but until now she had had no idea of the strength of feeling inside her mother. There were times when she'd wished Bea would stand up to Nelson, but she never did. She had misunderstood her mother's acceptance as a sort of love, but now Ruby could see something entirely different. She put her arms around her mother's shoulders. They were like ice.

'Mum, you're freezing,' she said. 'Get back into bed. I'll do it.'

'But I can't sleep,' Bea said plaintively. She looked around. 'He's still here.' With an angry movement, she pushed a shirt into the pillowcase. 'His body may be with the undertaker, but I can still smell him.'

'Then let me help you.' Ruby got her mother a dressing gown and made her put it on. They made short work of what remained of Nelson's things, and then Ruby took the suitcase and three pillowcases downstairs and put them in the scullery. She would put aside a few of his best things to sell, and the rest could go in the suitcase to be passed around for the neighbours. Anything too tatty could be used for rags. Someone might as well benefit from his death. It wasn't much to show for a life; made even less by the sentiment behind getting rid of it. Ruby made some tea, filled the stone hot-water bottle and went back to her mother. Bea was back in bed, but not sleeping. Ruby could see that she was shivering.

'What are we going to do, Ruby?'

'I don't know, Mum,' said Ruby, wrapping the hot-water bottle in a piece of blanket and putting it by her mother's feet, 'but please, don't worry. Something will turn up.'

'Yes, but what?' said Bea. 'We don't have to pay rent, but your job won't keep the three of us.'

'I'll look for a better job,' said Ruby, 'or we could take in a lodger.'

'A lodger?' cried Bea. 'But where would we put him?'

'Let's talk about it in the morning,' said Ruby and, indicating the cup on the bedside table, added, 'Drink your tea.' She knew her mother wouldn't like the idea she'd had, and she didn't want an argument now.

'No,' Bea insisted, 'let's talk about it now. Where would we put a lodger?'

'I was thinking we could use the front parlour,' said Ruby and, seeing the look on her mother's face, she added quickly, 'I know all your best stuff is in there, but a good lodger would mean a steady income.'

To her surprise, Bea nodded.

'Or we could use Percy's room. He said he was going to be in digs.'

'No,' said Bea vehemently. 'I want a home for my boy to come back to.'

'Supposing he got married,' said Ruby. 'We

148

could use his room then.'

Her mother looked shocked. 'Is that what he said? That he was getting wed?'

'Well ... no,' said Ruby, 'but Percy is very good-looking. I can't see him being on his own for long.'

Her mother relaxed with a smile.

'See?' said Ruby. 'I told you we'd work something out.' She leaned over the bed and kissed her mother as she would a frightened child who had had a nightmare. 'Now don't worry.'

Bea caught her hand. 'You're a good girl, Ruby,' she smiled. 'It's a good job you don't have any plans of your own.'

Back in the warmth of her own bed, Ruby struggled to get warm again. What a change – how different things were. Because of her father's death, her whole world had been turned upside down. Yes, it was a good job she had no plans of her own; and the sad thing was she probably would never have a chance to reach for the stars now.

Although the other girls complained that it was unfair that she hadn't been given any time off, Ruby was glad of her work at Warnes. It gave her time to think. As she vacuumed and dusted, she pondered the anomalies surrounding her father's death. She knew Nelson couldn't swim – few fishermen ever learned, in case they tempted fate – but it had come as a real shock that he had drowned. She'd never actually been on his boat. He'd always considered it bad luck to take a woman out to sea; or at least that's what he'd told

149

her, when she'd begged him to take her with him, as a little girl. She'd been around long enough to know that Nelson treated the sea with great respect. He never took unnecessary risks and he was meticulous about his fishing gear. The weather wasn't perfect that day, but until the morning it wasn't that bad, either. Ruby just couldn't work out what had gone wrong. And something else was odd: he never fished alone. For her father to have set sail, Percy must have been there.

She remembered that the two of them had had a row that night. A lot had been said, and Percy had gone off in a huff, but the fact that she'd seen him creeping back later that night must have meant that Percy had come home for his fishing boots. What else would he have come back for? Of course that didn't answer the question as to why he had been so shifty about it, and why he hadn't come forward to tell everybody how his father fell overboard. Why didn't he raise the alarm? Where was Percy now? It seemed very odd that he hadn't even bothered to make contact with their mother. Percy was hot-headed, but he had always been a loving son towards her.

Ruby did her work quickly and quietly, without any thought. Strip the bed, remake it with clean laundry, dust the bedside tables and chairs, not forgetting the picture frames, and make sure the skirting boards were clean. Then it was the bathrooms: put out clean towels, Vim the toilet bowl and gumption the bath, wash the floor. One by one the rooms were done and the doors closed.

As she worked, she thought about her mother and her little sister, May. Bea had apparently taken her loss very well. Ruby didn't want to think about that strange look of elation that her mother had hidden behind her hand. It was most likely nerves. She remembered some years ago, when Linus Todd had been killed by a motor car, his wife Letty had laughed her head off when they told her. Aunt Vinny had to slap her across the face to stop her. Hysterics they'd called it. Perhaps her mother had felt the same. Poor Letty Todd was only a shadow of herself now, and on the parish because she was too ill to work. Ruby didn't want her mother to end up the same way. Bea wasn't robust enough to get a job and besides, if she did, who would look after May? One thing was for sure: until Percy showed up again, they would have to fend for themselves, and Ruby's wage couldn't keep them all. She'd have to stop her German lessons, of course. If only she had kept the whole of that five pounds. Everything happens for a reason, so they say, and that money would have been more than helpful, if she'd kept it.

May seemed to be taking everything in her stride. She enjoyed being the centre of attention, and she certainly was when she was with Susan Marley. Susan was what the people around them called a 'homely' woman. She was plump and enjoyed a good laugh. It was hard to remember a time when Susan wasn't laughing. She was warm-hearted and generous, the sort of neighbour who stepped in when anyone was in trouble. She had been married, but her husband had died a long time ago, when Ruby was a child. She'd probably been told what happened, but she

151

couldn't remember now. Susan loved children, but she herself was childless. The kids in the street hung around her door because they knew she would give them a home-made cake or a biscuit or, better still, invite them in and let them play shops or dressing-up in her chaotic front room. Most of the mothers used Susan as an unofficial children's nurse, and so when she was with Susan, May had no shortage of playmates or babies to help look after.

Ruby had talked to May about their father. 'Pa's gone to heaven to be with Jesus,' she told her. 'He didn't want to go, but he had to. You do understand, don't you, darling?'

May had nodded gravely and gone off to play with a little boy who was hanging around Susan Marley's door. She only made one other reference to her father, and that was when she heard one of the neighbours saying to Bea, 'He's in a better place.'

'Is heaven nice?' May had asked Ruby, as she'd tucked her into bed that night.

'They say it's a beautiful place,' said Ruby.

'Do they have flowers in heaven?'

'I'm sure they do.'

'And fish?'

Ruby was a little puzzled by the jump, but she smiled. 'Yes.'

'Then Pa will have plenty to do,' said May, rolling over and pulling the bedclothes over her shoulders.

The watery dawn crept silently through a chink in the curtains of her bedroom. She stirred, opened her eyes and looked at his picture. She could have sworn she had just heard his voice again, but maybe it was the stuff of dreams. She reached out her hand and turned the frame slightly, so that she could see him better. The hand that adjusted the picture frame was ageing. She had wrinkles now, and her skin was lax. He, on the other hand, hadn't aged at all. He smiled that same unseeing smile from behind the glass, looking more like a boy than the man she remembered.

'Good morning, my darling.' And her heart almost stopped beating as she heard him whisper back, 'Good morning, Freddie.'

As Ruby stepped out in the corridor with only one more room to clean, she felt a presence behind her. She turned slowly and jumped. A woman was watching her from the top of the back staircase. Ruby half-expected to see Mrs Fosdyke. The housekeeper had a propensity for sneaking up on her staff, trying to catch them out, but instead Ruby faced an attractive young woman.

'Oh, Ruby,' she cried, 'it's so good to see you again.'

It took a couple of seconds for Ruby to realize that the young woman was Imogen Russell. She was dressed in a striking coat of midnight-blue with a matching hat. The dress underneath was silk, in a matching colour with white polka dots. Her hair and face were flawless and, as she came nearer, Ruby caught a whiff of expensive perfume. She also became aware that her own mouth had dropped open.

'I'm so glad I found you,' Imogen smiled. 'I've

153

been back to the hotel a couple of times. I always came up the back stairs, in case I got you into trouble.' Standing next to Ruby, she whispered conspiratorially, 'I didn't want anyone asking a lot of awkward questions.'

As she took Ruby's hands warmly in hers, Ruby smiled back. 'Oh, Miss. You look so well.'

'I am well,' said Imogen. 'You saved my life that day, Ruby. No, no, don't shake your head like that – you did. You really did.'

'I only did what anyone else would have done,' said Ruby modestly.

'We both know that's not true,' said Imogen. 'That's why I simply had to come back and thank you in person.'

'Your father...' Ruby began.

'I want to give you a gift for getting me to hospital in time,' said Imogen, pushing something into Ruby's hand.

'There's no need, Miss,' said Ruby, but Imogen insisted.

'That's very kind of you, Miss,' said Ruby. 'Are you fully recovered?'

They both knew what she meant.

'I was an absolute idiot,' said Imogen. 'He was married, of course, although I didn't know it at the time. When I told him what had happened, he seemed to think we could carry on as before.'

'I'm sorry,' said Ruby.

'Men are all absolute rotters,' said Imogen, a flicker of anger chasing the smile from her lips.

'Not all of them, Miss,' said Ruby sagely. 'You'll find a better one.'

'I hope so,' said Imogen. 'My father is taking me

abroad for a while: the south of France and then on to Italy. He seems to think a trip to Europe will perk me up, after my appendix operation.' She laughed gaily and Ruby joined in.

'He never found out then,' said Ruby, 'what really happened?'

'No, thank God.'

'I'm sure you'll make an excellent recovery, Miss.'

Imogen made as if to go, then turned back. 'Why don't you come with me, Ruby? I could take you as my maid.'

'Oh, Miss, I can't.'

'I don't know why I didn't think of it before,' said Imogen. 'Oh, do come. It will be the most amazing experience for you. You'll see Paris and Cannes, and then Rome and Venice. You'd love it, I'm sure you would. Oh, do say yes.'

Ruby caught her breath. 'Oh, Miss, it sounds wonderful,' she began, 'but I have ... responsibilities.'

'You're married?'

'No, Miss.'

It was then that Imogen caught sight of the black band on Ruby's left arm. 'Oh, Ruby,' she cried. 'I'm so sorry. What happened?'

'My father,' said Ruby. 'He was a fisherman and he drowned a few days ago.'

Imogen Russell looked genuinely shocked. 'You poor girl. If there is anything I can do...?'

Ruby faltered. What could she say? Miss Russell was clearly very wealthy, and her own family didn't even have enough money to bury her father, but it really wasn't the done thing to ask for financial help. She wouldn't dare. But there was one thing, and the earnest look on Imogen's face made her bold.

'Would you ...?' Ruby hesitated.

'Yes – anything.'

'Would you send me a postcard?'

'A postcard?'

'I should love to have a postcard from Paris or Rome,' said Ruby.

'Of course I will!' cried Imogen. 'Give me your address, and consider it done.' She fished around in her bag and drew out a small notebook and a propelling pencil. Ruby selected a blank page and wrote down her mother's address in a firm hand.

'Do you have family?' Imogen asked.

'I live with my mother, my older brother and my little sister,' Ruby told her as she wrote.

'When your responsibilities are over,' said Imogen, scribbling her own address onto another sheet of paper, 'let me know, and I'll give you a job. You deserve more than this, Ruby. Come and work for me, and you'll see the world.'

'Thank you,' said Ruby, scarcely able to believe what had just happened. She glanced anxiously around the corridor. 'Now, if you'll excuse me, Miss – Mrs Fosdyke may be here at any minute.'

'The dreaded Mrs Fosdyke,' Imogen grinned. Acting on impulse, she rubbed Ruby's arm affectionately. 'I am so sorry for your loss.' Then, hurrying back down the hallway, she gave Ruby a final wave at the top of the back stairs and was gone.

It wasn't until she came to change her handbag that Cousin Lily remembered her promise. How could she have so easily forgotten the man who had accosted her outside the Town Hall?

The past couple of days had been hectic. Her employer, Miss Rothermere, was leaving for Yorkshire and, as her personal servant, Lily was expected to get everything ready. The house in Richmond Road had a cook/housekeeper who came in every day, but as the only living-in member of staff, Lily was left with all of the packing. Mr and Mrs Drury, Miss Rothermere's nephew and his wife, had Lily dashing about morning, noon and night. 'Auntie's books need to go in that trunk, Cutler. The red one is for her china.' 'Cutler, where are Auntie's best shoes?' 'I can't find Auntie's amethyst brooch, Cutler. Which jewellery box did you put it in?' Lily was exhausted with it all.

The stroke had rendered Miss Rothermere almost helpless. She could speak, but her words were slurred and she often became very emotional. Until the Drurys had come to Worthing, Lily would take time to listen to the old lady and eventually she would understand what she wanted, but Mrs Drury considered anything done slowly meant that Lily was slacking. 'Come along, Cutler, don't stand there dithering. We haven't got all day.' Her constant carping meant that Miss Rothermere was reduced to tears, and Mrs Drury's glare implied that whatever had upset 'poor Auntie' was Lily's fault. There had been times when Lily wished she could have gone to Yorkshire with her employer, but now she was glad she'd never even been asked. For two pins, Lily would have walked out, but she hoped that if she stuck it out for a few days more, they would give her a handsome tip when they left. They could certainly afford it, according to the chauffer who had brought them down from Yorkshire. Mr Drury was more grateful than his wife. When he was in the room or they passed each other in the corridor, he would give Lily a wink or a warm smile, if his wife wasn't looking; and once or twice when they were together in close proximity, she'd felt his hand on her back or he would pat her bottom.

Of course, Lily wasn't stupid. She knew better than to encourage him. She didn't want him turning up in her bedroom in the dead of night, but a little harmless flirting never did anyone any harm.

Saturday had been particularly trying but, alone in her room, Lily had decided to make sure her mourning clothes were ready for Uncle Nelson's funeral on Monday. Miss Rothermere was leaving at ten and the service started at noon, so she would have no time on the day.

'Just for the service, mind,' Mrs Drury had said, when Lily had asked permission to go. 'We need you back here after lunch. The removal van arrives at ten-thirty and then you must clean the rest of the house before we go.'

Lily pressed her dress and hung it carefully in the wardrobe. That was when she decided to exchange her brown handbag for her black one and found the letter. She stared at the writing on the front and felt the bulky corner. What was inside? She held it up to the light, but it didn't help much. Who was that man? She'd never seen him before. Surely she would have known if he'd

158

been a relative. She tried to recall what he'd looked like: smart, middle-aged; his dark hair was thinning, but he was quite good-looking for his age – not exactly handsome, but attractive. He had a soft voice and was well spoken. An educated man. He obviously knew Aunt Bea, but she'd had to tell him who Ruby was, so he must have been a very old acquaintance. She fingered the envelope again.

'Cutler,' came the dreaded voice, 'bring Auntie some hot chocolate, will you?'

Down in the kitchen, Lily laid a small tray with a cup and saucer. The milk had boiled, so she poured a little onto the cocoa and worked it into a paste before adding the rest. The kettle was singing when she'd finished. Miss Rothermere liked her cocoa half-and-half. She didn't know what made her do it, but when she held the envelope over the steam, the gum around the edge melted and the envelope opened quite easily. Inside, Lily found a letter written in a beautiful copperplate hand – the sort of handwriting her teacher at school had struggled to make her copy, although, when she tried, the letters were always jumbled. The bulky thing in the corner turned out to be a pretty locket on a silver chain. Then she heard Mrs Drury coming along the corridor, her heels tap-tapping on the linoleum floor. When Mrs Drury poked her head around the kitchen door, Lily was pouring boiling water into the cup.

Alone in her room and in her nightie, Lily held the locket to her neck and admired herself in the mirror. It was heart-shaped and bulky, but try as she might she couldn't find the means to open it.

159

Perhaps it wasn't meant to open. The envelope, which she had shoved into her pocket when she'd heard Mrs Drury's footsteps, had resealed itself. It didn't look as if it had been tampered with at all. What should she do? She didn't want to steam it open a second time. She might not be able to reseal it. What should she do with the locket? She looked at herself in the mirror again. It suited her so well. It would go nicely with her best dress. No ... she couldn't. It would be like stealing, and she wasn't a thief. It did look good, though. Surely Aunt Bea wouldn't mind if she borrowed it for a while. It belonged around the neck of someone young and pretty. She couldn't imagine it on anyone as old as Aunt Bea, and Ruby wasn't one for wearing jewellery. What was the point of leaving such a lovely locket languishing in a drawer? Anyway, if she didn't say anything, how would Aunt Bea know?

CHAPTER 11

Rex Quinn stared out of the window to the street below. There was hardly anyone about and the few people who battled the elements pulled their coats around their bodies and hurried on. In the distance, the brown and churning sea crashed onto the beach, pulling the pebbles back with it. The Savoy was nice, but he wished he had booked into the hotel across the road. He would have had a better sea view from Warnes. No one was fishing today. The sky, the colour of pewter, glowered over the town with the threat of heavy rain. It was warm in his hotel room, but it looked cold outside and he hadn't slept well. There was too much going on in his mind. Would she come? He turned and, picking up his dressing gown, washbag and towel, headed for the bathroom.

Later on, spruced up and ready for his meal, he sat facing the door. If she came, he wanted to see her at once. He was jumpy. Every time someone moved in the corridor, his head shot up. He'd ordered the morning papers, but even though he'd read the lead story a dozen times, he had no idea what it was about. His breakfast was generous, but he couldn't really taste it. She *must* come.

He had no idea what to do with his day. The hotel manager suggested that he might like to motor out to Arundel or, if the weather improved, take a stroll along the Parade and see the devastation on the pier.

'People came from miles around to see it,' the manager smiled. 'They say that in the week after the fire, over four thousand people paid their tuppence to walk along what was left of it.' He chuckled. 'I reckon it's the only pier in the country that can manage to make thirty-four pounds in a week for half an attraction.'

Rex smiled thinly. He wouldn't be going out. What if she came and he missed her?

'Here for the boxing?' one of his fellow guests asked him as they left the dining room and headed for the visitors' lounge.

'Boxing?'

161

'Saturday night,' said the man. 'At the Egremont.' He was dressed in a thick tweed suit and sported a tobacco-stained moustache, which he'd skilfully twirled into two points. 'There's a room on the first floor. Of course it's not like the old days, but it's got a cracking atmosphere. I used to go there as a lad with my grandfather. I saw some good fights there. I remember...'

Rex heard him talking, but he wasn't listening. Surely Bea wouldn't refuse to come. He began to worry about the girl; she'd seemed a bit airheaded, but she was a relative. Or so she'd said. What if she'd never passed the letter on? Oh God, he hadn't thought of that before. He'd been an absolute fool to give it to her. He should have given it to Bea in person. The trouble was, he didn't know how she would react, if he got that close to her. Not yet. It was too soon. What on earth had he been thinking of? The man had only been dead a week or so. Bea didn't need to know he was here yet. This was hardly the time to settle old scores. The truth could wait for another day, or another weekend ... couldn't it?

The day of Nelson's funeral was overcast, but dry. Albert Longman and three fishermen were the pall-bearers. There was a reasonable turn-out, although Ruby had a shrewd idea that most of the people were there out of sympathy for her mother, rather than paying respect to her father. Nelson's waspish tongue had led to a falling-out with just about every fisherman along this part of the coast at one time or another.

The vicar of St Matthew's, a man who had

162

never met Nelson and hadn't a clue about his life, painted a picture of a loving husband and devoted father. Had she been there, May might have recognized one of those terms, but nobody else did. The church was so still you could have heard a pin drop. The silence was broken only by the persistent cough of someone who was desperately trying to control it. Ruby turned her head and recognized Linton Carver, one of the lads from her father's old regiment during the Great War.

They buried Nelson in the new cemetery at the bottom of Crockhurst Hill. Jim had come to the church, but not to the cemetery. He'd asked for the time off, but as he wasn't related to Nelson, Mr Hayward, Jim's boss, had only allowed him an hour and a half, so there wasn't enough time to go to the graveside. It comforted Ruby to see Jim, and they exchanged a shy smile as he headed back to the studio.

Ruby thanked everyone at the graveside and shook Linton's hand. Judging by his pallor, he was quite ill. 'I'm sorry,' she smiled. 'I can see that you're not too well. It was good of you to come.'

'I was with him at Ypres.' He patted his chest. 'Us old comrades stuck together.'

'Yes, of course,' said Ruby.

Albert Longman bumped into her. 'Excuse me, Ruby. Your mother is sitting in the car. Shall I tell everybody to come back to yours?'

'Yes, thank you, Albert,' she said and, reaching out to touch Linton's arm, she added, 'You will come, won't you, Mr Carver?'

'Perhaps not, love,' he said, patting his chest

163

again. 'Not feeling quite the ticket.'

'Can we give you a lift?' Ruby asked. 'There's room in the car.'

'Much obliged, I'm sure,' he replied.

There were some lovely flowers at the graveside, and even the girls at work had sent a wreath. She guessed that Winnie must have made it. The message was simple – *RIP* – and they'd all signed it: Edith, Phyllis and Doris. Of course none of them had been able to make the funeral. They would all be working, but for a fleeting moment Ruby thought she'd caught sight of a lone woman patting her hair as she stood by the archway near the chapel. At the time she'd been distracted by the pall-bearers lifting the coffin and, when she'd turned her head to look, the woman had gone. She'd frowned. Why on earth had Mrs Fosdyke come to her father's funeral? She didn't know him; she'd never met him. Ruby frowned crossly. Surely Mrs Fosdyke wouldn't go to all this trouble just to check up on her. On second thoughts, she wouldn't put it past her. The old bag!

While her mother waited, Ruby pulled the little cards from the flowers and put them into her bag. She planned to give them to her mother later on. She straightened up and came face-to-face with a man she had never seen before.

He lifted his hat. 'George Gore,' he said. 'Nice service.'

He explained that he too was an old soldier who had been in service with Nelson, and he had just travelled from Derbyshire to Worthing on business. When he'd arrived he'd realized that his old comrade-in-arms had drowned at sea.

164

'We're so glad you could come, Mr Gore,' said Ruby. 'My father never talked about his experiences during the war, but he would have been pleased that one of his old friends had come to pay his respects.'

'I can't say I'm a friend,' said George mysteriously.

'Oh?' said Ruby, slightly taken aback.

Albert Longman interrupted them. 'Excuse me again, Ruby, but I've just come to say goodbye. I have to get back to the office.'

'Yes, yes, of course,' said Ruby, taking his offered handshake. His skin was warm and clammy and it took all her strength not to shudder. 'Thank you so much for all your kindness. Without Percy, I don't know what we would have done without you.' She meant it. She might not like Albert much, but he had been a solid rock to both her and her mother. She became aware of George Gore again. 'This is an old acquaintance of my father,' she said. 'He's come a long way to pay his respects.'

Albert gave him a polite nod.

'We were together at Bellewaarde Ridge,' said George, averting his eyes.

Albert stepped aside, distracted by the wreath sent by the girls at Warnes. He leaned over to read the card.

'That's near Ypres, isn't it?' Ruby said to George Gore. The name was familiar, but only because her mother had once told her that her father had been there. 'Are you staying in Worthing?'

'Yes,' said George. His voice was flat. 'I'm in the area for a couple of weeks.'

165

'Thank you for taking the trouble to come,' said Ruby.

'Give my respects to your mother.' He lifted his hat again and was gone.

Ruby was puzzled. Why come all this way if her father wasn't even a friend?

'I'd best be off now,' said Albert, suddenly standing so close to her that he made her jump. 'Remember, if you want me, you know where to find me.'

Ruby looked down as she walked away. She hoped he wasn't getting any ideas.

The mourners regrouped at Newlands Road.

'What's happened to Percy?' Aunt Vinny's conspiratorial whisper in the kitchen was directed at Ruby, while Bea was out of earshot. The two of them were waiting for the kettle to boil again. It didn't take much to empty the teapot, for it wasn't up to coping with large numbers of people.

Ruby shrugged. 'Jim Searle went looking for him for us,' she said, 'but nobody seems to know where he is.'

'I thought it might be deliberate,' said Aunt Vinny. 'Nelson never was much of a father to him.'

'That didn't stop Percy trying to please him,' said Bea, coming into the room. 'All his life that boy did his best to make his father proud of him.'

'You should have told him,' Aunt Vinny said darkly.

'Vinny!' Bea snapped.

Her sister was unrepentant. 'He had a right to know.'

166

'A right to know what?' said Ruby.

'Nothing,' said Bea. 'And it's none of your business either, Vinny.'

Aunt Vinny slammed the teapot lid down and swirled the teapot. 'It never should have happened.'

'Vinny, I'll thank you to keep your opinions to yourself,' said Bea stiffly. 'Ruby, hurry up and get that tea out there.' She thrust a full tray of teacups at her daughter. 'Go on, go on – everybody's dying of thirst.'

Ruby found herself being pushed out of the kitchen and the door closed sharply behind her. She smiled as she handed out the teas, and made a valiant effort to ignore the sound of angry voices coming from the kitchen.

Cousin Lily hung back as people left the house, offering to help clear up in the kitchen. Bea excused herself and went upstairs. With Ruby at the shallow stone sink and Lily holding the tea towel, the cousins worked steadily, and gradually the pile of plates, cups and saucers stacked on the wooden draining board dwindled.

'What are you going to do, now that Miss Rothermere has gone away?' Ruby asked.

'I've put my name down at the domestic agency,' said Lily.

'Which one?'

'The Central in Warwick Street,' said Lily. 'Mr Drury gave me a good reference, so I should have no trouble finding another post.'

'You could end up going abroad,' Ruby said wistfully.

'Why on earth would I want to do that?' asked Lily.

'Of course,' said Ruby, 'I forgot about your engagement. You won't want to be parted from Hubert for too long, will you?'

'I don't think I shall marry Hubert,' said Lily.

Ruby feigned surprise. 'Oh?'

'We're not entirely suited,' said Lily with a sigh. 'I know he'll be absolutely devastated, but it can't be helped.'

Ruby suppressed a small smile. 'Be careful you don't get yourself a reputation,' she warned mildly.

'Of course I will,' said Lily. 'What about you? With Uncle Nelson gone, will you stay at Warnes?'

'For a bit,' said Ruby putting the tea leaves into the slop bucket underneath the sink and rinsing the teapot. 'But it's not a great wage.'

'I don't know how you do it,' said Lily. 'Such long hours, and having to go back again in the evenings. You have to stay so late. You can't go dancing or to the pictures. I'd hate it.'

'I do go to the pictures,' Ruby chuckled. 'I don't always see the whole film, but I do go to the pictures.'

They had started putting Bea's best china back into the bottom of the sideboard.

'What about May?' asked Lily.

'Seven years old?' Ruby grinned. 'She's a bit young to send out to work.'

'Uncle Nelson wanted her to have piano lessons and stuff,' said Lily.

Ruby was brought up short. 'Did he?' This was the first she'd heard of it. How come Cousin Lily

168

knew something she didn't? Suppressing her irritation, she said, 'How do you know?'

'I was there when he told her,' said Lily. 'She was very excited.'

Ruby straightened up and closed the sideboard doors. 'I don't know how we're going to manage that, without Father's income,' she said. 'May will have to wait a while.'

'Is she still with Susan Marley?' Lily called, as she took the dirty tea towel into the scullery and lobbed it into the copper, ready to boil.

'She comes back tomorrow,' said Ruby. 'Mum didn't want her upset by the funeral.'

'But she knows her father is dead?'

'Oh yes.'

'My mum can't understand why Percy's not here,' said Lily. 'I must say, I'm a bit surprised too.'

'We can't find him,' said Ruby. She knew it sounded like a lame excuse, but Jim had assured her that he had been back to the BUF building in Warwick Street time and time again, but no one knew where Percy was ... or they weren't saying.

Ruby and Lily smiled at each other awkwardly. They'd been together for all the big events of life – births, weddings and now a funeral – but they had little in common. That wasn't to say they didn't like each other. They got on well enough, but their conversation was stilted and awkward. Their mothers, who were sisters, had a rather volatile relationship, which might have explained the cousins' awkwardness. Bea and Vinny were always terse and abrupt when they met, but let anyone criticize the other behind their back and they would fly. It seemed they loved each other fiercely, but found it hard to show it. Nobody really understood why, nor did they trouble to find out. It was just the way it was.

Ruby was looking at Lily's dress. There was a rustle every time she moved. It clung to her body like smoky clouds and the fabric rose on her hip, giving it an air of sophistication. Even in deepest black, Lily was pretty. Ruby knew that the dress was most likely second-hand but, with her trim figure, Lily was able to pick up some choice frocks.

'Can I go up and see Aunt Bea before I go?'

'She may be asleep,' Ruby cautioned.

'I won't be a minute,' said Lily, grabbing her handbag.

Ruby didn't argue. She was feeling tired herself and wanted to sit down for a while. It had been a long and exhausting day, but she'd wanted to write to Miss Russell to thank her for the two pounds she'd given her the last time they'd met, only she couldn't find her address anywhere. It was a shame because Imogen's generosity meant that Nelson's funeral costs were all but met.

'I'm sure I left it on the dresser,' she told herself. 'It was right here, by the teapot.' She moved the best teapot to one side, lifting the lid and peering inside, but the slip of paper wasn't there. Frustrated, she sighed. If she'd lost that address, she couldn't write to Miss Russell and eventually they'd lose touch altogether.

Bea was lying on the top of her bed, but she wasn't asleep. She lay staring at the ceiling. She had taken her mourning dress off, and it was thrown carelessly over the chair. She was in her petticoat, with the floral eiderdown pulled over her to keep herself warm in the chilly bedroom. They only heated one room in the house, although today there was a fire in the front parlour as well. She turned her head as Lily knocked on the door softly.

'Are you off now?' asked Bea. 'Thank you for your help, dear.'

'You're welcome,' said Lily. She hesitated for a second, then came right into the room and shut the door. 'Aunt Bea,' she began awkwardly.

'What is it?' said Bea, suddenly anxious.

'You remember the day of the inquest,' Lily went on. 'When I came out of the Town Hall, someone gave me something. A letter.'

Bea sat up. 'A letter?'

Lily opened her purse and handed her the envelope.

'Who gave it to you?'

'A man,' said Lily. 'I've never seen him before. He was nicely dressed, with fairish hair. You must have known him a long time ago because, when he saw you, he asked me who Ruby was, so he didn't know her.'

Bea touched her mouth with her fingers and her eyes grew wide. 'Did he tell you his name?'

Lily shook her head. 'But he said, when you read the letter, you would know who had given it to me.'

'What's in it?' Bea said.

Lily shrugged. 'I don't know. I can't read, remember? The letters always move about on the page.'

171

'Thank you, dear,' said Bea, relaxing. She put the letter on the chest of drawers next to the bed and lay back down.

'Aren't you going to read it?' Lily couldn't hide her disappointment.

Bea yawned. 'Later. I'm too tired right now. Thanks for bringing it to me, and for all that you've done today.'

As Bea closed her eyes, Lily leaned over her and kissed her cheek. With one last glance at the propped-up envelope, she left the room, closing the door quietly behind her.

CHAPTER 12

Bea looked up at the Savoy Private Hotel. It was small and, unlike the giant Warnes Hotel across the road, it had a homely look to it. She had timed her visit so that there was no danger of bumping into Ruby. Right now she knew her daughter was at work, so there was no chance of seeing her on the street.

Bea had dressed with care. Under her dark-brown woollen twill coat with its sheepskin collar and trim, she was wearing a dark-green dress with a wide vintage-lace collar. Her head was covered by a close-fitting hat in a light-brown jersey, which teamed up nicely with her suede lace-up shoes and matching handbag. She was still in mourning, so she had a black armband on the sleeve of her coat. Taking a deep breath, she walked briskly up the front steps.

A woman sat behind the desk in the foyer. She leaned forward and smiled as Bea entered the hotel. 'Good morning, madam.'

'Good morning,' said Bea. Already her heartbeat had quickened. It was strange being treated as a guest, for Bea was more used to the role of a servant who bobbed a curtsey at important people. Although she had never been inside a private hotel before, she knew how to behave. 'I'm here to enquire about a guest,' she began. 'I believe he is staying here.'

The woman waited, her artificial smile fixed.

Bea took another breath. 'Dr Rex Quinn.' There – she'd said it. She'd said his name aloud for the first time in eighteen years. Nelson had forbidden her to mention his name ever again, and she had given him her promise. Well, Nelson was dead now, so she was under no obligation to keep it secret any more. It felt so deliciously wonderful that she almost wished Nelson was still alive to hear her say it. She could almost picture his face, purple with rage and indignation.

The receptionist was running her finger down the register. Bea was caught a bit off-guard. The hotel wasn't that big; surely she would know which room Rex was in, without having to look it up?

'Dr Quinn left town on Sunday,' she said, looking back up.

Her words hit Bea in the chest like a hammer-blow. She had to stop herself from crying out. Gone? He had been here, and now he was gone? Oh no, no... This was too cruel ... too much to bear.

173

'He was here for eight days,' said the woman.

Bea clutched at her chest. She had come as quickly as she could. If only Lily had given her the letter straight away. 'Did...?' she began in a quavery voice.

'Are you all right, madam?' said the woman, glancing at the armband on Bea's coat. 'Would you like to sit down? Shall I get you a glass of water?'

Bea struggled to regain control of herself. 'Did he leave a forwarding address?'

The receptionist shook her head. 'I'm sorry, madam.' With as much dignity as she could muster, Bea turned to leave.

'Madam,' the woman said again, 'please rest for a minute.' She came round the desk and guided Bea to a chair. It was next to a potted plant, which obscured her from the road. Her nose was tingling and she had a lump in her throat. She fumbled for a handkerchief. 'Wait while I get the proprietor,' said the woman.

Bea was vaguely aware that the receptionist had rung a bell as she came round the desk, but as she pressed the handkerchief to her mouth to stop a scream from coming out, everything else disappeared. He'd gone; she'd missed him. Why hadn't he come to the house? She shook her head. Don't be silly. He doesn't know your address. He only knew you lived in Worthing. If he had been here for a week, why hadn't he spoken to her at the inquest? It was unbearable to think that they'd both been in the same room, but she hadn't seen him. If only he'd come up to her then...

Someone else appeared at her elbow. She was

holding a small glass of something the colour of amber. 'Here, dear,' she said kindly. 'My name is Miss Taylor, and this is my hotel. You've had a bit of a shock. Have a little drop of brandy to steady your nerves.'

'She was asking for Dr Quinn,' said the receptionist.

'Did you give her the note?' Miss Taylor asked.

'What note?' said the woman.

'What note?' Bea repeated.

'Really, Iris, you never listen to a word I say. I clearly remember telling you about it. I put it in the pigeonhole.'

'The blue envelope?' asked Iris.

'Yes,' said Miss Taylor. 'Well, go and get it. Don't keep the lady waiting.' Bea sipped the brandy. 'That girl will be the death of me,' said Miss Taylor and then, seeing the black armband on Bea's coat, her face coloured. 'Oh, I'm sorry, dear. I didn't mean anything...'

'It's all right,' said Bea. 'You've been most kind.'

Iris reappeared with a blue envelope.

'Before I give it to you,' said Miss Taylor, 'may I ask for your name?'

'Mrs Beatrice Bateman,' said Bea, not once taking her eye from the envelope.

Miss Taylor handed it to her. Bea's hand trembled as she took it, and she instantly recognized the copperplate hand. She pressed it to her chest and stood up. The blood drained from her head, and Miss Taylor cried out as Bea wobbled precariously. 'Oh, my dear...'

'I'm all right,' said Bea as her head cleared. 'I just stood up too quickly, that's all. I'm fine,

175

really I am.' Calling out a thank-you, she headed for the door.

'You really should take your time, dear,' Miss Taylor called after her, but Bea wasn't listening. All she wanted was to get home and read his letter. She dropped it inside her bag and, despite the two-inch heels on her shoes, almost ran home.

Once back in her kitchen, Bea didn't even bother to take off her coat before she tore open the envelope:

My darling girl,

I waited for the weekend, hoping that you would come, but I suppose it's too soon. I am sorry to intrude so quickly into your grief, but I am an impatient man. I realize now that you must have time to get over your loss, and of course I want to protect your good name. If we are to have the best chance of a happy life together, I need to allow you to say your goodbyes properly. For this reason, I won't add any pressure until you are ready.

I shall come back next year, and perhaps by then we can meet without impropriety. I have booked a room for the weekend of October 6th, 1934. Until then, all my best love, Rex.

An anguished cry roared from Bea's mouth. *A year – another year...* No, no, he couldn't do this to her. A whole year... Oh God, this was too cruel. It was too much. She couldn't bear it. She was filled with pain and despair and suddenly heard this terrible howl that went on and on.

The back door burst open and her other neighbour, Florrie Dart, rushed in. 'Oh, Bea,' she cried. 'It's hit you at last, hasn't it? There, there, my dear. It will get better, I promise. Let's get you upstairs and into your bed, and I'll send for the doctor.'

A postcard from Miss Russell! Ruby took it down from the mantelpiece and turned it over:

Staying near the Sorbonne. Beautiful streets and lively night-life. Jazz is very popular here. Think of you often, dear Ruby. Thank you for what you did. Best wishes, Imogen R.

Ruby turned the postcard back and looked at the picture of the Eiffel Tower reaching up into the sky. If only she could see it for herself...

Someone tapped on the window, making her jump. When she opened the front door, Isaac Kaufman snatched his hat off.

'Hello!' she cried. 'Come in, come in.'

He stepped inside hesitantly.

'Sit down,' said Ruby, taking him into the kitchen. 'Let me get you some tea.'

'I came to offer you my condolences,' he said. 'Mr Searle told me of your loss.'

'Thank you,' said Ruby.

The reminder of her father's death was never far away, yet it still brought her up short when someone mentioned it. The weight of guilt because she hadn't cried was beginning to lie heavily on her chest, like a jagged canker. She should have cried by now, shouldn't she? When she'd seen his coffin again in the church she'd felt as if she couldn't breathe, but the tears had refused to come.

She put a match under the kettle and lit the gas. 'It was so kind of you to come,' she said. 'I know I've only had a couple of lessons, but I may not be able to carry on with my classes, and I was just thinking that I should let you know. You've saved me having to write you a letter and putting the stamp on the envelope.' Her laughter was both brittle and sad. She was prattling, but she couldn't seem to stop herself. 'I'm sorry to let you down.'

'No, no, dear lady,' he protested. 'It is *I* who am sorry.'

She looked at him helplessly. She wanted to ask him for her money back, but how could she? He probably needed it more than she did. But, whatever happened from now on, she couldn't afford to carry on with the lessons. It would be hard enough trying to keep going, without paying for such unnecessary luxuries.

'I cannot invite you to Mrs Grimes's,' he said, oblivious to what was really being discussed.

Ruby lowered herself into the chair opposite. Although it was clean, his shirt was crumpled. It looked un-ironed. He was wearing a different suit, and Ruby guessed he had bought it from a second-hand repository with the two pounds she had given him in advance. (No chance of getting her money back then, even if she had the courage to ask for it.) Isaac's face was haggard and he had dark circles under his eyes. At first he met her steady gaze, but then lowered his eyes and fiddled with his hat, which lay on the table in front of him.

178

'What's wrong?' she asked softly.

He managed a small smile. 'You have troubles of your own,' he said apologetically.

'Tell me,' she coaxed. 'Have you heard something about your family back in Germany?'

'I have no family now, Miss Bateman,' he said simply. 'They are all dead. I came to England for peace, but now I must leave.'

'Leave? Why must you leave?'

'Mrs Grimes,' he sighed. 'She has a new lodger.'

'And?' said Ruby.

'The lodger and Mrs Grimes ... they like each other,' said Isaac, clearing his throat with an embarrassed cough. 'I am in the way. He makes trouble for me.'

Ruby bristled with indignation, but as she busied herself making the tea, a plan was forming in her mind. The kettle boiled and, as she poured the tea, her mother came through the back door with a washing basket on her hip. Isaac leapt to his feet.

'Mother, this is Isaac,' said Ruby. 'He's a friend of Jim's.'

Bea put her basket on the draining board and wiped her hand on her apron before shaking hands. She was pale and her face was expressionless, just the way Ruby had found her when she'd come home a couple of days before. Mrs Dart had told her that her mother had finally wept for her father, and that the doctor had given her a sedative. Since then, Bea went through the motions of doing what she was supposed to do, but it was obvious that something had died within her. Their friends and neighbours told Ruby it was just the

179

grief, but she had a funny feeling it was more than that.

Once again Isaac offered his condolences.

'Isaac is a refugee from Germany,' said Ruby. 'He is also looking for lodgings.'

Bea seemed astonished. 'Oh, my dear,' she said, 'we're not ready yet. My husband ... the room...' Her voice trailed off.

'Please, madam,' said Isaac, obviously embarrassed, 'I intrude.'

'Perhaps if you came back at the end of the week,' said Ruby, 'we would be ready then.'

Isaac shook his head. 'You don't have to...' he began.

'My mother and I had discussed getting a lodger.' Ruby spoke directly to Bea, giving her a quizzical look. 'I feel sure we could be ready by Friday. Do you have anywhere to stay until then?'

'Miss Bateman,' Isaac began again, 'you are very kind, but I have little money.'

'What happened to the Parks and Gardens department?' Ruby frowned.

'I still work there, but the money...' He shrugged.

'I've been thinking about your skills as a boot-maker,' said Ruby.

'Boot-mender,' he corrected her. 'I am – how do you say? – a cobbler.'

'I've heard people around here saying they could do with a cobbler,' said Ruby. 'They want a man who will charge sensible prices and who is good at his job.'

Isaac shrugged. 'I have no tools.'

He looked defeated, but Ruby was on a mission now. 'There's a place on the corner of Lyndhurst

180

Road and High Street,' she said. 'We call it The Ark, because they have just about everything you could wish for there. What would you need most?'

'A cobbler's last,' said Isaac. 'Leather, nails, a good knife...'

'I'm sure we could find enough to get you started,' said Ruby.

'But where will I do it?' cried Isaac.

Ruby sat down, clearly stumped. Bea smiled to herself and began to fold the washing ready for ironing. Isaac sipped his tea.

May came in from the small courtyard garden and interrupted them. 'Can I have some tea for my dolly's tea party?'

'Bring your teapot and I'll give you some,' said Ruby. A moment or two later the tiny china teapot appeared, and Ruby filled it with lukewarm milky tea. 'That's all there is,' she cautioned. 'Don't drink it too quickly.'

'It's not for me – it's for dolly,' said May crossly. 'She drinks it.'

'Well tell her to be careful to make it last,' said Ruby with a smile. 'Where are you having your party?'

'By the shed,' said May, skipping out of the back door.

Ruby looked up at her mother. 'The shed,' she said. 'Isaac can mend his boots there.' Bea was nodding.

'I do not understand,' said Isaac.

'There's an old shed outside,' said Ruby, getting excited. 'People can come in through the back gate.'

'It's still full of your father's fishing gear...' said Bea. Her voice died away.

'Percy made it clear he doesn't want to fish,' said Ruby, 'so what's the point of keeping it? We could sell it and use the money for something else.'

Isaac put his head in his hands. 'Aye-eeh-aye, what is this?' He put his hand in his pocket and drew out two pound notes. 'I came to give you these back,' he said, 'and now what have you done?'

Bea raised her eyebrows. 'Where did that come from?'

'I'll explain later, Mother,' said Ruby. 'Isaac, you keep it. I still want my lessons and we can do them here. Use the money to buy your equipment.'

Isaac looked up, his eyes moist with tears. 'It will take me a long time to pay you back.'

'We know,' said Ruby.

'Pay her back for what?' Bea said, but neither of them was listening.

'We'll do it properly,' said Ruby. 'Give you a rent book, and everything. So ... what do you think?'

'I think you are amazing, Miss Bateman,' he said.

'Isaac, Ruby ... will one of you tell me what is going on?'

Half an hour later, when Isaac had gone and Ruby had explained everything, Bea shook her head. 'It's going to be a lot of hard work, getting ready for this. And what about our Percy?'

'You heard Percy say that he wanted to move

out, Mum,' said Ruby.

'But that was before your father died,' said Bea.

Ruby chewed her lip anxiously. 'We don't know if he's ever coming back,' she said softly. 'He promised you that he'd write. It's been weeks since he went, and you haven't heard a thing.' It was always a bit of a struggle not to feel cross with her brother. She couldn't blame him for going, and he had told her as long ago as the day of the High Salvington outing what was on his mind. Father had made his life a misery, and in times past Percy had even taken the blame for some of the misdemeanours she'd committed. He knew how much she'd hated being shut in the coal-hole, and she'd loved him dearly for accepting a tanning – and even the belt once – to spare her having to sit in the cold and dark for hours on end. In one sense, it wasn't Percy's fault that he wasn't here right now. He clearly had no idea their father was dead, but, by clearing off like that, he had in effect left her with all the responsibility.

Bea nodded miserably. Ruby put her arm around her mother's shoulders. 'Don't you see, Mother?' Ruby smiled. 'It will help us in the long run. Once Isaac's got going, he'll be paying us two lots of rent: one for the room, and another for the shed. That can't be bad now, can it?'

Bea shook her head and dug Ruby in the ribs. 'You're always organizing somebody, aren't you?' she scolded good-naturedly. 'Bossy boots!'

CHAPTER 13

It was the best half a crown Percy had ever spent. He had read Oswald Mosley's book, *The Greater Britain,* from cover to cover. What inspiration. What common sense. What genius! The more he read, the more he admired the man who had penned the words: 'A corporate state and a government with absolute power to carry out the will of the people'. Now that really would get things done. If only those in power had listened to what Mosley had proposed when he was in government two years before, the country would be in much better shape. Faced with two million unemployed, Mosley had put forward a grand plan to get things moving. After the stagnation of the twenties, following the crippling debts brought on by the Great War, his ideas seemed so logical. Raise the school leaving age and embark on a huge programme of slum clearances – it was a bold move, but the fools in Whitehall had thrown it out, in what Mosley called a 'spineless drift towards disaster'. Percy's blood boiled every time he thought about it. He closed the book and smiled to himself.

'Finished?' said his room-mate.

Percy nodded. 'Pretty good stuff.' He swung his legs down and got to his feet with a stretch and a yawn.

The day he had walked out of his home, Percy

had decided – just to spite his father – to join the Blackshirts. One thing was for sure: he didn't want his father turning up at headquarters and demanding that his son get back to fishing. And so, thumbing a lift or two, he'd walked for miles to get to London. After meeting a few Blackshirt members, he'd spent a period of time at their training centre in Whitelands House, the building formerly used by the college of the same name. Now renamed the Black House, it was only a stone's throw from Chelsea Barracks, with its own sleeping quarters, a drill hall and sports facilities. He paid his way by working in the kitchen and doing menial tasks that no one else wanted to do, like cleaning the bathrooms and toilets, as well as knuckling down to a strict routine of physical training and instruction. As if that wasn't enough, he also had the opportunity to learn to drive and, because the leadership wanted its trainees to have an all-round knowledge of everyday life, Percy got to discover what lay under the bonnet as well.

During his very limited free time, he enjoyed walking in the extensive grounds and ate with the other men in the canteen. Of course he still had to pay thirty bob a week for his board and lodgings, but it was worth every penny of the money he'd saved. He'd almost forgotten the money; in the heat of trying to get away from Nelson, he suddenly realized that he'd left the money in its hiding place, and had to go back to the house to fetch it. He'd been terrified of being caught, but his father had already gone fishing. Ever since Linton Carver had told him that his father had done something awful with the other lads during

185

the war, Percy had hated him even more. He'd tried to press Linton about what actually happened, but he wouldn't be drawn. Percy could only guess, and his imagination knew no bounds. What a hypocrite! All that claptrap about being on the side of right and good, and all the while his father had a dark, hidden secret.

After years of being put down, ridiculed and squashed, Percy was proud to think he could be part of something that was going to make a real difference in the country. Although not a great reader, now that he'd finally waded through *The Greater Britain* he was positive that, once Mosley had convinced the British people of his sincerity, the takeover of power by the BUF would only be a matter of time.

The door burst open and Lance Corporal Willis came into the room.

'Lieutenant Johnson wants to see you, Bateman.'

With her mother resting upstairs, Ruby noticed that her father's best Sunday coat was still hanging on the nail by the back door. Somehow it had been missed in the great clear-out that her mother had started. Ruby took it down and studied it carefully. He'd seldom worn it, preferring older, more familiar things, even though they were shabby. A button was hanging by a thread, but that was easily remedied. Once the button was sewn back on, she went through the pockets, but there was nothing of any consequence. She brushed the coat with the clothes brush. The next time the suitcase came back, she would put it inside, and then everything that had belonged to

Nelson would be out of the house.

As he followed the lance corporal through the house, Percy was racking his brains, wondering why he'd been sent for. He had earned the respect of his leaders and was often praised for his enthusiasm and agility, so he couldn't imagine why he'd been summoned to see Lieutenant Johnson. After a brisk march down a long corridor, he found himself in the officers' room. Percy stood smartly at the desk and waited.

'At ease,' said Johnson languidly.

Percy relaxed. Was he going to be offered promotion and a more responsible position, or was he going to be asked to leave?

'Someone from your family has been making enquiries about you,' said Johnson. He leaned back in his chair and sighed. 'He has been to staff HQ in Worthing several times during the past few weeks.'

So his father was looking for him. The idea of Nelson turning up several times to look for him was hugely satisfying to Percy. He felt justified in leaving instructions that he was to remain uncontactable, whatever the circumstances. Perhaps now that his son wasn't at his beck and call, the old man would appreciate him a bit more. Having no contact with the rest of his family was a small sacrifice to pay and, once his mother saw what he had made of his life, Percy felt sure she would understand. After all, it was only six weeks – and what could possibly go wrong in six weeks?

'The memo-writer doesn't say why there have been enquiries,' said Johnson, looking at his fingernails, 'but I'm sure, if there were something amiss, he would have mentioned it.'

'Yes, sir,' said Percy smartly.

'You're nearly at the end of training, aren't you?' said Johnson.

'Five more days, sir.'

It had been a proud moment when Percy had gone to his first rally as a fully fledged Blackshirt steward. The shirt itself cost only a few shillings, and was fastened by a row of buttons on the left shoulder. It had been designed by Mosley himself and modelled on his fencing shirt, because it could be worn without a collar and tie. And it prevented anyone being half-strangled in the rugby scrum that often accompanied the meetings.

'You could agree to make contact straight away,' said Johnson, sitting up straight and picking up his baton as he rose to his feet, 'but I'm sure a few days more won't make any difference.'

'Yes, sir.'

'If, on reflection, you change your mind, talk to the lance corporal. That's all. Dismissed.'

'Yes, sir. Thank you, sir.'

'What's it to be then, Bateman?' Lance Corporal Willis asked, as he and Percy left the building.

'I'd rather stick with it, without any distractions,' he said.

'Good man,' said Willis.

Percy enjoyed the camaraderie in the barrack rooms. He had made two particular friends, Edgar Mills and Barnabas West – known as Barney to his friends. They were about his own age and, until they'd joined the BUF, both had been unemployed. Edgar came from the East End, which he said was 'swarming with bloody foreigners and Jews now', and Barney came from Kent.

'Everything all right?' asked Edgar, as Percy walked back in.

Percy nodded.

The men were relaxing after a hard day of physical training and lectures. Percy stripped down to his vest and sat at a small table to write a letter, while Edgar, already in pyjamas, lay on his bunk reading a book. Barney was sitting on his bunk in his bare feet while he darned a sock.

'What are you fellows going to do, when you leave here?' asked Barney.

'A pal of mine knows a chap who is looking for long-distance lorry drivers,' Percy said. 'I got him to promise to take me on.'

'Lucky sod!' said Edgar, putting his book down. 'I ain't got nuffink yet.'

'You need to talk to Mick Clarke,' said Percy. 'He's got contacts in the East End. There's a whole network you can tap into, now that you're a Blackshirt. What do you fancy doing?'

Edgar shrugged.

'There's plenty of builders looking for brickies,' said Barney. 'I fancy the idea of building for the future.'

'There's a rally over in Shoreditch next week,' said Percy, writing the address on an envelope. 'They're looking for volunteers to help keep order.'

'Those big rallies can get violent,' said Edgar. There was a hint of anxiety in his voice.

Barney leaned over the side of his bunk and

189

nudged him playfully. 'You great lummox! You've heard what Mosley says: "Ejection will only…"'

'"…be carried out with minimum force."' The other two joined in, to finish the oft-quoted sentence, and then laughed.

'You'll only get trouble if the Communists are there,' said Percy in a more sober mood. 'They come in and stir up the locals.'

'Who's the letter for?' asked Barney. 'Girl-friend?'

'My mother,' said Percy. 'I promised her I'd write. My father has been to our local HQ asking after me.'

'Nothing wrong, I hope,' said Edgar.

'I'm sure if there was, my father would have said,' said Percy. He licked the gum on the envelope and stuck it down and then, propping it on his locker, added, 'I might hang onto it for another couple of days, until I've got the address for my new digs.'

'No point in buying two stamps just for your mother, eh?' Barney teased.

'But you've already stuck it down,' said Edgar.

'Blimey,' Percy laughed. 'So I have.'

'Where do you come from, Perce?'

'Worthing,' said Percy. 'It's about thirteen miles from Brighton.'

'Nice,' said Edgar.

'Not much there,' said Barney, holding up his sock for them to admire, 'except the fishing.'

'I wouldn't mind a bit of fishing,' said Edgar. 'I had a go at it once. Only in the canal, mind, but it was quite good.'

'You can keep it, as far as I'm concerned,' said

Percy, his expression darkening. 'I hate fishing. My old man is a fisherman.'

'You don't fancy following in your father's footsteps then?' said Barney.

'No, I bloody well don't,' replied Percy. He could feel the old anger rising in his chest. 'I hate the sea. I hate the smell of fish.' He dropped his voice. 'And I can't say I felt that great about the old man, either.'

'Give you a bad time, did he?' asked Edgar.

'Something like that,' said Percy, standing up. 'All I know is, no matter what I bloody well did, there was no pleasing him.'

The two men watched him balling his hands into fists.

'Some blokes are like that,' said Edgar. 'Was he in the Great War? My uncle was never the same when he came back. He ended up in the nut house.'

'He never talks about it,' said Percy bitterly, 'and I never ask.'

'Perhaps you should, mate,' said Edgar. 'He might be a bloomin' hero.'

Percy scoffed out loud.

'I reckon the next time you see him,' said Barney with a reckless abandon, 'you should ask him.'

'There won't be a next time,' Percy frowned. 'As far as I'm concerned, my old man is dead. It's all over between me and him now, and he can rot in hell for all I care. If I never see him again as long as I live, even that will be too soon.'

He pulled a towel from his locker and threw it over his shoulder.

'But surely you'd want to go back and see your mother?' said Edgar, a little shocked by the vehemence in Percy's voice. 'What about your brothers and sisters?'

'Perhaps he hasn't got any,' Barney observed.

'I've got two sisters,' said Percy, picking up his washbag. 'Ruby is seventeen and May is seven.'

'Well then,' Edgar pushed, 'you'll want to see them, surely?'

'I'm telling you now,' said Percy, his eyes flashing, 'while my old man is alive, I'm never going back.' He headed for the door, then paused. 'I have my reasons, but don't ask me.'

'You'd better hurry up with your ablutions,' Barney called. 'They'll be playing "Sunset", and it's lights out in ten minutes.'

The door closed.

Edgar glanced at Barney. 'Blimey. I've never seen him that worked up before.'

'Not much love lost there then,' Barney observed.

Edgar pulled down the blanket on his bed. 'Poor ol' Perce. I wonder what his old man did to him.'

It was Ruby's first day off for weeks that she didn't have to go to an inquest, see the undertaker, attend a funeral or have to sort out something to do with her father's death. Freda Fosdyke had refused to give her any extra time off to settle her father's affairs. With Percy being away, everything fell on Ruby's shoulders, and she was tired: tired of having to put on a brave face; tired of having to think ahead; and tired of work. Apart

192

from the rest of the formalities when the inquest would resume next Thursday in the new Town Hall, Ruby was back to the old routine.

She relaxed in bed for a bit, while her mother took May to school. Her *Pall Mall* magazine, which she'd smuggled home, had all but fallen to pieces, but she glanced through the pages again. There had been a terrible moment when her mother almost used it to light the fire, so now Ruby kept it upstairs with her other one.

'What on earth do you want to keep that old thing for?' Bea had asked. 'You've already read it, haven't you?'

Yes, she had ... but that didn't stop Ruby wanting to read it over and over again. She was excited today. Jim had the same day off, and they planned to catch the bus to Brighton. The summer season was over of course, but in the run-up to Christmas the shops would be festive and it would be a welcome change of scene. Ruby dressed warmly because the weather was chilly, although thankfully it was dry. She hurried towards the pier head, where they had promised to meet. Jim waved as she came into view and she returned his greeting. Her excitement mounted. A whole day with Jim. What could be nicer?

He paid her fare and they sat at the top of the Southdown bus. Someone got off at Shoreham, which meant they could sit in the front seats. Ruby felt like a queen surveying her country as they looked down on the narrow streets and the winding road beside the port. Then they came to the wider roads of Hove and Brighton itself, busy with traffic and heaving with shoppers. Once they saw the great statue of Queen Victoria looking out to sea, Ruby knew it wouldn't be long before they got out. The West Pier, then the Palace Pier, and they'd arrived at Pool Valley bus station. It was time to get off.

'Shops or pier?' asked Jim as their feet touched terra firma.

'Pier,' said Ruby. It was no contest. She longed to feel the wind in her hair and to fill her lungs with the salty sea air.

'It's the next inquest on Thursday,' she reminded him, as he paid their tuppence each to walk on the Palace Pier.

He nodded.

The ice-cream kiosks, the kiss-me-quick hat stalls and the deckchairs were gone, but Jim bought a stick of rock for May, and Ruby bought them both a plate of cockles, after she'd noticed his lean and hungry look as he spotted them. The seller sprinkled them with a little white pepper and some vinegar, and they sat on a wooden bench to eat them. 'When I was a kid living in the Home,' said Jim, 'we used to do this.' He had his back half turned and, when he turned back, he pretended to take a winkle from his nostril, looked at it and ate it.

'Ugh, you're disgusting!' she laughed as she gave him a playful shove. 'I hope somebody gave you a smacked bottom.'

'Nobody saw us except we kids,' he said with a grin.

'Were they all right with you?' she asked anxiously. 'I mean, they weren't unkind to you or anything?'

Jim shook his head. 'It wasn't a bed of roses, but it was all right. The only thing I missed out on was having my own family. I never felt like I belonged.'

'I wish Percy was here.' Her voice was small.

'I've been back to the BUF HQ four times now,' said Jim, 'but they still won't tell me where he is.'

'I don't think that's right,' Ruby complained.

'Neither do I,' said Jim. 'All they do is tell me he's safe and being well cared for.'

'He's missed Father's funeral,' said Ruby, 'and it looks like he's going to miss the inquest as well. Do they realize his father has died?'

'I've told them every time,' said Jim.

He reached for her hand and enclosed it in his own.

Ruby's heartbeat quickened. His hand was warm and big and gave her a delicious feeling. It was almost worth not having her brother around if Jim did this sort of thing. She didn't think Percy would be heartbroken about his father, but she thought he should know about his death. Technically he was the head of the family and should take on his responsibilities. Why should it fall solely on her shoulders? Perhaps he'd enjoy fishing, now that he didn't have to be with their father. She knew Nelson's caustic criticisms were the cause of a lot of the trouble between them.

'How are you getting along with Isaac?' Jim asked.

'We've got him fully installed in the old parlour,' Ruby smiled. 'He thinks it's heaven on earth. Do you know, the only thing he brought from

Germany to remember his family by was a half-finished place mat that his wife made.'

'So sad,' said Jim.

'Right now,' Ruby went on, 'he's trying to get the outhouse ready to use as a workshop. It's a bit small, but he reckons he can fit everything in.'

'It's a marvellous thing you're doing,' said Jim, giving her hand a squeeze.

Ruby's heart soared. 'It benefits us all,' she smiled.

Their cockles eaten, they stood again and strolled along the rest of the pier. A few fishermen were dotted along the boards, but it didn't seem to be a good day for catching anything. Having 'done' the Palace Pier, they strolled along the front to the West Pier. It started to rain.

'How about we find somewhere to eat?' Jim said. 'And then I'll take you to the pictures.'

Ruby snuggled into his arm. 'I'd like that,' she smiled.

Down one of the narrow side-streets Jim found a small cafe with checked oilcloth on the tables. It looked clean and he could afford the prices. They ate egg and chips, and then they saw Paul Robeson in *The Emperor Jones.* Ruby loved his singing and enjoyed the story very much. On the bus home, Jim put his arm around her shoulders and she dozed, contented. They had spent enough time talking, so they walked back to her place in a companionable silence. By the front gate he slipped his arms around her waist and drew her close.

'This has been the best day of my life,' he said softly. 'You're a fantastic girl.'

196

Ruby took in her breath, and then tenderly and gently his lips met hers.

Once she was indoors and Jim was whistling his way down the street, he didn't notice a shadowy figure following close behind.

CHAPTER 14

In contrast to the opening of the first part of Nelson's inquest, the weather on the day it was reconvened, Thursday November 23rd, was cold and wet. People entered the room on the right of the new Town Hall on Stoke Abbott Road, shaking their umbrellas and removing wet coats. The floor in the entrance became wet and dirty in no time. Ruby pushed her damp hair away from her face, and water ran along the brim of Bea's hat, trickling onto her collar.

The chairs were set out in rows. They were very modern, made of tubular steel with beige canvas seats and backs. There weren't many, but Ruby noticed that if more were needed, there were plenty of others stacked together at the back of the room. The room itself had bare walls, and because of the weather outside it was dark. After a while someone put on the electric lights, although there were so few that it made little difference. Afterwards she tried to remember if the walls were wooden or just painted a dark colour. The floor was covered in dark-brown linoleum, and the light coming in through the rectangular windows was diffused by their small Crittall frames. They were ushered into two seats near the front, facing the trestle table that served as a desk for the coroner.

Once settled, Ruby turned to see who else was in the room. A couple of policemen, some of the fishermen she'd seen on the beach that morning, and Coxswain Taylor of the Shoreham rescue boat, the man who had come to their house. A group of men sat to the left of the coroner's chair, and Ruby guessed they must be the jury. She recognized a few of them as well: Mr Whittington, the fishmonger from Montague Street; Mr Watts from the shoe shop in Chapel Road; and Mr Pressley, who had a jeweller's shop in South Street. There were others she knew, but couldn't put a name to the face. She wished with all her heart that Jim was coming, but she knew he would be working.

The coroner, Dr Thomas Fox-Drayton, arrived promptly at ten-thirty and enquired whether the jury had been sworn in. After explaining why they were all assembled once again, he began by asking Bea some questions. She confirmed Nelson's age, occupation and his address and that he had been in good health.

'How long had you known the deceased?'

'We'd been married for twenty years,' said Bea. 'Since 1913.'

'Would you say your husband was a competent fisherman?'

'He had been a fisherman all his life,' said Bea. 'He and his father and grandfather before him. My husband's family have fished in Worthing for a hundred and fifty years.' She went on to tell the court that, during the Great War, Nelson had served with the Northumberland Fusiliers and had been in action at Ypres, most notably at Belle-waarde Ridge. Ruby heard a couple of people behind her audibly drawing breath as her mother went on, 'My husband was wounded in 1915. And after a period of recuperation, he returned to the regiment – or what was left of it – but in a non-fighting capacity for the rest of the war.'

A hush had fallen over the courtroom. Ruby hadn't known any of that.

The coroner cleared his throat. 'Would you say that Mr Bateman understood the perils of the sea?'

'He had a great respect for the sea,' said Bea. 'He never took risks.'

'Was the deceased sober when you last saw him?'

Bea pressed her handkerchief to her nose. 'Nelson was teetotal.'

Ruby was asked the same sort of questions. All went well until the coroner said, 'What was your father's mental state? Was he upset about anything, when he set off that night?'

The question left Ruby stunned. What could she say? She'd promised to tell the truth, but if she told them what really happened, it wouldn't look good. Her father had been really angry with Percy – in fact he'd all but chucked him out of the house. Feelings had been running very high, but between Father and Percy that was normal. She couldn't help remembering that the coxswain had hinted at suicide. What if the coroner decided that her father had been so upset that night that he'd

199

done a dreadful thing? How would they live with it?

'Miss Bateman,' the coroner broke into her jumbled thoughts, 'was there something different about your father's demeanour as he set out that night?'

'Yes,' she said softly. She lowered her head and stared at her hands. She had to tell him; she had no choice. 'My brother had told him he didn't want to be a fisherman any more, so they'd argued.' She glanced up at her mother. Bea stared back, expressionless.

'Did the argument become violent?'

'No!' cried Ruby. 'Absolutely not.' It could so easily have done so, but she didn't mention that. Thank God Percy had told Father not to hit him ever again. If she'd had to tell the court they'd come to blows, it would have looked really, really bad.

'And what was the consequence of that argument?'

'My brother packed his bags and left home that night.'

'Is it possible that, when he was out in that boat, your father could have been distracted by the fact that your brother no longer wanted to follow in his footsteps?'

'My father knew how Percy felt, long before that night.' She wanted to say, *My father never held grudges,* but that wasn't true, and any number of the fishermen along the coast would have testified that she was lying. 'I suppose it's possible he could have been thinking about Percy,' she began again, choosing her words carefully, 'but he

200

wasn't the sort of man to let anything else bother him, once he was in that boat.'

'Did your brother go out with him that night?'

'No, sir.'

'Thank you, Miss Bateman,' the coroner smiled.

The next person to give evidence was Silas Reed, a Worthing fisherman, and the one who had raised the alarm.

'Percy and Nelson were fishing close by me,' he said.

'Miss Bateman has told the court that she didn't think her brother was fishing that night.'

'Well, Nelson had someone in the boat,' said Silas, clearly flummoxed. 'My eyesight may not be what it once was, but I saw someone else standing in that boat. Who else could it be but young Percy?'

Ruby held her breath. Why was he saying all this? Everybody else had said Percy wasn't on the boat.

'What was the distance between your two boats?'

Silas shrugged. 'Half a mile? A bit more maybe.' He went on to describe how, once he'd come ashore, he'd run to the pier and the blue police box to raise the alarm. Young Albert and some of the other men had secured the boat.'

'Young Albert?' enquired the coroner.

'Albert Longman,' said Silas. 'He went to Nelson's house to tell Mrs Bateman, and young Ruby here came to the beach to see for herself.' He shook his head sadly. 'Weren't nothing anybody could do. He were washed ashore later that day.'

Silas stepped down, and the coroner looked up. 'Is Percy Bateman in court?'

'No, sir,' said Bea. 'We've sent for him, but nobody seems to know where he is.'

'Have the police made enquiries?' The coroner looked directly at the police inspector, who shifted in his seat, looking uncomfortable. 'In view of the question mark hanging over this case, I suggest that the police make this a matter of urgency,' Dr Fox-Drayton snapped.

Albert was next. It struck Ruby for the first time that they hadn't seen much of him lately. She hadn't given him a thought, which was rather unkind, considering how helpful he had been in the beginning. She felt a bit guilty about it. She should have enquired after him.

Albert explained that on the day in question he'd had a problem sleeping and had gone for a walk along the seashore, hoping to see the rise of the dawn over the water. 'That's when I saw a boat,' he went on. 'It was coming ashore with the tide, and I realized that it was empty.'

The coroner wrote something down. 'What did you do then, Mr Longman?'

'I ran down the beach and into the water, to drag it ashore,' said Albert. 'The weather had deteriorated and a storm was brewing. I recognized it as the *Saucy Sarah*, Mr Bateman's boat, but there was no sign of him or his son.'

There was a low murmur around the courtroom, then Albert continued, 'I shouted for help, and when we'd got it up the beach I ran to the Batemans' house.'

'Are you a fisherman, Mr Longman?'

'Heavens, no,' said Albert. 'I did go out with Mr Bateman and his son once, but that was in my

202

capacity as a newspaper reporter. I was very sick and I hated it.'

There was a titter of laughter in the room.

'In that case,' said the coroner, 'I commend you for your bravery, and I shall take steps to see that you are rewarded with ten pounds from public funds.'

Albert blushed a little and went back to his seat. At the same time the Town Hall clock struck twelve and the coroner adjourned for lunch.

It was too far to go all the way back home, so Albert offered to take Bea and Ruby to Mitchell's, opposite the library in Chapel Road. Ruby tried to refuse, but her mother had already accepted. It was a popular place at lunchtime, but they were lucky enough to find a vacant window seat. Archie ordered a pot of tea and a round of sandwiches. Ruby declined to eat.

'Are you all right?' asked Albert anxiously.

'I'm fine,' Ruby smiled. 'I just can't face eating, that's all.'

The waitress bustled away.

'I'm worried that they're going to say Nelson did it deliberately,' said Ruby.

'But he didn't,' said Bea.

'I know that, and you know that, Mother,' said Ruby, 'but the coroner kept on asking about Father's state of mind.'

'I don't think it's anything to worry about,' Albert smiled.

The waitress came with their tea and two rounds of egg sandwiches.

As soon as she'd gone Ruby said, 'I've been

203

over and over what happened that morning and I just don't understand it.'

Albert concentrated on his sandwich while Bea poured the tea.

'Two heads are better than one,' Ruby went on. 'Three is even better. Please help me ... please...'

Albert looked up. 'All right. Fire away.'

She took a deep breath. 'Father and Percy had a falling-out, but we're sure Percy didn't go fishing – agreed, Mother?'

Bea nodded.

'So who was the person in the boat that Silas saw?'

'Silas is as blind as a bat,' said Albert. 'He imagined it.'

'Father couldn't have sailed that boat alone,' said Ruby. 'You need more than one person to get the trammel nets out.'

'Who's to say he was using the trammel nets?' Albert asked.

Bea shook her head. 'Ruby, dear, you have to let this go. Whatever you say, it won't bring your father back.'

'Yes, but if someone else was in the boat,' Ruby began again, 'it could mean that–'

'Ruby!' said Bea sharply. 'Enough.'

Ruby sipped her tea sulkily and said no more. It didn't stop her thinking, though. As she nursed her anger, she listened to Bea and Albert making small talk about the weather and what Bea was going to do next. Before she knew it, it was time to get back to the Town Hall. As her mother went to the toilet, Ruby couldn't resist tackling Albert one last time.

'What do you really think happened to my father?'

Albert regarded her steadily. 'He was alone on that boat,' he said. 'Ruby, it was nothing more than a tragic accident.'

Ruby nodded sullenly.

'By the way,' said Albert as Bea emerged from the toilets, 'where is Percy?'

'We think he's joined the Blackshirts,' said Bea. 'Or at least that's what Jim Searle believes.'

Albert raised an eyebrow. 'I wouldn't take too much notice of what Jim Searle says,' he said confidentially. 'You know he's a Barnardo's boy.'

Ruby spun around. 'That's not very fair,' she protested angrily. 'He can't help that. Anyway, I heard tell that you were put in care when you were a boy.'

'I was adopted,' said Albert tetchily.

'What's this?' asked Bea, drawing closer.

Albert put his hands up in mock-surrender. 'Just be warned, that's all.'

Ruby turned on her heel and left them.

As soon as proceedings began again, Silas Reed's son, William, gave evidence.

'I don't like to contradict my father, sir,' he began. 'He's a good man, but I was there and there was only one person in that boat.'

'Your father seemed very sure he saw another person,' the coroner observed.

William seemed slightly embarrassed. 'My father's eyesight isn't what it used to be, sir,' he said. 'On his way here, he bumped into a lamp post and apologized.'

The coroner thanked him, and William sat down to the sound of laughter.

Next the court heard how Nelson's body had been pulled ashore by two Goring fishermen later that day.

'He had a head-wound,' said one man. 'I thought he was dead as soon as I saw him.'

'Dead as a doornail,' said the other.

Dr Hare recounted how Nelson had been brought to his surgery and, after a thorough examination, he'd pronounced life extinct at four-fifteen that afternoon. 'Death was due to drowning,' he said. 'The blow to his head probably rendered him unconscious and then he fell into the sea and drowned.'

'Could the blow have been inflicted by a third party?' Dr Fox-Drayton asked.

Ruby held her breath. If he said 'yes', Percy could be in serious trouble.

'It's possible,' said Dr Hare, 'but in my opinion it is more likely that he slipped and bumped his head on the side of the boat as he went overboard.'

At a quarter to three the jury members were sent out, only to return about twenty minutes later. They returned a verdict of 'death by drowning'. In closing, the coroner aimed a few remarks at the police inspector.

'The jury have exonerated Percy Bateman from all blame, but it seems to me that he should be found. It must be distressing for his mother that her son does not yet know of his father's death, so I am calling upon the police force to look for Percy Bateman and make sure he knows what has happened. The verdict of this court is that Nelson Bateman was drowned as the result of an accident.'

With that, he rose to his feet, leaving the hushed assembly.

CHAPTER 15

Ruby returned to work with a sense of relief. Mrs Fosdyke made no reference whatsoever to Ruby's loss, nor did she enquire about her experiences at the inquest. Her only concession to the events that had dominated Ruby's life for the past few weeks was that, although she still checked Ruby's work, she was less vindictive with her punishments.

The girls who worked with Ruby – Edith, Doris and Phyllis – were kindness itself.

'We read about the verdict in the paper,' said Phyllis. They were all together in the sitting area, cleaning and tidying, before they were able to move on and clean the rooms.

'Phyllis!' Edith said sharply.

'It's all right,' said Ruby, shaking a cushion and rearranging it on a chair. 'I don't mind talking about it. My one dread was that they might have thought he'd done himself in.'

'You mean suicide?' said Phyllis. 'Gosh, I'd never even thought of that.'

'Now that you're back,' said Doris, 'you should come out with us. How about coming to the

Assembly Hall sometime? Tomorrow night they're playing some hot jazz. You'd love it.'

'I saw something about that in the paper,' said Edith, polishing a silver cigarette box. 'The council doesn't like it. They're trying to get it banned.'

'That new Councillor Budd is sticking up for us,' said Doris. 'He won't let the miserable old farts get their way.' A Blackshirt and a member of the BUF, Captain Budd came to dine in Warnes Hotel quite often. Clean-cut with Brylcreemed hair and a generous moustache, he had made his mark in the town by standing up against those who made pontifical proclamations about the moral degeneration of young people.

'He's really young, for a councillor,' said Edith. 'My neighbour's sister cleans for him and he's only in his thirties.'

'Anyway, why shouldn't young people have fun?' said Doris. She picked up a pencil lying on the table and tucked it over her top lip and under her nose. 'Red-hot jazz is absolutely spiffing,' she said, in an exaggeratedly posh voice.

'It is my opinion,' said Edith, in a pompous voice, 'that young people should go in for healthy dances such as ... the Lambeth Walk.'

By now all three girls were in hysterics.

'Have you seen Edith's ring?' Doris suddenly asked.

'You got engaged?' Ruby cried.

Edith blushed and nodded.

'To thingy from the bacon counter?' Ruby blurted out.

'To Bernard Gressenhall from the bacon counter,' Edith laughed.

'Oh, Edith,' cried Ruby, 'that's wonderful!'

'Well, go on then,' said Doris. 'Show her the ring.'

The girls gathered around Edith as she pulled at a chain around her neck and released a ring from under her uniform. It was a round opal with little diamond chips around the edges. Ruby gasped. 'Oh, Edith, it's beautiful. So when is the big day?'

'Not for ages yet,' Edith sighed as she put the ring away. 'My mum says we should wait until I'm twenty-one.'

'Twenty-one!' Doris cried. 'But that's practically dead and buried.'

Ruby saw Phyllis giving her a nudge in the ribs. 'We're trying to persuade her,' said Edith, 'but at the moment she's adamant.'

They all made sympathetic noises. Ruby felt particularly sorry for Edith. That meant it would be at least three years before she was old enough to marry. It was a long time to wait for someone. As she dusted the sideboard she thought of Jim Searle, with his fair hair flopping over his forehead and his merry eyes. She remembered his warm and tender kiss and, shivering with delight, wished with all her heart that she wore his ring on a chain around her neck. Perhaps three years wasn't so long after all. If he asked her to marry him, she would wait until the end of time.

'Roob,' said Edith, making Ruby snap out of her daydream, 'if you polish that sideboard much harder, you'll get right through to the cutlery drawer.'

'Sorry,' Ruby muttered. 'Miles away.'

'Did your Percy ever turn up?' asked Phyllis.

Ruby shook her head.

'Somebody told me he'd joined the Blackshirts,' said Doris as she dusted the picture frames.

'We thought so too,' Ruby sighed, 'and Jim Searle has been up to their HQ about four times, but nobody seems to know anything about him.'

'You mean Percy still doesn't know about your father?' said Doris.

Ruby shook her head.

'That's awful,' said Phyllis.

'My uncle is a member of the BUF,' said Edith. 'Do you want me to ask him about Percy?'

'Would you?' said Ruby. 'That would be wonderful. My mother's nearly out of her mind with worrying. It seems so awful that Father is dead and buried and Percy still knows nothing about it.'

'You do know they have *two* offices in Worthing,' said Doris.

Her comment came as a bombshell to Ruby. 'Two offices?'

'Oh yes,' said Doris. 'The one in Warwick Street is the Worthing HQ, and I forget what the other one is for.'

'That's the Sussex and Hampshire area office,' said Edith. 'Twenty-seven Marine Parade. That's where my Uncle Seth works.'

'But that's only a stone's throw from here!' cried Ruby.

'You could go after lunch,' said Edith. 'Want me to come with you? If Uncle Seth is there, he's sure to help.'

'Would you?' Ruby cried.

The door burst open and for a second all four

girls froze, thinking it was Mrs Fosdyke come to check on them, but it was only Carlo, the head waiter.

'You nearly gave me a flippin' heart attack,' said Doris, clutching at her chest.

'I 'ave that effect on women,' Carlo grinned. He was at least fifty, with a portly stomach. He blew her a kiss.

'In your dreams,' said Doris and they all laughed.

'Come on, girls,' said Ruby. 'We'd better get on, or she'll have our guts for garters.'

They filed out of the room and separated. 'Don't forget to come to the Assembly Rooms, if you can,' said Doris.

'D'you know what?' said Ruby. 'I might just do that.'

Bea took a cup of tea across the yard to where Isaac was busy whitewashing the walls of the shed. She had spent the morning writing Christmas cards and letters, telling distant family about Nelson and the verdict at the inquest. Eight letters sat on the kitchen table, waiting to be posted. She'd written nine letters, but couldn't find George Gore's address, even though she'd searched everywhere. Perhaps Ruby had put it somewhere safe. As Bea walked in the door, Isaac gave her a slight bow.

'How are you getting along?' she asked, putting the cup on one of the rungs of the ladder. 'It looks a lot lighter already.'

'It is *gut*,' smiled Isaac. 'I cannot thank you enough for your kindness, madam.'

Bea waved her hand dismissively. 'My daughter is right. It suits us all, and when you have customers queuing down the road, we'll double the rent.' She laughed softly until she realized by the horrified expression on Isaac's face that he had taken her seriously. 'No, no,' she cried. 'It was a joke!' He still seemed puzzled. 'An English joke,' she repeated as she held her stomach and imitated a belly laugh. 'To make you laugh.'

Realization dawned, and Isaac obliged her with a small chuckle. He reached into his jacket pocket, pulled something out and handed it to Bea. When he dropped it onto her palm she was surprised to see that it was a ring.

'What's this?' she asked.

'It is all I have,' he smiled, 'but it will give you plenty no, much money. See, the stone, it is a ... diamond.'

'No, no,' said Bea, trying to give it back. He had so few possessions, and she knew that his only other treasure was a partly finished place mat that had belonged to his late wife. 'You can pay me when you can.'

Isaac waved her hand away. 'For you,' he insisted. 'You trust me more than any other person. For that I thank you, but this is for my room and my shop.'

'Actually, I've been thinking about a name for the shop,' said Bea, changing the subject.

'Name?'

'You have to have a catchy name – something people will remember,' she said, already wishing she hadn't started this. 'You'll need a sign outside.'

Isaac nodded. 'Kaufman boot repairs,' he said, waving his hand over an imaginary sign, but Bea wasn't impressed.

'Of course it's only a suggestion, but I wondered if it might be better if you chose something that rolls off the tongue a little easier.' She didn't want to upset Isaac, but Jim had let slip that Mrs Grimes had asked him to leave because he was Jewish. If Isaac was to start again in this part of town, he'd have a much better chance with a more English-sounding name. He gave her a quizzical look, so she added, 'You don't have to do anything, unless you want to.'

He nodded again. 'It is *gut*,' he said, adding a helpless shrug, 'I will do it.'

'You could try naming the shop after someone you love,' she suggested. 'Your wife, perhaps. What was her name?'

'Griselda,' he said.

Bea took a deep breath. It was hardly the sort of name that slipped off the tongue, and it sounded very un-English.

'Maybe your husband's name?' Isaac smiled.

'No!' said Bea a little too quickly. Their eyes met and she gave a nervous laugh. 'Nelson isn't a very inspiring name.'

He bowed his head in respect. 'Bateman?' said Isaac.

Bea frowned. 'I don't think so. After all, it's your repair shop, not ours.'

'Your little girl,' he began again, 'she calls me Mr Coffey.'

'That's only because she finds your name difficult to remember,' Bea apologized.

213

'It's all right,' said Isaac. 'I don't mind. I use that name. Now I am Isaac Coffey.'

Bea smiled. 'And the shop?'

'I think about it,' said Isaac.

Bea turned to leave.

'Excuse me, madam,' Isaac said awkwardly. 'I hear you.' Bea turned back. 'I hear you through the walls.'

Bea opened her mouth to say something, but he put his hand up to stop her.

'At first, when I lost my family, my heart ... it is broken for my wife, my child. It never goes, but it gets far away. Now I remember without pain.'

Bea regarded Isaac carefully. Who knew what horrors he had experienced? Compared to what he had gone through, she had been much luckier in life.

'Thank you,' said Bea, her voice thickening with emotion. 'And I'm sorry for your loss.' She gave his arm a slight squeeze and left. As she strode across the yard, she could feel the tears coming again. She didn't stop them; she didn't need to now. Everyone thought she was grieving for Nelson, but in truth her heart was breaking for Rex. She had already waited eighteen long years and, because he hadn't even left his address, it looked like she really would have to wait one more.

The run-up to Christmas was hectic. At Warnes the staff were expected to stay on and help put up the Christmas decorations. Nobody minded too much, because they had a bit of fun doing it and the guests were most appreciative. Some gave generous tips, and so Ruby, Edith and Doris, along

214

with the porters, took it in turns to stand on ladders to hang silk flowers and glittering streamers from the ceilings. The tree was huge and they decorated it with tinsel and tiny candles clipped to the branches. At the top was a huge star. Winnie had excelled herself with her winter flower arrangements: fir cones, holly, Christmas roses and fir branches filled every vase and windowsill.

'Are you going away for Christmas?' Edith asked.

'No,' said Winnie, patting her hair. 'I prefer to be on my own.'

Only a few of the guests were staying all day at the hotel. The others would be having breakfast and then travelling to relatives or friends in the area, to spend the day with them. It was planned that those who stayed would enjoy a lavish meal, followed by entertainment from a local choir and Mr Beales, a local magician.

Mrs Fosdyke would be away too. She was apparently spending a few days with a friend, and the girls decided that was the best Christmas present in the world.

The preparations at home were far more modest. Bea had made mincemeat for the mince pies; and the cake, although baked a little later this year because of the circumstances, was ready for decorating. They had the promise of a small ham from the local butcher. Aunt Vinny and Cousin Lily were coming too. They wanted to bring their fair share, but it was decided that they would wait until Christmas Eve, in the hope of getting a small chicken at less than the normal asking price of one and sixpence a pound.

Once she had done the beds at Warnes in the morning, Ruby would be allowed home a little earlier. She wasn't expected to deep-clean on Christmas Day. She would have to go back to turn down the beds in the evening, but that wouldn't take too long. Although the decorations at Newlands Road were home-made, the house looked festive with a few crêpe-paper streamers and a large concertinaed bell in the centre of the room. There were cards from distant relatives and, of course, May hung her stocking in anticipation of a visit from Father Christmas.

The only thing missing was Percy.

CHAPTER 16

May looked up at her through sleepy eyes. Ruby was stiff and achy from sitting for so long in one position. Her little sister had been resting her head on Ruby's chest, and Ruby's arm was around her shoulders. They were in the bedroom, and Ruby had been reading bedtime stories. She let the sleepy child slide onto the pillow and pulled the bedclothes up to her chin.

'Night night, darling,' she whispered.

May grunted. Ruby put the book back in the bookcase and made to leave the room.

'You didn't say prayers,' said May, suddenly awake again.

Ruby grinned to herself. She knew it was a ruse to avoid going to sleep, but the child was quite right; they hadn't said prayers. She went back and sat on the edge of the bed with her head bowed. May put her hands together and closed her eyes.

'God bless Mummy and Ruby, and help me to do my sums at school,' said May. 'God bless Mr Coffey, and help him get lots and lots of boots to mend.' She paused, thinking. 'God bless all the fishermen and keep them safe.'

'Amen,' said Ruby, but May wasn't finished yet. 'God bless all the fishes in the sea and all the animals. And God bless my dollies and...'

'I think that's enough, darling,' said Ruby. 'I'm sure God will take care of everything.'

'Amen,' May said reluctantly.

Ruby kissed her forehead and stood up.

'When is Pa coming back?'

The question stopped Ruby in her tracks. She stared down at May. She looked so sweet, with her hair fanned out over the pillow. Her upturned face, now wide awake, was full of innocence. Ruby could hardly believe what she was hearing, let alone what she was seeing in May's face. The question was serious. Surely she knew. Surely she understood.

'May, you already know,' she said quietly. 'Pa is never coming back.'

May's eyes grew wide and then she frowned. 'But Mummy said he'd gone to be with Jesus.'

'That's right,' said Ruby.

'But at Sunday school Miss Pepperwell said Jesus came back after the third day. So when is Pa coming back?'

Ruby's thoughts were in a spin. This was awful. Clearly the child hadn't understood at all. It explained a lot: May had hardly ever cried for Pa and, now that she thought about it, she had wondered about May's slightly bemused stare whenever their mother was upset.

It was obvious that the child had been struggling with the euphemisms they had all used to soften the blow, and that she hadn't understood the permanency of the situation.

She sat back on the bed and took May's hand in hers.

'What Mummy meant to say was that Pa won't ever come back. He's gone to heaven.'

'But I want him to come back,' said May. 'Can he come at Christmas?'

'Pa loves you very much,' said Ruby, struggling not to cry herself, 'but he can never, ever come back.'

May's eyes were brimming with tears and her bottom lip quivered. 'But Jesus did,' she insisted.

Ruby swallowed hard. It was time for plain speaking. 'Jesus was a very special person,' she said. 'Pa can't do what Jesus did.' She took a deep breath. 'Do you remember when Cousin Lily's little cat died? You saw Aunt Vinny bury her in the garden, didn't you? We did that because she had gone for good. Pa is like that. The day you went to Susan Marley's, we buried Pa's body in the ground.' May's eyes grew wide and, suddenly guessing what she might say next, Ruby added, 'Poor Pa is dead.'

'Forever?'

'Forever,' said Ruby firmly. 'I'm sure he would love to come back and see you, but he can't.'

The tears in May's eyes spilled over and Ruby

218

gathered her in her arms. She wept for a minute or two, and Ruby wept with her. May wept for Nelson, while Ruby wept for May. But, all at once, May pushed her away.

'It's not true!' she shouted; 'You've made it all up. Pa *will* come back. He will come for Christmas. I know he will. He promised me a yellow bicycle. He's not dead, I tell you, he's not, he's not!'

There was a sound by the door and Bea came into the room. Ruby stood up and looked helplessly at her mother. 'She doesn't believe Father is dead,' she said.

'He's not dead,' May shrieked. 'Tell her, Mummy. Tell her!' Ruby opened her mouth to say something, but May wasn't finished yet. 'Go away,' she yelled. 'Go away. I hate you. I hate you!'

Their mother took May into her arms and the little girl began to sob uncontrollably. Profoundly shocked and upset, Ruby left the room and went downstairs. Thankfully there was no one in the kitchen. Mr Coffey, as everyone called him, had already retired to his room. Ruby sat at the kitchen table with her head in her hands. Although she couldn't make out what was being said, she could still hear May's shrill voice and sobs, and her mother's soothing tone of voice. Listening to them through the walls, Ruby suddenly felt a mixture of grief, pity and self-pity. A lot of self-pity… 'He promised me a yellow bicycle,' that's what May had said. Why had Father been so different with May? She thought back to her own childhood and couldn't remember getting one single present from her father. Oh yes, she had had presents for

Christmas and birthdays, labelled 'with love from Mummy and Daddy', but she couldn't remember one thing he'd given her himself. Why had he never loved her? She wasn't imagining it and she wasn't being paranoid, but she'd finally found the courage to put the way she felt into words, even if it was only inside her own head... Her own father had never loved her. She knew he wasn't a very nice man, but the difference between his relationship with her and Percy and his relationship with May was poles apart. He'd been just as horrible to Percy.

Ruby blew her nose and put her saturated handkerchief into the copper boiler, ready for washing. Getting a clean one from the drawer, she blew her nose again and sat down in the chair by the fire. Oh, Percy ... she thought miserably. Where was he, and why didn't he get in contact? When she and Edith had gone to the Sussex and Hants area HQ of the BUF that day, she had high hopes that they'd be able to track down Percy quite easily. She'd given as much detail as she could to the woman at the desk, a rather severe-looking person dressed all in black. At one point the woman stood to get something from a filing cabinet, and Ruby had been mildly surprised to see that she was wearing black slacks as well. Her close-cropped hair was held away from her face by a hair grip, and the only relief in her sober outfit was a raised pattern, knitted in dark green, on her black jumper and the bright-red lipstick she wore. Hardly the sort of outfit for a secretary, Ruby thought, although the woman had copied down meticulously everything she had said and promised to get in touch.

It was understandable that Percy had wanted to leave home, but why hadn't he written to Mother? Ruby thought back to the time when Percy had met her from work and told her he was leaving. She remembered he'd said that he had found out something about their father and wished he hadn't. What could be so awful that Percy couldn't bear to be under the same roof as him any more? And that he should lose contact with the rest of the family?

It was quieter upstairs now. She could still hear her mother's muffled voice, but May was silent now.

In some respects, life without her father was a lot easier. Mr Coffey's rent, when it came, would give them a reasonable income and, so far, they hadn't struggled. The sale of Pa's best clothes – the items she didn't put into the suitcase – had brought in a few pennies, and people did what they could to help. She'd received some good tips at Warnes, and there was still Nelson's boat and locker to clear out, if Percy didn't come back. Some of the fishermen slipped them a fish or two from their catch. A couple of days ago someone had left some whiting on the doorstep, wrapped in newspaper; and last week they'd dined on fresh lobster.

Her mother's sudden grief a few days after the inquest opening had surprised Ruby, but she guessed that Bea's feelings for her father had run deeper than she'd thought. After all, they'd been together for eighteen years. Ruby wasn't sure she could love someone who treated her the way her father had treated her mother. Of course, she hadn't grieved for her father herself. If she were to cry, it would be for little May, having to come to terms with the harsh things of life; or for Percy, driven away by her father's unkindness. She might be tempted to cry for herself, and an already wasted life; how different things might have been, had she been able to go abroad with Miss Russell. She glanced up at the two postcards on the mantelpiece. The second one had come a couple of days ago. The picture on the front was of a sun-kissed beach called Saint-Tropez. She had pronounced it 'Saint Tropezz' until Mr Coffey pointed out it actually sounded like 'San Tropay'. It looked wonderful, with its little fishing boats and the white sand beyond, in front of ancient-looking creamy-coloured buildings. The message on the back was short and sweet: *As promised, dear Ruby. Best wishes, Imogen R.*

Ruby sighed. How fabulous it must be to just pick up a case and travel the world, but that pipe dream was dead and buried, alongside her father. She heard her mother's footfall at the top of the stairs and pulled herself together again. Wiping her wet face, Ruby blew her nose heartily. It was no use moaning and groaning about things that could never be. She had to get on with it and do the best she could. Life wasn't that bad. She had a job and some good pals. She had a nice home, and she still had her mother. Best of all, she had Jim. What more could a girl want?

As her mother came into the kitchen, Ruby jumped to her feet. 'I'll put the kettle on, Mum. Fancy a cup of tea?'

Percy could hardly believe what he had just been told. Up until now his life had changed beyond all recognition. He had done his basic training and completed his driving lessons. He was confident that, even if he had to take this newfangled driving test, he would pass with flying colours. He no longer felt like an outsider. The movement held to the belief that all men were equal and, for the first time in his life, Percy found that his opinion mattered. He loved the camaraderie, the friendships and the feeling that he was part of something much greater than himself. There were a few things that disturbed him, but they were tiny in comparison to the things he enjoyed.

The movement was growing all the time. They had started earlier in the year with a few thousand, but now the BUF numbered some 10,000 members and was still growing. Percy himself was seen as a trusted and fervent enthusiast. Although he had never been personally introduced to Mosley, he had been to dozens of rallies held in honour of the great man and had already travelled all over the country with his entourage. Right now he was in York, some 260 miles from Worthing. After hearing Mosley's speeches it was easy to be filled with a passion for the country and to be willing to die for the cause, if necessary, so he wasn't surprised by the adjutant's call to the office.

'We are pleased with your progress, Bateman,' he began, 'and would like to offer you promotion.'

Percy couldn't help but let his chest swell with pride. 'Pleased', 'progress' and 'promotion' were unfamiliar words to Percy, in the normal course of events. What would his father say now?

'Thank you, sir,' he said smartly.

'The major is thinking of sending you back down south,' the adjutant went on. 'Maybe to London or the Home Counties.'

'I understand, sir,' said Percy.

'The major has mooted that you should receive a small stipend, and of course you will get your board and lodging. Shall I tell the major you have no other commitments, Bateman?'

'That's right, sir.'

'No family?'

'I have a father, mother and two younger sisters,' said Percy. 'They don't know I'm here. I wanted to prove myself before I went back home, sir.'

'Well, you've certainly done that, Bateman,' said the adjutant. 'Your father should be proud of you. You've done quite well, for one of the lower classes.'

His remark jarred and Percy felt a stab of anger. The pompous ass. He resisted the temptation to answer back, knowing that he and his mates called the adjutant a 'chinless wonder' behind his back.

The adjutant's secretary sitting at another desk cleared her throat noisily.

'What is it, Muriel?' he asked.

'There's a communication from the Sussex and Hants area HQ concerning Mr Bateman,' she said. 'I have it here.' She held up a piece of paper. 'It seems that Mr Bateman's family have been trying to contact him.'

'I was aware that my father has been calling at HQ for me,' said Percy, 'but I felt it right to delay contact until after my training period, sir.'

The adjutant took the sheet of paper from her and looked at it. He held it at arm's length, struggling to see without his glasses. Percy waited while the adjutant opened drawer after drawer in his desk, until he finally found his spectacles in the breast pocket of the jacket hanging on the back of the chair.

For the first time it occurred to Percy that it might be more than annoyance that had made his father so persistent. Had something happened? Why were the family so anxious to find him? Perhaps he should have kept in touch after all. It had been two months since he'd left home. He had supposed his mother would worry, but Ruby knew he wasn't going to the ends of the earth; she knew he'd come back. Perhaps he should have posted that letter he'd written when he was living in the Black House, but somehow or other he'd never got round to it.

The adjutant put on his glasses. 'Oh,' he said brightly. 'It seems your father is dead.'

Percy was appalled by the savagery of the words. He stared at the man, unable to speak.

The adjutant held the paper between the forefinger and thumb of both hands. 'It appears he drowned at sea.' His tone of voice was unfeeling, and more than a little bored.

'Here, give me that!' Percy snapped. He snatched the paper away.

'Bateman,' shouted the adjutant, 'how dare you! That paper is an official communication.'

Percy read it quickly:

Regret to inform P. Bateman of the sudden death of

Nelson Bateman, father, drowned at sea in September. An inquest will be held on November 23rd.

'This letter is dated October 12th,' he said angrily. 'That's more than two months ago. Why wasn't I informed sooner?'

'You've just said yourself,' the adjutant said casually. 'You said you didn't want any contact with your family.'

'But my father had just died,' Percy spat out. 'Surely anyone with a ha'p'orth of common sense would know that would be an exception.'

'This movement is dedicated to the overthrow of an antiquated governmental system and useless institutions,' the adjutant said haughtily. 'We have better things to do that run after every Tom, Dick and Harry and their petty family affairs.'

'Petty family affairs!' Percy was beside himself with rage. 'I should have been informed immediately.' Behind him the secretary began typing furiously. 'I am the head of the household now. My mother and sisters have been left to fend for themselves. I should have been there, damn you.' Letting go of the paper, it fluttered to the floor. Percy turned on his heel and marched out of the room. As the door closed behind him, the adjutant turned to the secretary with a wounded look.

'Well, really!' he exclaimed. 'They'll all be wanting a bloody nursemaid next.'

It was almost time to go back to Warnes. As she roused herself from her afternoon nap, she heard his voice quite clearly. It came, as it always did, in that twilight moment between being sound asleep and waking. Her heart soared. She hadn't heard from him for at least a fortnight and was beginning to feel that he'd left her again; she had even toyed with the idea of going back to Mrs Knight's seances. It was only the thought of that hot, stuffy room and the strangers gathered around the table knowing her business that stopped her making an appointment.

When he came, she had learned the hard way that, if she tried to see him, he would leave. It was always a struggle to stay in the same position; she had to remain absolutely still, hardly daring to breathe, and yet be alert enough to hear him. If she opened her eyes, he would go as quickly as the night-time shadows flee when the dawn appears. She strained her ears, waiting for him to say her name – the pet name that only she and he knew. If he said that, she would know it was him. Then the voice came. It was only in her head, and yet it was clearer than ever before. She could scarcely take it in, but there was no mistaking that it was him.

'Freddie, there is something else I want you to do.'

CHAPTER 17

It took May several days to stop being angry with Ruby. She would glare at her big sister or refuse to speak to her. Ruby found it very hurtful. It was as if May blamed her for their father's death.

On the Saturday before Christmas, Ruby took May to Hubbard's to see Father Christmas. He was in a pretty grotto on the second floor. They were met by an elf who, after taking Ruby's one and sixpence, asked her how old May was. As Ruby told him, a second elf standing fairly close by took a present marked '6+' from a pink tub, and May went inside.

They found themselves going down a little tented walkway flanked with pictures of characters from children's picture books, such as Cinderella, Pip, Squeak and Wilfred, The Mad Hatter and Blackbeard, the famous pirate mentioned in *Moonfleet*. Eventually they were ushered into a room by a woman dressed as a fairy. Father Christmas was sitting on a red-and-gold throne surrounded by presents. As she approached, he leaned forward and took May onto his knee. 'And what would you like for Christmas, my dear?' he said kindly.

May gazed up at him in wonderment. 'A yellow bicycle,' she said, 'like Pa promised me.'

Father Christmas glanced up at Ruby, who shook her head.

'Well, my dear,' said Father Christmas. 'I'm afraid the elves forgot to make enough yellow bicycles this year. I'm terribly sorry, but if you could wait until next year, I'll see what I can do.'

For a second May looked crestfallen.

'I know it's very hard,' he went on, 'but you seem like a big, brave girl. Do you think you could wait until next year?'

May nodded sullenly.

'I have a special badge for brave children,' he

said, handing her a red badge with *Father Christmas at Hubbard's* on it. He pinned it onto her coat and May smiled. She climbed off his knee and he handed her the present that Ruby had seen the elf take out of the pink box, and then they emerged from the grotto.

They walked home almost in silence. Ruby felt terrible. Father Christmas had handled it well, but the fact remained that May had had yet another disappointment.

'How was it?' asked Bea as they walked indoors.

'Father Christmas said he didn't have any yellow bicycles,' May said. She puffed out her chest as her mother took off her coat. 'He gave me a special badge instead.'

While Bea admired the badge, Ruby made a secret vow that if her little sister still wanted a yellow bicycle next year, she would get one.

'What's that?' asked Bea, pointing to her present.

'Father Christmas gave it to me,' said May. 'Can I open it now?'

'Why not,' said Bea, sitting her at the table.

May tore away the paper to reveal a jigsaw puzzle. It only had twelve pieces, so it was a bit babyish for May, but Ruby was delighted to point out that in the picture of a village post office, the postman had left his red bicycle leaning against the postbox.

'That's just like the one I want,' said May gravely.

Percy packed his case quickly. He had managed to get a ticket for the morning train to London.

It would be packed with day-trippers on their way to see the Christmas lights in the capital. Percy could hardly believe that his father was actually dead. He couldn't grieve for the man, but it altered his life dramatically. When he'd left home he'd been so angry, but now that he'd been apart from them for a while, he'd mellowed. What would his mother and sister do? They couldn't possibly cope on their own.

He had never liked fishing, but perhaps he could learn to like it, if he was on his own and away from his father's caustic tongue. In fact, the more he thought about it, the more he liked the sound of being a fisherman in his own right. Fishing could bring in good profits. He might buy a better boat and more up-to-date fishing gear. Worthing wasn't such a bad place to live, either. He didn't love it as much as Ruby did, but he had a few good friends and the house would be his, one day. Of course he'd have to look after his mother, but he didn't mind that at all. She'd made a dreadful mistake in marrying a man like his father, but since he'd been in the BUF, Percy was now a man of the world. His mother, he'd decided, was a good woman. She'd put up with a lot over the years and didn't deserve the way Nelson had treated her.

Had he known about his father's death, he wouldn't have spent the past few weeks up north. When he'd finished his basic training in the Black House, he had been offered the opportunity to help set up an office in York, and he had jumped at the chance. Now that he knew his father was dead, things were different. However, if he was forced to go back home, he could volunteer at one of the BUF offices in Worthing. The place had become a bit of a hub in the organization, and there was no doubt that the movement would go far. He set the alarm for six and climbed into his bed with a contented smile. Tomorrow would be the start of the rest of his life, and things were looking good.

Now known as John Coffey, Isaac had made great strides since becoming the Batemans' lodger. Using some of the money Ruby had given him for German lessons, he'd been to The Ark, a chaotic repository on the corner of Lyndhurst Road and High Street, and picked up a rusty old shoe-last and a couple of pairs of real leather shoes, which he'd skilfully cut up to use for repairs. Woolworths furnished him with toecaps, nails, glue and rubber soles, which, although not of the best quality, would keep him going for now. He charged a very small price to his first customers, for two reasons. First, he wanted to become known; and second, the repairs wouldn't be of his usual high standard until he was able to get some first-class materials. He worked part-time, using his free time from the council's Parks and Gardens department. It worked well; December and January were going to be lean months, and there was little to do in the greenhouses then. As a result, his hours had been cut anyway.

It had been three weeks since he'd arrived at the Batemans', penniless and dependent on hand-outs, but already he was getting a reputation and, more importantly, valuable customers. Fortunately all the shoe-repair shops in Worthing were close to the town centre, so John's enterprise didn't interfere with anyone else. People in the area soon found their way to his little back-gate shop.

Ruby was a good pupil. He taught her German using colloquial speech, rather than beginning with the rudiments of grammar, but even as she mastered the words, he could tell that she had a natural flair.

'Can you tell me the way to the pier?' he asked in German.

'Go through the alleyway and follow it all the way to the sea,' she told him confidently.

'*Sehr gut,*' he said, clearly impressed. '*Wie spät ist es?*'

'It is 1933,' she told him in German.

'No,' he corrected. 'I asked for the time.'

'*Es is zehn nach sechs* – it is ten past six.'

'Now,' he said, '*erzähle mir von deiner Arbeit im Hotel Warnes.*'

'I clean the bedrooms,' she began.

'German, German,' he said.

'*Ich mache die Schlafzimmer sauber* – I make the beds and tidy the bathroom. *Ich mache die Betten und räume die Badezimmer auf.*'

'*Gut,*' he smiled.

Ruby grinned. '*Ich bin ein sehr gute freche Mädchen.*'

John started laughing. 'I think you mean *Zimmermädchen – chambermaid,*' he said.

'What did I say?' asked Ruby in English.

'It doesn't matter,' said John, 'but believe me, you are a chambermaid.'

At the end of the week he handed Bea a box of chocolates and his first rent.

'I shall pay what I owe as soon as I can, dear lady,' he said, giving her a short bow. 'I am forever in your debt.'

Bea signed the rent book and handed it back to him. 'I know you are not a Christian man,' she said firmly, 'but we would like you to spend Christmas Day with us. It's a family time, and we won't hear of you being on your own.'

'You are very kind,' he told her, as his eyes filled with unshed tears.

As far as Ruby and Bea were concerned, they were determined to make Christmas special this year. Ruby had invited Jim to spend Christmas with them as well. His landlady had informed him that she would only cook his breakfast and then she was off to her sister's for the day. With no family of his own, Jim faced a lonely day in his room, but Ruby and Bea refused to let him. Christmas was the time for all their dreams to come true.

Of course there were some things they couldn't have. Bea wished she could send a Christmas card to Rex. May wanted Pa to turn up with that yellow bicycle he'd promised. And Ruby longed for Percy to come back home.

'Mind the doors. Mind the doors!' The porter walked up and down the platform, warning people not to stand too close to the edge as the incoming train pulled into the station.

George Gore looked up and down the platform anxiously. He had no idea what his visitor looked like, but he was keen to hear what he had to say.

233

The letter had come as quite a shock. He had thought that, with Nelson Bateman's passing, the whole damned thing was over and done with. What they had done had haunted him ever since that terrible day in 1915. With Nelson gone, and poor old Linton on his last legs, he had welcomed the idea that he could put the past behind him, once and for all.

It had been 1915, and Whit Monday. Back home in dear old Blighty, people would be going to the carnival; they would endure nothing more taxing than having a go at the coconut shy or riding on the carousel. The night before it happened, he relived the memory of kissing his best girl by the hoopla stall the year before. One year was all that separated the green grass of Fryer's Field and the mudbath of shit and blood, where he now waited for the next push. He hadn't slept for days, and at a quarter to three in the morning Jerry began a ferocious artillery bombardment. If that wasn't bad enough, while every man scrambled to his post, Victor had been among the first to realize what was coming. A favourable wind had alerted him to the smell, long before the others even had an inkling.

'My God! Gas,' he'd cried. 'Gas attack!'

The lads had been lucky enough to get their respirators on fairly quickly – Linton Carver being one of the last – but the defenders further down the trench weren't nearly so quick. Large numbers of them had been overcome before they could even get the things out of the boxes. What followed was a terrible day. Despite their heroic efforts, Jerry broke through around Bellewaarde Lake and they had to wait until early evening before the counter-attack could be mounted. Even that was doomed to failure. Fighting in bright moonlight, they suffered heavy losses. It was then that the chain of events that was to ruin all their lives began.

Now he strained to see who was getting off the train. The station was packed with day-trippers on their way to see the Christmas lights in London. They knew that the train from York would already be crowded, so everyone was anxious to get aboard before the station staff turned people away. Despite repeated warnings, people on the train still opened the doors before it had stopped. Admittedly most passengers only opened it in a small way, but there was always the danger that a door might fly open and hit someone on the platform. It was rush hour and the platform was crowded.

'Hold a copy of *The Times* in the air as the train comes in,' the mystery man had written to him. 'I have something amazing to tell you about the day Victor died.'

The London express thundered into Newark, people surged forward and George lifted his paper. It all happened so quickly. He moved with the crowd, but then felt a hefty push in the small of his back. Someone cried, 'Look out!' but it was already too late. George was propelled towards an oncoming open door, which hit him squarely on the side of his head. The person holding the door realized what had happened and let go. The door swung open with full force, pushing George into the side of the train. From there he was poleaxed to the floor.

A woman screamed and people moved back. As the porter came running, someone knelt beside George where he'd fallen. Although he was helpless and had no words, George knew he was dying. The pain was indescribable; his head felt like it was exploding, and he could taste his own blood in his mouth. He was aware that someone was beside him on the platform. His rescuer leaned and whispered in his ear. None of the horrified crowd heard what was said, but George did.

'That was for Victor, you bastard.'

CHAPTER 18

The train delay was annoying, especially for the day-trippers. Despite their anger, it wasn't possible to let the London express go until the police had finished their investigations. A doctor had been called and he pronounced the man dead.

'Yes, I was right behind him,' said Percy, 'but I didn't see what happened. One minute he was there, then he charged forward.'

'He was pushed, that's what,' said a woman in a headscarf.

'I saw the train door opening,' said a gruff-looking older man.

'That's when I shouted,' said Percy.

'You shouted,' said the inspector, jotting it down in his notebook. 'And you are?'

'Percy Bateman,' he replied.

'Chestnuts, roasted chestnuts – thruppence a

236

bag!' As the vendor's cry echoed around the platform, the tightly packed crowd dispersed and
diverted their attention to him.

The stationmaster peered over the heads of the
few people clustered around the inspector. 'How
much longer are you going to be, Squire? Only I
gotta get this train moving.'

'Give me one more minute,' said the inspector.

To his horror, Percy and the other witnesses
were escorted into the station waiting room. A
policeman followed them in and stood with his
back to the door, effectively barring their exit.

'How long are you going to keep us here?' demanded the gruff man. 'I have a regimental
dinner to attend in London.'

'The inspector wants your names and addresses,' said the constable. 'He won't keep you
any longer than necessary.'

Outside on the concourse the rest of the passengers were piling back onto the train.

'Look here,' said Percy, moving forward, 'we're
going to miss the train.'

'My husband will be waiting for me with the
pony and trap,' said the woman anxiously.

The policeman squared himself up. 'Sit down,
if you please, sir.'

'But...' Percy began again.

'I said, sit down – if you please, sir,' the policeman repeated emphatically.

'Can't *you* take our names and addresses?' said
the woman in the headscarf. 'I'll go to my local
police station and make a statement. I must get
home tonight.'

'The inspector will be here shortly,' said their

stubborn jailor.

'Get out of the way, you moron,' said the army man. He tried to move the constable, but the man stood firm. There was a bit of jostling and some colourful language, but the guard was already waving his green flag and blowing his whistle. The train juddered, and they heard its throaty roar as it headed up steam and began to move away from the platform. The woman burst into tears, and the men rose up as one person and rushed the constable. Just then the door burst open and the inspector came into the room.

'Right, you lot,' he shouted. 'Any more of that and you can all spend a night in the cells.'

They were all angry and frustrated, but what could they do? Clearly the inspector had the upper hand. The train was gone and, if they were to catch the next one, they had no choice but to give their statements. It was going to be a long day.

Jim met Ruby from work, to walk her home. He quite often did so now and it gave them both an opportunity to talk over the events of the day. In the run-up to Christmas there was plenty going on. It was raining, so they huddled together under Jim's big umbrella.

'How are the German lessons going?'

'I haven't had that many,' Ruby confessed, 'but I've enjoyed them so far. John refuses to take any more money.' She laughed nervously. 'He says I'm a natural.'

'Go on then,' Jim chuckled. 'Impress me.'

'*Ich wohne in Worthing*,' said Ruby. 'I was born in Worthing. *Wo wohnen Sie* – where were you born?'

Jim nodded and pulled a face. 'I *am* impressed,' he said.

Ruby felt a little glow of pleasure. 'What did you do today?'

'Not a lot,' said Jim. 'We didn't get anybody in the studio. It's too close to the Christmas holiday, so I spent the day clearing up. We've got a big order in the New Year.'

'Oh?'

'The Blackshirts are encouraging their people to be photographed in uniform, so several have booked themselves in for the week after,' said Jim. 'We've been lucky enough to get a few of the knobs coming.'

'Is that good?' asked Ruby. They were crossing High Street and moving into Upper High Street and had to wait for a bus to pass. The rain had become even more penetrating. The hem of Ruby's coat was saturated and brushed across her already-wet legs as she walked, making it very uncomfortable.

'If the picture gets in the paper, or printed somewhere else,' said Jim, 'it should bring in more business.'

'You're beginning to sound like more than an employee,' Ruby joked.

'I was going to tell you something when we got home,' said Jim, 'but I can't wait.'

'Good news or bad news?' Ruby asked cautiously.

'Good,' said Jim. 'You remember that photograph I took of you on the burnt-out pier?'

'The one you called "Beauty and the Beast"?' Ruby asked.

'You remember I entered it in a competition?' Jim went on excitedly. 'Well, it won a prize.'

Ruby stopped dead. 'Jim, that's wonderful!' she cried.

'It didn't come first,' Jim added quickly, 'but it got second place.'

She reached up and kissed his cheek.

'It deserves a better kiss than that,' he said. The sound of the pouring rain on the umbrella didn't matter, as he put his arm around her waist and drew her close. His lips were warm and tender, and even a trickle of cold water from the tipped umbrella running down the back of her neck didn't spoil the moment.

'Put that girl down, Jim Searle,' said a gruff voice coming out of the darkness towards them. 'You don't know where she's been.'

'Percy!' cried Ruby, as the two of them broke apart. All else forgotten, she threw herself into her brother's arms.

Their laughter and happiness spilled over as Percy walked through the front door of the house. Bea was beside herself with joy to see her son – all apologies and explanations momentarily brushed aside. Percy was kissed and hugged so hard that he thought before long he'd have no breath left in his body. May came downstairs and threw herself into her big brother's arms. 'You came back!' she cried. 'Did you bring me a present?'

Once he had been stripped of his wet coat, they could see Percy's uniform.

'You actually joined the Blackshirts?' said Bea faintly.

'I did,' said Percy. He had been plonked into the

best chair and given a towel to dry his hair. A modest brandy had been placed beside him. 'But I've jacked it in. I told them I have family commitments, so I'm back home now.' May climbed onto his lap and helped to dry his hair. 'I'm sorry about Father,' he told Bea. 'I only found out two days ago.'

'I went to the BUF HQ at least four times,' said Jim indignantly. 'I guessed you were there, but they wouldn't help.'

'And Edith and I tried the area office,' said Ruby.

'I would have come back, but they withheld the information from me,' said Percy. 'I was damned annoyed, I can tell you.'

'Why didn't anyone tell me you'd looked for him?' Bea complained.

'We weren't absolutely sure Percy was there, Mother,' said Ruby, 'and we didn't want to worry you.'

Bea placed a brown paper bag in front of her son.

'What's that?' he asked.

'Your father's effects,' she said. 'We thought we should keep them for you.'

Percy pushed them away. 'I don't want them.' He picked up the brandy and downed it in one. 'I originally wanted to complete my training before I made contact with you again,' Percy went on, 'but they should have overridden that. No one seemed to understand the urgency of the situation. How are you coping?'

'We've taken a lodger called John,' said Bea.

Percy's mouth dropped open. 'In my attic room?'

Bea shook her head. 'We got rid of the front parlour,' she replied and, noticing his shocked expression, she added, 'Nobody ever used it, and I got quite a few pounds for the furniture.'

'It was the only way we could survive,' said Ruby, putting the brown paper bag in the drawer, out of sight. She felt uneasy. Was her brother angry or simply a bit surprised?

'Your mother and sister have been pretty amazing,' said Jim. Ruby was spreading Percy's wet coat over the clothes horse near the fire. 'My landlady virtually threw John out on the street.'

Ruby gave him a nudge. She didn't want Jim to mention that John was Jewish. Percy was a Blackshirt, and so was Mrs Grimes's new lodger and he had some very disparaging opinions about the Jews.

'If they hadn't opened up their home to him,' Jim went on, 'I dread to think where John would be.'

'Why did she chuck him out?' asked Percy. 'Couldn't he pay the rent?'

'It wasn't like that,' said Bea.

'She had a fancy man,' Ruby said quickly. 'John was in the way.'

'He's a good man,' Bea continued. 'He's opened a little cobbler's shop in the shed at the back. He's already proving to be very popular, and we'll soon get double the rent: one for the room and the other for the shop.'

Percy burst out laughing. 'And here's me, thinking you couldn't do without me.'

'Oh no,' cried Bea, 'don't say that, Son.'

Percy stood up and kissed her cheek. 'It's good

242

to be home, Mother.'

While everybody had been talking, Bea had warmed up the leftover stew from dinner-time. She placed a dish on the table and encouraged her son to sit up and eat. It was a small portion but, with two doorsteps of bread, it would do nicely.

'Back to bed now, young lady,' she said to May. Percy let her down and went to the table. May protested, but knew it was no use arguing. The grown-ups smiled one to the other as her thunderous footsteps reached the top of the stairs and her bedroom door closed firmly.

'This looks good,' said Percy, reaching for the salt cellar. 'I'm absolutely starving, and you won't believe the journey I've just had.'

Bea was alone in her bedroom. It was the day before Christmas Eve, and the next day, Sunday, the shops would be shut. If she needed anything more for the holiday, today was the last day she could get it. This promised to be the best Christmas for a very long time. Ruby had gone to work; May was playing with her dollies under the kitchen table; and Percy had gone out. The wonderful thing was, she had all her family at home, and Bea was determined to make this Christmas one to remember.

She was looking at John's ring. Should she sell it now? It was very tempting. She was almost at the end of the trinkets she'd found among Nelson's things in his drawer. She had recognized some as his mother's jewellery, but the rest was a bit of a mystery. Still, it had kept the wolf from the door. Ruby had no idea how or why they still managed to eat fairly well and keep the bills paid, but as winter came on, it would get harder. Bea could already feel her chest getting tighter, and the coal in the coal-hole was going down quickly. Now that John was here, she couldn't expect him to live in a cold room, so she had two fires to keep going.

She turned the ring over in her hands. It could easily bring in fifteen shillings – maybe a lot more. She had planned to use it only if she had to. She'd wanted to hang onto it and give it back, if ever that was possible, for the poor man had so little. As difficult as things were for her, she and her family still had each other, and there was no danger of her family being taken from her. Thank God she owned the house. She had already eked out what little Nelson had left behind, but there was still the boat and his fishing gear in his locker on the beach. Now that Percy was back home, he would need that. The thought cheered her up. Of course, what on earth was she thinking? When Percy started fishing again, they would have food – and plenty. She wrapped the ring up in a clean handkerchief and pushed it to the back of the drawer.

As she took her hand out again, her fingers brushed Nelson's pocket watch. She would wrap it up in some paper and give it to Percy as a Christmas present. He and Nelson didn't always see eye-to-eye, and the watch had little value, but it was something to remember the man who had fed and clothed him all his life.

Downstairs, she opened the jar on the mantel-piece and peered inside. There was three shillings and sixpence left. She would buy a little fresh fruit, as a special treat. It would be nice to use the fruit bowl again. Fruit had been the first thing to go when Nelson died. It was funny, but life was one of two extremes. When Nelson was alive, she'd had plenty, but was desperately unhappy; and now that he was dead, she was a lot happier, but life was a struggle.

She glanced at her reflection in the mirror. She'd lost weight. It wasn't a drastic loss, but she was a lot slimmer. Eating only two meals a day had its benefits, but by going without herself, to make sure the family had enough, she hoped she wouldn't end up like some. Mrs Stanton had eight children and had dropped dead in her own kitchen – malnutrition, they'd called it. Her husband had been out of work for three years and, with all those mouths to feed, they'd made her sell just about every stick of furniture in the house before she could qualify for the dole. Even that was means-tested, and their eldest boy's paper-round money was deducted from the amount they received.

Bea shook away the dark thoughts. Thank God that wasn't going to happen to her. She would be all right. With John's money and Percy fishing again, things were looking up, not down. Taking the money from the jar, she called May to come out from under the table and, grabbing their coats and her bag, they set off for the shops.

CHAPTER 19

Ruby thought the hotel room was empty, but by the time she'd been working there for a few minutes she realized that she wasn't alone. Mrs Harper, a frequent guest at Warnes, was rummaging through a washbag in the bathroom.

'Oh,' said Ruby, surprised. 'Excuse me, madam. I'll come back later.'

She opened the door wide. Outside in the corridor, Winnie was putting the finishing touches to a flower arrangement. Ruby turned to leave, but when Mrs Harper looked up at her, Ruby was surprised to see that she was in tears.

'Have you seen it, dear? I know I put it down somewhere.'

Ruby came closer. 'Seen what, madam?'

'The brooch,' said the old lady. Judging by her clothes, she was clearly a wealthy woman and her fingers, wrist and neck were already covered in heavy jewellery. 'I can't find Louisa's brooch.'

'Have you tried looking in your handbag or the dressing table?' Ruby suggested kindly. She didn't think anyone would find a brooch in a washbag.

They returned to the bedroom and Ruby helped her, but to no avail. Ruby was on her hands and knees looking under the bed when the door burst open.

'Come along, Mother,' said an irritable female voice. 'For goodness' sake, hurry up. The car will be here soon.'

'Yes, dear,' said Mrs Harper. 'I've just got to put on my shoes, that's all.'

'I'll wait for you downstairs then.'

The door closed and Ruby got up from the floor. 'I'm sorry, madam. It's not under the bed.'

'Oh dear, oh dear,' said the woman, clearly distressed. 'My daughter gets so cross when I lose things.'

'If I do find it,' said Ruby, 'what shall I do with it?'

'Pop it in the drawer beside the bed,' Mrs Harper said. 'It goes in the little red box.'

Muttering distractedly, the guest put on her shoes and hurried from the room. Mrs Harper had left a fox-fur stole and an umbrella on the bed, so Ruby tidied them away. As usual she had to strip the beds and put on new clean linen. She pulled the sheets off and remade the bed. When she took off the pillowcase, something fell onto the sheet. It was a pearl-and-amethyst brooch. Smiling to herself, Ruby opened the bedside drawer. There were two red boxes inside. She picked up one, but it had another brooch inside. The second box was empty, and she was just putting the pearl-and-amethyst brooch inside when a cold voice behind her said, 'What are you doing, Bateman?'

Ruby whirled round to find Mrs Fosdyke staring at her.

'I... It's not how it looks,' she stuttered. 'I found it on the bed, and I was putting it back.'

Mrs Fosdyke raised an eyebrow. A small smile played around her lips. 'You don't know how many times I've heard that one,' she said coldly.

'But it's true,' Ruby cried. 'I wasn't taking it. The guest asked me to help her look for it, and I found it caught inside the pillowcase.'

The door was still open, and Ruby saw the florist packing up the rest of her things. 'Winnie, you'll vouch for me, won't you?' she said. 'You heard the guest say that her brooch was lost.'

Winnie stood with a bewildered expression on her face. 'What brooch?'

Ruby looked helplessly from the florist to Mrs Fosdyke. 'I had the door open,' said Ruby, 'and the guest was upset because she'd lost her brooch.'

Winnie began to look uncomfortable. 'I'm sorry, dear,' she said apologetically, 'but I'm afraid I didn't hear anything.'

Ruby's heart sank.

'Leave everything as it is and come straight to the office,' said Mrs Fosdyke.

'But I haven't done anything wrong,' Ruby cried helplessly.

'Now, Bateman,' she snapped.

They emerged into the corridor just as Mrs Harper was coming back. 'I left my stole and the umbrella,' she said, looking flustered.

'I found your brooch, madam,' said Ruby.

'Bateman!' Mrs Fosdyke snapped again.

But Ruby wasn't going to go down without a fight. 'I've put it in the drawer, in the red box.'

'Um?' said Mrs Harper. 'Oh, thank—'

She was interrupted by her daughter coming up the stairs. 'What are you doing now, Mother? Do hurry up.'

'Yes, yes, of course.'

'Shall I show you where I put it?' Ruby insisted.

248

'What's going on?' asked Mrs Toynby, Mrs Harper's daughter.

'I caught this girl going through your mother's things,' said Mrs Fosdyke. 'I am just about to call the police.'

'I didn't steal anything, madam,' cried Ruby. 'Your mother was distressed because she couldn't find her brooch. I helped her to look for it, but we couldn't find it. As soon as she'd left the room, I found it caught inside the pillowcase.'

By now a couple of other guests had gathered in the corridor.

'Bateman – the office,' said Mrs Fosdyke, anxious to get Ruby somewhere far less public.

'Have you been mislaying things again, Mother?' said Mrs Toynby. 'Cedric is right. You are going doolally.'

'No!' cried Mrs Harper. 'I have no idea what the girl is talking about. I forgot to bring my stole, that's all. Really, Louisa, you're making a terrible fuss about nothing.'

She went back into her room and the door closed.

Ruby felt sick. This couldn't be happening. If the woman denied everything, she would be labelled a thief. She'd be sacked. She mustn't lose this job. Without a decent reference, she'd never get another job. Oh God, if they called the police, she might even end up in prison.

'No, wait,' cried Ruby. 'Please ... you must believe me. I didn't take anything.'

'Bateman,' said Mrs Fosdyke, 'the office.'

The older woman came out of the room and made for the stairs. 'Please, madam,' cried Ruby.

'You must tell them. If you don't, I shall get the sack.'

Mrs Harper glanced at her daughter. 'Whatever this is about,' she said defiantly, 'it's got nothing to do with me.'

Her daughter glared at Ruby and they both went downstairs. Miserably, Ruby followed Mrs Fosdyke to the office.

Percy had a lot to do. First he went down to the beach to inspect his father's locker and boat. Few of the other fishermen were around. It was December 23rd, after all. Those who were there were quick to acknowledge him, and a couple expressed their sadness at Nelson's passing. The boat was fine, but a lot of the fishing gear was missing.

'They say it were all gone when they pulled he out of the water,' said a burly fisherman known as Bluey. He and a friend were still trying to sell the fish they'd caught on Saturday, though – being Christmas – most housewives were thinking more in terms of chicken or pork for their meals. 'Must have took it wi' he when he fell.'

Percy frowned. 'Did he have someone with him?' Bluey glanced at his companion and shifted awkwardly, making Percy sense something was wrong. 'What is it?'

'Silas Reed told the coroner it were you in the boat wi' him.'

'Me!' cried Percy indignantly. 'Of course it wasn't me. I was on my way to London.'

Bluey's companion sniffed loudly. 'You know what Silas and his eyesight is like. The man couldn't see the *Mauretania* if it sailed up the Rife.'

250

'All the same,' Bluey insisted, 'the police were supposed to be wanting to talk with you.'

'Well, nobody came looking,' said Percy tetchily. He opened the locker and found what was left of Nelson's fishing tackle inside.

'You going out on the water?' asked Bluey.

'My father always wanted me to fish,' replied Percy.

Bluey's companion sniffed again and Percy felt himself bristle. If they said one word about his lack of fishing skills – one word... Having checked the bottom of the boat, he locked up again and left the beach. *It will be better without him*, he told himself as he strode towards the town, but he knew it was said without much conviction.

Ruby sat in a shelter looking out to sea. She was cold and she had never felt so miserable in her whole life.

How had this happened? She had been so happy when she'd come to work this morning. Percy was back, which meant she and her mother had got the Christmas present they'd wanted most. Only last night, this year promised to be the very best Christmas ever. It was probably wicked to say it, but her father wasn't there to spoil anything.

Now that Percy was back, Ruby wished she had a way of contacting Miss Russell, who had sent her a Christmas card from Cape Town, South Africa, no less. It had pride of place on the mantelpiece, and Ruby had snatched a couple of minutes to look Cape Town up when she was working in the lounge area at Warnes. She had little time to read much, but she enjoyed looking at the black-and-white photographs of what was described as the University of Cape Town, with its impressive Athenian temple entrance, and the Worcester shopping centre, which looked much like any English town, apart from the snow-capped mountains in the distance. Miss Russell was going to spend the holidays in a place called Pretoria, where she would be staying with friends in the famous Erasmus Castle; as a postscript she had added the word *'spookhuis'*. Ruby was convinced it was German until John pointed out that it was an Afrikaans word meaning 'a house with a ghost'. Ruby smiled to herself and shivered with delight at the thought of it. She sighed. Even if she could contact Miss Russell, she would have no chance of working for her, now that she'd got the sack. She'd need a good reference.

She had known that Mrs Fosdyke had been gunning for her ever since she'd been rewarded for helping Dr Palmer. She blew her nose and shivered. What would Jim say? He was on the way up now. He had just won a prize in a national photographic competition. It suddenly occurred to her that, in the excitement of seeing Percy, she'd never got round to asking him what he'd actually won as a prize. Perhaps the picture would be in some sort of exhibition, or even in the paper. Good for him! All at once her blood ran cold. Supposing they found out that the 'Beauty' in the photograph had just been labelled a thief and had been sacked from her job? That could mean she would ruin Jim's chances of success as well. The thought of it brought fresh tears and further self-condemnation.

The men in his dormitory had had a whip-round and had given him a generous amount of money when they'd heard the news of his father's death, so Percy joined several dozen other men on the shop floor of Woolworths. At this time on Christmas Eve, they had the place to themselves. The younger men were at the perfume and cosmetic counters, buying talcum powder and lipsticks for their girlfriends, while the older, more obviously married men went for the household items like a new feather duster or drinking glasses. A few men hung around the boxes of chocolates, while the more daring of them looked at the lacy scanties.

Percy bought a box of toffees for May, a Yardley's talc-and-soap set in a presentation box for Ruby and a big box of the new Black Magic chocolates for his mother. The assistant on the chocolate counter was particularly helpful, because she wrapped up the box of chocolates for him. He stopped in a tea shop for a cup of tea and then, having called in at the off-licence to buy a couple of bottles of beer, made his way back home.

Ruby still sat in the shelter. She looked across the water to the pier, still black and broken from the fire. The workmen had put up fencing to stop the public from walking on two-thirds of it, while they slowly removed everything but the steel frame from the Southern Pavilion. It stood out in stark relief against the sky, like the ribcage of a much-loved but dead animal. A morbid thought crossed her mind. They were alike, she and the pier, stripped bare and exposed to the critical eye of the town. That thought made her cry some more.

Later, all cried out, she made some decisions. She wouldn't tell the family what had happened. They didn't need to know yet, and she didn't want to ruin their Christmas. She would make something up – tell them she'd got a bit of holiday. She'd go back to Warnes after Christmas and apologize to Mrs Fosdyke. She had nothing to be sorry for, but with two and half million other people out of work in the country, she couldn't afford to nurse her pride. Mrs Fosdyke would most likely refuse to have her back, but she might go easier on the reference. It was obvious that the hotel guest was confused. Hadn't the waiters in the dining room said so, on more than one occasion? She'd point this out – politely – and hope that Mrs Fosdyke would be reasonable. If she couldn't get her job back, Ruby would trudge the streets night and day until she found something – anything would do. Her heart sank and she realized she was back at square one. No one would give her a job, not even a dreadful job, without a reference.

One good thing: now that Percy was back home, he would return to the fishing. Ruby sighed. If only she were a man, she could go fishing too. A small smile worked its way onto her lips. Perhaps Percy would take her on as a 'mate'. Why not? She knew some fishermen believed that women were not physically or emotionally capable of sailing, but she would have no trouble disproving that stupid idea! However, there was a stronger disincentive to joining her brother. It was traditionally believed that having a woman on board

254

brought bad luck. Ridiculous, of course; and the myth had probably only gained legs because a woman on board a larger ship could be a distraction, or even the cause of jealousy between members of the crew. That wouldn't happen on the *Saucy Sarah*, because she would be with her own brother. Besides, this was the twentieth century. Percy was a man of the world and, as such, surely he would have no truck with such superstitious nonsense. No, the more she thought about it, the more she liked the idea. She wouldn't need a reference to be a fisherwoman.

Ruby wiped her nose one last time and stood up. Problem solved. She would enjoy her Christmas and then tell everybody her plan. If this was as bad as it got, she'd be all right. Surely nothing could get worse than it was already.

CHAPTER 20

The suitcase was leaning against the kitchen dresser. When Ruby opened it, her father's coat had gone and so had the dresses. In its place she found a lovely silk nightdress and some jumpers. One was hand-knitted in a pretty blue wool with a silver thread, but there was an ugly mistake in the pattern running down the front. Ruby decided to swap it with the boring black shoes she had worn at Warnes. She wouldn't be needing them now and, if she unpicked the blue jumper, she could make something else.

The Christmas celebrations began on Christmas Eve. Just before May went to bed they heard carol singers in the road. Bea opened the front door and they listened. 'Peace on earth and mercy mild...'

'Oh, I hope so,' Bea whispered.

To the family's delight, the singers sang 'Away in a Manger' and 'As with Gladness, Men of Old', before moving on. May went up to bed. Percy went to the pub. Ruby put the finishing touches to the room. Having come home a bit earlier, with the excuse that she'd been given the time off as a Christmas gesture, she and May had spent the afternoon making the room look quite festive. They'd already hung crêpe-paper chains and now they added a bit of holly to the mantelpiece, taken from the tree three doors down, and some ivy picked from the archway beside the railway line leading into Ivy Arch Road. They'd put Epsom salts onto some fir cones they'd found on the road nearby. Ruby knew that if they spread them thickly enough, when they dried it would look like snow.

She put a plate of cobnuts, collected in September and left to ripen, next to her mother's armchair, and the home-made sweets she'd made the previous week in the centre of the table. Standing back to admire her handiwork, Ruby smiled. It was perfect.

The day itself began with May thundering downstairs to see if Father Christmas had been. Ruby turned one sleepy eye towards the clock. Five-thirty. She groaned and turned over, pulling the

256

bed-sheets back over her head. The room was freezing. She dozed, but she wasn't allowed to stay there for long. She was called downstairs by her mother at six-fifteen, with the promise of a cup of tea if she came down to watch her sister open her presents.

They sat huddled in the kitchen, Percy included, yawning and trying to look enthusiastic while May unwrapped everything. Whenever possible, Bea carefully folded the paper that could be used again, although some pieces had obviously done several Christmases already and were rather the worse for wear. She put what she could into a drawer, ready to iron some day, and then it would go upstairs to be stored until next year.

Ruby and Bea loved their presents from Percy, given to them both still in the Woolworths bag. The jumper that Ruby had knitted her mother was fine, although it was slightly bigger than she'd thought. Her mother had given her the brooch Grandma used to wear. She had always planned to give it to Ruby on her twenty-first birthday, but in these difficult times it was all she had. It was a pretty flower-shape with pink-and-white stones. Although it had no great value, it meant a lot to Ruby, because it brought back memories of the white-haired old lady who had cuddled her and told her she loved her, on the magic days when she came to Worthing when Ruby was a child. She also had a surprise present from the suitcase. The shoes she had worn at Warnes were given to her, neatly wrapped in an apron.

'I thought they'd do as a spare pair, love,' Bea whispered, as Ruby gaped in surprise. 'I swapped them for a headscarf.'

'Thanks, Mum,' said Ruby, hiding a small smile. Clearly her mother hadn't recognized them – why would she? She never cleaned them or anything.

Percy was handed a small but bulky present from his mother. He was staggered to see his father's pocket watch emerging from the paper. 'He would have wanted you to have it,' said Bea with a smile.

'Thanks, Mother,' said Percy, putting it into his trouser pocket.

Of course May had the lion's share of presents. Her stocking contained a magic painting book, which only required the use of a wet brush to bring out the colours impregnated on the page; a pair of tin scales, with two little jars of sweeties to measure out; some plasticine; a skipping rope with real wooden handles; a little shell necklace; and an apple and a tangerine. Under the tree she found the tin of toffees from Percy, a puzzle from Aunt Vinny and Cousin Lily, a whole set of knitted doll's clothes from Ruby and a toy sewing box from Bea.

Percy stoked the fire and put on some more coal. Normally Bea would have been alarmed to see so much of their meagre supply going on at once, but, she reminded herself, it was Christmas. After a while Percy yawned and went back to bed. May got her dollies out and began dressing and undressing them in their new clothes, while Ruby shut herself in the scullery to have her wash. Dead on the dot of eight, and just as Ruby came out of the scullery, John came out of his room and sat at the table. Bea put his break-

258

fast – two boiled eggs and a doorstep slice of bread – in front of him and poured the tea.

'Happy Christmas,' she said shyly. She pushed a small gift in front of him. 'I know you don't celebrate it, but it's the way we do things around here.' John opened his mouth as if to protest, but Bea stopped him. 'It's the season of peace and goodwill towards all men, and I want everybody in this house to be family today.'

John seemed genuinely moved. The gift was wrapped in a small piece of blue tissue paper, exactly the same as the tissue paper that covered the brooch her mother had given Ruby. John undid the string holding it together and revealed a pair of cufflinks that had once belonged to Nelson. He had hardly ever worn them, but seeing them again gave Ruby a bit of a jolt. Apart from the watch, she knew that her mother had got rid of everything else Nelson had owned. Percy appeared, fully dressed, in the doorway.

'They are not new,' Bea was saying apologetically, 'but you are welcome.'

John's hand trembled as he picked them up. 'Madam, I have never come across such kindness. Thank you, thank you.'

He seized Bea's hand and kissed it. Ruby saw her brother stiffen.

'Percy,' cried Bea, retrieving her hand, 'you haven't met our lodger yet, have you? John, this is my son Percy. Percy, this is John Coffey. John is a cobbler and has just started up a business in the old shed outside.'

John rose to his feet and bowed stiffly. 'I am pleased to meet you,' he said, holding out his hand towards Percy.

Percy hesitated for a second, but took the proffered hand and shook it. 'Where are you from?'

'Germany,' said John.

'Germany?' said Percy.

Ruby held her breath. John nodded.

'Mosley is very keen on Germany.' Percy's face broke into a smile. 'I am very pleased to meet you.'

Once breakfast was over, Percy decided to go and see some friends, and John went for a walk. That left the kitchen free for Bea and Ruby to get the dinner started.

'Aren't you having any breakfast, Mum?' Ruby asked as she cleared the table.

'I had mine earlier,' said Bea.

At ten Aunt Vinny came round with a rather scrawny-looking chicken. 'The last but one left,' she said. 'He's hardly got a leg to stand on,' she chuckled, holding one thin leg in the air, 'but I got him for two bob.' And they all laughed.

'Anyway,' said Bea, 'I've already got a small bacon joint, so we shall be feasting today.'

While Bea put the bacon in the double saucepan, her sister chopped off the chicken's head and got it ready for the oven. Ruby was already seated at the table, preparing the vegetables.

'Where's Cousin Lily?' Ruby asked. 'I thought she was coming to help.'

'She's out with her young man,' said Aunt Vinny.

Ruby could barely hide her surprise. 'So she's still going out with Hubert Periwinkle?'

'Hubert Periwinkle!' said her aunt. 'Oh no, dear. She packed him up ages ago. Just lately she's been seeing Albert.'

'Albert?' said Ruby.

'Albert Longman.'

Ruby was aware that her mouth had dropped open. Albert Longman? She could hardly believe her ears. Cousin Lily was stepping out with Albert Longman, with his funny haircut and his smarmy smile. 'How long has she...?'

'I thought you knew,' said Aunt Vinny innocently.

'They've been together ever since that first inquest. He came round that night. Most comforting, he was.' She gazed into the distance, all starry-eyed. 'Our Lily is real smitten with him.'

And so are you, by the look of it, Ruby thought darkly. So, within weeks – nay, days – of declaring his undying love to her, Albert was courting Cousin Lily! 'Are they getting engaged or anything?'

'Not yet,' said Aunt Vinny, 'but she's confident.'

Her mother had said nothing, but Ruby could see she was just as surprised. So much for Albert's broken heart!

'Is Lily spending the day with his family then?' asked Bea.

'Oh no, dear,' said Aunt Vinny. 'He's taken her to church, that's all. They'll be here in time for lunch.'

Ruby rose quickly from her chair and put the potato peelings into the bucket under the sink. She didn't want her mother and aunt to see the smirk on her face. Cousin Lily and Albert in

261

church... Now that would be a sight for sore eyes.

She closed the door, shutting out the sound of Christmas carols and people in the street wishing each other a happy Christmas. What did it all mean anyway? Men on camels and a baby lying in a straw bed – she didn't want peace on earth. All she wanted was her lover back. How could she enjoy herself, when he had been blasted to kingdom come?

She turned the key in the lock so that she wouldn't be disturbed. She would sit very still and concentrate. Maybe she would hear his voice again. That would be the best Christmas present ever. Her writing pad was in the drawer. She got it out and put it on the table next to her chair. If he spoke to her, she could put it down on paper. That way she could read and reread his words again and again. Picking up her favourite fountain pen, she closed her eyes. A slow smile crept across her lips as she waited.

Cousin Lily stretched luxuriantly and gazed at the man in bed beside her. He was sleeping now, exhausted after their passionate lovemaking. Her body still stung from his penetration and, as she thought about what they had just done, her excitement rose again. She'd fought him off for several weeks, but finally he'd worn her down. They'd planned this day for some time, fooling her mother into believing they were going to church. They'd made a big thing of it being Christmas Day and needing to thank God for his gift, and set off in time for the service. They'd hidden in a nearby twitten, and as soon as her mother had left the house, they had crept back upstairs and into Lily's room. She had been excited and a bit scared, but Albert was an accomplished lover.

He'd been breathtakingly strong, apologizing and lusting after her all in the same breath, as he undressed her and took her on the bed. She had been thrilled and terrified all at the same time. When it was all over she'd lain still, staring at the ceiling, as his body – empty of all power – sagged on top of her. He'd lifted himself off her, kissed her and rolled over to sleep. Lily had slept a little herself, but then the enormity of what had happened began to sink in. Suppose she got pregnant? Suppose he talked about her in the town? Suppose, now that he'd had his way, he left her and went off with someone else? Suppose her mother found out? He woke to find her tearful and trembling but, with honeyed words, he'd soon made her melt in his arms once more and they'd made love again.

When it was done, he'd whispered, 'Happy Christmas, darling,' and Lily knew he would love her forever.

CHAPTER 21

The meal was set for one o'clock and everybody had assembled by twelve-thirty. Jim Searle came bearing gifts, which, despite May's loud protests, were added to the ones under the Christmas tree to be opened at teatime. Albert and Percy seemed slightly surprised to see each other, but apart from that and the fact that Nelson was missing, it was a normal Christmas Day.

'Nice to see you again,' said Albert, shaking Percy's hand. 'Where have you been?'

'To begin with, I was in London,' Percy explained, 'and then I moved to York.'

He told them a little about the rallies he'd been to and the training he'd undertaken with the BUF.

Albert shook his head. 'Each to his own, but that's not the life for me,' he said. 'I'd hate being told what to do all the time.'

The chicken and bacon were a great success (John declined the bacon) and they enjoyed the roast potatoes with cabbage, carrots and parsnips. Bea put the last of a brandy miniature over the pudding and set it alight. Aunt Vinny had brought a tin of sterilized cream that she'd won in a raffle some time ago, which topped it off nicely. When the meal was done, everyone agreed it had been splendid. Normally the men would retire to the front parlour, but now that it was John's room, they had to make a few changes, and with all the extra chairs in the kitchen there wasn't a lot of room.

After May had begged to go out in the street with her new skipping rope, Percy decided he needed some exercise on his bicycle and invited Jim to do the same. Unfortunately Jim had come on foot and didn't think his landlady would want to be disturbed if he went back to his digs. John suggested that the family needed some time together without him, but Bea wouldn't hear of it, although she did concede that it would help her if he rested in his room until teatime. Albert, who had spent a good deal of his time watching every move Ruby made, took Cousin Lily out for a walk.

Because Bea had eaten the biggest meal she had had in a long time, she started to feel unwell. Aunt Vinny took her upstairs, which only left Ruby to do the washing up. Jim tugged at a tea towel to dry the dishes.

'You don't have to do that,' she said.

'I want to,' said Jim, giving her a quick kiss on the lips. She'd been longing for him to do that ever since he'd arrived.

'You forgot to tell me what the prize for the photographic competition was,' she said, smiling up at him. 'What did you win?'

'A course,' he said mysteriously and, seeing Ruby's puzzled expression, he chuckled. 'First prize was twenty-five pounds' worth of the latest photographic equipment and a chance to work with a top fashion photographer.'

Ruby's mouth dropped open. 'Twenty-five pounds! But that's a king's ransom.'

'Second prize,' he said, 'my prize, is a week with Thomas Kendrick.'

'Who's he?'

'Only just about the best wildlife photographer around,' laughed Jim. 'He lives in a small hamlet near Wimborne in Dorset. I get to stay at his home and learn some of his techniques.'

Ruby had mixed feelings, but she beamed and hugged him close. 'When do you go?'

'January the twelfth.'

'That's marvellous, Jim,' she said. 'I am so pleased for you.'

She had wanted to confide in him about her job, or lack of one, but considering what he'd just told her, that would be unfair. She knew him well enough to know that he would postpone his trip to be there to support her. But this was his moment – his opportunity to walk that lesser-known pathway. She couldn't spoil it for him, and besides it was only for a week. He'd be back in no time.

Job done, they sat beside the fire. 'Want to go for a walk?' asked Jim. They were having to whisper because, when she came back downstairs, Aunt Vinny had dropped off to sleep in her chair.

'Do you?'

'Not fussed.'

'Anyway, the others will be back soon,' she said, sitting down.

Taking an anxious glance at her sleeping aunt, Jim knelt on the rag rug in front of Ruby and took her hands in his. 'Will you write to me?'

She laughed softly. 'You're only going for a week.'

'I'd still like a letter from my best girl,' he said earnestly.

'You'd better tell her then,' she teased. 'Of course I'll write, even though you won't have time to read it.'

They heard voices and Aunt Vinny stirred, closing her open mouth and opening her sleepy eyes. Jim was back in his chair, his face the picture of innocence, as he sat bolt upright with his hands clasped firmly in his lap. Ruby had her hand over her mouth to stifle the giggle welling up inside her. Aunt Vinny turned her head to look at the clock and, while her back was to him, Jim blew Ruby a kiss.

After a tea that nobody really wanted, they opened the remaining presents. Once she had seen what Jim had given her, Ruby could hardly recall what her other presents were. She loved the Yardley's powder in a big box, with its own powder puff. It must have cost Jim a fortune. Cousin Lily squealed with delight when Ruby took of the cellophane wrapping and let her smell its perfume. Ruby had given Jim a fountain pen, but it wasn't a patch on what he'd given her. Lily had given Albert a tie, and he had bought her a book.

'How lovely!' she cried. 'I've always wanted to read that one.'

When she saw the expression on Albert's face, Ruby looked away. Everybody (except Jim) knew that Lily couldn't read, and she was a past master at hiding the fact, but there was something un-kind in his smile.

Christmas Day was almost over and so, to round it off, they got out the dartboard and decided to play: the men against the ladies. May, grumpy and protesting that she wasn't a bit tired, was packed off to bed. John was about to go back in his room until Jim pointed out that they needed him to make up the team.

The women's team was at a distinct disadvant-age. Half the time Cousin Lily couldn't even get her darts on the board, although Ruby had a feel-ing that she was playing up to Albert. They all enjoyed the laugh, anyway.

'How's the job going, Albert?' Percy asked.

'So-so,' said Albert, 'with it being Christmas. I've been assigned to nativity plays and children's parties.'

'Oh, dear,' Jim sympathized.

'It makes a change from missionary teas and WI meetings,' said Albert drily.

'My mother has been telling me how well you looked after her and my sisters when my father died,' said Percy. 'I want to thank you.'

Albert waved his hand dismissively, but, throwing a glance at Ruby, he said, 'My pleasure.'

'I can't imagine how the accident happened,' Percy went on.

'One of the old boys thought you were in the boat with him,' said Jim. 'He told the coroner as much, anyway.' He threw his darts, getting a treble twenty, a double five and a one.

'I heard that,' said Percy. 'Bluey said it was Silas. But I was in London at the time and I can prove it.'

'Odd, isn't it?' Albert remarked. 'Anyway, not to worry. The coroner didn't believe it, and that's all that matters.'

'Let's not talk about sad things today,' said Cousin Lily, getting ready to take her turn at the dartboard. Everyone moved well away from it.

'You're right,' said Bea.

Aiming her dart, Cousin Lily closed one eye and hit the door frame.

The day after Boxing Day, Ruby slipped up the service stairs at the back of Warnes Hotel. She timed it so that Mrs Fosdyke had finished doing

268

her rounds and would be in the office upstairs, with the MD.

She had dressed with care, making herself look as presentable as possible. Her hair was neat and tidy and she was in her Sunday-best clothes, with her shoes highly polished. Ruby looked up and down the corridor to make sure nobody was around. The cleaning trolley was outside room 32. Mrs Harper was in room 36, just a little further along. Ruby walked briskly, her heart already beating faster. She mustn't get caught and stopped before she could talk to Mrs Harper. She knocked softly on the door. 'Come in,' said a quavery voice, and Ruby stepped inside.

Mrs Harper was still in bed. She seemed pale and was clearly not well, but she smiled as Ruby came closer. 'Hello, dear. How are you?'

'I'm fine,' said Ruby. 'Mrs Harper, I need your help.'

The old lady sat up. 'Do you, dear?'

'Do you remember losing your brooch?' Ruby asked.

'Did I?'

Ruby chewed her bottom lip anxiously. 'Yes, you did. I was cleaning in the bathroom, and you were worried that your daughter might be cross.'

There was no reaction. Mrs Harper stared at Ruby with a blank expression.

'I helped you to look for it,' Ruby ploughed on. 'I looked on your coat lapel and we looked in the drawer.' She expected some kind of response, but there was absolutely nothing. What should she do now? She smiled at the old lady. Mrs Harper smiled back.

'I've got a bit of a cold,' said Mrs Harper. 'Did you bring the morning paper with you, dear?'

Ruby knew then that it was hopeless. She turned towards the door. 'I'll send somebody up with it,' she smiled.

'Do I know you, dear?' said Mrs Harper.

'You did,' said Ruby, swallowing hard, 'but that was a long time ago. I'm afraid I have to go now. Goodbye.'

'Goodbye, dear,' said Mrs Harper, settling back down in the bed.

Ruby closed the door and rested her head on the frame, until she heard another door opening further down the corridor. Instinctively she knew it was Mrs Harper's daughter. She dared not be caught talking again to her mother. Mrs Toynby knew that Ruby had been sacked, and to be found in Mrs Harper's room again wouldn't look good. Ruby walked back down the corridor with her head held high and, as she reached the back stairs, she heard Mrs Harper's door open and her daughter say in a sing-song voice, 'Time to get up now, Mother. We're going to see your nice new home today.'

As she fled down the back stairs, Ruby heard somebody coming onto the landing. The sound of a handle hitting the side of a bucket told her it must be either Winnie or Edith. Ruby toyed briefly with the idea of saying hello, but then decided it was better not to let anyone know she was there.

Outside in the cold winter morning, Ruby knew her time at Warnes was well and truly over. It had been a mad idea to try and persuade Mrs Harper that she had made a dreadful mistake. The poor old soul's mind had finally gone and, with it, any hope of getting her own good name restored, so there was little point in apologizing to Mrs Fosdyke. Ruby desperately wanted her job back, but she knew hell would freeze over before Mrs Fosdyke would give her another chance, and there was no way she was going to grovel. Her next stop would be the domestic employment agency, but she had little hope of getting a placement without a reference.

Percy had spent the morning preparing the boat and the nets, or what was left of them. He'd have to buy some more trammel nets. They were gone, presumably when Nelson went overboard. The lobster pots were still there, and he found a couple of mended nets in the locker. At this time of year he could get some good cod, but it was better to fish at night when the cod came closer to land. He might manage to catch whiting as well, but he wouldn't make the same mistake as his father and go fishing alone.

Coming back home, he spotted Ruby walking ahead of him and ran to catch her up. 'Hey up, Sis. Why aren't you at work?'

At first Ruby didn't answer, but when Percy grabbed her arm to stop her walking on, she burst into tears. They were fairly near a small cafe in High Street, so he pulled her aside and they went in. The heat and fumes from a paraffin heater hit them as they walked through the door. Ruby opened her coat and took off her scarf and gloves. Percy ordered two teas, and Ruby explained what had happened. Her brother listened with a shocked expression.

'But surely they could see the old duck was doolally?' he said angrily.

'That only makes her all the more vulnerable,' Ruby said, wiping her eyes with her handkerchief. 'Unless she tells them what really happened, they're going to believe the worst, aren't they? It's dreadfully unfair, but what can I do?'

Percy put his hand over hers. 'Take your time, Sis,' he said. 'Have a good look around Worthing for a job and, if that doesn't work, try further afield. What about nursery work? There are plenty of glasshouses around here.'

'There isn't much planting and picking in January,' she said. 'Ask John.' Their tea arrived and Ruby welcomed its steaming warmth.

'Your wage isn't so vital, now that I'm back home,' he said.

'You're a good man, Percy Bateman,' said Ruby miserably.

'I don't know about that,' he said.

'How about I come on the boat with you?' she said. 'You need a mate.'

'But you're a woman,' Percy laughed.

'I had noticed,' said Ruby.

Percy's expression changed. 'It's bad luck to have a woman on board.'

'Oh, stuff and nonsense!' said Ruby. 'This is the twentieth century, Percy, not the Middle Ages. Surely you don't believe all that superstitious claptrap?'

Percy gave her a long, hard stare. 'I'm not taking a woman aboard,' he said firmly.

'But...' Ruby began.

Her brother raised his hand to silence her. 'You heard me,' he said. 'Now drink up and stop worrying. It'll be fine.'

CHAPTER 22

Linton Carver was scared. Somebody knew.

He never had letters. He'd lived in the same house all his life and the only time the postman ever brought anything with his name on, it was a bill. When he was a boy he'd come from a large family, but no one ever wrote to him. Unless his Aunt Mabel told them otherwise, they probably thought he had died in the Great War, or perhaps in the worldwide flu epidemic in 1918. Maybe they'd died themselves. Millions of others in the Empire had. He'd never got in touch to find out.

Linton had never had a lady friend, either. In fact he might still have been a virgin himself if it hadn't been for that woman in the barn. The shame of what he had done eighteen years ago still haunted him. It was the stuff of all his nightmares.

It was only 1914, but they'd been desperate to get away from the guns and the gas, and the smell of chewed-up body parts of the people who had once been friends. Victor had been the first to take off; and the others, including Linton himself, just followed. They'd walked through the woods and, as the sounds of battle grew fainter, they'd heard the birds. He couldn't remember

273

the last time he'd heard birdsong. It had brought tears to his eyes.

Then Victor had told them he wasn't going back and had smashed up his rifle. It was an act of pure defiance, but perhaps if he had known what was about to happen, he might have thought twice about doing it. Whoever sent this letter must have known all about it.

Linton turned the envelope over in his hands and trembled. The postmark read: *Worthing, 6.30 p.m., January 6th, 1934.* Oh, God, whoever posted this lived in the town. They weren't far away. Perhaps they'd actually seen him in the street. The envelope didn't contain much. One sheet of paper with just two words, and it meant only one thing – someone knew what they'd done: 'Remember Victor.'

He was suddenly desperate for the toilet. His stomach churned and his bladder felt fit to burst. He went outside and into the yard. It might be the depth of winter, with temperatures low enough to freeze a penguin's balls, but the outside lavatory still reeked of dung and Jeyes fluid. He yanked off his coat, pulled down his braces and trousers, only just making it as he sat over the hole in the wooden seat. As he defecated, his legs shook, not with the cold, but with fear.

Who had sent it? Who knew? He'd been so sure that, with Nelson gone, he was safe. What was that person going to do? What happened to Nelson: was it an accident or not? And, if not an accident, then it must be murder. Linton hadn't had much of a life since he'd been gassed, but he wasn't ready to die, not yet.

He was crying now; huge, gulping silent sobs that racked his whole body. It always got to him like that, when he remembered.

They had stayed in the barn until nightfall. They knew they had to go back before they were missed, but they had to work out what to say about Victor's rifle. They'd settled on a plan and were about to set off when the woman came into the barn, leading a horse. They'd watched her take off the saddle and begin rubbing the animal down with some straw. After a while Nelson began to rub his dick, matching her movements on the horse's back, stroke for stroke. Then George did the same thing. It wouldn't have mattered, but one of them moaned and suddenly the woman realized she wasn't alone.

Linton's first thought was that they had to make her understand she mustn't tell the authorities they'd been there, but there was a language barrier. Besides, the others had other ideas. It all happened so bloody quick. They'd barged past him, and Nelson had grabbed the woman while George held her down. She'd begged them to stop. He couldn't understand a word she'd said, but he recognized the panic in her voice and he'd seen her tears. He and Victor had told them to stop, but as he watched what Nelson was doing, something stirred in his own loins. Victor tried to pull Nelson off, but George shoved him so hard that he fell against the horse and, already spooked by their angry voices, the animal lashed out with his hoof. Victor was knocked out cold. George and Nelson swapped places and, while Nelson held her down, George did it too. Linton's mind was on fire. He'd never felt such strong feelings. For the first time in his life he was fully aroused, and the more he watched, the more inflamed he became. Then they were inviting him to take what he wanted. The woman was quiet now. She just lay there. She wasn't struggling any more. They told her she'd enjoyed them so much, she was begging for more and... And...

He shuddered and started to cough. It was bloody cold in the privy and he'd finished. He reached for the torn-up newspaper hanging on the nail, to wipe himself clean, but he didn't go back indoors. Instead he leaned forward and, putting his head in his hands, wept quietly as the shame overwhelmed him once again. *May God forgive him, because he couldn't forgive himself...* And now he'd had this letter. Somebody else knew.

'Ruby, what's wrong?'

She looked up at Jim's anxious face and smiled. 'Nothing. I'm just thinking how much I'm going to miss you, that's all.' They were in Warwick Studios, a rare time of being alone. Jim's boss, Leonard Hayward, was doing a family portrait at a client's home, and Ruby had come to help Jim pack. It turned out that he didn't need any help, as he had already packed his little case, which was back at his lodgings, and he wasn't taking any equipment with him to Wimborne. They both knew it was just an excuse to be together one last time before he left.

Jim had made tea and, after showing her a magazine with his winning picture next to an article, they'd sat together on the horsehair sofa.

His ardent kisses grew stronger and he had his hand on Ruby's breast when she stopped him gently. 'Jim, we mustn't.'

'I know, I know, but I want you so much, Ruby,' he said. He kissed her some more and this time his hand strayed onto her thigh.

She pulled away again.

'You're trembling,' he said, pulling her head onto his chest and making himself more comfortable on the hard sofa. 'I know you're worrying about something. I want you to know that I would never hurt you, Ruby. I want you more than I can say, but I will never make you do something you're not comfortable with.'

Ruby picked at a loose bit of wool on his Fair Isle pullover. 'It's not that,' she said.

'Then what?'

The words stuck in her throat.

'If we are to go any further with this relationship,' he said gravely, 'and I sincerely hope we will, we must have no secrets. I don't want to be with anyone who doesn't tell the truth and keeps things from me.'

She sat up and looked at him. 'Oh, Jim,' she said, touching his cheek. 'I'm sorry. I didn't know how to tell you...'

'Tell me what?'

'I ... I've lost my job.'

'The hotel is cutting down on staff?' he queried. 'But you always said they didn't have enough.'

'I mean, I've got the sack,' she said quietly.

He stared at her uncomprehendingly. 'The sack? But why? What happened?'

So she told him. 'When did all this happen?'

'Christmas Eve,' said Ruby.

'Christmas Eve! My dear girl,' he cried, 'you've kept this to yourself all this time?' He looked genuinely upset. 'You should have told me.'

'I'm sorry,' she said, her bottom lip quivering and her eyes filling. 'I didn't know how to.'

'Promise me,' he said, taking both her hands in his, 'promise that you won't ever do this again.'

'But I didn't take the brooch,' she cried helplessly. 'And if you think–'

'No, no,' he cried. 'I meant that you should have told me about losing your job. You must tell me everything. My darling girl, I want you to be my wife some day. I can't bear to think that you were suffering all this time and I knew nothing about it.'

She was aware that her mouth had dropped open. 'Your wife?'

'I love you, Ruby Bateman,' he laughed. 'Don't tell me you didn't realize that?'

'I didn't,' she whispered. 'I didn't dare to hope... Oh, Jim, this is the most wonderful day of my life.' She was laughing and crying at the same time. She flung her arms around his neck and kissed his cheek. He found her lips and returned her kisses with a growing passion. She knew she should stop him, but now it was doubly difficult. He loved her; he wanted to marry her. Her blouse was coming undone.

'Ruby, oh, Ruby,' he moaned as his fingers went under her chemise and found her hardened nipple. His tongue filled her mouth and every part of her mind was racing; her body began to yield; she was giving herself to the feeling he'd created... And then they heard the key in the door.

They sprang apart. Ruby pulled her clothing together. Jim stood up and, running his fingers through his untidy hair, called out, 'You're back early, sir. Is there something I can do to help?'

Ruby heard a man's voice say, 'I've still got a few boxes in the car. Give us a hand, will you?'

While Jim headed towards the corridor leading to the street, Ruby grabbed her blouse and made her way to the WC. Safely behind the locked door, she dressed and made herself respectable again, before going back out. She could hear the two men bringing photographic equipment into the studio. She glanced at her reflection in the mottled mirror hanging from a nail over the sink. Her cheeks were flushed. She splashed cold water onto her face and reduced the colour a little. Her heartbeat had slowed, but the blood in her veins pulsated with the knowledge: *he loves you... Jim loves you...*

'Hey up, Percy.'

Percy looked up to see Barnabas West, his old friend. Percy hadn't seen him since they'd shared a billet together in the Black House. Barney was coming across the pebbles and onto the beach. His cheerful greeting had made Percy jump.

'Barney,' he smiled and struggled to his feet to shake his hand. It was a welcome interruption. Percy's fingers were frozen and the chill wind was eating into his bones. 'What on earth are you doing in Worthing?'

'Looking for you,' said Barney, pumping his hand. 'You're a hard man to find.'

'I can't think why,' said Percy. He had been sit-

279

ting with his back to the sea, still cleaning and repairing the fishing gear, ready for a change in the weather. 'You knew my family were fishermen, didn't you?'

Barney shrugged. 'You may have mentioned it.'

Percy felt a little uncomfortable calling himself a fisherman. In fact he had only managed a couple of trips since he'd been back home. He'd gone out with a young lad close to school leaving age, who was at a loose end, but they hadn't caught much. Percy had begun to realize that he not only hated fishing, but he just didn't have the knack for it. Either that, or it was as the other fishermen said, and the boat was cursed.

'I reckon Nelson caught the king of the mackerel,' Silas had told him, 'and never threw him back.' He'd shaken his head and sucked hard on his pipe. 'Bad omen that.'

Percy had tried to laugh it off as a silly superstition, but with the kind of luck he was having right now, it was getting harder and harder to dismiss the thought.

'Is this your boat?' Barney remarked.

'It is now,' said Percy. He spat into the wind and, as if to spite him, it started to snow.

Barney looked around. 'Is there a tea room or a cafe around here? Somewhere we could talk?'

He helped Percy put everything back into the locker and they set off for the Seagull Cafe on the Brighton Road. It sounded a lot more attractive than it looked, but Percy welcomed the mug of tea, which warmed his hands as he waited for the plate of egg and chips Barney had ordered for him.

'They want you to come back to HQ and work for the movement,' said Barney through the haze of blue smoke between them, a mixture of burnt fat in the frying pan and cigarette smoke.

'I'd like to,' said Percy, 'but I can't afford it. My father was drowned and it's up to me to carry on, for the sake of my mother and my sisters.'

'Listen, Perce,' said Barney, leaning forward in a confidential manner, 'the movement is growing faster than anyone ever dreamed. The membership already stands at nearly twenty thousand. Twenty thousand!'

Percy choked on a chip. So it really was coming to that...

'They reckon, if things carry on this way, it'll be fifty thousand by the summer,' Barney went on, 'maybe a hundred thousand by the end of the year and I'm not exaggerating, either. The point is, you don't have to come back as a volunteer. You can get paid.'

'I'm not good at paperwork,' said Percy, shaking his head.

'It's not paperwork they want you for,' said Barney. 'It's recruitment.'

Percy stopped chewing and looked up at him.

'We've got the ex-army blokes to drill them, but we need more men. We need one of their own, who can tell them what a difference they can make. We need a working-class man to attract working-class men into the ranks.'

'And you think I can do that?'

'We know you can,' said Barney. 'You were top dog at the Black House, and people looked up to you. You're fit, clean-living, a no-nonsense sort of a bloke – just the kind of man we want.'

Percy kept his eyes on his plate. 'There are some things I don't agree with,' he began.

'You and me both, pal,' said Barney. 'But everybody is entitled to have a personal opinion. Fascism doesn't deny the right to free speech; in fact we champion it.'

Percy jabbed at the yolk of his egg with a chip and they both watched the yellow liquid run onto the plate.

'Where is the perfect organization anyway, Percy?' said Barney persuasively. 'If you find it, don't tell me to join. I'll mess it up on day one.'

'Fishing has been in my family for generations,' said Percy, finally looking up at his friend.

'Like Jesus said,' Barney grinned, 'Fascism will make you a fisher of men.'

Their eyes met, as Barney's blasphemy hung between them.

Percy smiled. 'All right,' he said. 'Give me a few days to think about it.'

CHAPTER 23

Bea had spent some time putting May's birthday presents away. It was Saturday, January 20th, and although May's birthday had been on the Tuesday, this was the best day for a birthday tea. Coming so soon after Christmas made it a little difficult, but Bea did her best to make the day special. It hadn't been much of a celebration, but she had managed to give her youngest child a small cake, some sand-wiches, and jelly and ice cream for her eighth birthday. May had invited three little friends over, and Ruby had helped by organizing some games. The old favourites were the best: Blind-Man's Buff, Pass the Parcel and Hunt the Thimble. It wasn't as lavish as her previous birthday had been, but Bea was confident that May had enjoyed her-self; and when her daughter blew out the candles on her cake, Bea had made a wish on her behalf that her birthday next year would be much better.

Bea had also got into the habit of keeping a weather eye on some of her neighbours. Times were hard for everybody and she couldn't do much, but sometimes a friendly face and a chat over a cup of tea were all that was needed. If they weren't too proud, she would rub the duster over the furniture and sweep up. Sometimes she would take the sheets home to wash. She never looked for payment or reward, but it often came anyway. She had been coming to Mabel Harris's place for years. 'There's a couple of self-seeded potatoes still in the ground,' Mabel had said one day. 'You dig 'em up and we'll share 'em.' The ground was hard and it was difficult to get the spade in, but the crop had served them well. The potatoes were a good size and healthy.

Mabel's little garden was a wilderness now. When her husband was alive, it had neat rows of potatoes, carrots and runner beans. Mabel herself had been a seamstress, but with the advancing years, her arthritis made it too painful to sew. As she gradually got rid of her sewing things, what-ever she couldn't sell she gave to Bea. Ribbons, poppers and buttons were always useful, and Bea put them in her sewing box.

Today Bea had little energy to work, so she satisfied herself with a bit of dusting and washing up some dishes left in the sink. After that, they sat down for a friendly chat.

'I hate to ask you this,' said Mabel, 'but I'm really worried about my nephew.'

'Linton?' asked Bea.

Mabel nodded. 'He's never been the same since the war, and his chest gets really bad in this weather. He hasn't been to see me for a couple of weeks, and my legs won't take me as far as Heene any more.'

'Are you thinking he's ill?'

Mabel shrugged her shoulders. 'To be honest, I don't know, Bea. He was with your Nelson at Ypres, and his death upset Linton something rotten.' She sighed. 'There are times when I think the gas didn't just affect his lungs, but his brain as well.'

'Why's that?' Bea asked.

Mabel got up and went to her dresser. It was lined with cups and saucers, with a card or two propped against them. Bea knew that some of them had been up there for donkey's years, but Mabel couldn't bear to throw them away. Pride of place was given to the last birthday card her husband ever bought, before he died. Mabel took off the lid off a Royal Albert teapot, her pride and joy, and tipped it up. It rattled as she moved it and something fell out. When she brought it to Bea, Bea was surprised. It was a piece of lead in the shape of a bullet. She frowned and looked up with a puzzled expression.

'When my Jack died,' said Mabel, 'I needed money, so I decided to sell some of his things. I found this in his best suit pocket. When I showed it to Linton – honestly, Bea, I thought he was going to pass out.'

Bea swallowed hard. She'd seen something like it before, but for a minute she couldn't for the life of her remember where. 'Why was Linton upset?' asked Bea.

'He wouldn't say,' said Mabel. 'I was going to chuck it away, but after Linton's reaction, something made me keep it.'

Bea turned it over in her hands. '"Victory,"' she read on the side. 'What does it mean?'

Mabel shrugged. 'With things as they are, I've got a lot of time to think these days,' she said, 'and I remember the odd things my Jack did, in the days before he died.'

Bea was intrigued. 'What things?'

'He was never one for flowery language, if you get my meaning,' said Mabel, 'but if he told me once, he told me a hundred times that he loved me.'

'Are you saying he had a premonition he was going to die?'

'I don't know what I'm saying,' said Mabel. 'All I know is that when I showed Linton this thing, it upset him so much that he hasn't been the same since.'

'I'll go to his place tomorrow,' said Bea.

'You're an angel,' said Mabel.

'I know,' Bea smiled. 'And modest with it too.'

With the coming of the long-awaited electrification of the railway line between Victoria and West Worthing on December 30th, the dignitaries who came promised all sorts of new amenities, which would bring new jobs to the area. An eighteen-hole golf course was promised on Lower Warren Farm in Broadwater; a hippodrome cinema was to be built in Rowlands Road; an Astoria cinema in Bath Place; and a palace of dreams called The Showboat in Liverpool Terrace, which, with its nautical design, porthole windows and such, would give the appearance of a great ocean liner. Everything was supposed to be up and running by June 1934, but Ruby couldn't wait that long. She needed a job and she needed it now.

In his first letter from Dorset, Jim had shocked her by saying that he planned to stay a lot longer in Wimborne. It seemed that the celebrated photographer had taken quite a shine to him and wanted to teach Jim a lot more than the prize allowed. The deal was open-ended, but Jim hinted that he might be away for some while.

He had already been gone for three weeks before Ruby finally found a job. She hated lying, but when they'd asked her for a reference, she told them that although she could get a character reference, she had been looking after her sick mother since she'd left school and this would be her first job. They accepted her on face value, and Ruby was to begin as a ward cleaner in the hospital on Lyndhurst Road the following week, on Monday the fifth. It wasn't much of a wage – less than she'd been getting at Warnes and, from the sound of it, she was going to have to work very hard – but she would be able to pay her way at last. This was going to be a long haul and, if she was going to marry Jim, it didn't matter anyway.

She still kept up her German lessons. John Coffey had a steady business now, but he still found time to set her a challenge and she knew it comforted him to speak in his mother tongue, even if it was only with a stumbling beginner. Since Ruby had lost her job Percy had been a bit grumpier and, although her mother accepted what Ruby had told her about needing a change from the hotel, she couldn't really understand why. Bea kept pressing her, but Ruby gave no explanation.

She started work at her new job at seven, making tea for all the patients on her ward. The night-staff were getting ready for the day-staff to take over at eight, so the first hour was quite challenging. After making the tea, Ruby had to collect the water jugs and glasses, alongside the empty cups, and wash them up. After that she cleaned the ward itself. She was thorough and methodical. Everything was wiped with a damp cloth and the floors were mopped and dried. At any time she might be called upon to clear up a mess, or to make toast and a boiled egg for someone who had just been admitted, or for someone recovering from an operation and who had missed the dinner trolley. The only time she left the ward was to empty bins, and she quickly taught herself to watch out for amorous doctors and to keep out of Matron's way.

Matron was a bit of a tartar, but she was never vindictive, like Mrs Fosdyke; and funnily enough, all that Ruby had learned in Warnes paid off. More than once Matron had complimented

Ruby on her neatly kept linen cupboard. And it didn't take long for Ruby to work out a better system of doing things. Her ideas ensured they never ran out of linen, or anything else, under her care. Working at the hospital didn't take much thought, but once she got into the swing of things, she enjoyed it. Some of the nurses were a bit snooty, but others were very friendly and it seemed that, once she had proved herself to be hard-working and conscientious, everybody liked her.

The hospital was closer to home than Warnes, which was just as well because the February weather was awful. Bitterly cold winds compacted the snow, which had fallen since the beginning of the year. The hospital was bursting at the seams with patients, especially the old, who had fallen on the ice and broken bones. Few of them survived; once infection set in, or in some cases shock, not even the best nursing could save them. Ruby had to get used to the most cheerful of souls going downhill very quickly. It was the one drawback of an otherwise enjoyable job.

Jim's letters were full of praise for his tutor. He was enjoying what he was doing. Wildlife photography was very different from the portraiture he'd been used to, and at the moment Jim wasn't sure which he liked doing most. *I want to marry you as soon as possible,* he wrote. *I have a little money saved, but I can't support a wife yet. We must be careful, my love. You must be the strong one.*

She knew what he meant. If they hadn't been interrupted that night, when Mr Hayward came home early, she could have been in all sorts of trouble. Jim was asking her to be the strong one, but Ruby wasn't sure she could be.

Edith from Warnes Hotel turned up at Ruby's place.

'We all miss you, Roob,' she told her. 'We couldn't believe what that old cow did. She told us you'd just walked out.'

'All in the past,' said Ruby, anxious not to discuss it in case she cried. 'How's Bernard from the bacon counter?'

Edith gave her a nudge. 'Promoted now,' she chuckled, 'so you won't be able to tease me any more. He's been given a more managerial position, so he'll be ordering from suppliers.'

'That's marvellous, Edith!' cried Ruby. 'Does that mean your mother might let you get married sooner?'

Edith shook her head sadly. 'Not a chance.'

'Oh, dear,' Ruby sympathized.

'Anyway, tell me something about yourself,' Edith said, and Ruby told her about Percy coming home, and about her new job at the hospital. Edith was fascinated to hear that Ruby was having German lessons, so Ruby dazzled her with a couple of sentences. 'You always were a clever bugger, Ruby Bateman,' she said admiringly, and Ruby blushed.

'How's Mrs Fosdyke?' she asked.

'It's better on the days when she doesn't turn up,' Edith shrugged. 'We always seem to be in her bad books these days. You always kept us in line.'

'And there you were, calling me a slave-driver,' Ruby laughed.

'You have to admit that you were good at organizing us, Roob,' said Edith quite seriously. 'And when you did, you never made us feel like something on the bottom of your shoe. I wish we had someone like you in charge.'

Ruby nudged her playfully. 'Go on with you.'

'It's true,' said Edith.

'Well, thank you,' said Ruby, deeply touched. 'You have no idea what that means to me.'

When she had gone, Ruby turned over the old postcards she'd had from Miss Russell. Such lovely exciting places, but it was no good wishing for something that was never going to be. She took them down to put them on the fire, but she just couldn't do it. Instead, she put them in a box. It was time to turn her back on the past and look to the future, wherever that might lie.

That night, despite her best intentions, Ruby lay in her bed thinking about what might have been. Why was it that all the major events in her life never seemed to work out properly? She had wanted to train as a typist, but her father had made her work at Warnes. He'd died just as she'd got the opportunity to work for Miss Russell, but she couldn't walk out and leave her mother. And now Jim wanted to marry her. She loved him a lot and looked forward to being with him, but she worried that even that would go wrong. *Dear God,* she prayed, *let everything go right this time.*

CHAPTER 24

Bea stirred the few potatoes, carrots and onions in the pot and sighed. She hadn't got a lot in the cupboard when she'd started the meal, and even less now. Her stomach rumbled. With Percy back home, she had thought things would get a lot easier, but if anything they were worse. The weather hadn't helped. Percy hadn't been able to fish, and he'd made no attempt to find something else to tide them over. What was even worse was that ever since he'd come home he'd become more and more morose and bad-tempered.

John was paying two lots of rent now, which certainly kept the wolf from the door, but with another hungry man in the house and two rooms to heat, it was getting harder to manage the housekeeping. Although she was working now, Ruby hadn't had a job for the whole of January. She brought home even less now than she did from Warnes. May needed new shoes, which had eaten into Bea's reserves, small as they were, and although during the day she survived at home on her own with no fire at all, the coal-hole was almost empty.

Of course she knew she was luckier than some. Poor Linton's chest was getting worse every week. She could only manage to walk to Heene on a Wednesday, and even that was a struggle, but Mabel had been relieved to hear that her husband's nephew was still alive and kicking. In the north of the country the Depression meant that families were literally starving. Bea kept a shilling on the mantelpiece, in case anyone needed the doctor, but she didn't tell the family how ill she herself was feeling. Dizzy and often light-headed or with a thumping headache, she was beginning to find everything a real effort. She was feeling down all the time, and even though she tried to shake it off, she knew it was getting worse. On top of that, she had lost weight. Her clothes hung on her now, although an extra jumper to keep the biting cold at bay hid it from the family. The one thing that kept her going was the thought of seeing Rex later in the year.

Life was difficult in other ways too. May was always complaining. Nelson had spoiled her rotten, giving her everything she asked for, and it was difficult for the child to adjust. 'Why can't I have a new book?' 'Why can't I go to the party?' 'Elsie Thomas has ribbons in her hair, so why can't I?' The questions went on and on, wearing Bea out with the continuous whining that accompanied them.

She tasted the stew with a spoon and it was delicious. The little bit of scrag end of mutton that she'd got from the butcher made all the difference. With a hunk of bread to pad it out, it would at least be a nourishing meal for John and the family. Ruby got paid today, so they could eat better tomorrow.

She heard Percy come in and called out a greeting. He took off his boots in the scullery and came into the kitchen.

'Not very warm in here,' he remarked. 'Has the fire gone out?'

'No,' said Bea, anxious that he might put more coal on the fire. 'It's taking a while to get going, that's all. How did you get on today?'

'For God's sake, Mother,' he snapped. 'Don't start nagging the minute I get in the door.'

'I wasn't,' Bea protested innocently. 'I only asked–'

'Well, don't!' Percy shouted.

Bea turned her back and, biting back her tears, stirred the pot again.

'Aren't you dishing up now?' Percy asked.

'We have to wait for John.'

'Why?' Percy demanded. 'If he can't be here on time, why should we wait? I want to go out to-night, Mother. Serve mine now.'

The door opened and Ruby called, 'Hello, Mum.' She came into the room, taking her scarf from around her neck. 'Oooh, not very warm in here.'

'That's what I said,' said Percy, shaking out his paper.

Bea said nothing. Ruby kissed her mother's cheek and handed over her unopened wage packet. 'Where's May?'

'Gone over to Elsie's place,' said Bea. 'I'm just about to fetch her. There's a letter for you on the mantelpiece.'

'Want me to go and fetch May, Mum?' asked Ruby cheerfully. 'I've still got my coat on.'

'No, love,' said Bea. 'I need to have a word with Elsie's mother. Lay the table, will you?'

Ruby took off her coat and hung it up. She took

her letter down from the mantelpiece and smiled. It was from Jim. She would read it later. Taking the cutlery from the drawer, she said, 'How's the fishing?'

'Don't you start,' Percy growled.

The two women glanced at each other with a knowing look, then carried on with what they were doing. Bea dished up a portion of stew for Ruby and Percy. Pushing the loaf of bread in front of them, she said, 'Eat up. Save enough for John and May. I shan't be long.'

'What about you?' Ruby frowned.

'I had mine earlier,' said Bea, putting on her coat. 'Won't be long.'

Percy took his plate to the pot of stew. 'Go easy on that,' said Ruby.

'There's not enough on my plate to feed a flea,' said Percy. 'And if I want to find a piece of meat, I'll have to send in the dogs.'

'Percy, please don't take too much,' Ruby insisted. 'I don't think Mother has had anything.'

He threw himself sulkily back in his seat. 'It's not my fault the weather's too bad to fish.'

'Times are hard,' she observed.

'Times are hard, times are hard,' he mimicked. 'What do you expect, with this bloody government? The whole country needs a damned good shaking.'

Ruby was shocked. 'What's the matter with you? You're like a bear with a sore head.'

'This is not what I planned for my life,' he said angrily.

'That's funny,' said Ruby. 'I feel exactly the same way. The only difference between you and me is that, being a man, you can make changes. Being a woman, I can't.'

'I've had my offers,' said Percy. 'They want me to work in the BUF HQ.'

'Why don't you then?' Ruby challenged.

He stared at her in shocked silence, a piece of torn bread still hanging from his mouth. He'd never before heard Ruby answer back. The door opened behind them and John walked into the kitchen.

'I'm sorry,' said John. 'Am I late?'

'Yes,' Percy mumbled.

'Not at all,' said Ruby, jumping immediately to her feet to get another plate of stew. John sat at the table, with a nod in Percy's direction. 'My mother has gone to fetch May from a friend's house.'

They ate in awkward silence.

'It is good,' said John.

'You're welcome,' said Ruby, conscious that there was little left in the pot, and her mother and May were still to come.

'It is good,' John repeated.

The door opened again as Bea and May came in, and May's shrill voice pervaded the room. 'Elsie has got a teddy at one end and she puts her dolly at the other end. It's not fair.'

'Lots of things are not fair,' said Bea patiently. 'Now sit up to the table.'

May hauled herself onto a chair and sat there with a pouty mouth.

'What's up with you?' Percy asked.

'She's cross because Elsie has a new dolly's pram, and she can't have one,' said Bea.

'It's a twin pram,' said May, 'and it's not fair.'

Her mother put a plate of stew, in front of May and smiled at John. 'More stew, John?'

Ruby's heart sank as John held out his plate. She dared not say anything, but if he had more, there would be virtually nothing left for her mother.

'I don't want this,' May scowled.

'Eat up,' said Ruby quietly in her ear. 'There's nothing else. You'll be hungry.'

May pushed the plate away from her so vigorously it tipped up and the contents went all over the tablecloth.

'May!' Ruby scolded firmly, and at the same time there was a loud thud, followed by the sound of a plate smashing onto the stone floor behind her. When Ruby turned round, her mother was on the floor, her white face turned towards the ceiling.

Percy leapt to his feet in shocked surprise. 'Oh my God, Ruby!' he cried. 'Is she dead?'

CHAPTER 25

Cousin Lily lay back on the pillow and closed her eyes. By her side Albert snored gently. This wasn't how she'd imagined it would be. There was no conversation between them now. She and Albert had been together for almost four months, and it had been a few weeks since she'd given herself to him for the first time. Back then he had been the perfect lover; a little hurried at times, but he'd said romantic things and talked of the day they would marry. She wanted to tell the family of their plans, but Albert wouldn't hear of it.

'I'll lose my job on the paper, and then we'll never get married,' he'd told her. 'I have to remain impartial. If they discover I'm stepping out with a local girl, they'll move me on or get a new reporter.'

'Don't newspaper men get married then?' she'd asked. 'Surely they're not expected to be like priests.'

'Of course not, but I'm still on my way up,' he'd insisted, 'and I have to be seen to be impartial. Please don't ruin everything for me, darling.'

'But I want to be married,' she'd pouted.

'And we will,' he'd said, pulling her closer.

'I'm scared I'm going to end up having a baby,' she'd said.

'You leave all that sort of thing to me,' he'd laughed, as he mounted her again. 'You're not in the pudding club yet, are you?'

She recalled how tender he had been in the beginning. He was different now; more irritated by her protests, and he'd begun choosing less desirable places for their lovemaking as well. This room was awful. She'd closed her eyes, because she couldn't bear to look at it. They were in some seedy hotel in the back of beyond, where the landlord wanted some of his money up front and the men in the bar leered at her as Albert took her upstairs. He'd brought no suitcase, so it was obvious why they were there.

She'd tried to say something before they'd made love, but Albert was in too much of a hurry. At one point he'd even told her to 'just shut up!' and she'd cried. He'd qualified what he'd said by telling her someone was listening at the door, but she didn't believe him. He was kinder after that, but Lily felt used and dirty.

Her mother had always taught her not to give in to a boy. 'Once they've had their way with you,' she'd cautioned, 'they'll either tell their mates you were easy and you'll get a reputation, or they'll get bored with you and find somebody else. Men never marry the girls they sleep with.' Maybe Mum was right. After four months of seeing Albert there was still no engagement ring on her finger.

And another thing: he kept asking her questions all the time. Had she heard from Percy? Where was he, and when would he be back? He was still asking questions when they both went round to Aunt Bea's with a birthday card for her on February 15th. Now that Percy was back home, was he going to take over where his father had left off? Was he out fishing tonight? Lily and Percy might be cousins, but she didn't know what Percy was doing or thinking every waking moment. The funny thing was that, after asking her all these questions about the family, when she'd told Albert that Aunt Bea had been taken ill and had to get the doctor, he didn't seem that interested. But if he wasn't asking about Percy, he was on about Ruby. Why had she left Warnes? Had she got a new job yet? What was she doing at the hospital? On and on he went, so much so that Lily was beginning to wonder if this was an obsession.

'Sometimes I think you're more interested in Ruby than in me,' she'd complained, but then

Albert would kiss her and run his hand up the inside of her thigh and into her scanties, and she'd forget everything else. She sighed and turned her head to look at him. If only their relationship was heading somewhere. He opened his eyes and smiled. He moved closer. 'One more time,' he whispered in her ear, 'and then we must go.'

Lily was busting for the toilet. 'I have to go to the bathroom first,' she said.

Albert rolled back and put his hand under his head with a sigh. Naked, Lily sat on the edge of the bed and reached for her coat. 'You'd better do that up,' he said sharply. 'You don't want any-one in the corridor seeing you like that.'

She stood up and buttoned her coat right down, then tied the belt tightly around her waist.

'Hurry up, won't you?' he grinned, his voice softer now.

She padded out of the room and closed the door. Albert glanced at the bedside table and the clock. He'd have to be quick, if they were going to do it again, and he was dismayed to realize that he was already going off the boil. Lily's locket was draped over the clock face and he pulled it towards him, to get a better look. It was silver but plain, and now that he looked at it more closely, he could see that the stone on the right side of the heart shape was a diamond. Who would give someone like Lily such a quality piece? It was hallmarked too: 1916. It had a seam around the edge but, no matter how hard he tried, he couldn't open the locket. There had to be a secret catch somewhere, but the thing was so smooth and he couldn't find anything. He was about to give up when he spotted it on the loop that joined the locket to the chain. He pressed it, but nothing happened. It was only when he slid the catch that the locket sprung open. He gaped, unable to believe what he was seeing. *Lily? It beggared belief. How could she have deceived him so well?* Albert stared open-mouthed for several seconds, before snapping it shut again. He was both astounded and horrified. *The bitch! The conniving little bitch.*

By the time she came back into the room he was almost fully dressed.

'Are we going already?'

He didn't speak, but his cold stare frightened her.

'What's wrong?'

'You know exactly what's wrong,' he said harshly. 'Now get dressed.'

She obeyed him, but by the time she was ready, Lily was in tears. 'What have I done? Please tell me, Albert. Why are you so angry with me? I don't understand.'

'Shut up. Shut up,' he snarled as he hustled her out of the room.

The men in the bar leered as they hurried through. Lily waited miserably by the door as Albert paid the barman.

'You come back later, darlin',' shouted one of the customers, 'and I'll give you a better time than he obviously did.'

Albert manhandled her through the door to the sound of their humiliating laughter.

Percy waited on the beach until someone came. This was a big step, but he had no choice. The weather was a lot better than it had been for ages, and the fishermen would be out on the water tonight. *Sod's bloody law,* he thought bitterly. Silas Reed was the first to come across the pebbles with his son, William, and Toby Granger.

'Hey up, Percy,' he called cheerfully. 'You sailing with the tide too?'

Percy shook his head. 'When I first came back here,' he said, 'you made me an offer on the boat, the tackle and the locker. Does that still stand?'

'Might do,' said Silas, pulling a face, 'but it's not in such good nick now, lad. It's nearly six months since Nelson went.'

'How much are you offering?' asked Percy.

Silas named his price – thirty pounds down on what he'd offered before.

'Done!' said Percy, almost before the breath had left his body. He shot out his hand and the old man shook it firmly as he spat on the stones.

Percy walked away, calling over his shoulder, 'I'll come round tomorrow for the money.'

'Well, I'll be blowed,' said Silas. 'That was easy.'

'You'd better check that boat first, Father,' chuckled William. 'Make sure he ain't put an 'ole in the bottom.'

Ruby's patient sat next to the fire, with a stone hot-water bottle covered by a blanket under her feet and a thick shawl around her shoulders. Ruby tried to spoon some broth into her mouth.

'I'm not a child,' said Bea, taking the spoon from her.

'But you can't be trusted, either, can you, Mother?' said Ruby. 'You kept telling us you'd eaten, but you hadn't.'

'I didn't want you to worry,' said Bea stubbornly.

'Oh, Mum,' said Ruby, taking her mother's hand. 'You gave us such a terrible fright. For one awful minute I thought–'

'Well, I wasn't, was I?' Bea interrupted tetchily.

Everyone in the room had been appalled to see Bea pass out like that. Ruby and Percy had carried her upstairs to her bed, while John had run for Dr Bloom. After a thorough examination, he'd pocketed his shilling and pronounced that there was nothing wrong with Bea that a square meal wouldn't cure.

'However, I advise caution,' he told her stunned family. 'It's obviously been a long time since she's eaten, so her stomach will have shrunk. Give her small meals. Little and often.'

Ruby had never felt so ashamed. What hadn't she noticed? Now that she thought about it, she hadn't seen her mother sit down with them at teatime since Christmas. Bea was always saying she'd just eaten or would have something later. It had made a difference, not having Ruby's wage to put on the table. And her mother had been annoyed when Ruby, to spare her feelings, had announced that she'd left Warnes because she'd wanted a bit of a change.

While Bea sat on one side of the fire sipping her broth, Ruby sat on the other, thinking her dark thoughts.

'What's wrong, Ruby?'

Ruby shrugged. 'Feeling a bit sorry for myself, that's all, Mum. Nothing seems to go right these days.'

'That's life,' said Bea philosophically.

'It was difficult when Father was alive,' said Ruby. 'It's even worse now.'

'We'll get by.'

'Maybe I want more out of life than just getting by,' said Ruby bitterly.

Bea smiled. 'I used to be a dreamer like you.'

'Father was right,' Ruby sighed. 'He always said I had notions above my station.'

'Huh!' said Bea. 'And what did he know?'

They didn't hear the back door open or Percy coming into the scullery. He was taking off his boots and hanging up his coat.

'Why did Father hate me, Mum?'

Bea looked up sharply. 'Don't be silly.'

'Listen, Mum,' said Ruby. 'After what happened to you the other day, the time for pretence is over. Things have to change in this family, and we might as well start by telling each other the truth.'

'I don't know what you mean,' said Bea huffily. 'And while you're flinging brick bats, what about you? You haven't exactly told us the truth, have you?'

Percy stood on the other side of the door with his hand raised, ready to push it open, but somehow he couldn't do it.

'You're right,' said Ruby and, taking a deep breath, she added, 'I didn't leave Warnes because I wanted a change. I was sacked.'

'Sacked!' cried Bea. 'Whatever for?'

'They said – or at least Mrs Fosdyke said – that I was stealing a brooch. But honestly, Mum, I wasn't.'

'If you say you weren't stealing it, then I believe

303

you,' said Bea stoutly.

'The old woman had lost it. I was helping her to find it when her daughter came into the room—'

'Ruby, my darling,' Bea interrupted. 'There's no need to give me all the details. I believe you.'

'Oh, Mum...' said Ruby, her face crumpling. She knelt beside her mother's chair and the two women embraced. Percy watched through the crack in the door and waited. 'Father would have loved to see me in this state,' said Ruby, looking up at her mother. 'He never liked me much, did he?' She paused. 'He was horrible to Percy as well. Why was he like that, Mum? He always spent time with May, but he never seemed to want Percy or me. Why did he treat both of us like dirt?'

At the mention of his name, Percy froze.

Bea began to cry softly.

'Oh, Mum,' said Ruby, 'I'm sorry. I didn't mean to upset you. Please don't cry.'

'It's all my fault,' Bea choked.

'No, Mum,' said Ruby. 'How can it be your fault? You've been the best mother in the world. Nobody could have been better.'

Bea shook her head. 'It is my fault,' she said, fishing up her sleeve for her handkerchief. 'He did it because I made him angry.'

'I don't understand,' said Ruby.

'He couldn't forgive me, you see,' said Bea.

'Forgive you for what?'

The atmosphere in the room was electric. Behind the door Percy held his breath and waited.

'I never was the paragon of virtue that you always think I am,' said Bea. 'I was young and foolish. Oh, Ruby, I was already carrying Percy when

Nelson and I got married. He always made out that I'd trapped him, but it wasn't like that. Then the war came, and he was a changed man. We tried to make it work, but it was impossible, and he never forgave me for having another man's child.'

Her words hit Percy like a slap in the face. A cold rage began to swell in his chest.

Ruby stared at her mother. 'You loved another man?' she said incredulously.

'I still do,' said Bea. 'And Nelson knew it too. God forgive me, I've never stopped loving him.'

The scullery door swung open and banged against the wall. Percy stood in front of them, his face like thunder. 'You never said a worse thing, Mother,' he spat. 'I was another man's child?'

'No, no!' cried Bea. 'You don't understand.'

Ruby jumped to her feet.

'Oh, I understand all right,' said Percy between his teeth. 'All my life I tried to please that bastard, thinking he was my father, but I never could, could I? And now I know why. It was all your bloody fault.'

'No, listen, Son,' said Bea, getting up.

'Well, I'm not stopping here no more,' said Percy. 'From now on, you and Ruby and May are on your own. I wash my hands of the lot of you. I owe you nothing, and I'm not sticking around here wasting my life trying to be something I'm not.'

'Percy...' Bea reached out her arm, but he pushed past her and bounded up the stairs two at a time. May came out of her bedroom crying, because she had been woken up. Ruby hurried upstairs to comfort her. As she settled her sister

305

back in her bed, Ruby could hear Percy moving around in his attic room. He re-emerged a few minutes later with his bags packed.

'Percy, you've got this all wrong,' said Bea, coming to the stairs to meet him. 'Please let me explain.'

'No explanation needed, Mother,' he said haughtily. 'You've said quite enough.'

'But it's not what you think,' she cried after him.

'Too late,' he said, as he reached the front door. He turned the second before he went through it. 'Oh, by the way,' he said, 'don't bother to come looking for me. I don't want to see any of you ever again.'

Then the door slammed and he was gone. Bea gasped and began to cry again.

'Don't worry, Mother,' said Ruby, helping her back into her chair. 'It was only temper. He'll be back in the morning.'

'Oh, Ruby,' said Bea brokenly. 'Do you really think so?'

'Of course,' said Ruby, hoping she sounded a lot more convincing than she felt. 'He'll be fine.'

'I should have told you the truth years ago,' Bea began. 'The trouble was, Nelson forbade me to speak of it. He could be such a cruel man.'

'Are you really saying that Percy was someone else's child?' Ruby asked cautiously.

Bea dabbed her nose with her handkerchief. 'No, no, Ruby. Percy was Nelson's boy,' she nodded. 'He was the reason why we had to get married.'

'You mean you were an unwed mother?' said

Ruby, trying not to sound shocked. Her mother had already admitted she wasn't perfect, but this was quite a revelation; the sort of thing nobody ever talked about.

Bea nodded. 'I was a silly girl with stars in my eyes, and he was so handsome and strong. He filled my head with beautiful words and carried my heart away with him as well.'

'Father?' said Ruby. It was hard to believe that the man who said such heartless things could ever have said anything beautiful.

'He was a bit of a poet back then,' said Bea. 'When we first got together, he wrote me love poems.' She smiled wanly. 'I've still got them. I'll show you sometime.'

'I don't remember him doing anything nice until May came along,' Ruby said bitterly. 'He always treated you badly, he never stopped shouting at Percy and he hated me.'

'He wasn't always like that, Ruby,' said Bea. 'The man who came back from the war wasn't the same man who had gone away. The war changed him. In fact, I think something dreadful happened out there. Whatever it was, he could never talk about it.'

'But if Percy was his son,' said Ruby, 'why did Father treat him so badly?'

'Nelson had no intention of marrying me,' said Bea. 'When I told him I was having a baby, he denied the baby was his, and told me it was only meant to be a bit of fun. When our families found out, his parents and my parents got together and they made us get married.'

'Oh, Mum,' said Ruby, kneeling in front of her

and putting her arms around Bea. 'I'm so sorry.'

'I tried to make him happy, Ruby, really I did,' Bea choked. 'But he said Percy had trapped him into something he didn't want, and that's why he took it out on the boy.'

They fell silent, each with their own thoughts, until Ruby suddenly knelt up. 'But I don't understand. You said you had another man's child.'

Bea held her gaze. 'Your father had been injured at Ypres,' she said, pronouncing the word 'Wipers', as they had done at the beginning of the war, before the men came back and explained the correct way of saying it. 'He was sent back home to recuperate and I went to see him.'

Ruby's legs were becoming numb, so she had to get up from the floor and sit in the chair opposite. 'Do you want something to drink while I'm up, Mum?'

Bea shook her head, pulled the cushion away and pushed herself back in the chair.

Ruby said, 'Go on.'

At first her mother hung her head and screwed her handkerchief around her fingers. 'That's when I met him,' she said quietly.

Ruby held her breath, but then her mother's head came back up and she looked Ruby in the eye.

'Rex Quinn. Your father.'

CHAPTER 26

Percy waited nervously in the foyer of the BUF area HQ. People were bustling in and out of the front door, and up and down the staircase facing the road. Barney was a long time coming and Percy was uncomfortable being left with his own thoughts. The white-hot anger he'd felt the night before when he'd walked out of the house had cooled a little, but as he rehearsed over and over again in his head what his mother had told him, it didn't take much to revive it. All those years he'd been struggling to please Nelson, and wondering what he could do to gain his father's respect, when all the time he was... He couldn't even bear to think the word.

It should have made him feel better, knowing that he wasn't Nelson's son. He'd never liked the man, but strangely enough the revelation that he was someone else's child had had exactly the opposite effect. He suddenly felt out of kilter, the odd man out, alone... And he didn't like it. He was angry with his mother for keeping it from him. She should never have kept a thing like that secret. He was also angry because the woman he'd idolized as the perfect mother had given herself to someone before she was married. She was no more than a common tart. He leapt to his feet and stared sightlessly out of the window. How many others had there been? Had she stayed faithful to Nelson?

Everything started going round and round his head again, until it felt fit to burst.

'Percy!' Barney's welcoming voice brought him back to the here and now.

Percy turned on his heel and smiled at his old pal, who was coming down the stairs with a clipboard tucked under his arm. He looked so smart in his BUF uniform. Every square inch of him was black: black shirt, black jodhpurs, shiny black calf-length boots, and his thick, dark hair slicked down on his head.

As he came towards him, Barney held out his right hand. 'Good to see you again. Have you thought about what I said?'

'That's why I'm here,' said Percy, taking his hand.

'Good news, I hope,' replied Barney, shaking his hand vigorously.

'Yes,' said Percy, 'but with one stipulation.'

'Oh?' Barney gave him a quizzical look. He wasn't used to people making demands, especially not this early on in the proceedings.

'I'll be a recruiting officer,' said Percy, 'but I want to do it as far away from Worthing as possible.'

'Oh, dear,' said Barney. 'Woman trouble?'

'Something like that,' said Percy, 'but it's all sorted now.'

Barney's face broke into a wide smile. 'Good man,' he said, giving Percy a hearty slap across the back.

'Ruby,' said Bea that morning, 'I know it's your day off, but would you do something for me?'

310

'What is it, Mum?'

Ruby had just taken May to her school in Sussex Road and was planning to do some things around the house to help out. Her mother was still weak, but refused to rest altogether. She was sitting in the Windsor chair with arms, which Nelson had always used, knitting a pullover for Percy. Having blanked out the fact that he had said he wasn't coming back, Bea had decided it would be cold at night on the boat and he didn't have many warm things.

'I promised Mabel I'd keep going over to Heene to see her nephew,' said Bea. 'She's been really worried about him, but being laid up like this, I can't really go.'

Ruby leaned over and kissed her mother's cheek. They had always been close, but Bea's revelation the night before had made their relationship even closer and they'd talked late into the night. When her mother had first told Ruby that she wasn't Nelson's child, but that her father was called Rex Quinn, Ruby had been completely stunned and rendered absolutely speechless. It was some time before she'd spoken.

'Nelson wasn't my father?' she repeated.

Bea shook her head.

Ruby closed her eyes, took a deep breath and let it out slowly. 'Oh.'

'Ruby?' her mother said anxiously. 'I'm so sorry. I should have told you before. I've let you down. I've let you down badly.'

'Oh no, Mum,' cried Ruby. 'You haven't let anyone down. It's such a relief.'

Bea frowned. 'You're not angry?'

311

Ruby shook her head. 'Did Nelson know I wasn't his?'

Bea nodded.

'That explains a lot,' said Ruby.

'I'm sorry,' Bea repeated.

Ruby got up from her chair and put her arms around her mother again. They were both crying as they hugged each other.

'I thought you'd be really angry,' said Bea.

'I knew he hated me,' said Ruby, stepping back to wipe her eyes, 'and now I know why. After the way he treated us all, why did you stay with him, Mum?'

'I had to come back, because I couldn't bear to lose Percy,' she said brokenly. 'He may not have liked the boy, but Nelson would never have let me take him with me. He said that if I left home, he'd take Percy to the workhouse.'

The clock on the mantelpiece struck midnight.

'Oh, Mother...'

'As soon as you were born,' Bea went on, 'he punished me. He told me I'd trapped him with one child and committed adultery to have another, and the hatred got stronger and stronger as the years went on.'

'But what about my father?' Ruby asked. 'Why didn't he come for you?'

'I couldn't let him,' said Bea. 'According to the law, Nelson was father to both you and Percy. When you were born, to protect you, I let Nelson put his name on the birth certificate. If Rex had come back for me, Nelson would never have allowed me to take you with me.'

'Even though I wasn't his child?'

312

'He would have sent you to the workhouse.'

Ruby shivered. 'Things must have improved when you had May?'

'He adored May,' Bea sighed, 'and now that I had three children, Nelson had made sure that I stayed with him for good. I never could have supported you all alone.'

'And Rex?'

Her mother's eyes filled with tears again. 'I had to send him away. Oh, Ruby, it was the hardest thing I ever did. I had to, but I couldn't abandon you and Percy to that man.'

'Why would someone enjoy being so cruel?' said Ruby. 'This was never a happy home. Oh, I know you did your best, Mum, but we were all on tenterhooks, weren't we?'

'During the war something began to eat away Nelson's very soul,' Bea said. 'I was in the wrong, of course, but it wasn't *just* what I did to him. There was something else, I'm sure of it.' She looked up at Ruby and smiled. 'You are so like your father. When I look at you, I see his smile and,' she touched Ruby's face, 'his lovely dark hair. You'd like him, Ruby. He's a wonderful man.'

Ruby's head was reeling. Nelson wasn't her father. What a relief – how wonderful. How absolutely bloody wonderful!

'Can I ask you something else?' she said. 'Would you be able to tell me about my real father, or is that too painful?'

Bea caressed her daughter's cheek. 'I'd love to talk about him.' She smiled wistfully. 'He was so kind and gentle. Good-looking too.'

'Did he die in the war?'

313

'Oh no,' said Bea. 'He's still alive.'

Ruby frowned. 'How do you know?'

'Because he came to Worthing to see us,' said Bea, stifling a huge yawn. 'Can we talk about it a bit later, Ruby? It's gone midnight and I'm so very tired.'

'He came here?' Ruby gasped.

'Not here,' said her mother, getting up. 'He came to Worthing at around the time of the inquest.'

'Why didn't you tell me?'

'I can't talk about it any more,' said Bea, wobbling on her feet. 'Tomorrow.'

Reluctantly, Ruby had to let it go. Her mother was exhausted and she knew she mustn't push her too much. The questions would have to be asked another time. Alone in her room, she had finally got round to reading Jim's letter. He was coming home. Her eyes filled with tears. What on earth would he think about all this?

Ruby had slept fitfully, waking several times during the night with questions still reverberating around her head. She had wanted to carry on talking to her mother about Rex this morning, but she would do the favour first. 'Of course I'll go and see Linton,' she smiled now.

A couple of hours later Ruby was knocking on Linton's door. His house, on the very edge of old Heene village, had a small front garden and a slightly larger one at the back, where he grew vegetables when his illness allowed. For a living, he made baskets. They were mostly functional ones, but until the Depression bit he'd also had a small following in the big shops, some as far away as Chichester.

Ruby had to knock firmly several times before she saw the curtain in the front room twitch. 'It's me, Uncle Linton,' she called. He wasn't a relation at all, but the old habit she'd been taught as a child – of calling all adults 'Auntie' and 'Uncle' – lingered. 'Ruby Bateman.'

The front door opened a crack and Linton, his face grey with the effort of breathing, looked out.

'What – do – you want?' he said with an effort.

'Mum's not well, and Auntie Mabel is worried about you,' said Ruby. 'Can I come in?'

He stepped back and Ruby walked in. The house was spotless. Some of his canes and almost-finished work stood in a corner of the living room. It was fairly dark inside because he'd kept the curtains drawn. Linton walked back to his chair and flopped down.

'You really don't look well,' said Ruby. 'I think I should get the doctor.'

Surprisingly he didn't argue.

Taking the front-door key with her, Ruby set off. The doctor, when he came, insisted that Linton should go into hospital and then left, promising to telephone from his surgery for an ambulance. Ruby went upstairs to pack a small suitcase with pyjamas and a washbag. When she came back downstairs, Linton looked even worse. She walked over to him and squeezed his hand. 'Is there anything I can get you?' she asked.

He indicated a drawer and, when she opened it, it was full of papers.

'Something in here?' she asked.

He nodded, his breathing rasping and full of

effort. She hadn't a clue what he wanted or where to start, so she pulled the whole drawer out and placed it on his lap. He sorted through the papers and settled on a buff-coloured envelope.

'Shall I open it?'

He shook his head.

'You want to take it with you?'

He shook his head again.

'Shall I give it to Auntie Mabel?'

Linton shook his head for a third time and pointed at her. 'For – you,' he said.

'All right,' said Ruby, guessing it must be his last will and testament. 'I'll look at it when I get home.'

She hardly had time to put the drawer back, and the envelope into her bag, before the ambulance arrived.

Left on her own, Bea put down her knitting and went back upstairs. She still felt dizzy at times, but she didn't feel quite as exhausted as she had done when she was first taken ill. She realized now that she had been an absolute fool to cut down on food by not eating herself. The thought of what might have happened to her was a sobering one. Percy and Ruby could look after themselves, but what about May? Most likely her sister, Vinny, would have offered to take May in. She would have moved in here herself, but the house belonged to the children and, if Vinny moved in, there was no guarantee they'd ever get it back, at least not without a fight. Vinny wasn't a wicked person, far from it, but faced with the prospect of having to go back to the two rooms that she and Lily lived in or

316

being in this house, Bea knew that Vinny would fight tooth and nail to stay.

Percy hadn't been back since he'd stormed out of the house, but Bea was confident that, once he'd cooled down, he would be back. She sighed. If only Rex was here. He would know what to do.

Upstairs in her bedroom, Bea pulled out her, undies drawer and tipped it upside down on the bed. It wasn't her underwear she was looking for; instead, fastened to the underside of the drawer, were some letters. The gummed strip holding them in place was yellow with age and was beginning to lose its stickiness. The letters had been there since 1917. The only contact she'd had with them was when she ran her fingers longingly under the drawer. She had dared not get them out, in case Nelson caught her reading them, but it had given her a satisfying thrill to know that she still had a secret. She knew them off by heart anyway. If he had found them, he would have torn them to shreds and called her ugly names; but he wouldn't have exposed her shame, for that would have reflected badly on him.

She thought back to the time when Eve Pickthall had been 'caught in the act', so to speak. Nelson had been the one to reintroduce 'rough music' outside her door. Back in the previous century, if someone in the community had done something very wrong, the locals would gather outside their door with dustbin lids and wooden sticks, and pots and pans and aluminium spoons, and make a loud noise; they would shout obscenities and keep it up for days, or at least until the object of their wrath was forced to leave town. Poor Eve had run down

317

the street, with the mob pursuing her all the way to the railway station. God only knew where she was now; but, unable to face his neighbours for the shame, her husband had jumped off Beachy Head a few weeks later. It was this memory that kept Nelson from exposing his own wife's infidelity.

Bea peeled the gummed tape carefully from the back of her letters. Ruby would want to know all there was to know about her father and, for the first time in years, she would be able to talk about the only man she had ever truly loved. She kissed the dear writing on the envelope and pulled out the first letter.

It was more formal than the others, because it informed her that her husband was in the hospital at Graylingwell near Chichester. At first she had panicked, for Graylingwell was known as the local asylum. Had the war driven her husband mad? The letter went on to say that Graylingwell was now a military hospital, and Nelson had sustained a serious injury to his side. He would need to stay there for some time, but she was welcome to visit him. There followed the visiting times, and in a footnote she read: *Cpl Bateman has carried out his duties to his regiment and the country with fortitude.* It was signed: *Dr Quinn, Capt.* That note had been added by hand, and they were the first words Rex ever wrote to her.

She would tell Ruby that at the time it had meant little. All that mattered was that her husband lay gravely ill in hospital and, according to the visiting hours, the only time she could go and see him was on Sunday afternoon. She had journeyed to Chichester the next Sunday, leaving little Percy with her mother. She had been filled with fear and dread, wondering what Nelson would be like. He had been bad-tempered with her when he was well, so what would he be like now that he was in pain and badly hurt? What sort of a future did they have? She was only twenty-five; would she have to nurse an invalid for the rest of her life, as well as look after a little baby?

The visit was everything she'd feared, and she'd left the ward battling her own tears. Dr Quinn had met her in the grounds and, may God forgive her, the moment their eyes met, something was kindled inside her. After that, every glance up at him only fanned it into flame. She had fallen madly, hopelessly in love the second she set eyes on him.

Afterwards she couldn't remember a single word he'd said – something about giving Nelson time and that, as his doctor, he could assure her that Nelson would get well. On the train back home all she could think about was Dr Quinn's kind face, his deep-brown eyes, the way his hair curled softly at the sides and how much she'd wanted to kiss him.

'Mum?' The sound of Ruby calling brought her back to the here and now.

'I'm just coming down,' she said. 'Put the kettle on, will you?'

She heard her lovely daughter – *their* lovely daughter – pouring water into the kettle and smiled. May would be coming back from school before long, but as soon as she and Ruby had some time together, she would tell her everything.

Ruby had the right to know about her father. Kissing the envelopes once more, Bea placed them carefully inside the drawer, this time on the top.

CHAPTER 27

Jim was back in town. Having been to Ruby's home to look for her, he was waiting outside as she left the hospital. Her heart leapt as she recognized his tall, lean frame slouching against the wall. He pushed against his shoulder to stand up straight and walked briskly towards her.

'Darling,' he said, taking her into his arms.

She went to him readily and, when he kissed her, all the old feelings came flooding back. As his time away had lengthened from two weeks to almost two months, she worried that her ardour had cooled. She still thought of him all the time, but as the weeks slipped by she missed him a lot less than she had done in the beginning. She supposed it was because there was so much going on in her life: her new job, her mother's illness, Percy taking off like that, and now the revelation about her father. There was so much to think about. She and her mother had finally spent a couple of evenings talking about Rex, and he sounded such a nice man that she couldn't wait to meet him.

Jim took her into the saloon of The Swan and ordered a milk stout for her and a pint of bitter for himself. They sat in a corner, leaning towards each other, oblivious of everyone else. Ruby had already told him some of her news in her letters. Of course he knew that she'd found a new job, and he was glad to hear she was doing well. He knew Bea had been ill, but he didn't know about Percy leaving in a huff, and he certainly didn't know about Rex. When Jim asked her how things were, Ruby decided that it was neither the time nor the place to talk about her mother's private life and skirted round the subject.

Jim listened politely, but it was obvious he wanted to talk about what had been happening in his own life. He was excited.

'As you know,' he began, when she asked him what he'd been doing, 'I had an old Leica camera, which was what I used for the "Beauty and the Beast" photo. It's not bad and, although it's at least eight years old, it can still give a pretty good picture.'

Ruby nodded and smiled. He carried on talking about cameras and the finer points of photography as if she understood.

'I would have carried on using that,' said Jim, his bright eyes dancing, 'but you'll never guess what Mr Kendrick did? He only gave me a 1932 Contax camera.'

'How wonderful,' said Ruby.

'I should say so,' said Jim enthusiastically. 'It's terrific. It's got a vertical eleven-blade metal focal shutter and...' he paused for effect, 'a bayonet mount, so that I can attach other lenses if I need them, and...' his voice had gone up in volume, 'a detachable back, so that I can change the film!'

Ruby looked suitably impressed. 'It sounds

very up to date.' It was good to see him so happy.

'There couldn't be a better camera – I'm sure of it,' he said, sipping his pint.

'How come you stayed so much longer?' said Ruby. 'I thought you said the prize was to spend a week with Thomas Kendrick.'

'It was,' said Jim, relaxing into his chair, 'but we got on so well. He not only paid me a small wage, but also said I was the son he'd never had, which as you can imagine was music to my ears. Oh, Ruby, when he persuaded Mr Hayward to let me stay on, he taught me so much. With everything he showed me, that man has given me the opportunity to really make something of my life. I promise that you and I will have a much better standard of living than I could ever have imagined.' He took a gulp of his beer. 'Has Percy gone back to fishing?'

Jim's face was serious as she told him about Bea collapsing and Percy leaving again.

'Why on earth would he do that?' he gasped. Ruby was about to dismiss it with a shrug of her shoulder, but Jim caught her hands in his. 'No more secrets, remember?'

So she told him. But not everything. Not about Rex.

'Have you been to the locker, to see if he's camping out?' Jim asked.

'I never thought of that,' cried Ruby. 'Of course! He's bound to be there, isn't he? Oh, Jim, can we walk there now? I just need to know that he's all right.'

Jim finished his pint quickly. 'Come on then, darling.'

It was unusual for Vinny to call in unannounced, especially in the early evening. Bea and Vinny were on good terms, but neither sister made a show of it. Bea supposed it was because their mother had been the same. She was rather buttoned-up, preferring to show her love for her daughters by what she did for them, rather than with hugs and kisses. Bea and Vinny were content to see each other at Christmas and Easter, and a couple of times in the warmer months, so it was a bit of a surprise when Bea opened the door and saw her sister on the doorstep.

'Ruby told me you hadn't been well,' she announced as she walked in, uninvited. 'Looking at you, I can't say I'm surprised. You're as thin as a rake.'

Bea smiled. 'Must be getting to be like you then,' she quipped.

Vinny harrumphed and took off her hat and coat. 'So what's wrong with you then?'

'Shall I make us a cup of tea?' Bea suggested.

'No, you sit down,' said Vinny. 'I'll do that.'

Bea knew better than to argue. She sat down again and watched as Vinny got everything ready.

Her sister eyed her as she put the teapot on the table. 'Are you sure you're eating properly?'

'I wasn't,' Bea admitted candidly, 'but I am now.'

'Things difficult?'

'They are a bit.'

'Your Ruby working?'

'She's at the hospital,' said Bea, 'but she gets quite a bit less than she did at Warnes, and that wasn't that good.'

'What's she doing?'

'She's a ward cleaner.'

'Sounds like you're all in a bit of a pickle.' A teacup was pushed in front of Bea. 'She's a good organizer, your Ruby,' said Vinny, sitting down with her own cup and saucer held high on her chest. 'I don't know why you don't persuade her to get a job where she can use her talents.'

'Perhaps you're right,' said Bea.

'I heard Percy was back.'

'He's gone again,' said Bea.

Vinny harrumphed again. 'That boy wants a good talking to,' she said. 'What the devil is the matter with him?'

Bea sipped some more tea and said nothing. Vinny had always been the bossy one, and it was no use trying to change her mind once she'd decided on something. Besides, Bea was too tired to argue any more. Yes, they were in a pickle. Yes, their reserves – meagre as they had always been – were almost exhausted, but she'd worn herself to a frazzle worrying about it and she couldn't do it any more.

'That lodger of yours still paying up?'

Bea nodded.

'Well, that's one good thing, I suppose. If Percy's gone off again, what about the boat and the locker? Can't you sell them ... or rent them out?'

Bea looked up sharply. She hadn't thought of that. How silly of her! That was the obvious thing to do. Renting them would be the best option and would bring in a steady income.

'You've only been in the house five minutes,' she smiled. 'Trust you to come up with the answer to a prayer.'

Vinny lifted her skirt and parted her legs, so that they would be warmed by the fire. 'I'm in a bit of a pickle too,' she said.

'Oh?' Bea was surprised that her sister was confiding in her. Usually Vinny was far too independent to share her own troubles, but now that she looked at her, Bea could see that she was really worried about something. 'Can I do anything to help?'

Vinny leaned back in her chair and stared into the fire. 'I'm worried sick about Lily,' she said.

Bea was tempted to begin asking questions, but something told her to be quiet and listen.

'I think she's been sleeping with that Albert Longman,' said Vinny. 'She denies it, of course, but I'm sure she's doing it.'

'Will he marry her?' asked Bea. She, of all people, should be the last person to throw stones. After all, hadn't she done the same thing herself, with Nelson?

Vinny shook her head. 'He isn't in love with her,' she said. 'I've seen the way he looks at her, and that's not love. But the silly girl won't have it any other way. Oh, Bea, what am I going to do? At best she'll get a bad reputation; and at worst, if she ends up having a baby, I can't give up work to look after it, and she'll be ruined altogether.'

Had anyone else confided in her in this way, Bea would have put an arm round them, but she knew her sister was not a touchy-feely person. Instead she got up and poured them both another cup of tea. 'Confront him,' she said.

Vinny looked up at her with a shocked expression.

'Find a time when Lily isn't there and confront him,' Bea repeated. 'If his intentions are honourable, he'll ask Lily to marry him; and if not, he'll run faster than a fox being chased by the hounds.'

'What if she finds out?'

'Who's going to tell her?' said Bea. 'I won't, and neither will you. He's not likely to admit to anyone that he's been seen off by a woman. Better a few angry tears now than a life ruined forever.'

Vinny nodded and sighed. 'You're right,' she said. They sat in companionable silence for a while until Vinny said, 'Well, that's you and me sorted.' She rose to her feet. 'Now you get yourself better, Bea, and I'll pop by next week.'

And with that, she was gone.

It was dark by the pier. She wasn't keen to be in such an uninviting place at night, but the desire to hear his voice again was so strong. This was a magic time. She hadn't felt so exhilarated since before he went away. Her heart was fluttering like a silly schoolgirl, her mouth was dry and her hands trembled. Without the lights along the boardwalk to the Southern Pavilion, it was a depressing place. The council had made a small start on the repairs, but in these harsh economic times, other more pressing needs in the town took precedence. Most of the buckled girders had been removed and the acrid smell of burning was long gone, but the blackened remains of the Southern Pavilion still pierced the skyline like the naked bones of a great whale.

He had told her to meet him under the pier. Her feet crunched on the stones as she walked off the Parade. She looked around nervously; nobody else was about. The ice-cream kiosks wouldn't open until Easter and, apart from the public toilets, there was no reason for anyone to be in the area. It was a creepy place. The wind off the sea penetrated between the seams of her clothing like icy fingers searching for warmth. It stung her face and tugged at her collar. Keeping her head down, she pulled her coat tightly round her body and trudged on.

She wandered about for a few minutes, before deciding that she was so cold she would have to go back home. The wind sighed and then she heard something. She leaned against the pier support and closed her eyes. His voice always came when she was still. If only she could stop her teeth chattering.

'You're late.' His reedy voice made her shiver. She knew it was all in her head, but this was the first time he'd been cross with her.

'Sorry,' she whispered anxiously. 'I couldn't get away.'

'Ah, well, you're here now.'

She held her breath, terrified that the moment would pass by. The wind fluffed her hair and she imagined that it was his hand on her face, stroking her skin, brushing her lips. She began to cry softly.

'I need you to do something else for me.'

She put her hand to her head and rocked slightly.

'Is it like the last time?' She blew her nose. 'I didn't like it...'

'Sweetheart...' he said huskily. 'Please – for me?'

And, sinking to the stones, she banged the sides of her head with her own fists.

CHAPTER 28

It took Ruby and Jim quite a while to walk the short distance to the beach and Nelson's locker because Jim kept pulling her into dark doorways to kiss her and tell her how much he'd missed her. Ruby protested, but only mildly. It was wonderful being loved like that, and each time he did it, it fanned her passion even more.

'I don't want to wait too long before we marry,' said Jim. 'I mean to start my own photography business.'

'Where would you get the money for that?' cried Ruby.

'Warwick Studios is closing,' said Jim. 'The Depression is making life difficult and Mr Hayward is retiring, but I've worked out a proposition for him. I would continue to run the business and, in exchange, he would get a percentage of the profits. That way, he keeps his assets, and I can be my own man.'

'Oh, Jim, that sounds amazing. Do you really think he'll agree?'

Jim shrugged. 'Thanks to everything Mr

Kendrick has shown me, I've given it my best shot. We just have to keep our fingers crossed.'

'I shall cross my toes as well,' said Ruby.

They finally arrived at Nelson's locker, but as there was nobody about, she guessed that the fishermen must be on the water. She hadn't a clue when it was high tide, but it looked fairly high right now. The men would have pushed off their boats as soon as the tide turned. There were a few lights out on the water, which only confirmed her worst fears.

'Looks like we've missed them,' she said. 'I'll have to come back tomorrow sometime.'

Jim was examining the locker. 'Ruby, I hate to say this,' he began, 'but it looks as if someone may have already pipped you to the post.'

'What do you mean?'

He was pointing to the name on the locker. Nelson Bateman's name had been painted out, and the name *William Reed* put in its place.

Ruby gasped in horror. 'When did this happen?' She looked around wildly. 'Father's boat has gone too!'

'It looks to me as if Percy has already sold the boat and locker,' said Jim. 'Unless William Reed simply helped himself?'

'He wouldn't do that,' said Ruby. 'I know the Reeds and they're honest people. But Percy had no right to sell that boat. If it belonged to anyone, it belonged to my mother.'

'Let's not think the worst yet,' said Jim. 'He may already have given your mother the money.'

'Yes,' she said, feeling relieved. 'That's what he's done. He's gone back home and told Mother

329

he's sorry and given her the money.' She shivered with the cold.

'Come here and let me warm you,' said Jim, opening his coat.

She snuggled into him and he drew his coat around them both. 'Oh, Ruby,' he sighed. 'I love you so much.'

When they got back to Ruby's home, Percy hadn't returned, so it followed that he hadn't given her mother any money. They didn't say anything, preferring to wait until the next day when Ruby had had the opportunity to question the Reeds. Instead they stood together, holding hands and looking coy, as Ruby told her mother that Jim had asked her to marry him and she had accepted. Bea was thrilled.

'Mum, I won't leave you in the lurch, I promise. But if at all possible, please don't make me wait until I'm twenty-one,' said Ruby. She remembered poor Edith's predicament. 'We are perfectly sure.'

'If you have good prospects and can provide for Ruby,' Bea told Jim, 'then I'll give you my blessing.'

Ruby and Jim glanced anxiously at each other. 'I'll move heaven and earth to be a good provider,' said Jim stoutly.

The next day Bea didn't seem to notice when Ruby went to work earlier than usual. But before going to the hospital, she made a long detour to the beach, where the fishermen were preparing their catch for sale. Once she'd chatted to them, her worst fears were confirmed.

'He sold it to me a couple of days ago,' said

330

Silas. 'I give the boat and locker to my boy. What Percy done with the money, I don't know, lass. 'Tain't none of my business.'

'It's fine, Mr Reed,' Ruby smiled. 'I just wanted to know what was happening, that's all.' She was having a job keeping her voice even.

How could Percy do such a thing? Surely he knew how difficult things were for her mother and May. She waved cheerily and set off for the hospital. Her heart was sinking, but it was no good getting upset about it. What was done was done, and they would just have to manage until May was old enough to go out to work. She could only hope that their run of terrible luck would end soon, but as she walked through the gates she would have given anything to give Percy a good biff on the nose.

Ruby hurried into the hospital. There was a familiar figure just in front of her. What was Mrs Fosdyke doing here? She was carrying a bunch of flowers. Ruby grinned to herself. Whoever she was visiting, the ward sister would be sure to turn her away until proper visiting hours began. Mrs Fosdyke hesitated at the crossroad in the corridors and, as she turned round to get her bearings, Ruby ducked into a doorway. She had no wish to speak to her old supervisor and she couldn't help feeling that Mrs Fosdyke might make trouble for her. As a result, she was a bit late arriving on the ward, but luckily nobody seemed to notice and, once she was working, her angry thoughts soon dissipated.

It was five-thirty and John was sitting on the train from Brighton. He had had a day to remember.

331

He had worked solidly and without a break since coming to Newlands Road and business was good. Of course he charged rock-bottom prices, but he had repaired a good few boots and shoes and had mended someone's Gladstone bag. He was also getting orders for leather-work, mending broken straps on laundry baskets and travelling cases, and such. His close proximity to the railway station worked to his advantage.

Mrs Bateman and her family were kindness itself and he was grateful, but John was lonely. He often thought of his beautiful wife Griselda, his sister-in-law Rachel, and Reuben, his little boy. He should have been there to protect them, but what could he have done? He had been working in his shop when the Hitler Youth had spotted Griselda, Rachel and the baby. What seemed at first like silly skylarking had quickly turned into something far more serious. Eyewitnesses said it was because one of the men did, or said, something she didn't like that Rachel slapped him across the face. God alone knew what he'd said to her, but his sister-in-law had always been quick-tempered. The young man had been furious, and he and his Hitler Youth friends had chased them all, like frightened rabbits. They had found Griselda's and the baby's bodies a week later. God alone knew what had happened to Rachel.

John had been angry and outspoken – probably too outspoken, because he'd ended up having to flee for his own life as a result. He missed Germany, and he missed Griselda and his little son dreadfully; and he missed his sister-in-law too. He often wondered what had happened to Rachel.

There was nothing left of the old life now. Nothing except the little place mat that his wife had embroidered; and he only had that because, when he was getting ready to run away, he was looking for something to wrap up some jewellery in. The place mat was the first thing he'd laid hands on. The jewellery was all gone; sold to pay his passage to England. Only the pretty mat remained. He also missed his faith, and he missed the Jewish community.

That's why he had decided to take the train to Brighton to give himself a little break. He wandered beside the sea, although, being so early in the year, there were few people about. At lunchtime he sat on the Palace Pier and ate a pie, and, after a short doze on a bench, ventured inland and wandered along King's Road. From there he turned up Middle Street and, to his utter joy, came across a pale-yellow brick building with a rose window. There were six windows on the ground floor and eight on the first floor, all topped with red-and-blue tiles. The heavy wooden door was flanked by pink columns, with fruit and flowers from Israel crowning the tops. What thrilled him most was the inscription over the door, which included the year when the building opened. The English would have written 1875, but the number above the door was 5636 – the date according to the Hebrew calendar. It was at this moment that he realized he had stumbled across a synagogue.

He didn't have long to wait before a fellow Jew came along and John was taken inside. He stood just inside the door, taking in the sights and smells of all that was familiar and precious to him. The synagogue was very ornate. The women's galleries were held up by cast-iron columns, and the paintwork had a marble effect. The whole place shimmered with gold and gilt. Up the marble steps, where the Torah Ark was kept, he could see a heavy brass Menorah. John could feel tears trickling down his cheeks.

They made him very welcome and, when he told them where he lived, someone offered to put him up on Fridays so that he could go to synagogue on Saturdays. Everyone, including John himself, agreed that to travel all the way from Worthing would break the conditions of the Law of Moses; but John, by now sorely tempted to revert to his real name of Isaac, could think of nothing he would like more than to be with his own people on the Sabbath. On the train back home he was a contented man, and the happiest he'd been since coming to England.

The night-nurse had done her rounds. Linton Carver still felt as if he was in a fog, but things were beginning to register at last. His breathing was easier since they'd filled the room with steam and it felt like he was emerging from a tight cocoon.

He'd been aware that young Ruby Bateman had been visiting him for some time. He couldn't talk to her, because it taxed him too much, but he was comforted to have her sitting next to him, sometimes holding his hand. She had come every single day since he'd been here. Tomorrow he would try and communicate with her. Linton liked her. She was a rare beauty, all the more attractive because she was totally unaware of the effect she had on men. He hadn't appreciated a good-looking girl for a long time, but now that his head was a little less muzzy, he wanted to tell her. He wanted to give her fatherly advice. Perhaps now that Nelson wasn't there any more, she'd let him. Nelson never had a good word to say about the girl. Linton couldn't understand why. Now if she was his daughter...

The door opened and someone slipped inside the room. The light was very dim, having been left that way so that he could sleep. Linton didn't like sleep. When he slept, he relived the horrors of war all over again. In his dreams he could smell the mud, the shit, the rotting bits of the bodies of men who had once been his friends; and sometimes he could even smell the bloody gas again. If he wasn't reliving the trenches, he was thinking about that girl in the farmhouse. She didn't deserve to die like that. Every time he thought of her, the shame of what they'd all done overwhelmed him. God would punish him for his part in it. That's why he fought to stay awake all the time. He was doing that now, staring at the cracked ceiling with its single light and plain white shade, and willing himself not to drift off.

A figure moved silently towards the bed and leaned over him. He couldn't see the face because she was wearing a face-mask, but he smelled the cheap perfume. Matron wouldn't like that. He'd heard nurses being told off for lesser crimes, like wearing hairslides or talcum powder. But perfume? He could almost hear Matron hissing, 'Go home and wash, Nurse. This is not a brothel.'

He heard a rattle as she picked up his notes on the clipboard at the end of the bed to look at them. Then she slipped a cool hand under his head, lifting it slightly to remove the pillow underneath. When it had gone, he was lying very flat and it wasn't so easy to breathe. The figure reappeared over his face again, and this time he looked up.

'Goodnight, Linton,' she said harshly. 'It's time for you to sleep.'

He didn't recognize her, but for some reason he suddenly felt very afraid. 'Do – I know – you?'

She shook her head and leaned closer. 'But you remember Victor, don't you?'

Panic rose in his chest. His eyes grew wide. He tried to shout, but his chest felt as if she'd put a boulder on it. He tried to sit up, but she had her hand on his shoulder. He felt the bed dip a little as she pressed the pillow over his face, and then he couldn't breathe at all. As he struggled to free himself, the sounds of battle grew louder and louder in his ears. He could hear men screaming, the relentless pounding of the guns, and Captain Markham barking his orders: 'Over the top, my lads. Over the top.' He clawed the pillow frantically. He knew he was suffocating. His head was banging and the pain in his chest was terrible. Then he heard the girl in the barn sobbing again. She was begging them to stop, but then Nelson said, 'Go on, lad. You know you want to.' His strength was ebbing away. He fought it as long as he could, but it was no use. Gradually the sounds of battle and the sobs of the girl faded as he embraced the welcoming silence.

CHAPTER 29

Ruby was so anxious to tell her mother about the boat that she could hardly wait to get home that night. She burst into the house, making Bea, who was helping May with her reading, jump.

'Sorry, Mum. Do you want me to finish that for May?'

Bea shook her head. 'Your tea is on the plate on the top of the saucepan. I'll take May to bed.'

'Mum,' Ruby began again, when Bea returned about ten minutes later, 'remember we said no more secrets? There's something else I have to tell you.'

'Oh?'

'It's about Percy.'

'If it's about the boat,' said Bea, 'I already know.'

Ruby was startled. 'But how?'

'Silas Reed came to see me,' she replied. 'He told me that you'd been to see him on the beach. He said that when he told you he'd bought the boat and locker, he could tell by your face that it was a surprise.'

'Oh,' said Ruby. She didn't know whether to feel angry or sad. After all, Percy had betrayed their mother most.

'He's a good man, is Silas,' her mother went on. 'He was very upset that Percy has gone off with the money. I told him he was under no obligation, but he wants to give us the occasional fish.'

337

'That's nice of him,' said Ruby.

'And I'm getting stronger every day,' said Bea. 'If I can, I shall get a bit of work myself in the summer.'

Ruby didn't argue. She couldn't imagine Bea getting a job and keeping it; her health was too up and down. But she gave her mother another hug and said encouragingly, 'Perhaps our luck has turned the corner at last,' even though she didn't for one minute believe it herself.

The next day Ruby was about to go in and see Linton and clean his room, but the door was locked.

'Mr Carver was found dead after the night-sister's ward round,' the sister told her. 'I understand he was a friend of yours, and that it was because of you that he was admitted in the first place.'

'Not exactly,' said Ruby, trying to take in what she'd just been told. 'My father...' She faltered, remembering that Nelson wasn't her father at all, but it would take too long to explain all that. 'My father served in the same regiment with him in the Great War. My mother asked me to check up on him, because she was indisposed.'

'The police may want to talk to you,' said the sister.

'The police?' Ruby was shocked. 'Why?'

'Mr Carver wasn't expected to live,' said the sister, 'but it appears that someone couldn't wait. It looks highly likely that he was murdered.'

'Whatever makes you say that?' Ruby gasped.

'His pillow was on the top of the bed and there

338

were signs of a struggle. Somehow the water jug was tipped over.'

Ruby's mouth dropped open. 'But who on earth would want to do away with a nice old man like that?'

'He wasn't that old, Ruby,' said the sister. 'His war injuries may have aged him and, because you're very young, he seemed old. Mr Carver was only thirty-eight. And I agree with you. I can't imagine why someone would want him dead.'

Ruby shook her head in disbelief. How was she going to tell her mother?

'If you know anything that might help the police with their enquiries, I urge you to tell them,' said the sister, bustling away.

Close to tears, Ruby said, 'Yes, Sister.' Poor Linton. Who could have done such a wicked thing and, more importantly, why?

The police, when they finally got round to speaking to her, were thorough, asking their questions in an abrupt and efficient manner. Ruby was utterly truthful and held nothing back.

No, she had no idea why someone would have wanted to harm Linton. No, he had never talked about his war experiences, and the war had been over for sixteen years – surely no one would hold a grudge that long. No, she didn't come back to the ward last night. She had seen Linton in the afternoon, and in the evening she was at home with her mother. Yes, her mother could verify that: Newlands Road, on the corner. Yes, as a matter of fact, John was their lodger. Yes, she had been in Linton's home. She had been there the day he came into hospital. Yes, it was she who had called the doctor. Yes, he lived alone. Well, he seemed to be able to look after himself. The place was very neat and tidy. It was only when his lungs played up that he had difficulty. No, he didn't seem worried about anything. She knew he probably wouldn't get better, but he had perked up a bit over the last few days. Relatives? Only Aunt Mabel. No, she wasn't exactly a real aunt – she just called her 'Aunt'. Mabel Harris. Yes, it was a different surname. Linton was related to her late husband; he was his nephew.

When they'd finished, the policeman asking the questions thanked Ruby for her cooperation. The one taking down notes totally ignored her as they walked off. She felt a little drained by the experience.

'Now that they've finally gone,' said the sister, coming up behind her, 'I want you to clean that room, Ruby. Give it a thorough going-over. I'll get one of the other girls to cover your other duties.'

Ruby wished the sister had said she could take a bit of a break, but with a heavy heart she collected her mop, bucket and cleaning things. First she took the bed linen and stuffed it into a canvas bag on trolley wheels, ready for the laundry; and then she began her systematic cleaning of the room. A couple of times she had the feeling that she was being watched, but apart from a fleeting shadow, there was no one around. She began by the door and worked her way round the room, so that nothing was missed. The walls, skirting boards, a chair, the locker, the overhead lampshade, the area around the light switches, the mattress and the bed itself – all were thoroughly washed down. It was as she turned the mattress that something, which must have been trapped underneath, fell on the floor and rolled under the bed. Ruby pushed the iron bedstead to one side and picked it up. She stared in disbelief. She'd seen one of these before. There was one in the envelope that had contained Nelson's effects. In fact, it was identical. A home-made, imitation lead bullet. Even the inscription on the side was the same: *Victory*.

Ruby arrived back home in a sombre mood.

'Dear, oh dear,' said Bea when she saw her. 'You look as if you've lost a shilling and found a ha'penny.'

Ruby explained what had happened to Linton.

'Murdered!' Bea cried. 'Does Mabel know?'

'I guess so,' said Ruby. 'She's his only relative, so I presume someone's told her.'

'Murdered,' Bea repeated. 'How? Why?'

Ruby told her what the ward sister had said.

'I'd better go round to Mabel's,' said Bea, snatching off her apron. 'The tea is almost ready. Call John when the potatoes are done. I'll eat mine later.'

May was playing outside with some of the other children. Ruby watched her mother leave, then checked the potatoes, before calling John and May for their meal.

An hour later, when Bea came back, Ruby took a plate from the top of a saucepan of boiling water. She put in in front of Bea. 'Careful of the plate, Mum.'

'Where's May?'

'In the scullery, having her wash,' said Ruby.

'John ate and went back into his room.'

John had got into the habit of keeping himself to himself. Bea often invited him to sit by the fire and he sometimes did, but not all that often. Ruby guessed he was still struggling to get over his homesickness and the loss of his wife and child. Tonight he had played a game of Snap with May while Ruby did the clearing up, but when the child was told to get ready for bed, he made his excuses and left.

Bea ate her meal slowly. It wasn't until May was tucked up in bed that the two women had an opportunity to talk. Ruby was hoping to hear more about her natural father, but first they had to talk about Linton.

'How did Aunt Mabel take the news?' asked Ruby as she poured them some tea.

'It wasn't unexpected,' said Bea, 'although she was a bit shocked when the police told her somebody had murdered him.'

'Did she have any idea who might do that?'

'None at all,' said Bea. 'The poor man had a terrible life. He was barely in his twenties when he was gassed. He never had a lady friend, never got married, and he was ill on and off all his life.'

'Mum,' said Ruby, 'I've got something to show you.' She got up from the table and went to her coat, which was hanging on the nail on the back door. When she put the lead bullet on the table in front of her, Bea gasped.

'I found it on the floor when I was cleaning Linton's room,' Ruby explained. 'It's like the one in the brown envelope they gave you when Nelson died, isn't it?'

Bea went to the dresser and opened the drawer. Coming back to the table, she tipped the contents of the brown envelope onto the table. The grey bullet rolled towards its mate. They compared the two of them.

'They both look hand-made,' said Ruby, 'and they are almost identical. What can it mean?'

Bea shook her head. 'Perhaps it's something to do with the war?'

'It seems a bit odd that Linton had it in his hospital room,' said Ruby. 'I packed his bag to go to hospital, and he certainly didn't have it when he left home.'

'Someone could have brought it in.'

'As far as I know,' said Ruby, 'I was his only visitor.'

Bea looked up. 'So, what are you saying?'

'I think the murderer gave it to him.'

Bea picked up one of the bullets and held it in the palm of her hand. The silence between them grew, until it was punctuated only by the slow tick-tock of the clock on the mantelpiece. They heard it whirring, and then came the dulcet chimes for nine o'clock.

'If the murderer left this bullet for Linton,' said Bea slowly, 'and Nelson had one in his pocket...' She looked up at her daughter.

Ruby finished the sentence for her. 'Then Nelson was murdered too.'

'I've seen another one,' said Bea. 'Mabel's got one. She found it in Jack's pocket after he died.'

'Was Jack in the war?' asked Ruby.

Bea nodded. 'He was a mechanic. He was stationed with Linton for a bit. I remember Mabel

343

telling me that he used to keep a weather eye on Linton.'

Ruby chewed the inside of her bottom lip. 'How did Uncle Jack die?'

'He didn't die in the war,' said Bea. 'He was run over by a truck on the Littlehampton Road, when you were a little girl.'

'Then do you think...?' Ruby began.

They both held their breath, hardly able to comprehend where this conversation was going.

'You'll have to go to the police,' said Bea.

Ruby shook her head. 'It's all a bit vague, though, Mum. I mean, what proof have we got, apart from these funny bullets?'

'You must admit it's a bit odd,' Bea insisted.

Ruby nodded and, picking up one of the bullets, studied it more carefully. 'What's going to happen to Linton now? Is Aunt Mabel able to bury him?'

'They're hoping to arrange the funeral sometime next week,' said Bea. 'I don't suppose he left a will, so everything will go to Mabel.'

It was then that Ruby remembered the envelope Linton had given her the day he went into hospital. 'I think I've got his will,' she said, giving her mother a brief explanation.

She had propped the envelope against the mirror in her bedroom and had totally forgotten it. She hurried upstairs to get it now. It had slipped down the back and fallen on the floor. Sitting back down at the kitchen table again, she opened it and took out a flimsy sheet of paper. The lettering was typed and was clearly done by an inexperienced typist. There were blotches and spelling mistakes all over the place. As Ruby read it aloud, she and Bea listened with mounting horror.

The streets of London were a far cry from the relative peace and quiet of Worthing. Percy loved it. There was always something to do and it seemed that London never slept.

The night before he began his new posting, Percy made a decision to throw himself even more fervently into the cause. He told himself he wouldn't care about the poverty; he would forgo the pictures and the pub with a happy heart because, from now on, he had a cause to fight for and a driving force in his life. He would make the BUF his whole reason for existence. It would be better than the choicest meal to him – its hold on him stronger than any family bond – and he would be happy to sacrifice the chance to have a sweetheart or a wife if that interfered with his purpose. He climbed into his bed with a warm glow. He'd show them. One day he would march down the streets of Worthing carrying the BUF flag, and every head would turn in his direction. They'd say, 'There's a man to be proud of.' He took in a breath and let his chest swell. Right there and then he was in deadly earnest and, if necessary, he would be willing to die for his ideals.

He had been plunged in at the deep end when he'd arrived in the East End, but he mastered quickly whatever he was asked to do. If he stood on a soapbox at the corner of the street market, he had no trouble at all in gathering a crowd of eager bystanders. The working-class man felt downtrodden and neglected, feelings with which Percy was well acquainted. Successive governments had talked of disarmament and had put forward plans for growth, but it hadn't filtered down to the ordinary man in the street. That man didn't care for world politics; all he wanted was decent housing, and food on the table. Most of all, he wanted a job.

As part of his new role Percy had to check that the new recruits who had pledged to give five nights' active service to sell the patriotic workers' newspaper, *The Blackshirt*, fulfilled their commitment. He also helped with some of the other organizational jobs. It was he who found some old furniture vans and had them converted, so that they could move groups of stewards to the different venues quickly and cheaply. Mosley himself was making upwards of 150 speeches a year, so finding a way of getting supporters to attend the meetings as unpaid stewards was no mean feat.

To begin with, Percy basked in the euphoria of it all. Where else would a dustman's son rub shoulders with the son of a duke, or a rich playboy use the same washroom as a plumber? But, as he became more familiar with the inner workings of the movement, another side began to emerge.

The BUF had acquired the nickname 'the Biff Boys', and there were times when Percy wasn't surprised. He recalled one meeting when the crowds sang the national anthem and a man, standing just in front of him, bent down to pick up his small child. Having put up his hands several times to be picked up, the little boy suddenly changed his mind and sat down on the floor to play with his toy train. As the strains of the music faded, two stewards marched towards the man and began to eject him from the meeting.

'What have I done?' the hapless man cried.

'Disrespect to the king,' was the angry reply and, with his little boy following behind crying bitterly, the man was hauled out of the meeting.

Such dictatorial behaviour seemed totally unreasonable to Percy, as did the segregation of party workers. He was among the leadership, but before long he discovered there were certain places where he wasn't welcome – not because of his lack of training, but because of his class. The officers' club, for instance, was the domain of the public-school members, and men like Percy were banned. For a movement that prided itself on equality, some members, it seemed, were more equal than others.

'We must set the example,' Mosley exhorted them, one evening back at HQ. The applause and table-banging thundered around the room. Percy sat smugly nodding his head until his leader said, 'I picture family life, with a man master of his own home, caring for his wife and children, and enabling his aged parents to live out their last days with dignity. This should be the sole aim of every member of the party.'

Percy squirmed in his seat. That wasn't a picture of *his* family life. He'd left home in a rage. He'd excused it to himself by saying that he was confused and had felt betrayed. Every memory he had of trying to please his father – from the pictures he'd drawn in his first class at school, to his joy at catching a huge cod that realized nearly ten pounds when it was sold – made him even angrier. The old man had said nothing. As a little boy, Percy had lain awake for hours trying to

347

fathom out why his father rejected him; and now he lay awake at night eaten up with shame and embarrassment. He was angry that he'd belittled himself for years by trying to make Nelson proud of him. Why had his mother never told him? Why had she carried on letting him believe that Nelson was his father? And who was this unknown man she had taken to her bed?

'We must lead this nation with integrity,' Mosley told them. And yet everyone knew the man was a notorious womanizer. Once again, it was a question of one rule for the rich and another for the working-class.

What would his illustrious leader say if he knew that Percy was a cuckoo in the nest? In his more rational moments, Percy liked to think it would make no difference at all. They were all bound together in a common cause to rescue the land they loved. But in his darker moods, he imagined the pointing finger and the shame of it.

Of course he'd punished his mother. He'd sold Nelson's boat and the locker for a reasonable price, fully intending to give her the money that night, but then he'd overheard what she'd told Ruby. He'd been so angry that he'd kept it, and it was that money which was funding his present circumstances. As a member of the permanent staff, he was paid; but, as a single man, he got a lot less than the married men. He supposed it was because they had responsibilities, and it was true that he had told himself the first night that he was willing to suffer the loss of everything for the cause. But still it rankled.

The person he felt really bad about was Ruby.

While he derived some satisfaction from punishing his mother, he did feel guilty about what he was putting his elder sister through. May was a spoiled brat; she deserved to get a dose of real life. But Ruby was different. He'd been mean to her, leaving her to cope with everything, and that wasn't fair. It wasn't the way a moral person should behave. It went round and round his head, until Percy got such a headache that he often had to resort to taking an aspirin.

News came that there was to be a large rally at Easter. The stewards were to have a change of tactic. Instead of working alone, a group of them were to band together under one leader. The hall was mapped out and each leader was given a specific area to control. To Percy's great joy, he was made leader of ten men.

'Freedom of speech is ingrained in our movement,' Mosley said more than once. 'I have no objection to a spot of heckling but, in the event of trouble, I shall give three clear warnings and then you need to eject the troublemaker.'

Percy studied the map, making a mental note of where the exits were in relation to his area of control, in case of an emergency.

'Remember,' Mosley told them, 'we don't start fights, we only finish them.'

CHAPTER 30

The conversation at the dinner table was awkward and strained. Ruby and her mother had only one thing on their minds, but this was neither the time nor the place to talk about it, in front of John and May.

'Any news of Jim and the partnership with Warwick Studios?' asked Bea.

Ruby shook her head. 'Jim asked, but Mr Hayward wasn't keen,' she said. 'He's promised to look at the books, but Jim doesn't hold out much hope.'

With the meal nearly over, John began to shift uncomfortably in his seat.

'I wish to tell you,' he began. Ruby and Bea gave him their full attention. He cleared his throat noisily. 'You have been most kind to me. I cannot repay–'

'There's no need,' Bea interrupted.

John put his hand up. 'Please, dear lady, let me finish. Please to sit.'

Bea had been removing the dirty plates from the table. She sat down again. Clearly this was important.

'I have been to Brighton,' said John. 'I found a synagogue.' Bea frowned, puzzled. 'It is the place where my people worship God,' he added by way of explanation. 'I did not know there were Jewish people here. I knew they were in London, but

350

not here.'

'You want to go and live in Brighton,' said Ruby, understanding perfectly.

John nodded. 'The people of Worthing, you ... have been very kind, but I would like to be with my own people. I should like a wife – a new family.' He looked at them anxiously.

'That's perfectly understandable,' said Bea. 'Of course you must go.'

John snatched her hand and kissed it. '*Y'var-ekh'kha ADONAI v'yishmerekha. Ya'er ADONAI panav eleikha vichunekka. Yissa ADONAI panav eleikha, v'yasem I'kha shalom.*'

Bea and Ruby hadn't a clue what he'd said, but they could tell by his expression that John was giving her a Jewish blessing.

'When will you go?' she asked.

John shrugged. 'Maybe next week.'

The two women smiled bravely. His going would mean a significant loss of income.

'Good luck,' said Bea.

'Yes,' said Ruby, 'all the best, and keep in touch, won't you?'

Later that evening, when Ruby and her mother were alone in the kitchen, they talked about John.

'I had hoped he might stay a bit longer,' said Bea. 'He was no trouble, and the money was useful.'

'Will you get another lodger?' asked Ruby.

'I suppose so,' said Bea. 'It's the obvious answer, but will I get one as good as John has been? And would we find someone to rent the little shop as well?'

The night before, they had agreed not to talk about Linton's letter until they'd slept on it. When Ruby had finished reading it, they'd stared at each other in stunned silence. After making their pact, Ruby had put the letter back in the envelope and they'd kissed each other goodnight, wishing themselves a good sleep. Of course neither of them had slept well; and the next day, although busy, had passed in a haze of 'what ifs' and the thorny question of what to do now.

Once they had eaten their evening meal, and May was in her bed and John was in his room, Ruby fetched the envelope from behind the best teapot on the dresser.

'Read it again, Ruby,' said Bea. 'Perhaps I can take it in a bit better now.'

Ruby read the letter aloud:

In May 1915 Victor deserted his post. He was a good mate and we knew the consequences, so we – George Gore, Nelson Bateman, and me – set off to bring him back before he was missed. We walked through some woods just to get away from the sound of the guns. When we caught up with him, Victor told us he wasn't ever going back and smashed his rifle on a boulder. That's a capital charge. We had a bit of a fight about it, and Nelson broke us up. He suggested going to lie low in this barn, where we could all work out what to do.

Then this woman came into the barn with a horse and started to rub it dawn. We hadn't seen a woman in God knows how long, and the sight of her put a fire in Nelson something terrible. Not to put too fine a point on it, he decided to take her down. Victor tried to stop him but he spooked the horse and it kicked him.

352

For a minute I thought he was a goner, but he was just knocked out. By this time, Nelson had ripped half the woman's clothes off and George was holding her down. She didn't half scream, so they got me to put my hand over her mouth. When Nelson finished, he held her while George had his turn and then they persuaded me. When it was all over, Nelson dragged the woman behind the stalls and when we left the barn, she was dead. Nelson carried Victor in a fireman's lift and we went back. Nobody ever found out what we'd done. I suppose the Boche got the blame. I've tried all my life to forget what happened, but I never could. I wished to God I hadn't touched her. I wished I could have been knocked out like Victor but, may God forgive me, I was as bad as the rest.

Back in the trenches we said that we'd gone after a couple of stray Hun. They didn't believe us, so Nelson told the CO it was all Victor's fault. He told them some yarn about Victor threatening us with his gun, and that's why we went after him. We all wanted to save our own skins, so we went along with it. They were only half-listening anyway. The bombardment was getting worse and they wanted it over and done with. Victor never said anything in his own defence. I honestly think he'd had enough. He just gave up, so he was charged with absenteeism on active service and damaging army property (his gun) and found guilty at a court martial. He was sentenced to be shot. That's when I was all for telling them it was wrong, but Nelson said that if they knew what had really happened, we'd all be on a charge and shot.

The firing squad was made up mostly of the Sunny Worthing lads. There were six of us altogether; the three of us who'd been in the barn with Victor and my uncle

353

Jack Harris, Chipper Norton and Charlie Downs. We marched to the quarry at dawn. Victor was led out of a shed and a couple of other blokes, who died in the trenches later on (may they rest in peace), tied him to a chair. They pinned a white handkerchief over his heart. That was our target area. The sight of the poor wretch tugging at his bonds made me sick to my stomach, but the six of us, on the order, raised our rifles. We was told that one man had a dummy bullet. I prayed to God that it was mine. As soon as Victor began to beg for his life, I just wanted it to be over. It was pitiful to see him, especially when he pissed himself.

The order came and I aimed and fired and, when the smoke cleared, Victor was still. The officer in charge, Captain Blatchington, was standing by to shoot him in the head with a revolver, if he was still alive, but the doctor said he was dead.

Before he died, I heard Victor shout, 'Mother of God', and then he called out somebody's name. 'Freddie', I think it was. I reckoned it must have been his brother.

I've been getting letters. Someone knows about this and is trying to frighten me. My uncle Jack was killed not long after he came home. They said it was an accident but I'm not so sure now. Chipper Norton fell into the sea and Nelson Bateman and George Gore have both died in less than a year. I don't think any of them went natural. If I go, warn Charlie Downs.

Signed: Linton Carver.

Ruby looked up. 'Did you know George Gore was dead, Mum?'

Bea shook her head. 'I only met him when he came to the funeral. Silas Reed knows him. I reckon it must have been Silas who told George about Nelson's passing. I could ask him.'

'What about Charlie Downs?'

Again Bea shook her head. 'I've no idea who he is.' There was a shuffling noise outside the back door and Jim called, 'It's only me. Can I come in?'

'Yes, dear,' Bea called back, and then they heard Jim closing the back door and taking his coat off. Ruby snatched at Linton's letter to hide it in the drawer, but her mother grabbed her wrist. 'If you're going to marry him,' she said, 'you can't keep secrets. He has to know everything.'

'Everything about what?' said Jim, coming into the room. He was rubbing his cold hands together and his cheeks were florid with the change in atmosphere. Walking towards Ruby, he kissed her with such tenderness it made Bea's heart ache.

'Sit down, Jim,' said Ruby, pulling out a chair, 'We have to talk.'

Cousin Lily was in tears. Albert hadn't turned up. He'd promised to meet her tonight, when they would discuss wedding plans, but as the evening wore on and she realized he wasn't coming, she'd put on her coat and gone to his digs to find him. She'd never been there before, but perhaps he was ill. She couldn't bear to think of him all alone in bed with a nasty cold or something. Of course his landlady would never allow her to go up to his room, but she could at least satisfy herself that he was being looked after, and Albert would be comforted to know she cared enough to come and see how he was.

Mrs Slater had been surprised to see her, and was even more surprised when Lily explained her reason for coming. 'I don't understand why you've come here, dear,' she said. 'Albert's not here. He moved out a couple of days ago.'

'Moved out?' Lily choked.

'He said it was because he was getting married and his fiancée lives in Hastings. The banns are to be read from this week, apparently.'

Lily had managed to keep her dignity until she got home, but as soon as she'd walked in the door she had broken down. Her mother had been wonderful. She'd comforted Lily without recrimination, especially when Lily confessed that she had let Albert have his way.

'Are you in the family way?' Vinny asked, as she held her daughter in her arms.

Lily shook her head. 'I've got "Auntie Flow" right now,' she said.

Vinny heaved a silent sigh of relief and resisted the temptation to give Lily a good talking to. She was a lucky girl, for she must have been sleeping with Albert for months. Most girls wouldn't get away with it for that long. Of course her daughter must never know that Vinny had taken Bea's advice. She'd cornered Albert a couple of days beforehand and confronted him about her daughter. When she'd told him that she knew what was going on, he'd gone white with embarrassment and apologized profusely. Vinny had told him straight, 'Marry the girl, or get out of her life and don't come back.' Well, it looked as if he'd made his choice. She felt sorry for her daughter but, like Bea had said, 'Better a few tears shed now than a ruined life.' Perhaps now Lily would find someone who would really love her.

Jim listened in stunned silence as Bea and Ruby explained everything. They told him about their suspicions surrounding Nelson's death and Linton's murder. He frowned as they showed him the bullet and the letter that Linton had given to Ruby.

'I can't believe this,' he began. 'I feel like I've walked onto one of those Hollywood film sets. You don't honestly expect me to believe that all these people have been murdered.'

'The police think Linton was murdered,' said Ruby.

'But not Nelson, surely?' he said, appealing to Bea.

'Nobody saw what happened on that boat,' said Bea.

'And Silas told the coroner's court there were two people in the boat,' said Ruby.

'Silas is as blind as a bat,' Jim chipped in. 'The jury didn't believe him anyway.'

Ruby glared at him. 'Everybody else thought it must have been Percy, but he was in London at the time. There's no reason why it couldn't have been somebody else.'

'Like who?' Jim challenged.

'I dunno,' said Ruby crossly. 'Whoever killed Linton, I suppose.'

Jim laughed. It was obvious he thought the whole idea a big joke. She could feel her face beginning to flush. She wished they hadn't told him now.

'What about the bullets?' Bea asked.

'They could be a war souvenir,' said Jim.

'There's only two men with them: Nelson and Linton.'

'Three,' Bea corrected. 'Mabel Harris has got one that belonged to Jack, remember?'

'You don't know if Chipper Norton or George Gore had one,' said Ruby. 'We didn't even know George was dead, until we got this.'

'Perhaps he isn't,' said Jim. 'You've only got Linton's word for it.'

'Aunt Mabel!' cried Ruby. 'She might know about the others.'

'I think you might be right,' said Bea.

'I don't think they have a postal service in heaven,' said Jim. He was looking at the letter again.

'You may think this is a great big joke,' Ruby retorted, 'but Mum and I are really worried.'

Jim immediately looked contrite. 'I'm sorry, darling. I didn't mean to be frivolous, but you have to be sure of your facts before you go jumping to conclusions.'

'Nobody is jumping to conclusions, Jim Searle,' Ruby snapped. 'We only showed you the letter because we thought you ought to know.' She snatched it away from him. 'Sorry to have bothered you.'

They were having their first ever row.

'You're not being very fair, darling,' Jim began.

'I'm not being fair!' Ruby screeched. 'Well, at least I care about people and how they die.'

Bea went out to the scullery and pretended to do some tidying up. After a few more heated words, it went quiet. She waited for a couple of seconds more and then looked through the crack

358

in the door. They were kissing. Bea smiled to herself. She had told Jim he had to prove himself to be a good provider before they could marry, but bearing in mind what Vinny had said about Lily, perhaps she should let them marry now. They could have the attic room. She would make it clear that she didn't expect Jim to support her and May, but at least they could all be together. But on second thoughts, Ruby was still only seventeen. Was she too young? She was the same age as she herself had been when she'd married Nelson. And didn't she know from bitter experience that, for girls of seventeen dreaming of their wedding day, life doesn't always turn out the way you want it to? Oh dear, what should she do? She sighed and the ache in her heart grew larger. If only Rex was here.

CHAPTER 31

Bea went with Mabel Harris to the inquest into Linton's death. She borrowed a bath chair from The Ark and pushed Mabel to Stoke Abbott Road. Getting her up the steps was a massive hurdle, but several neighbours and friends, as well as a well-meaning stranger, manhandled Mabel and the chair into the room. Being back at an inquest less than six months after Nelson had died gave Bea a sense of déjà vu, only this time she was better able to cope. The coroner, Major Jeffries, was as considerate as Dr Fox-Drayton had been, and the proceedings were a lot quicker. Having explained that this was not a trial, but only to ascertain the cause of death, and after hearing from the police and the doctor who certified Linton's death, he pronounced a verdict of 'murder by person or persons unknown' and released the body. Linton had been suffocated with his own pillow.

Back home at Mabel's place, Bea made them both a cup of tea. Fluffy, Mabel's tabby cat, jumped into her lap. 'I can't believe it,' said the old lady. 'Who on earth would want to hurt Linton? A more gentle soul you couldn't wish to meet.'

Disregarding the confession in his letter, which of course Mabel hadn't seen, Bea was inclined to agree. 'I'm sure the police will soon find the culprit,' she said, 'but in the meantime, we need to get on with arrangements for the funeral.'

'He had a policy,' said Mabel, 'and he had money. We can give him a good send-off.'

'Did he leave any instructions?' Bea asked. 'Was there a will?'

Fluffy purred loudly as Mabel stroked her. 'Oh, yes,' she said. 'Linton was very organized. He left you and the girls a little something.'

Bea's jaw dropped. 'What?'

'He left a bit of money for you,' said Mabel. 'Not a fortune, but it may come in handy.'

Bea couldn't help smiling. 'I can't believe it.'

'Oh, come on, Bea,' said Mabel 'You were kindness itself to him in the past. I lost count of the meals you made for him, until your Nelson put a stop to it. He hated the way Nelson treated you, Bea. I think he left you some money to give you the chance to get away from him and start again.'

'I only did what anyone else would do,' said Bea.

'Oh no, my dear,' Mabel insisted. 'It was more than that, and Linton knew it. He left me the house and I'm pretty sure he left you fifty pounds and the girls twenty pounds each.'

Bea took in a breath. What a surprise. What a blooming wonderful surprise! They drank their tea and discussed the plans for the funeral.

'"Abide with Me",' said Mabel. 'He liked that hymn, and "Lead, Kindly Light". He used to sing that sometimes when he was working in the garden.'

'What are you going to do about the house?' Bea asked.

'I'm not sure,' said Mabel. 'I may rent it for a while and then sell it. I haven't decided yet. I don't like the idea of a stranger living in it, but there's nobody else in the family, d'you see?'

Bea nodded sympathetically. 'Do you want me to write to anyone to tell them Linton has passed away?'

Mabel looked down at her twisted arthritic fingers. 'Well, I don't suppose I could do it with these hands.' She listed several people and gave Bea the money for a writing pad, envelopes and stamps. 'You're an absolute godsend.'

'It's no trouble at all,' said Bea. 'What about that old friend who came to Nelson's funeral – George something?'

'George Gore?' said Mabel. 'Oh, my dear, don't you know? Poor George is dead.'

'Dead?' Bea was scarcely able to breathe. So

Linton was right: George Gore was indeed dead.

'I had a letter from his wife,' said Mabel. 'She wanted me to go to the funeral, but – things being as they are – I couldn't manage to go all that way.' She shook her head sadly.

'How did he die?' Bea asked innocently. 'I mean, he looked hale and hearty at the funeral. When did he pass away?'

'It was on his way back from Nelson's funeral,' said Mabel. 'His train was delayed and the platform was crowded with day-trippers. He was standing too close to an incoming train, and someone opened the door as it came into the station. The poor man died almost immediately.'

'I never knew,' said Bea.

'That's funny,' said Mabel, 'I would have thought your Percy might have said something. He was on the platform at the same time. He was a witness.'

'Really?' said Bea. She was trembling a little and got up to wash the teacups, in case Mabel noticed. Why hadn't Percy mentioned it? Ah, now hang on a minute – he didn't even know George, did he? She relaxed again. 'You say you heard all this from George's wife?'

'And he's got three little kiddies,' said Mabel sadly.

Bea turned to face her friend. 'Mabel, can I have her address? I should like to write to his wife and offer my condolences, seeing as he and Nelson were brothers-in-arms.' It was a long shot, but she might be able to find out if George had had one of those lead bullets.

'Of course,' said Mabel. 'It's in the top drawer

of the dresser. In a brown address book – you can't miss it.' As Bea wiped her hands and went to fetch it, Mabel said, 'You may as well take it with you. It'll save you writing all those addresses twice.'

Bea's hand trembled as she pulled out the address book. The book itself was falling to pieces and the pages were yellow with age.

'I keep meaning to get a new one,' said Mabel. 'Half the people in there are dead, anyway.'

'I promise I shall take great care of it,' said Bea, tucking it into her handbag.

John was on his way to Brighton. Some things were hard to give up, but he had decided this was to be a completely new start. Bea and Ruby were sad to see him go, but they knew it was the right thing for him to do. He looked a lot better than he had done the day he arrived nearly four months ago, and the friends he'd made – along with some of the neighbours – turned out to say goodbye. His new friends from Brighton turned up with a lorry that was open to the elements, but it didn't matter because the weather was fine. It didn't take them long to load up his few things, and then he was ready to go.

'You are a fine woman, Mrs Bateman,' he said, shaking her hand.

As he let it go, Bea pushed something into his palm. He made as if to look at it, but she held his hand closed and said, 'For later.'

John ruffled May's hair and told her to be a good girl, then shook Ruby's hand and told her that any time she was in Brighton she should look him up.

Ruby promised to keep saying the words he'd already taught her in German, but she knew it would be very difficult to learn any more, without being able to hear how it was supposed to sound. He wished her good luck and climbed into the back of the lorry. Bea could have sworn there were tears in his eyes. They stood in the road, waving until the lorry was out of sight, then went indoors.

As he reached the end of Chesswood Road, John opened his hand. Bea had given him what looked like a small piece of rag. When he pressed it, the core was hard. He unwrapped it carefully and there was his ring. By the time the lorry had reached the seafront, John was crying softly.

The front parlour seemed bare without him, but he'd left it neat and tidy. There was a small bunch of spring flowers on the table and a luggage label saying 'Thank you' tied around the neck of the vase. It stood on a small embroidered place mat that Bea had often seen him fondling with tears in his eyes. It was cream, with dainty pink and blue flowers. The maker was obviously a very skilled needlewoman. The mat wasn't properly finished, but even so Bea loved it. She was just walking away from the room when she spotted an envelope on the mantelpiece over the fireplace. It had her name on it and she recognized John's handwriting. When she tore it open, she found fifteen shillings inside. It made her catch her breath. That was the sum she would probably have got, had she sold the ring all that time ago. How on earth...? But of course John couldn't have possibly known that she'd always planned to give it back to him, if she could. She'd kept the ring upstairs ever since he'd given it to her, and he had no idea how many times she'd come close to selling it. What an amazing coincidence. Bea was so moved that she sat on the edge of the bed, staring into space, for some time. It was only when a tear splashed on her hand that she realized she was crying.

Cousin Lily looked ill. Ruby was shocked when she saw her. She had called into Aunt Vinny's to tell them that Linton's funeral was to be held the following Tuesday. Nothing elaborate, but a service at St Botolph's church in Heene, followed by an interment in the graveyard across the road. Linton had been a regular church member ever since the war, and although most people were buried in the new cemetery at Offington Corner, in special cases the Church of England allowed some to be buried in the old churchyard. Everyone agreed that Linton would have liked that – everyone except Ruby, that is. She didn't know him that well, but she thought he would have been embarrassed by all the attention and, now that she knew something of his history, she was able to make an educated guess as to why.

Aunt Vinny was still at work in the laundry, which was why Lily opened the door to the house. As Lily was an usherette in the cinema now, most of her working hours were in the evenings, with the occasional afternoon matinee. She didn't often get the matinees. The women who had worked at the Dome for some time tended to hog those shifts.

'You look terrible,' Ruby blurted out. 'Are you all right?'

'I wish I was dead,' said Lily dully.

'Lily, whatever's happened?' cried Ruby. 'I thought you and Albert were happy and that everything was wonderful... At least, that's what some of the neighbours told me.'

Lily burst into tears and Ruby put her arm round her shoulders.

'He's gone,' sobbed Lily.

'What – dead?' said Ruby, visibly shocked. 'Albert's dead?'

'No, no,' said Lily, reaching up her sleeve for her handkerchief. 'He's left Worthing. He's left me.' And with that she began to howl.

'I'm sure if it was meant to be–' Ruby began lamely.

'That's what Mum said,' Lily interrupted. 'She says there's plenty more fish in the sea and all that...' Her face crumpled. 'But I want Albert.'

'Oh, Lily...' said Ruby.

Lily blew her nose noisily. 'He was worried that you'd spoil it for us. I know you were sweet on him, because he told me.'

Ruby almost choked. 'I never wanted Albert,' she said. 'Father... Father wanted me to go out with him, but I never thought of him in that way.'

'Well, I did,' said Lily beginning to cry again. 'And he loved me. It wasn't true what his land-lady said. It was *me* he was going to marry.'

Ruby put her arms round Lily again. 'I'm so sorry.' As soon as Lily had calmed a little they sat down. 'What did his landlady say?'

'That he was going back to his fiancée in Hast-ings,' said Lily, wiping her eyes again. 'But it's not true.'

'So where do *you* think he's gone?'

Lily shrugged.

'Maybe he's ill,' Ruby suggested.

'He isn't ill. He sent me a note, but I can't read it,' said Lily.

'Oh.' There was no answer to that one. Lily left the room and came back a few minutes later with the letter. She handed it to Ruby. She did feel sorry for Lily, but Lily was a terrific-looking girl and Ruby knew that, as soon as they knew she was free, half the young men in Worthing would be beating a path to her door. Right now she looked a bit of a mess, with her bright-red nose and little piggy eyes because she'd been crying so much, but with her blonde hair curled and a pretty dress on her trim figure, Lily wouldn't stay single for long. 'Are you sure you want me to read it?'

Lily nodded. 'Read it out loud.'

Dear Lily, he'd written. *I won't be coming round any more. You know the reason why. Albert.*

Ruby read it twice, then handed it back. 'I suppose he was trying to be kind,' she said. 'At least he let you know he won't be coming back.'

'But I don't know the reason why,' Lily howled. 'I just want to die.'

'No, you don't,' said Ruby. 'It's really not as bad as that.'

'But I gave myself to him,' she said dramatically. 'I thought we were going to be married. No other man will want me now.'

'Of course they will,' said Ruby crossly. She was upset for her cousin, but really, she was milking it for all it was worth. 'And besides, if you don't tell anybody, how are they going to know?'

'I should have known that this would happen,' Lily went on bleakly. 'Even when we were in bed together, he was always talking about you and your family.'

'Pardon me?' said Ruby, startled.

'"Where's she working now?"' said Lily, mimicking Albert sarcastically. '"What time is she off? Is she going to marry Jim?" On and on he went.'

Ruby pulled a face. 'I'm sorry,' she said. 'I always made it very clear that I wasn't interested. He was too old.' She felt her face colour. Lily was practically the same age as her. 'I mean, you're nearly a year older than me,' she went on, 'and that makes all the difference.'

Lily nodded miserably. 'I just want him back.'

CHAPTER 32

It was busy at the hospital. The wards were crowded and extra beds had been brought in to the middle of the room. Worthing had been suffering from a bad dose of carelessness. People were having accidents left, right and centre. It was strange how things like this happened, especially when there was no common underlying cause. The previous summer, a sudden hot spell brought patients suffering from sunburn, sunstroke and dehydration; during the winter the admissions went up because of falls on the ice and broken limbs, and in February there had been a cluster of influenza patients. In the run-up to Easter there was no real reason why the hospital should suddenly double its intake, but it did.

It made life difficult for the ward maids. Ruby struggled to get between the beds and it was hard to keep the floors clean, with so much extra traffic. She worked hard as usual, but once again she became aware that she was being watched. She would often 'feel' someone behind her, or standing in a doorway; but, if she spun round, that person would be gone or going. It made her feel uncomfortable and not a little nervous. Was she doing something wrong? She always took great care about her appearance, pinning her hair under her cap and making sure she changed her coarse apron frequently. She tried to see to any extra requests as quickly as was humanly possible, but for the first time since she'd come to the hospital Ruby was unsettled.

At home, although money was a lot tighter without John's rent, in some respects things were easier. She and her mother got along well. Bea's health had improved, so she was able to take on a lot more of the household responsibilities, which meant that Ruby could occasionally have a little free time to herself.

Now that spring was just around the corner, it was time to do the spring-cleaning. The accumulated soot from the open fires had to be washed from the walls. Picture frames, mirrors and the mantelpiece, which had collected a film of grime through the winter months, had to be thoroughly cleaned. There were carpets to brush by hand and beat in the open air. And all that had to be done alongside the normal washing. Each week the sheets were boiled in the copper in the scullery, put through the mangle a couple of times, rinsed by hand and put through the mangle again, before they could be hung out to dry. Spring-cleaning meant that the window curtains and the heavy door hangings, which helped to conserve the heat during the cold weather, had to be washed as well. Bea was able, for the first time in many months, to do her fair share. As Ruby cleaned the windows with one part vinegar to four parts water, she understood why the government discouraged married women from working. If she was a young mum, it would be difficult to do everything at home and hold down a job.

Jim came round most evenings, but the enthusiasm he'd brought back from Wimborne was beginning to wane. It wasn't that he didn't believe in his own ideas, but, with virtually no resources, it was hard to see how he could even begin to fulfil his dreams.

'I think people like us – when they're on holiday – want more than a picture postcard,' he told Ruby one evening. They were all sitting together in the kitchen. May was in bed, and Ruby was doing the ironing with the flat irons on the range. 'What they want is a picture of themselves at the seaside.'

'The likes of us could never afford a camera,' Ruby laughed.

'Exactly,' said Jim. 'That's why I'm convinced there's a vast untapped market out there for holiday snaps.'

'Don't just talk about it,' said Bea. 'Give them what they want.'

'With all due respect, Mrs Bateman,' said Jim, 'my boss would never allow me to use his studio to feather my own nest. Photographs for the lower classes are not something he'd want to be associated with.'

'Did anything ever come of you possibly taking over, when Mr Hayward retires?' asked Bea.

Jim shook his head. 'He isn't interested in being a sleeping partner,' he said. 'He wants to cash in his assets and enjoy the rest of his life.'

'I don't suppose I blame him,' said Bea. 'He's worked hard all his life.'

'He's putting everything up for sale very shortly,' said Jim, 'which is why I thought snapping day-trippers would be a good idea.'

'There must be some way you could do it,' said Bea.

'What would you need, if you did do it?' asked Ruby.

'A darkroom, for a start,' said Jim. 'If I take pictures along the promenade, the holidaymakers are only there for a few days. They'll want to take their pictures home with them.'

'Is that possible?' asked Ruby.

'If I had a helper,' said Jim. 'I can't take the pictures and do the developing at the same time. And hiring a place to do the developing would need capital.'

'You could use John's shed, couldn't you?' said Bea.

Jim and Ruby stared at her and then at each other. 'That's a very generous offer, Mrs Bateman,' Jim began, 'but you could get good rent money for that room. I'm not in a position...'

'If you were family, we could all share in your venture.'

Ruby gasped. 'What are you saying, Mother?'

'I'm saying that if you and Jim were married sooner rather than later, we could all help out.'

'It's one hell of a risk,' said Jim.

'All marriages are,' Bea grinned.

Jim's face coloured. 'I ... I didn't mean that,' he began.

'I know,' said Bea. 'I was teasing.'

'I still need capital,' said Jim, shaking his head.

'Linton left me a little money,' said Bea. 'I'm willing to risk mine to give you a leg up.'

Jim's mouth dropped open.

'I didn't know that!' cried Ruby. 'Oh, Mother, that's wonderful. You deserve it.'

'I'm not sure how much it is,' said Bea, 'but Mabel thinks it may be as much as fifty pounds.'

'Fifty pounds!' cried Ruby. 'Oh, Jim.'

'He's left some to you and May as well,' said Bea. 'I shall save May's in a Post Office savings account. It could be twenty pounds.'

'Then you must have mine too,' said Ruby. 'Sixty pounds could go a long way.'

'*Each*,' said Bea. 'He left you twenty pounds each.'

By now Ruby was laughing. Jim looked totally speechless, but there were tears in his eyes.

Bea smiled benevolently. 'So what's it to be, Jim?'

He grasped Ruby's hands and kissed them. 'Would you like to marry me this year, Ruby?'

'Oh yes, Jim Searle. Yes, a thousand times yes!'

With Linton's funeral over, and his will finally settled, the family turned their thoughts to Ruby's wedding. It was going to be a low-key affair. Ruby decided to make her own dress, and Aunt Vinny volunteered to make a bridesmaid's dress for Cousin Lily. Lily was less fragile now and, as a matter of fact, she had a new beau, although she was determined to take things a lot slower this time. Nick Wilkins was already besotted with her.

Friends and neighbours had promised to help with the food by doing a loaf of sandwiches or a dozen cakes for the reception, and Jim's boss said he would take a studio portrait picture for them on the day. They chose Saturday, August 5th; the following Monday was the summer bank holiday, which meant that Jim and Ruby could have a couple of days off before going back to work. By way of a honeymoon, Jim booked a coach trip with Cecil Turner's coaches, which happened to be going to Eastbourne for the day.

Edith and the other girls were thrilled when Ruby told them about the wedding. Ruby had sneaked into the hotel the back way, and they were all in the staff-room when she told them.

'If you have it after three o'clock, we should all be able to come,' said Phyllis. 'Oh, please say you'll invite us.'

'Of course I will,' laughed Ruby. 'And I want you all to come to the reception, if you can.'

'We should be able to come for a while,' said Edith, 'but then we'll have to get back to turn down the beds.'

'Count me in too,' said Doris. 'I love a good party.'

'Who's having a party?' The door squeaked open and Winnie made everybody jump as she came up behind them. She was carrying a vase of dead flowers and was on her way to the utility room to dispose of them.

'You nearly gave me a heart attack,' Doris exclaimed as she clutched at her chest. 'I thought you were old Flossie Fosdyke.'

'Ruby is getting married,' said Edith, 'and she's invited us all to the wedding.'

'Everyone?' said Winnie. She turned to Ruby with a quizzical arch of her eyebrow.

'Everyone,' said Edith.

'How lovely,' said Winnie. 'Then I should love to come.'

'You're welcome,' said Ruby.

'I'm afraid I cannot buy you a present,' said Winnie apologetically.

'That's fine,' said Ruby. 'Just come.'

'I could always do your bridal bouquet.'

'What?' Ruby gasped. 'Would you? Would you really?'

They heard the sound of footsteps coming down the hall. 'Oh, Lummy Charlie – quick,' Phyllis hissed. 'It's Mrs Fosdyke.'

The girls busied themselves with various bits of equipment, in an attempt to make it look as if they all had a legitimate reason for being there, while Ruby hid behind the door of the open cupboard.

'What are you all doing in here, pray?' Mrs Fosdyke boomed. 'Hurry up, all of you. Breakfast has started, and you need to be doing the rooms. Fox, where is your cap? And Parsons,' she called after Edith, 'I shan't tell you again: don't run – walk.'

Behind the door, Ruby held her breath and prayed. If Mrs Fosdyke saw her there, she would probably accuse her of trespass and demand that she go to the office, and that would make her late for work. As it was, Ruby would have to run like mad to get to the ward on time. Mrs Fosdyke's eagle eyes searched the room. Winnie ignored the housekeeper and continued washing out the smelly vase, ready to use for some new blooms. After a few seconds Mrs Fosdyke left the room and Ruby emerged from her hiding place.

'Is it a big wedding?' Winnie asked.

Ruby shook her head. 'Just some friends and neighbours.'

'I suppose things are a bit difficult, now that your poor father has died,' Winifred began.

Ruby was at a loss to know what to say. She didn't know the florist very well and was tempted to think it a little impertinent of her to raise such a subject. 'We get by,' she said.

'I'm sure you do, dear,' Winnie smiled. 'Now tell me, what colours would you like in your bouquet?'

'Ruby, would you come into my office?'

It was late afternoon, and the sister had stopped Ruby working in the kitchen. She had been washing up a couple of plates, knives and forks. Oh dear. She'd turned up five minutes late this morning. She had run all the way to the hospital, arriving hot, perspiring and out of breath, but she was still late getting onto the ward. Had someone reported her? Had her past caught up with her at last? Maybe someone from Warnes had told them

375

that she'd been accused of theft and sacked. Her face suddenly felt clammy. *Please, God, don't let this be happening.* She had been so happy, what with the wedding and all. She glanced around as she left the room. It was spotless.

The short walk to the sister's office seemed like a mile as her thoughts raced hither and thither, trying to work out why she was being summoned.

'Close the door, dear,' said the sister as they entered her office. The friendliness of her tone made Ruby relax. If she spoke so kindly to her, she probably wasn't going to give her the sack after all. She closed the door and stood to attention in front of the desk. It was only then that she realized that Matron was sitting in front of her. Her heart sank.

'Ruby, we are delighted with your work on the ward,' said the sister, 'but we feel that you are capable of much more. Unknown to you, the sisters from other wards have been watching you at different times of the day.'

Ruby blinked in surprise. So that was why she'd had the feeling she was being watched.

'And,' the sister continued, 'they would like you to teach their ward maids how to run their wards. We've all had a word with Matron here, and she has agreed that you should receive a promotion.'

'We are aware that you are still very young, but we want you, to supervise all the wards in the hospital,' said the matron. 'We are putting you in charge of ordering the linen, making sure every ward is as clean as your own. And, where standards fall short, we want you to show the other girls how to do it. Do you think you can manage to do that, Ruby?'

She could hardly believe her ears and she certainly couldn't contain the smile that raced across her lips. 'Yes, Matron,' she said with as much restraint as she could manage. 'I'm sure I can.'

They spent some time discussing terms and conditions, and decided that she should start her new post at the beginning of May. When Ruby walked out of the sister's office, she was no longer a humble ward maid, but the wards supervisor of Worthing Hospital. The sad thing was that she wouldn't have the post for very long. It was a pity that the Board of Governors and the government didn't allow married women to work in hospitals.

Ruby's promotion had sent everyone into a frenzy of excitement and congratulations. All their neighbours agreed that she deserved it and wished her all the luck in the world. A week later it was Bea's turn to be excited. When Ruby came home from work, she couldn't wait to show her something.

'I've had two letters,' she said, even before Ruby had taken her coat off.

'Two?'

May was clambering onto her sister's knee to show her something she'd made at school. It was a piece of canvas, which had some large holes. May had embroidered it in coloured wool. The pattern wasn't symmetrical, though it was obviously meant to be, but it was both eye-catching and colourful.

'That's gorgeous,' cried Ruby. 'I love that blue kiss you've made in the corner.'

'It's a place mat,' said May.

'I can see that,' said Ruby. 'It's really lovely.

What did your teacher say?'

'She liked it,' said May, a little pink glow of pride rising on her cheeks.

Ruby hugged and kissed her. Their relationship had improved a lot since May had finally understood that Nelson was never coming back, and she was a lot nicer to Ruby these days. 'You're the best and the cleverest sister in the world,' said Ruby, and May giggled.

'Sit up now,' said Bea, putting the hot plates onto the table.

May slid from Ruby's lap and pulled out her own chair.

'Aren't you going to put your dinner on your place mat?' Ruby asked. She lifted the plate and May arranged the mat underneath. 'You said you had two letters, Mother.'

'You remember I said I had Mabel's address book,' said Bea. A cloud of steam enveloped her as she tipped the cabbage into a colander standing in the sink. 'Well, I wrote to George Gore's widow to offer my condolences. I mentioned you-know-what, and she's written back to say she wants to see us.'

A plate of sausages, cabbage and mash appeared in front of Ruby and May.

'Where does she live?' asked Ruby.

'York,' said Bea, 'but she doesn't want us to go there, thank God. She's coming here.'

'Here?' cried Ruby. For a split second the thought of it horrified her. Where would they sleep? Would she have to postpone her wedding?

'I mean they're coming to Worthing,' said Bea patiently. 'They've booked a guesthouse, and she's

378

bringing the children for a week during the summer holidays.'

Conscious that May was all ears beside them, they ate their meal making small talk about school dinners, the price of potatoes and when Ruby's new job would actually begin. After dinner, May was sent to the scullery to have a wash, while Bea and Ruby did the washing up.

'Did you ask Mrs Gore about the bullet, Mum?'

Bea shook her head. 'All I said was that it was a terrible coincidence that three of the pals had survived that awful war, only to die within months of each other.'

Ruby looked thoughtful. 'I don't understand why Jim is so sceptical about it,' she said. 'The more we delve into it, the clearer it seems to me. Someone has got it in for them.'

'But we don't really understand why,' said Bea. 'If it was to do with the war, surely they would have done what they wanted to years ago.'

Ruby nodded vaguely. 'You said you had two letters, Mum?'

'When I was going through Mabel's address book,' said Bea, 'I came across another familiar name. Colonel Blatchington.'

Ruby caught her breath, recalling the letter Linton had given her the day he was taken into hospital: *The officer in charge, Captain Blatchington, was standing by to shoot him in the head with a revolver, if he was still alive.*

'Do you think he's the same person?' she whispered.

'It's a very unusual name,' Bea remarked.

'But you said Colonel Blatchington,' Ruby cautioned.

'The war was over sixteen years ago,' Bea said. 'Plenty of time for promotion.'

'I was two years old,' said Ruby wistfully. 'Mum, I get the feeling that this is about more than what happened in the barn. Uncle Jack wasn't there, was he?'

'But he was part of the firing squad that shot Victor,' said Bea. Ruby nodded. 'I wrote to the colonel,' Bea went on, 'telling him about Linton's passing, and of course I mentioned Nelson as well.'

'And?' said Ruby.

'He sent his condolences,' said Bea.

'Oh.' Ruby felt totally deflated and disappointed.

'But,' said Bea, clearly enjoying her little bit of drama, 'he said that he has Percy in his office, and he complimented me on my hard-working and trustworthy son.'

Ruby's face broke into a wide smile. 'Oh, Mum, that's amazing! I wonder if Percy knows the colonel had a letter from you?'

'I should think so,' said Bea.

'Do you think he will write?'

'Probably not,' said Bea. 'You know how stubborn Percy can be.' She wiped the draining board with a cloth and threw the washing-up water away. 'But I know where he is and that he's safe. That's enough for me.'

May was back. 'Can I have a story?'

'Did you clean your teeth?' her mother asked.

'Yes,' said May, baring her teeth for inspection.

'I'll do the story, Mum,' said Ruby. 'You have a

sit-down.'

Mounting the stairs behind May, Ruby smiled to herself. Her mother was right. Percy might still be angry, but at least they knew where he was. She'd ask Mum for the address and then leave it a couple of weeks, before writing to him herself and asking him to give her away at the wedding.

CHAPTER 33

Dear Percy,

I hope this finds you well, as it leaves me. This is to let you know that Jim Searle and I are getting married on August 5th at St Matthew's church. We are having a small celebration afterwards in the church hall and I would dearly love you to give me away.

Jim is going into his own photographic business, and I have had a promotion at the hospital. Mother and May are well and send their best love. You are my dear brother, and I miss you.

With fondest love, Ruby

Percy stared in fascination at the glass and wrought-iron dome. He had never seen such an amazing building in his life before. His gaze wandered along the mosaic frieze at the top of the brickwork, just under the roof; someone at the Black House had told him it depicted sixteen different skills. He couldn't remember them all, but he knew the sculptures represented all walks of life, from brick-makers and farmers to engin-

381

eers and musicians. Careful not to miss his footing as he looked up, Percy wandered around part of the building, trying to read the inscription: *Opened by Her Majesty the twenty ninth of March in the year MDCCCLXXI. Thine O-Lord is the greatness and the power and the glory and the victory and the majesty...*

Pausing by one of the many doors, Percy flicked a speck of dust from the sleeve of his shirt and smiled to himself. Only five months ago he was bobbing around the Worthing lump – a range of underwater chalk cliffs that rose well over ten feet, about five miles off the Worthing coast – trying to catch cod and herring, lobsters and crabs. Just look at him now. This was the Royal Albert Hall, for goodness' sake – the place where the Italian world heavyweight boxer, Primo Carnera, had knocked out Reggie Meen in 1930. The place where leading artists from all over the world had played, sung and performed since it opened, way back in the Victorian era. Now inside the hall itself, Percy turned his eyes towards the three tiers of seating, and 'the gods' above them. Tonight it was his turn. Oh, not to perform, but to be part of the vast organization that would facilitate Oswald Mosley and the leading members of the BUF. Tonight, at 7.30 p.m., their illustrious leader would make a grand entrance, bathed in the smoky-blue beams of the arc lights and heralded by a fanfare, and preceded into the hall by six of his most trusted men carrying flags. Percy would be one of them.

A young man, no more than seventeen or eighteen, hurried towards him. 'Excuse me, sir.' Percy turned and the Blackshirt stood smartly to attention and handed him a letter. Glancing down, Percy recognized the writing instantly, but he couldn't look at it now.

He was well aware that the Communists and left-wing Labour Party members had pledged to hold a counter-demonstration, but the men under his leadership were more than capable of dealing with any trouble. He had taken great pains to train them in the art of being polite but firm. There was, he told them, no need to descend into violence. Violence never solved anything. And he should know. All his life he'd faced Nelson's belt and the lash of his father's tongue. The only thing it had achieved was to create in Percy the desire to get even. People were already flocking to Oswald's clarion call in droves, but if they got beaten up, or if they saw others being bashed about, they'd stay away. They came from all walks of life – the rich and famous rubbing shoulders with ordinary people. He'd met people he'd only read about in the newspapers, like Sylvia Pankhurst and Mary Richardson, the widely known suffragettes of a bygone age. The latter had become head officer in charge of the women's section, which she guarded like a bulldog.

Percy only occasionally threw an adoring glance at a BUF girl. The women's uniform was rather masculine, with its black shirt and tie, black belt and grey A-line skirt; and although many of them plastered their hair with Gripfix, so that it would stay tidy no matter what, sometimes – just sometimes – a softer beauty shone through. The truth of the matter was that he was beginning to feel not only slightly disillusioned, but also lonely.

Behind him someone dropped something with a clatter, bringing him back to the here and now. The letter was still in his hand.

He tapped the envelope on his palm. The writing was Ruby's, although the original address had been crossed out and redirected to the Black House. What was so important that she should try to get in touch with him again? Could it be that his mother was ill? The last time he was home she had seemed far from well. If she was dead, he could do nothing about it, and he could do without the interruption of a funeral. And if his mother was dangerously ill, and Ruby was imploring him to go home, he didn't want to see her anyway. He was still too angry. The feeling of betrayal was still too keen.

'Anything I can do for you, sir?'

Percy started as a much older man came and stood by his elbow. He smiled and shook his head. As the man turned to go, Percy took one last look at the envelope, then folded it in half and thrust it into his pocket.

Rex Quinn always felt he had a sixth sense when it came to Bea Bateman. He had planned to return to Worthing later in the year, but increasingly he felt that he should arrange to go back sooner. It hadn't been easy, leaving her to her grief. He hoped she had made a good life with Nelson and the children. He recalled the astonishment he'd felt when she'd chosen to go back to her husband all that time ago. Nelson always seemed a rather churlish sort of fellow. When he'd arrived at the

384

hospital, everybody thought he was on his last legs, but the man obviously had the constitution of an ox. He'd not only made a full recovery, but he'd gone back to France as well.

Rex had been brought up as a God-fearing Congregationalist and, as such, he'd made a valiant attempt not to see Bea again. He'd read and reread the story of David and Bathsheba in the Old Testament, and determined in his heart that history would not repeat itself. King David had lusted after Bathsheba and had sent her husband back into the seat of battle, where he was certain to be killed. Rex had no say in what happened to Nelson once he was fit, but, to his everlasting shame, he wasn't sorry to see him shipped back out to the trenches again.

He and Bea had enjoyed a wonderful spring and summer together in his home. Little Percy had enjoyed playing on the beach and they'd eaten strawberries and made love in his conservatory, sometimes under the stars. The disaster began when first of all Bea discovered she was pregnant, and then her husband announced that he was to be repatriated back home. Rex had begged her to stay with him, promising a good home for her and the boy, but she'd told him that she knew her husband only too well. She couldn't leave her child, and Nelson would never allow her to take Percy with her. Rex had wanted to keep in contact with her, but Bea wouldn't hear of that, either. Nelson, she told him, was vindictive. If he ever found out who the father of her child was, that man was as good as dead.

Rex had been terrified that Nelson would beat

Bea, or do her such harm that she would lose their baby, and so it was with enormous relief that he heard she'd been safely delivered of a little girl. He'd only seen Bea once more after that. It was about nine years ago, when he'd bumped into the whole family in Hastings. Bea had tried to look casual, but Rex always feared she might have given the game away, because although he'd been polite, Nelson seemed on edge the whole time. Rex had never married, for Bea was the only woman he would ever love. But he'd heard sometime later that Bea and Nelson had gone on to have another child. He was glad for her and hoped she was happy.

He reached for the telephone and dialled the number of an old friend. After several minutes of chit-chat about nothing in particular, Rex became more direct.

'Look here, old man,' he said congenially, 'I need a bit of a break. Do you think you could come here for a fortnight as my locum in August?'

Albert Longman felt like a traitor. It was several weeks since he'd left Worthing. He had successfully avoided bumping into Lily, but as soon as he'd heard on the grapevine that Ruby was actually going to marry Jim, he couldn't bear to stay away. He'd tried to put her out of his mind, but he couldn't. He would have to go back and see Dr Haydon again. Even as he stepped off the train, he knew he should have done this a long time ago.

The hospital was a forbidding Victorian building, but there had been some recent redevelopment on the site. A noticeboard stood to one side of the driveway: *Graylingwell Hospital for the Mentally Ill.*

Albert rang the bell and a woman came and unlocked the door. He explained that he had an appointment with Dr Haydon and was shown in. Walking briskly, the woman led him down a long corridor where a domestic was polishing the linoleum floor with an electric buffer. A few people shuffled about; some had vacant expressions and appeared to be drugged, while others greeted him cheerfully. Of those who passed the time of day, Albert was struck by their accents. Some were obviously middle- or maybe even upper-class. Oddly, it comforted him to realize afresh that mental illness was no respecter of class or status.

The corridor seemed endless, but at last he was shown into a small office and asked to take a seat and wait. Dr Haydon came in a few minutes later and Albert stood to shake his hand.

'I hope this visit isn't what I'm thinking it is,' said the doctor.

Albert shook his head sadly. 'I'm afraid it is, Doc. I just don't know what to do.'

CHAPTER 34

Ruby was getting desperate. Her wedding day was getting ever closer and she still didn't have anyone to give her away. There was no reply from Percy – not even to her second letter – and the family had a distinct shortage of male relatives.

Everything else was tickety-boo. Her dress was almost ready: just the hem to do and the cuffs on the sleeves. May's dress was done, and Cousin Lily's only had to have a second fitting before it could be completed. Her mother and Aunt Vinny had spent a rare day together in town and had bought their outfits. Bea had a lovely frock from Smith & Strange in South Street. Their clothes were normally way out of her league, but she had spotted a blue cotton dress with its own little bolero in the window; it was only twelve shillings and elevenpence and it fitted her perfectly. Aunt Vinny went for a navy dress with a white trim, and they complemented each other quite well. After that, the two of them had gone to the Dome to a hair-waving demonstration called 'Waves of Desire'. An elderly woman who had been 'Miss 1900' in her youth sat with a lovely girl who had just been crowned 'Miss 1934'. They acted as models for the Eugene system of waving. Bea and Vinny would have loved to have a permanent wave but, at twelve and sixpence, it would cost almost as much as Bea's dress!

Edith popped round to admire Ruby's dress. It was hanging in the front parlour, which nobody used now.

'It's gorgeous, Roob,' Edith said. 'Oh, you're so lucky.'

Ruby squeezed her friend's arm sympathetically. 'It'll be your turn soon.'

'I hope so,' said Edith confidentially. 'I can't hold him off much longer.'

The two friends giggled. 'What's it like with Jim?'

'We haven't done it yet, but we struggle sometimes,' said Ruby. 'Still, we don't have long to wait.'

'Do you think it hurts?' asked Edith. 'When it goes in, I mean.'

'I don't know,' said Ruby with a shiver.

'Bernard showed me his once,' said Edith, lowering her voice and coming closer. 'Oh, Ruby, it was huge.' Ruby made no comment, and her friend suddenly looked anxious, as if she'd betrayed a confidence.

'So is Jim's,' said Ruby.

'And hard,' said Edith.

'And pink,' said Ruby, whereupon they had a fit of the giggles.

'Who is going to give you away?' asked Edith, suddenly serious again.

Ruby shrugged. 'I've written to Percy twice, but he doesn't reply. Either that, or they don't give him my letters. That's what happened the last time.'

'Would you like me to ask Bernard?' said Edith.

Ruby took in a breath. Of course! Bernard would be ideal. 'Do you think he would do it?'

'I'm sure he would,' said Edith.

Ruby flung her arms round her friend's shoulders and hugged her. 'That would be wonderful.' She had only met Bernard a few times, but he seemed very nice. He obviously loved Edith dearly. It wasn't an ideal situation but, with no other men in her life, it solved a very pressing problem.

'Then consider it done,' said Edith.

Ruby paused as they walked out of the door. 'The only thing is,' she began, revelling in the naughtiness of their conversation, 'after what you've just told me – you know, about Bernard's thingy – I won't be able to get it out of my mind.'

'In that case,' said Edith, 'I'll make a pact with you. You stop thinking about Bernard's thingy and I'll stop thinking about Jim's.' And, giggling helplessly, they joined Bea in the kitchen.

The crowds waited patiently. It was nearly time for the Albert Hall meeting. Percy stood in a long line of Blackshirts that snaked around the whole building. He had his back to the door with his feet slightly apart and his hands behind his back, and he remained at his post until the vast crowd had gone in, which happened with surprising speed.

As a flag-carrier, Percy then hurried to meet the others. The great man himself arrived not soon afterwards. This was the first time Percy had seen him this close up. Mosley, tall with disturbingly dark staring eyes, a Roman nose, swept-back hair parted in the middle and a full moustache, was in full uniform, including jodhpurs and jackboots. As they waited for their cue, Mosley held his body stiffly. It was clear that he was becoming irritated by the delay, which Percy put down to nerves. He was nervous enough himself.

'What are we damned well waiting for?' Mosley demanded. He glared at Percy. 'Who's doing the bloody fanfare?'

Percy didn't have a clue, but he knew he daren't say so. Mosley didn't suffer fools gladly.

Someone else waiting with them accidentally trod on Mosley's toe and he exploded. 'Good

God, am I surrounded by bloody fools and im-
beciles?' He rounded on Percy again. 'You,' he
barked. 'Yes, you, boy. Get out there now. Go on,
go on...'

Percy's face flamed. No one had called him
'boy' since his father died. He didn't like it then,
and he sure as hell didn't like it now.

At that moment the fanfare began and Mosley
shoved Percy in the back. He was propelled
through the curtain, and the roar that greeted him
sent an instant tingle down his spine. Holding the
flag upright with as much dignity as he could
muster, he walked down into the arena and
headed towards the massive organ, which seemed
to be using every single one of its 9,000 pipes as
it thundered a deafening peal. Another roar went
up as everyone stood to their feet and he knew
that Mosley had entered the hall. The arc light
swung away from him and Percy was left on his
own to negotiate the stairs by memory, until his
eyes became used to the gloom. The crowd, by
now in a frenzy of excitement, chanted, 'M-O-S-
L-E-Y, Mosley', as they clapped their hands and
stamped their feet.

Percy reached the platform and someone came
forward to receive his flag and place it in a
specially constructed stand. His face was still hot,
and he was furious. What Mosley had said was still
ringing in his ears: *You, boy. Get out there now...*' He
felt rather than saw Mosley come up behind him,
and once again that rasping voice was right behind
his ear. 'Get out of the way, you nincompoop,'
Mosley hissed, his mouth tight with rage. As he
turned to wave to the crowd, one of Mosley's

personal bodyguards pushed Percy to one side to make way for Mosley to climb the steps onto the platform. 'Silly ass,' he said as he walked past.

'Silly ass, yourself,' Percy snapped and knew in that moment that he was going to walk away from all this. Without so much as a glance in Mosley's direction, Percy turned on his heel.

It took a while for the crowd to settle and then Mosley began his speech. He never used notes, but in no time at all he had his audience completely spell-bound. By the time the heckling started, Percy was almost at the back of the hall. He watched as the stewards moved in and removed the troublemakers. They did everything efficiently and with great skill, but it still troubled Percy.

A group of Blackshirts came up the stairs in front of him, carrying a struggling body. As they stumbled by, Percy was disturbed by what he saw. The person was a young woman. Her clothes had been ripped from her upper body, exposing her underwear. One man had his huge hand pressed over her mouth and nose. Her head was being forced back, which must be causing her a great deal of discomfort, if not pain, and she clearly couldn't breathe. Her eyes, wide and terrified, met Percy's as he held the door open for the men to pass. They rushed her to the entrance and dumped her unceremoniously on the ground outside. Anxious that she might be badly hurt, Percy went to help. She was still on the ground, gasping for breath, and there was blood all over her hand. As soon as she saw Percy leaning over her, she recoiled.

'It's all right,' he said softly. 'I'm not going to hurt you.'

She looked up at him and he was horrified by the gaping wound on her cheek. The cut was bad, but even so, she was breathtakingly beautiful.

'I think I had better get you to hospital,' he said. 'Are you able to walk down to the street? I can hail a taxi from there.'

The girl stood shakily to her feet. She was clearly weakened by her experience. Percy put his arm out to assist her and, although she nearly fainted a couple of times, they made their way to the road. As soon as they arrived at the hospital, the girl was whisked away.

'You can wait there,' said the nurse, indicating a row of chairs. She smiled admiringly at Percy's uniform. 'I wish I could have been at the rally. I think Mosley is rather wonderful.'

Percy said nothing, but glanced up at the clock. The meeting would be drawing to a close by now.

The staff at Warnes Hotel were very helpful. Rex had arrived late on Thursday night and had woken up in the morning with a heavy head-cold. When the chambermaid, a delightful young woman called Edith, found him still in bed, she enquired if he needed a doctor. Rex felt like death warmed up and told her so. Prescribing himself hot lemon-and-honey drinks, aspirin and plenty of rest, he climbed back into bed.

Rex decided he couldn't go to see Bea like this, and whatever had drawn him back to the town would have to wait. On Friday he woke up feeling a lot better. Edith made his bed and took his dirty washing to the hotel laundry. She had already made sure he had *The Times* and had been kind enough to look out a couple of books for him to read. *The Encyclopaedia of British Bees* looked as if it would be a bit dry, but *The Shape of Things to Come* by H. G. Wells looked a lot more promising and, at 420 pages long, Rex settled down for a good read.

Rex decided to sit by the balcony so that he could see the sea and watch the promenaders. For that reason he was glad he'd chosen Warnes rather than the Savoy this time.

'You seem to be in a bit of a hurry today, Edith,' he said, as she put his drink on the table beside him.

'Oh, I am, sir,' she smiled. 'A friend of mine is getting married tomorrow and I am to be a bridesmaid.'

'Ah,' said Rex with a nod.

'Mrs Fosdyke has given me a lot of extra jobs, to make up for the fact that I'm going off early,' said Edith, glancing around the room to check that everything had been done.

'Then I'm very grateful that you've looked after me so well,' said Rex, feeling slightly guilty.

'And that's not all,' Edith went on. 'As my friend's father has passed away and her brother can't be found, my fiancé is going to give her away.'

'Well, it sounds to me like you've got everything under control,' Rex smiled indulgently.

'Yes, sir.' Edith hesitated. 'Will that be all, sir?'

'Yes, yes,' said Rex. 'Don't let me keep you.'

'Yes, sir. Thank you, sir,' said Edith, giving a

little bob.

He smiled as she left the room, a smile that quickly died as he heard the housekeeper's ringing tones of disapproval.

'You'd better get a move-on, Parsons, if you want that time off tomorrow. Number thirty-six hasn't been touched yet, and then there's the linen cupboard to tidy.'

'Yes, Mrs Fosdyke,' he heard Edith say.

'You girls expect far too much these days.'

Rex frowned. The woman was hardly being reasonable. It was *his* fault poor Edith was behind with her work, and yet the girl herself hadn't made him feel the least bit awkward about it. There was a sharp rap on the door and a tall, thin woman in a dark-grey uniform entered the room. There were dark circles under her eyes and her skin had a rather unhealthy pallor, as if she didn't get enough fresh air. 'Good morning, sir,' she said with a smarmy smile.

Rex took an instant dislike to her.

'My name is Mrs Fosdyke, and I'm the housekeeper. I know you have been unwell and I came to see if everything is all right.'

'I must compliment you,' he said, watching her chest already swelling with pride, 'on your charming staff. I couldn't have been better served. Nothing has been too much trouble for Edith – is that her name?'

Mrs Fosdyke's mouth tightened. 'That is as it should be, sir.'

'On the contrary,' smiled Rex. 'I'm sure she has a very heavy workload, but she has gone out of her way to help me. I believe I heard you say she has some time off tomorrow?'

'She's going to a wedding.'

Rex held Mrs Fosdyke's stony stare with a pleasant smile. 'I hope helping me doesn't get in the way of that. I do so hate unfairness, don't you?'

Two bright-pink spots appeared on her cheeks as Mrs Fosdyke prepared to leave. 'Please, pick up the telephone if you require anything else, sir,' she said, closing the door softly.

CHAPTER 35

The hospital staff had decided that the girl should stay in overnight. Percy was given special permission to see her before she went up to the ward. Once again, when he walked into the cubicle, she recoiled. No woman had ever reacted to him like that before, and it made Percy feel very uncomfortable.

'I'm sorry my colleagues were so rough with you,' he said. She was bewitchingly beautiful, with her large, dark eyes and flowing black hair. The wound on her cheek had been cleaned and dabbed with iodine. It was only now that he noticed she already bore a facial scar, which had been reopened by the rough handling she'd received. It began at the corner of her right eye and went down her face, onto her neck, and disappeared under her blouse. When it was inflicted it must have been a life-threatening injury.

'I'm grateful for your help,' she said with an air

of defiance, 'but I hate all that you stand for in that uniform.'

Percy was shocked. When he'd joined the BUF, apart from a few Communist agitators and some mischief-makers, there was little opposition to the Fascist movement. They attracted more trouble now, but he'd always put that down to the opposition becoming more organized. Recently he'd had his own misgivings, but he'd felt that he would be swimming against the tide by voicing them, so he'd knuckled down and tried to make a go of things. After the way Mosley had treated him tonight, though, he knew he wouldn't be going back. But he was curious to know why the girl was so vehemently against them. 'You are not from this country,' he observed. 'Do you mind telling me why you dislike them so much?'

'In Germany, where I come from,' she said, 'Hitler's jackbooted followers have already killed hundreds of innocent people. You think your Mosley is going to bring about a utopia, but he will only bring misery and death.'

Percy shook his head vigorously. 'If you don't mind me saying so,' he said, 'I think you exaggerate.'

The girl leaned forward and pointed at the scar on her face. 'You wouldn't say that if you had this.'

Percy was speechless.

At that moment the nurse asked him to leave. He was upsetting her patient. 'I'm sorry,' he said helplessly. He turned to go, then stepped back. 'Can I see you tomorrow?'

She leaned back on the pillow with a tired sigh.

'Don't come in that uniform.'

His heart soared, but he was halfway out of the ward before he realized he didn't even know what she was called. 'What is your name?'

'Rachel,' she said. 'Rachel Stein.'

He spent the whole night in a state of turmoil. There was no doubt that the BUF meetings were attracting a lot more violence. Mosley talked about strong government and upending the social structure of the country, and, while it was true there was a lot wrong with it, for a while now Percy had been forced to admit that he wasn't exactly comfortable with his leader's proposals. That night he had been given one of the most coveted positions, as flag-bearer, and yet he had been treated with contempt and ridicule. Not only was the movement open to question, but so was its leader. Rachel represented the face of the downtrodden, and he didn't like the way she had been treated.

Visiting hours were a long time coming, but when he reached the ward and the sister opened the doors at 3 p.m., Percy could hardly contain his excitement.

Rachel was right at the end of the ward. As he strode towards her, his heart pounded. He'd brought her flowers and some grapes.

'You look quite handsome in your suit,' she smiled.

Percy felt his face colour. He loved the soft lilt in her voice. He loved the way her hair, loose and long, rested on her shoulders. He loved her smile, and her eyes.

They made small talk and then Percy asked

her, 'Can you tell me what happened to you? You were very positive that Hitler is a bad thing for Germany. Do you mind telling me why?'

She blinked, as if she was unsure of his motives.

'I'm serious,' he said quietly. 'I know I joined the Blackshirts, but...' He shrugged helplessly.

'I was with my sister and her baby,' Rachel began. 'It was becoming more and more difficult for Jews to make a living in Germany. The Hitler Youth made trouble all the time.'

'You are Jewish?'

'Yes,' she said, with a defiant toss of her head. 'You have a problem with that?'

'Not at all.' Percy shook his head. He'd been surprised more than anything else. 'Go on.'

'We were walking together: Griselda, the baby and I,' she began. 'They came out of nowhere – pushing us, trying to grab the baby out of Griselda's arms, calling us "Jewish whores". One of them tried to put his hand down my blouse, so I slapped his face.' Rachel turned her head away and Percy could see that her chin was shaking.

'If it's too difficult...' he began.

'No,' she said, collecting herself again. 'I'll tell you. I want to tell you. They dragged me into a shed and tore off my clothes.'

Percy's eyes widened. *Dear God ... what was she going to tell him?*

'Then one of them – the one with the knife – did this.'

'But why?' asked Percy incredulously.

'Because I am Jewish,' she said simply. Her eyes were bright with unshed tears, but she stared straight at him. 'They hate the Jews and the Gypsies, and the cripples and the mentally ill. They want to kill us all. We don't fit in with the master race, d'you see? This is what your Mosley wants too.'

'I've never heard him say anything like that,' said Percy stoutly.

'Of course not!' cried Rachel. 'He needs to get into power first, then he will do it.'

Percy stared at her, horrified. He leaned back in his chair. 'What happened to your sister?'

'She took the baby and ran away,' said Rachel. 'She ran across a railway line. One of the men that followed was hit by a train.'

'How awful. But it must have been a bit of a relief.'

Rachel's eyes filled with tears as she shook her head. 'When one of them is hurt, they always take revenge,' she said sadly. 'A week later the police found Griselda and the baby in an alley; they had been beaten to death. Of course they never caught the person responsible. Then someone told me my brother-in-law had been arrested. I was terrified...' Her voice trailed off. 'And when I heard that our house was marked for demolition, some friends helped me to escape. I was the only one who made it to England.'

Percy's hand went to his head and he looked down. He had no words. He was appalled by what she'd said, but he believed everything. All the things he didn't like about the BUF came marching out like an army.

She leaned over and touched his shoulder. 'I've given you a shock,' she said quietly. 'I'm sorry. You are a good man. You came to help me and I am grateful.' Her face was pale, but she was no coward. Terrible things had happened to her, but her eyes still blazed with passion. He could see now why she had been at the meeting. She was determined to make sure that people understood the dangers of Hitler's rise to power and, by default, Mosley's too. Now that she was in a place of safety, she had every right to choose anonymity and the quiet life, but something told him Rachel would never do that, and he admired her all the more.

'How *did* you get to England?'

As he sat in the chair beside her, listening to her story, Percy realized two things. First, he was going to have to change direction once again; and second, and perhaps most surprising of all, he had fallen head-over-heels and hopelessly in love with Rachel Stein.

The sisters and the nurses from the hospital had given Ruby a tremendous send-off. She had cake and flowers, good wishes and a present of a bale of towels. It seemed grossly unfair that, just because she was getting married, the law of the land was making her give up a job she loved. The Marriage Bar meant that women working in the public sector were not allowed to carry on after marriage. On the other hand, it did mean that she could give Jim's photography venture 100 per cent of her attention. He had already created a darkroom in what had been John's little workshop, and he had begun to teach Ruby how to develop film. If she became proficient, it meant Jim could spend more time at the seafront with the day-trippers.

Bea had persuaded a neighbour to create a

canvas booth that hung on a wooden frame. She planned to sit inside and sell the finished photographs, and take orders for more copies. Ruby had worked out a system of cross-referencing, so that they could even manage a postal service and be sure of getting the right photographs to the right people. They had started on a small scale just after Easter, and it was already a well-oiled machine. Choosing a name had been a bit of a headache, but they had settled on 'Magic Memories: a photography service to capture your seaside moment.' The weather was mixed, but there were some warm days and, every moment he could, Jim was standing on the promenade with his camera.

Their wedding day was warm, but overcast. They had begun the day with Bea washing Ruby's hair. She used rainwater from the water-butt outside and put some vinegar in the final rinsing water. The night before, they had pulled out the galvanized tin bath and had each taken a turn: May first; then, while Bea put her to bed, Ruby soaked; and then Bea had the water last.

A succession of friends and neighbours came in during the morning of Ruby's wedding day, which kept Cousin Lily busy with the teapot. Ruby couldn't remember what everybody talked about, but she had never felt so happy. She kept hoping that Percy would come in the door, but deep down she knew he wouldn't. Still, she was determined not to let it spoil her big day.

'How's Nick?' Ruby asked Lily, with little confidence that he'd still be around.

'Fine,' said Lily. 'We're going to get married.'

Ruby raised an eyebrow. 'And don't look at me like that,' Lily whispered teasingly. 'You were right. When it happened he didn't know.'

'You mean you're...?'

Lily glanced across the room towards her mother, but Aunt Vinny was deep in conversation with Susan Marley. 'We've only just started – and oh, Ruby, he's wonderful.'

'Be careful,' Ruby cautioned.

'Oh, Nick won't let me down,' said Lily.

Ruby sighed. She had hoped Lily had learned her lesson, and that with a brand-new relationship she wouldn't give herself too soon.

Just after lunch, they dressed Ruby in her wedding dress. It was plain white satin with sleeves to the elbow. The bodice was fitted, and she had a sweetheart neckline with a stand-up collar. On her head she wore a coronet of orange blossom trimmed with silver thread. She looked stunning, and everyone agreed that no one would ever believe she'd made the dress herself. All she needed now was her bouquet. She glanced at the clock. It was already one thirty. The wedding was at three and they still had to walk to St Matthew's.

Winifred Moore arrived at the house soon afterwards and didn't disappoint. Ruby was thrilled with her bouquet. It was massive, reaching from her waist as far as her knees, and was made up of creamy roses and white carnations, caught together with maidenhair fern and ivy.

'Oh my goodness!' cried Bea, clapping her hands. 'You look wonderful.'

Winnie had also prepared two more bouquets – one for Edith and another for May – using white carnations, but when the child held her flowers in front of her, Winnie decided it was much too big. Despite protests that it would be all right, she pulled it apart over the sink and quickly re-created a smaller, more attractive posy. Everyone agreed that May looked fantastic. Edith wore blue satin with a blue halo headdress, while May's frock was gold satin with a gold halo headdress.

It was time to walk to the church. The sink was still full of flower bits and stems.

'You go on ahead,' said Winnie. 'I'll clear up the mess and let myself out.'

'Are you sure?' asked Ruby.

'Of course, my dear,' smiled Winnie. 'You run along – and be happy.' Ruby moved to kiss her, but Winnie moved deftly out of the way.

'Thank you,' said Ruby. 'You've been so good to me. How can I ever repay you?'

Winnie waved her away and stood by the door as the wedding party set off. At the end of the street, Ruby turned to wave, but Winnie was already gone.

After a while, there was a soft tap on the door. Wiping her hands on a tea towel, Winnie opened it cautiously. 'Oh, it's you.'

Ruby arrived at the church at two fifty-five and Bernard was waiting outside for her. He looked very handsome in his suit, and had a carnation in his buttonhole. As he smiled down at her, Ruby knew exactly why Edith loved him. He was the strong, dependable type.

'All right, lass?'

Ruby nodded and they made their way down

the aisle. The church was dark inside. There was little light, and the walls were of plain red brick. Their friends and neighbours waiting in the pews rose as one when she walked in, and the organist struck up 'Here Comes the Bride'. She saw Jim come from the front pew and turn to watch her walking towards him. She was trembling with nerves, and her shaking bouquet gave her away.

'Hello, Ruby Bateman,' he whispered as she stood beside him. 'May I say that you look exceptionally beautiful today.'

The wedding party walked back to the Foresters' Hall, where Susan Marley and their other neighbours had laid on a spread fit for a king. The speeches, the music and the dancing went on until late in the evening. For Ruby it was the best day of her whole life.

'Thanks for being my bridesmaid.' She had cornered her old friend in the ladies' cloakroom. 'I'm so grateful to Bernard for giving me away, as well.'

'Oh, Roob,' Edith beamed, 'you look so lovely, and I can't believe how handsome my Bernard looked. You will come to my wedding, won't you?'

'Try and stop me,' said Ruby, giving her a hug.

As the happy couple left the hall, Ruby aimed her bouquet at where Edith was standing, but Cousin Lily caught it. Perhaps it was just as well. Lily seemed very happy with Nick, and she deserved some happiness of her own after the way Albert had treated her. Thinking about it, it occurred to Ruby that she hadn't seen Albert lately. Where had he gone? Had he left Worthing for good? Maybe he really did have a fiancée in Hastings.

Back at the house, Ruby and Jim got ready for bed. In between kisses they took it in turns to wash in the scullery and then retired to their very own room for the first time. To Ruby, it was her palace, her little piece of heaven on earth. She'd lit candles on the mantelpiece and their soft glow, reflected in the overhead mirror, gave the room a cosy feel.

Jim was a gentle lover. Ruby could tell that he was as hungry as she was, yet he didn't rush her. He built her desire, until she thought she would die for want of him, and when he finally lifted her nightdress over her head, she felt no embarrassment at all. When he entered her, it stung a bit, but she was transported. It surprised her how well her own body accommodated him, and they both shivered with delight as he made love to her. It didn't last very long, but Ruby was content.

As they lay in each other's arms, they heard Bea and May come home. Bea put the radio on and Ruby's favourite singer, Connie Boswell and the Boswell Sisters, filled the room. 'Blue moon...'

Jim kissed his new wife tenderly as the sounds of his mother-in-law getting May ready for bed gradually faded and the words of the song grew in intensity. He rolled on top of Ruby and gazed lovingly into her eyes.

They heard a click and Bea turned off the radio. A few bumps from the ceiling, and a creaking floorboard or two, didn't hinder their second session of making love, which was even sweeter than the first. As she reached an amazing climax that she didn't even know existed, Ruby couldn't help but utter a cry of ecstasy. At almost the same moment, Jim cried out too. For some time they lay spent in each other's arms, still naked and glowing.

'I love you, Mrs Searle,' Jim whispered into her hair.

The candles were guttering and so, unashamed, she climbed out of bed to blow them out. He caught her hand and drew her back, leaning up on his elbow and kissing her breasts, her tummy and her pubic hair. 'Oh, Ruby. Ruby, my love.'

'Greedy boy,' she giggled.

He let go and picked up something from the bedclothes. 'What's this?'

He held it up and Ruby froze. 'Where did that come from?'

'It must have rolled from under the pillow as you got out,' said Jim.

He looked up at her and saw her look of horror. It was one of the lead bullets. Jim sat up and snatched the pillow away from the bolster.

'Perhaps someone put it there as a joke?' he suggested.

Ruby climbed back into bed, a little unconvinced, but as soon as her new husband started kissing her again, all else was forgotten.

CHAPTER 36

Bea had enjoyed her daughter's wedding. Although she had been at the forefront of the plans and preparations, when she arrived at the kitchen door, her sister Vinny packed her off.

'You go out there and enjoy yourself,' she said. 'This is your daughter's wedding. You shouldn't be working.'

They'd never been kissing sisters, but impulsively Bea pecked Vinny's cheek.

'Oh, get away with you!' said Vinny, waving her away, but Bea couldn't help noticing the faint smile etched on her lips.

The rest of the wedding breakfast had been everything she'd wanted, and more. It was quite a gathering, with at least forty of them. The sandwiches were lovely and moist, the cakes seemed never-ending, and the tea brewed in a large galvanized teapot was good and strong. The buzz of conversation convinced her that everyone was enjoying themselves. After the speeches they toasted the bride and groom, using some of Susan Marley's elderberry wine, and then Ruby and Jim cut the cake. Bea had made it herself and, thankfully, there was plenty to go round. She was glad she'd used the square tin rather than the round one. It made it so much easier to cut small slices.

Cousin Lily leaned over her aunt and put a

piece of cake in front of her. 'There you are, Aunt Bea. It looks fantastic.'

Her pretty locket swung out in front of her and Bea froze. 'Where did you get that?' she whispered angrily.

Lily's face coloured and she straightened up. When she'd put on the locket that morning she hadn't given a thought to the fact that Bea would be at the wedding. Turning on her heel, she headed for the kitchen again. Bea followed. Luckily the room was empty.

'I asked you where you got that locket,' said Bea. Her face was flushed and angry.

'I'm sorry, Aunt Bea,' said Lily, clearly embarrassed. 'I didn't think you'd mind. That man gave it to me.'

'What man?'

'The man who gave me that letter after the inquest.'

Vinny came up behind them. 'What letter?'

'He didn't give it to *you*, did he?' said Bea, ignoring her sister. 'That locket is mine. You were supposed to pass it on to me, weren't you?'

'What's going on?' asked Vinny.

Bea held out her hand and Lily, her face a picture of misery, handed the locket to her. 'I wasn't going to keep it,' she said. 'I only borrowed it.'

Bea raised one eyebrow. 'You shouldn't have taken it at all,' she said tartly. 'I'm very disappointed in you, Lily.'

'Will someone please tell me what's going on?' Vinny insisted.

'I'm sorry,' said Lily, her eyes glistening with unshed tears. 'I didn't think you'd mind.'

'You never even asked me,' said Bea, turning to leave.

Vinny turned to her daughter. 'Lily, what's this about?'

Outside the kitchen door Bea held the locket close to her chest for a few seconds, before composing herself and stepping back into the wedding reception. Behind the door Lily and her sister were having harsh words. Bea was more than a little annoyed with Lily. Holding her locket for the first time in eighteen years, Bea was experiencing an acute sense of loss, but she took a deep breath. No, she mustn't cry. She wasn't going to let anything spoil Ruby's wedding.

By six o'clock they had cleared the trestle tables to the side of the hall. Then the men brought in a barrel of beer, which gave everyone a bit of fun when Silas Reed tapped it and sent a fountain of frothy amber liquid all over himself. As the evening wore on, and other members of the fishing community, friends and neighbours joined in the dancing, the wedding party became very merry and, later, a little mellow.

Bea stayed behind with the other women to help clear up, giving Ruby and Jim time to settle into their little room without embarrassment. May was exhausted, but excited to be up so late. At 10.30 p.m., the time they were to vacate the hall, everything had been put away, wiped down and swept up. Friends and neighbours helped Bea carry the leftovers back home and, to lessen the risk of encouraging mice, she spent a few minutes putting everything into a tin or the meat-safe, or under a cover.

She'd put the wireless on as soon as she'd got in to save Jim and Ruby's blushes. With May washed and tucked up in bed, she then made her way to her own room.

She took the locket from her handbag and held it up to the light. She knew it was worth a fortune. It came from Boodle & Dunthorne, a bespoke jeweller in Liverpool, and Rex had given it to her shortly after she'd had their baby. That was the last time they were together. Bea turned the secret catch and saw the picture of her baby for the first time in eighteen years. Ruby's innocent stare turned back the years, and Bea pictured herself looking at it while Rex was with her. On the opposite side was a little curl of Ruby's dark hair. Bea touched it gently and, feeling the tears running down her cheeks, wiped them away with the heel of her hand. She'd made Rex take the locket with him.

'Give it back to me when we are free,' she'd told him. *Oh, why had that silly girl kept it for herself?...* If only Lily had given it to her straight away, she might have got to the Savoy before Rex left Worthing. He might have even made it to his daughter's wedding and walked her down the aisle.

As she got ready for bed, Bea comforted herself that if – no, *when* – he came back to Worthing, the hotel's management had promised to give Rex a letter that she had persuaded them to keep in the safe. Dog-tired, even though she felt frustrated and upset, Bea slept soundly.

Percy had woken up with a problem. Apart from the fact that he wanted to keep on seeing Rachel,

411

he had to find himself a job and somewhere to live. The sickening violence he'd seen at the Royal Albert Hall had left him profoundly shocked. He hadn't said anything to them that night, but his friends in the Black House were actually boasting about what they had done.

'I was with Smith and his mates,' said one man. 'As soon as that fellow in row C started shouting, the four of us jumped on him.'

'I saw you,' said another man. 'I would have helped, but just as we were coming over, some young chap stood up and shouted, "Hitler means war," so we had to shut him up good and proper.'

'Did you tell him to leave?' Percy asked.

The steward laughed. 'Don't you worry – we gave him the full treatment.'

'I told you to ask people firmly to leave, and then escort them off the premises,' said Percy tartly. 'Those were Mosley's clear instructions.'

'Oh, we were very firm about it,' laughed Smith.

Percy frowned. This was descending into anarchy. He wasn't stupid. Yes, the Blackshirts had already gained a reputation for being a bit rough, but he had hoped that, with strong leadership, his team at least would set an example. It was obvious now that it was never going to happen. While it was true that he had left the building to see if Rachel was all right, the meeting had already descended into a shambles long before he went. Hecklers were being treated with brutality. From what he had seen, there was never a tap on the shoulder and a polite request to leave quietly. What made it worse was that, once a man had his arms pinioned, he was in no position to avoid the punches of everyone and anyone who fancied throwing one. Percy had felt from the word go that the movement had its flaws, but all this violence was getting out of hand. Ruby had once told him that he was too headstrong. 'You get too passionate, and then you forget everything else,' she'd said. 'Take things a little slower.' Well, today he would take her advice. He was supposed to attend a meeting to discuss the strategies of the night before, but instead of going along there, he dressed in civvies and headed for the hospital.

Bea was up early the next morning, helping Ruby to make a packed lunch using some of the leftovers from the wedding breakfast. The happy couple were heading out to Eastbourne on one of Cecil's coaches for the day. By eight o'clock the pair of them were running down the road hand-in-hand. They had to be at the Dome by eight-fifteen and would be out all day.

Bea watched them go with a little concern. They had been rather quiet at the breakfast table. Of course they were tired from yesterday, but it was more than that. She knew Ruby well enough to know when she had something on her mind. Was everything all right in the bedroom department? Had Jim disappointed her? He seemed nice enough, but you could never really tell. She had only known two men, in the biblical sense. One had been rough and unkind, while the other had been a caring and gentle lover. Chalk and cheese. Bea sighed and hoped that Jim was kind to Ruby.

She made herself a cup of tea and, with May still

413

fast asleep, dozed a little in the chair. The locket was around her neck and it comforted her to feel it every now and then. She decided she would take May to the beach. She could miss Sunday school for once. It was funny, but even though the sea was right on the doorstep, they hardly ever found time to enjoy it. What was that old saying about coals to Newcastle? She and May could take the last of the sandwiches, and there were a couple of sausage rolls as well. She yawned. Every day she spent an awful lot of time in the Magic Memories booth, taking orders and selling Jim's seaside snaps, but she never ventured out onto the pebbles or to sit in a deckchair. All that seemed very inviting today, and it wouldn't be long before May came thundering down the stairs.

She heard someone shuffling their feet outside the front door. Oh no – she didn't want visitors now. She was tired. Perhaps it was her sister, come back to see if there was anything else waiting to be done. There was a soft knock on the door and Bea called out cheerfully, 'Come in, it's open,' at the same time thinking: *Go away...*

She kept her eyes closed as the visitor came in. 'There's some tea in the pot,' she said, sure it was Vinny. 'Help yourself.'

When the person who had entered the room didn't speak, Bea opened her eyes. She took in her breath and gripped the arms of the chair in disbelief. The room was suddenly filled with the sound of soft laughter.

'Hello, Bea,' Rex smiled. 'You look as beautiful as ever, even with your eyes shut and your mouth wide open.'

She rose shakily to her feet as the blood pulsated in her head and her chest tightened. She could hardly breathe. He opened his arms and she came to him. Touching his chest, she said, 'Is it really you?'

'Yes,' he said huskily. 'It's me, my darling. I've come to collect you, and this time I won't take no for an answer.'

She moved slowly into his arms, savouring the moment as he enfolded her. She could feel his breath on the top of her head, and his arms felt warm and protecting. As he pressed her to him, she could hear his heart beating wildly in his chest. They stood in silence together for several seconds. Bea closed her eyes again and was intoxicated by the smell of him. He released her and they stared into each other's eyes. Then he bent his head and gave her the lightest, gentlest kiss, which sent all her senses to the moon and back. They looked at each other again and then his next kiss was far more eager. The third was hungry and full of the promise of what was to come. Bea melted in his arms until a child's voice behind her said, 'Mummy, what are you doing?'

CHAPTER 37

Victor's widow always woke with a feeling of contentment, which quickly vanished. She rolled over the bed to look at her husband's picture. She reached out and pulled it to the edge of her bedside table. He looked so handsome in his uniform, and she was becoming more and more aware of how young he looked. Her hands were becoming wrinkled with age and a couple of the veins stood out. She was growing older, while he had remained twenty-nine for the past twenty years.

They had been together for ten years and she had loved every minute. They'd married in St Mary's in Ferring and lived in the village, where he worked as a sexton for the parish. He'd been born and brought up in Worthing and didn't want to move too far from home. She was his senior by five years, but she had the passion of a much younger woman. To be frank about it, she adored sex. She could never get enough of it. Victor used to laugh when she'd beg him not to stop. 'Keep this up, gal,' he'd joke, 'and you'll have me in an early grave.'

She never refused him, and they had had their moments in some wonderfully romantic places. The most daring had been in some farmer's barn in Wisborough Green. It was a country walk with a difference and they had nearly got caught. The farm dog had barked below the loft where they lay naked on the straw, and would have given the game away had not its master, waiting outside with a pony and trap, called sharply for it to come. They had giggled like naughty schoolchildren scrumping in an orchard. How she'd loved the sense of risk and abandon.

While she had enjoyed the lovemaking, she wasn't so happy about the consequences. At first, Victor withdrew before ejaculation. It was much better when he stayed inside her, but then her son came along. She still wanted her husband, but as she got bigger, he was afraid it would hurt the baby. The result was that she resented her child even before he was born. He was a weak child anyway, stupid and whiney. She did what she was expected to do to nurture him, but her mind was always on her lover.

Her life would have been perfect if it weren't for the war. Damn the Kaiser and his cohorts. Damn Kitchener and his war poster. She'd been utterly devastated when Victor had come home to say he'd joined up alongside the lads from Sunny Worthing and, if that wasn't bad enough, after his basic training was sent to France. She'd carried on, writing a letter to him every day, and longing for the time when they could be together again. Then came the official letter:

Madam,

I am directed to inform you that a report has been received from the War Office to the effect that your husband was sentenced, after trial by court martial, to suffer death by being shot, for desertion, and the sentence was duly executed on May 29th 1915.

I am, Madam, your obedient servant, Lt-Col F Faber

Shot for desertion? Victor didn't even die at the hands of the enemy, but was shot by a firing squad made up of his own countrymen. She had been poleaxed. For days she couldn't function, and she was eventually sent to Graylingwell Hospital, which was doubling up as a military hospital at the time. The civilian patients were eventually moved on, but not before she had met a few injured soldiers walking in the grounds. It was then that she discovered the awful truth. Not only was her husband shot by the British Army, but the men who made up the firing squad were his own pals – the very men who had persuaded him to go to war in the first place. His greatest and most serious misdemeanour had been smashing up his rifle.

At first she was numb. That was followed by a rage so strong she felt as if she was drowning in it. Over the years it had settled down, only to become like the magma in a volcano – still there and hot, waiting for the moment when it was time to erupt and spew out hellfire and judgement.

Her son had grown up by the time she came out of hospital in 1922. Everyone was thrilled when she 'recovered'. Someone from Hastings had looked after the boy, and he was working. Her release came at the same time that the war memorial was unveiled in Alexandra Park by the Earl of Cavan. Other men would be honoured, but as a convicted man, her own darling would never be remembered. Although she hid it well, the anger she still felt convinced her that she was far from 'cured', and for nearly ten years she had done what was expected of her, even though the desire to dance on the graves of those who had taken her husband never went away. Jack Harris was the first. He'd been hit by a lorry but the others lived on.

When she got the job in Worthing she was elated. No one there knew her now. She had put on nearly four stone and her hair was white, but she could relive the memories of a happier time. A neighbour had persuaded her to visit Mrs Knight, but nothing ever happened in her seances. But then, when she least expected it, Victor had come to her. She still remembered the thrill when he'd spoken to her the first time.

Her son kept asking questions, of course. Checking up on her, he was. She didn't want him hanging around, but he was a persistent little sod. She was glad in the end, as his ability to track people down came in useful. Some of the firing squad had died in the war and then, one by one, the accidents kept happening. She didn't care, of course. Why should they have long and happy lives when Victor was in his grave?

Chipper Norton was next. Victor had told her what to do. She'd been looking out for him for several days and when she overheard someone talking in the post office as she queued for a stamp, she was delighted. 'Me and the wife are off to Portsmouth with Chipper Norton and his missus to celebrate. It's a coach trip – very reasonable. You should come. There's plenty of seats left.'

'Umm,' said the friend. 'I might just do that. Which coach company is it?'

'Southdown,' said the friend.

In her position it was easy enough to take a day off work, so she had booked a ticket straight away. She'd spotted the friends booking up a trip around the harbour and had bought a ticket for that too. Chipper was leaning against the rail of the ship, looking out to sea. Little did he realize that the piece of rail doubled as the gate where they put up the gangplank. She would never have thought of the idea but, at Victor's suggestion,

419

she'd stood beside Chipper and released the catch. Of course she could never tell anyone what really happened, but as he cried out and fell, he would have seen her smile. It was so satisfying to watch him sink like a stone into the murky water, his raincoat billowing out and, as it took on water, sucking him under the waves. She'd held her breath as the rescue attempt got under way, but it was to no avail. Chipper was well and truly dead by the time they pulled him out, and when she told them that she'd seen him playing with the catch like Victor told her to, and how she'd warned him to be careful, they believed her.

Victor had planned Nelson's demise very carefully. In common with other fishermen, he was very superstitious about having a woman on board. During a stroll or two along the seafront he'd pointed out that there was a tarpaulin at one end of Nelson's boat, which covered the fishing gear. At the last minute she'd changed her mind and decided to go to his house with a knife, but she had been surprised to hear Victor's voice as she waited in the shadows. She wasn't really concentrating, but he'd spoken to her all right: 'Go back to the beach, Freddie, and get into the boat.'

She'd had to run like the wind to get to the boat before Nelson did and hide herself, but she'd managed it. She heard later that Nelson and his son had fallen out that night. He was alone in the boat and, when she stood up with the white sheet over her head, he'd been so startled and terrified that he'd got himself tangled in his own nets, in the panic to get away, and toppled over the side.

He might have managed to scramble back on board, but once he'd realized that she wasn't a ghost, she'd panicked and pushed the weighted nets overboard with him. She was no sailor and had a bit of a job getting back to the shore, and had to abandon the boat a little way out. The water was terribly cold and the swim to shore almost finished her off, but the tide was coming in and she made it. When she got home, she wondered whether to tell their son everything, but something told her that she must keep her secret.

She'd had a stroke of luck when George Gore came to Nelson's funeral. Once again, Victor told her what to do but she'd had to follow George almost all the way back to his home before she got an opportunity. As luck would have it, the trains were delayed and, as they waited on the platform, she spotted someone with an open carriage door as the train pulled in. With Victor's encouragement, a good push did the trick. They always screamed when it happened, and that gave her a headache, but afterwards, when she was resting and she heard her husband's voice again, it was worth it.

Dispatching Linton Carver was easy. She'd been calling on him for months and nobody takes any notice of a middle-aged woman visiting a sick man in hospital. She just had to wait for Victor to tell her when. Then she'd heard the girls at work talking. 'Roob reckons Percy is in the BUF head office. Her mum had a letter from a Colonel Blatchington, telling her so.'

She'd pricked up her ears. Blatchington was the officer in charge when they had killed her best

421

beloved. True, the Blatchington the girls were talking about was a colonel, but after all these years he was bound to have been promoted. A decent sort of bloke, Victor had called him once; but what sort of decent bloke would stand by, ready to shoot a defenceless man in the head to make sure he was dead? She'd asked the girls a few questions and had discovered that Ruby's wedding was being organized in haste. The stupid girl was probably pregnant. Ruby wouldn't have much money to spare, so her offer to do the flowers free of charge was gratefully received.

She'd deliberately made the child's bridesmaid's bouquet far too big to give her an excuse to stay behind and have a look around Nelson's house. Once alone there, she'd searched the drawers on the dresser, found a brown address book and, sure enough, Blatchington's address was there. So was a letter in Linton's own hand.

The letter was a revelation. Linton had been nothing if not thorough in his confession, and her hatred of them all burned with a passion. She'd heard most of it before. For some time she had been encouraging Linton to talk to her, playing the part of a sympathetic matron with a deeply held religious need to help her fellow men. To him, she'd been a gentle simpleton who dispensed tea and cake as he unburdened his soul. Through Linton she'd already found out about Nelson and George, but he'd never spoken about Blatchington; and Charlie Downs was a new one to her as well. She toyed with the idea of putting the letter on the fire, but in the end she couldn't resist taking it with her. She'd heard someone try the door handle and froze. They'd all be coming back soon, and she had to leave. She'd been in the house for ages and there was no reason why she should still be there. Then a voice called through the wood, giving her no option but to open the door. Now she wished she hadn't.

She picked up Victor's photograph now and kissed the glass. 'Darling, I've made a stupid mistake. Help me. Tell me what to do to make it right.'

CHAPTER 38

Rex took Bea and May to the beach. Not in Worthing, but to a secluded beach at Elmer Sands partway between Littlehampton and Bognor. The place had remained unspoiled until ten years before, when the farmer sold some land to people who had built a few weekend cottages. More recently he had sold more land to developers, who had expanded it and called it Elmer Sands Estate. A line of trees screened the new estate from Bailiffscourt, and roadways had been created. Building was slow, because of the chronic shortage of builders (so many having been killed during the war), and the houses themselves were simple. Heating them by paraffin stoves and using only pump water merely added to the rustic feel of the place.

'My parents brought me here as a child,' he told Bea as he unpacked the car.

He had certainly come prepared, with picnic hamper from Warnes and two folding chairs.

'Warnes...' she remarked. 'Last time you stayed at the Savoy.'

'I fancied a change,' he replied.

'I left you a note at the Savoy.'

He stared at her in surprise. 'A note?'

'I went to see you last year, and they put a note in the safe for you.'

'Oh, Bea, I'm sorry.'

'What if I had been unable to come today?' Bea laughed as he spread a plaid rug on the sand.

'Then I should have had another very lonely Sunday,' he said, straightening up and kissing her lips. 'Right, young lady,' he said to May, 'you need a bucket and spade.'

There was a small kiosk nearby and, taking May by the hand, Rex walked her to it. She came back kitted out with everything she would need for a happy time: bucket, spade, shrimp net and even a tray to put her 'catch' in. He'd also bought her a sunhat and a windmill. May was beaming as if it was Christmas Day.

'What do you say?' Bea reminded her.

'Thank you,' said May dutifully and, as she headed towards the water's edge, Rex sat down next to Bea.

'You've been very generous to her,' she smiled.

'Of course, you do realize it was all a dastardly trick, just to get you alone,' he said.

'I would expect nothing less from a captain in the British Army,' she replied coyly.

'Ex-captain,' he corrected her, 'and I'm not sure I deserve such an accolade. When I was in office, I did something unforgivable.'

Bea glanced at him with a puzzled expression.

'I seduced another man's wife and fell hopelessly in love with her.'

'She didn't take much seducing,' said Bea. 'I have it on good authority that she was already head-over-heels in love with you.'

He caught her hand and drew it to his lips. Bea watched as he kissed her fingers. 'My poor darling. Was it awful?'

'It wasn't easy,' she conceded, 'but I still had the hope that we might be together one day. That's what kept me going, but I never thought it would take this long.'

'Eighteen years,' he said, shaking his head.

'I was cruel,' she said. 'I should never have made you promise to wait for me. I should have let you go and live your life. Please forgive me.'

'Nothing to forgive,' he protested. 'I would have waited anyway.'

'Nelson never let me forget what we did. After he knew I was pregnant with Ruby, he didn't touch me.'

Rex looked out to sea, where May was crouched over a rockpool. 'But you went back to him in the end?'

'Remember when we bumped into you?' said Bea quietly. 'We were in Hastings visiting friends, and we saw you going into someone's house – a patient, I suppose. You had your doctor's bag.'

'I remember.'

She shook her head sadly. 'Nelson must have seen something in my eyes – my reaction to you... I don't know. I tried to laugh it off, pretend it never happened, but he was so angry.'

'So May...?'

She looked down at her lap. 'Nelson was a big man. That night he forced me. It was easy enough.'

He seized her hand. 'Oh, my poor darling...'

Bea looked up at him and he saw the tears standing in her eyes. 'She doesn't know,' she said deliberately, 'and she must *never* know. I love my daughter, Rex. It's not her fault.'

He nodded and looked back at the little girl playing in the rockpools. 'Your secret is safe with me, but I hate the thought of what he did to you,' he said brokenly.

Bea reached for his hand. 'You mustn't dwell on it, my love,' she soothed. 'It's all in the past now. You're here, and you still love me. That's all I want in life.'

'How can you brush it aside so easily?'

'I saw what holding onto a hurt did to Nelson,' she said, 'so I made up my mind to forgive him. It wasn't easy, but it released me from him. Please don't feel sorry for me. I'm no martyr. I made a choice to love you, and I made a choice to save my children from the workhouse. I made a deliberate decision not to hold anything against him. I don't regret anything. Nelson only did it the once. He was insanely jealous, and yet he hated me for trapping him into marriage. I'd made up my mind to leave him, once May was old enough to fend for herself. But although he never hurt her, I was too afraid to take the risk.'

A far-away child's voice called, 'Mummy, come and look at this.'

They both stood up. 'How did he come to die?'
'Ruby and I think he was murdered.'
'Murdered?' Rex gasped.
'Mummy ... look!'

Bea was pulling her shoes off. She put her finger to her lips. 'I'll tell you later.' Then, calling to May, she said, 'Coming, darling. Have you caught something nice?'

May was skipping in the road with her friends when Ruby and Jim slowly made their way back home. They were both tired. Eastbourne had been crowded with August bank-holiday visitors and the weather was kind to them. Cecil's coach might have been a bit of a relic, but it was clean and comfortable and he was a careful driver. Their picnic on the beach had been a pleasure and they both enjoyed the newness of their married relationship.

However, the discovery of the bullet in the bed had dominated their day. They had rehearsed the names of everybody who had come to the house the day before, and the list was so long that it felt as if the rest of the world and his wife had passed through the doors. Friends, neighbours, Susan Marley, the florist, the chimney sweep who had come to wish them good luck, several fishermen who had sailed with Nelson, all the girls from Warnes ... the list went on and on. Everyone had had access to the bedroom, because their coats had been thrown across the bed and Ruby couldn't resist showing some of them her new 'home'. As far as she and Jim could see, not one of them was a threat, let alone a killer. They'd gone over and over it until Ruby's head hurt, so they'd made a pact not to speak of it again, only to find themselves drifting back to it once more.

May waved and ran towards them.

'Hello, Pipsqueak,' said Ruby. 'Did you and Mummy have a nice day?'

'We went to the beach with Mummy's friend.'

'Did you now,' said Ruby.

'It wasn't our beach,' said May. 'It was miles and miles away, and we went in a big car.'

Ruby chuckled. 'Oh, yes?'

'We *did*,' May insisted. 'And I went fishing in a rock-pool and I caught a baby crab, but Mummy said I had to put him back, because that's where he lives and he would miss his home.'

Her mother had come to the door. 'May, you can stay outside for another five minutes and then it's time for bed,' said Bea. 'Ruby, Jim, I need to talk to you.'

Ruby's heart sank. Something was wrong. Had something happened to Percy? 'What is it, Mum?' she said, going indoors and pulling off her hat.

She listened open-mouthed as Bea told them about Rex turning up.

'Did he know it was my wedding?'

'No, love,' said Bea. 'He was most upset to miss it. Apparently he was here in Worthing, but he was ill and had to stay in his room at the hotel.'

'Oh, darling, what a terrible shame,' Jim murmured.

'Is he all right now?' Ruby asked anxiously.

Bea nodded. 'He turned up soon after you'd gone, and he took May and me to Elmer Sands.'

Ruby felt a stab of jealousy: Rex was *her* father.

Jim must have sensed how she felt because she felt him reach for her hand. In the run-up to their wedding she had told him everything she knew about her mother and Rex. Surprisingly, for a man, Jim thought it was romantic. 'I'm glad your mother has known real love,' he'd said. 'She deserves it. Your father... Nelson was never very nice to her.'

'The thing is,' Bea went on now, 'he wants to meet you both.'

'When?' Ruby asked eagerly.

'I told him you might be too tired, but he'd like us all to have dinner with him at the hotel tonight.'

Ruby gasped.

'He's sending a car around in about...' she glanced at the clock, 'forty minutes.'

'Forty minutes!'

'If you'd rather leave it for now,' said Bea, 'we've arranged that you could meet him tomorrow instead.'

Ruby glanced at her husband. 'I can't wait until tomorrow and, besides, it's bank-holiday Monday. All the day-trippers will be on the prom wanting their "Magic Memories".'

'This is far more important, Ruby,' said Jim. 'He's your father.'

Ruby suddenly realized that her mother was all dressed up. She was wearing the dress she had bought for the wedding, and her hair was neatly curled.

The next half-hour was manic. Ruby and Jim dashed around each other concentrating on getting ready before the car came. Susan Marley came round to babysit, while Bea put May to bed.

The child complained and pleaded to come, but by the time everyone was ready, she was already tucked up and Susan was reading her a story.

No one could have been more shocked than Ruby when the car pulled up outside Warnes Hotel. But if any of the staff who greeted them were surprised to see their ex-chambermaid walking through the doors as a guest, they certainly didn't show it.

As they were shown into the dining room, a man sitting at a table near the window stood up. Ruby's eyes never left his as they made their way through the tables. He was tall, with a military bearing. He had dark hair, greying at the temples, and he was clean-shaven. He was wearing a dinner jacket with a dark tie on a snow-white shirt. Ruby waited as he kissed her mother on the cheek and shook hands with Jim. Then Jim stepped aside and Ruby came face-to-face with her real father for the first time. They smiled at each other shyly, then Rex opened his arms and she stepped towards him with a shiver of excitement. His hug was warm and inviting, and yet sensitive to her feelings. He smelled of the carbolic fragrance of Lifebuoy soap. This was the hug she had longed for all her life; the hug Nelson could never have given her – her father's hug.

'I'm so pleased to meet you, Ruby,' he smiled. 'Your mother has told me so much about you. I can't believe I missed your wedding. I am so sorry.'

'Please don't worry,' said Ruby, her eyes shining. 'It couldn't be helped.'

They sat opposite each other, and several times

during the evening Ruby realized she was staring at her father. They talked about everything: her childhood; how much he loved her mother and missed her; how hard it had been to wait for the right time; his days in the army; and his life now as a country doctor. They talked about Ruby's job at the hospital, Jim's life in the children's home, and Rex keeping alive the memory of Bea with the help of the locket...

Ruby frowned. 'The locket?'

Bea took something from around her neck. Ruby hadn't noticed it before – or had she? It was vaguely familiar. Her mother showed her the hidden catch and she found herself looking at the picture of a baby.

'That's you,' said Rex. 'That was all I had of you, for all these years.'

Ruby ran her finger over the curl of hair.

'You had dark hair, even as a baby,' said Bea.

'Didn't Lily...?' Ruby began.

'On the day of Nelson's inquest, Rex gave that locket to Cousin Lily to give to me,' said Bea crossly, 'but the little minx kept it.'

Ruby leaned across the table to show Jim her picture.

The meal they ate as they talked was amazing. Ruby had occasionally seen what was being served at Warnes, but she had never tasted it for herself. The choice was unbelievable: hors d'oeuvres, consommé – a sort of watery-looking soup – or cream of rice *amandine,* followed by fillet of whiting, duck with green peas or English roast beef, all served with either fresh vegetables and boiled potatoes or lettuce and tomato salad. Dessert was

431

Viennese tartlets, fruit jelly and whipped cream or ice cream.

A little later Jim changed the subject. 'Do members of your regiment keep in touch with each other?' He glanced at his wife; Ruby would know where this was going. He was trying to find out if there was any way of contacting Charlie Downs.

'Sometimes,' said Rex. 'There's the regimental club and, of course, the wonderful work the British Legion does helps to keep friendships alive.'

'So if I wanted to find someone,' Jim ventured, 'would the Legion be able to help me?'

'I imagine so,' said Rex. 'Or if you knew which regiment your friend was in, you could try writing to them. Why? Are you thinking of tracing your own father?'

'Just curious,' said Jim brightly. 'I have no idea who my father is. The Searle family tree begins with me.'

They drank wine with the meal, but Ruby thought it wasn't as nice as Susan Marley's home-made elderflower wine. Then they were invited to take their coffee in the lounge.

Ruby was following the group when she realized she'd left her scarf on the back of the chair. As she came out of the dining room into the corridor, Mrs Fosdyke came down the stairs. Her mouth visibly tightened when she saw Ruby.

'What are you doing here, Bateman?' she hissed as she advanced towards her. 'How dare you!'

'Is everything all right?' Rex was standing in the doorway.

'This girl,' Mrs Fosdyke spat contemptuously, 'has no business to be here. She is trespassing.'

The maître d' came out of the dining room as Rex said in acid tones, 'This girl is with me. She is my guest, and I'll thank you to treat her with respect.'

With the maître d' apologizing profusely and Ruby blushing a deep crimson, Mrs Fosdyke gaped from one to the other.

'I think it's you who should give my daughter an apology,' said Rex, glaring at her.

Mrs Fosdyke's lips curled. 'Your daughter?' It was obvious by her tone of voice that she didn't believe him for one minute.

Ruby opened her mouth to say something, but Rex interrupted. 'Yes, my daughter.' He turned to the maitre d'. 'Do you usually allow your guests to be insulted like this?'

'I do most humbly apologize, sir,' said the maitre d' and, turning to Mrs Fosdyke, he added, 'Mrs Fosdyke?'

'I know this girl,' said Mrs Fosdyke. 'And you are *not* her father. Her father is dead. He was nothing more than a common fisherman.'

'Mrs Fosdyke!' said the maître d' indignantly.

'I wouldn't be so quick to make judgements,' said Rex tartly.

'Mrs Fosdyke!' said the maître d'. 'Apologize – this minute.'

'It doesn't matter,' Ruby said quietly. 'Really.'

Recovering her composure, Mrs Fosdyke pulled back her shoulders. 'I never apologize,' she said, haughtily, 'and especially not to a cocky little strumpet who once worked here as a chambermaid.' And with that, she walked away, leaving everyone open-mouthed.

433

CHAPTER 39

'The bloody woman deserves the sack!'

Rex Quinn was almost beside himself with anger. His loud voice filtered through the wall and into her room.

It was the next day and he was back at Bea's place. Jim had gone to work, Percy was out and May was playing outside, but Ruby was still in her room. All the way back from the hotel the previous evening she had fought back her tears, pretending that she was all right. But she wasn't. Mrs Fosdyke's words had hurt her deeply. Why did she hate her so much? Ruby only ever treated her with respect and obedience. Jim had done his best to comfort her, but even he was at a loss to understand. Why had Mrs Fosdyke been so rude?

Hearing her father's voice now, Ruby opened the door and was just about to walk into the kitchen when she heard Rex say, 'Of course I have lodged a complaint. The woman's behaviour was appalling. I've never heard such a tirade of abuse.'

'I think I may be the cause,' said Bea quietly, and Ruby froze.

'You?' said Rex. 'Oh, my darling, why on earth would you think that?'

'I grew up with Freda Fosdyke,' said Bea. 'Years ago she set her cap at Nelson, but I was the one he married. It broke her heart.'

'Well, I'll be damned,' said Rex.

Ruby came into the room and her mother put on a bright smile. 'Hello, love. I'm glad you had a bit of a lie-in. Sit down and I'll pour you some tea.'

Ruby sat down, and Rex kissed his daughter's cheek.

'We were just saying...' her mother babbled on.

'I heard what you were saying, Mum,' said Ruby, 'and I want you both to stop worrying about it.'

'I'm seeing the manager this morning, before I finally leave,' said Rex firmly, 'and I'll be telling him that I'm not having my daughter spoken to like that.'

Ruby smiled. To hear him talk about her like that was music to her ears. All her life she'd wanted a father who cared about her – one who would stick up for her – and now she had one. 'I'd rather you didn't,' she said. 'I don't want to give Mrs Fosdyke a moment more of my life.'

'But the woman–'

'I don't work there any more,' said Ruby. 'It really doesn't matter. I refuse even to think about it.'

'It's my fault,' said Bea, sinking into the chair.

'No, Mum,' said Ruby. 'Mrs Fosdyke is a cow and a bully. While I worked at Warnes, I let her opinions rule my life. Well, I won't do it any more. Bullies look for someone to bully. Well, not me; not any more. She can think what she likes. I refuse to let it bother me.'

'You're an amazing young woman,' said Rex. There was no disguising the admiration in his voice.

'Not at all,' said Ruby.

'The woman deserves the sack,' he insisted.

'Perhaps she does,' said Ruby, 'but if I get her the sack, I shall never be free of her. I'm cutting all links with her, right here and now.' She looked up at her parents' astonished faces and smiled. 'Now, we'd better get a move-on or we'll miss the day-trippers.'

Although Rex was only in Worthing for one more day, it was imperative that Jim spend the day on Marine Parade with his camera. The day-trippers would be in town, despite the overcast skies and the usual bank-holiday drop in temperature. The Sunday trading laws had prevented them from putting up the booth yesterday, so even though it was cold and miserable, the bank holiday was still an opportunity for Magic Memories. They simply couldn't afford to miss the opportunity to get the business going.

Surprisingly, Rex had elected to join them later that morning, taking a turn in the booth with Bea and looking after May at the water's edge. Ruby spent her time developing the morning pictures, ready to sell before 4 p.m., when the coaches parked up by the pier, waiting to take visitors home, actually departed. She flew backwards and forwards from Newlands Road on her bicycle. It was a lot quicker than walking.

'Bea, my darling,' said Rex, as he helped her pack up ready to go home, 'it's time we talked about our future.'

Having settled in her own mind the way she was going to deal with Mrs Fosdyke, Ruby was still in a bit of a quandary. She was blissfully happy to be Jim's wife, and settling down to married life was both fulfilling and satisfying. He was teaching her to develop the films and she was becoming more skilled by the minute. She'd designed some little cards that advertised Jim's burgeoning business, to give to potential customers, and she'd taken over keeping the books. Ruby tried to be as encouraging as she could, but she knew Jim was worried. That was why she didn't tell him about the thing that most concerned her.

That they'd both seen the bullet in the bed was enough to cause them concern, but as she'd made the bed the next morning, Ruby had found a slip of paper. It had been crumpled by their own bodies as they lay in bed and slept on it, but when she read the words – just three of them – written there, it sent a chill right through her: *Ruby Searle, widow.* There could be no doubt about it; someone was making a deliberate threat.

She kept it to herself and worried for about a week, until she could make up her mind what to do. Jim had enough on his plate already and, for the first time in her life, her mother was happy. Ruby couldn't bring herself to spoil things for them. That left her with no one to talk to – no one who'd give her sound advice. Aunt Vinny loved a good gossip, so Ruby couldn't even talk to her.

Then she bumped into Albert Longman.

He had been coming out of the offices of the *Worthing Gazette* just as Ruby walked by. They'd passed the time of day and, as he lifted his hat to leave, she made a decision. He was a reporter; he investigated things. He was older, a man of the world. If anyone knew what to do, Albert would. They parted in the street, but almost at once Ruby called him back.

He turned, licking his fingers and plastering his hair down at the front.

'Albert,' she began, 'I know we've had our differences, but can I talk to you about something in confidence?'

He looked a little taken aback, but quickly recovered. 'Of course, Ruby,' he said as he smiled that smarmy smile. 'Any time you like. After all, we're old friends, aren't we?'

Once again Percy was making big changes in his life. He'd walked out of the barracks without a backward glance and, as luck would have it, had found himself a job and a place to live all on the same day. It wasn't much; just a job as a warehouse man and night-watchman, and the room he had 'on the job' was hardly fit for a dog. But it was a beginning.

He didn't tell her exactly what he was doing, but he loved it when he saw Rachel. They would walk and talk for hours. Occasionally he would take her to the pictures, and sometimes she would let him hold her hand. During those times she told him a great deal about herself. He heard about her happy childhood, and how things changed when Hitler came to power.

'We heard stories about people being taken away in the dead of night,' she told him, 'but you never think it will happen to you.'

'Why doesn't anybody stand up to him?' asked Percy. He found it hard to believe that anyone could gain so much power – absolute power – so quickly. But, as Rachel explained about the systematic elimination of all opposition, he began to feel increasingly uncomfortable. The sweeping-away of the old traditions – the 'dead wood' of society – and recreating it into a new world order were all terms Mosley had used. He wanted a Britain where Fascism was king, and where his word alone became the oracle for the nation. It sounded just the same thing that Hitler wanted: different name, different country, different leader, but the same result.

Percy began to ask himself real and, until now, unspoken questions. What if Mosley did become leader? What would happen to the king, to Parliament, to the government itself? If all the old ways *were* swept away, who would rule Great Britain? He shivered. Of course there was a lot wrong with the institutions of the nation, and everyone agreed they all needed a good shake-up, but how could you sweep away 400 years of democracy in a bloodless coup? And what would you put in its place? It all sounded very romantic from the platform, but what was the reality? Now at last Percy realized that he had been carried away with an ideology that was at best highly suspect and, at worst, downright dangerous.

For the first time since he'd arrived in London he missed his family. Rachel had lost all of hers; he had simply turned his back on his. What a fool he had been. What a hypocrite too. He was a man of the world; he'd slept with a few girls and, if Rachel would let him, he would jump at the chance to sleep with her. He didn't much like the idea that

439

he was another man's child, and he was of the opinion that a woman should be faithful, but by sleeping with women himself, hadn't he done the same thing as those he scorned? Then there was the money from selling Nelson's boat and locker. He shouldn't have kept it. If he wasn't Nelson's son, then it wasn't even his property. He knew his mother and sister were almost destitute and, by taking that money, he might well have pushed them into the workhouse. He didn't feel much like the all-conquering hero these days. He felt shabby, irresponsible and a thief.

As Percy held his girl in his arms while she wept for the friends and family she would never see again, this side of the grave, he wished with all his heart that he'd never got himself mixed up in another man's thirst for glory.

Ruby and Albert met in Lancing on Thursday. She had taken the bus, and he the train, and they met in a small cafe on the high street. He was waiting as she walked in, and stood up to offer her a seat. The waitress hovered and Albert ordered tea for two and a toasted bun.

'I feel dreadful, sneaking off like this,' she said.

Albert tried to grasp her hand. 'You know I'm always here for you, Ruby,' he purred.

She snatched her hand away. 'Please remember that I'm a married woman, Albert,' she said haughtily. 'Let's keep this solely on a business footing.'

'Of course,' he smiled, closing his eyes as he did so.

'I need your expertise, that's all.'

'And you shall have it,' he said with that same irritating smile. 'What can I do for you, Ruby?'

It took a while to explain everything and, to give Albert his due, she was delighted that he listened to every word she said. It was a little disconcerting that he never took his eyes off her, but he didn't interrupt, or ridicule her in any way.

The waitress came back and Ruby poured them both some tea, while Albert put some jam on his already-buttered bun.

'The real problem is that something has changed,' she said. 'I ... we had thought this was all to do with someone exacting their own warped brand of justice, on behalf of Victor – whoever he was – but there's something else.' She fumbled in her bag and put the bullet on the table. 'Jim and I found this in our marriage bed,' she went on.

Albert raised his eyebrows. 'But neither of you had anything to do with Victor's death.'

'Exactly,' she said. 'We were willing to believe this was a practical joke or something, but what Jim doesn't know is that I found this as well.' She placed the crumpled piece of paper in front of him.

Albert studied it carefully, repeating the words aloud.

'Ruby Searle, widow.'

Hearing it said aloud, Ruby shivered. 'What does it mean?'

Albert looked thoughtful. 'I can hazard a guess,' he said, 'but it's rather odd.'

'That's what I thought,' said Ruby. 'It means someone has got it in for me, doesn't it?'

'In for Jim, more like,' said Albert.

441

'I think someone means to do him harm.'

Albert looked up. 'I'm afraid they do,' he said. She was heartened to see genuine concern etched on his face, so she told him everything she knew.

Albert sighed.

'What do you think I should do?' she asked.

'Have you been to the police?'

Ruby shook her head. 'Jim thinks it's not a real threat. I mean, it could be someone's idea of a sick joke.'

'It's a bit unsavoury,' said Albert.

'I've got a letter that Linton wrote,' she said. She also told him about Linton's address book. 'I was thinking that if you could go through it, you might be able to find out who is doing this. It has to be connected.'

Albert lifted his cup to his lips. 'Of course I will. You can count on me to protect you, Ruby.'

'Can you find Charlie Downs as well?' she went on. 'Mum and I can probably reach Colonel Blatchington ourselves. Percy has had some contact with him. I think we really should warn them. And one other thing: can you find out who made that bullet?'

Albert put his cup back in the saucer. 'Ruby, the thing is home-made. There's no maker's name, no manufacturer's number. Anybody could have done it – even a child.'

She sighed. 'I just don't know which way to turn.'

He reached for her hand again. 'We're old friends, Ruby,' he said. 'I want you to know that I'm here for you. If you get anything else, let me know.'

'What about Jim?'

'Jim is a big boy,' said Albert. 'I'm sure he can look after himself. Don't worry.'

Ruby suddenly felt very grateful. 'Thank you.'

'Don't worry. I'll have a scout around,' Albert went on. 'With that address book, I may be able to find out about the other men involved in this sordid affair. Keep in touch.'

Ruby nodded.

'Drink your tea,' he said. 'I'll meet you here next week. You can bring the address book and the letter with you then.'

'I can't come for a couple of weeks,' said Ruby. 'It's Mum's wedding. But I can come the week after.'

'All right.' Albert nodded. 'I must say, I am a bit surprised to hear that your mum is getting married so soon.'

'It's been a year,' said Ruby tartly.

'I suppose so,' Albert nodded.

'You won't tell anyone, will you?' Ruby asked anxiously. 'About us meeting, I mean. I don't want Jim getting any wrong ideas.'

'Our little secret,' said Albert, running his finger across his mouth. 'My lips are sealed.'

As she waited at the bus stop Ruby was glad she'd thought of Albert. She loved Jim with all her heart and, although she knew that Albert had once harboured feelings for her, and there were things about him that irritated her, he had turned out to be a good friend.

CHAPTER 40

Percy was more in love with Rachel than ever. He had even been taking lessons from the rabbi. It wasn't hard to accept what he was being taught, but he wasn't yet sure if he wanted to convert. He didn't consider himself a religious man, but if he could not have Rachel unless he converted, then he would do it. She didn't seem to mind one way or another.

The tide was turning. After the chaotic scenes in the next BUF gathering at Olympia, the *Daily Mail* changed its allegiance and began to thunder against the movement. That had ushered in a new period of unrest and anger. Percy wasn't surprised when bitter clashes between English supporters of Fascism and their opponents took place in the East End. As more German Jewish refugees fleeing Nazi persecution began to arrive, many of them settling in Spitalfields and Hampstead, they brought with them a long history as entrepreneurial middlemen, and London provided excellent financing opportunities. It was easy for jealousies to fester. The Blackshirts said you would never find a poor Jew, and Percy was beginning to see why. He loved the way Rachel's people helped each other and, because of his connection with her, Percy found himself working in one of the new 'sunrise' industries. He'd got a job working for a wholesaler, supplying food and drink. His driving skills came in useful, as he bought top-notch ingredients from Covent Garden and ferried them around London to a small chain of restaurants. His employer liked that fact that Percy took pride in his work by cleaning his van every night when he returned to the depot, so it wasn't long before talk of promotion was in the air.

He was overjoyed when at last Rachel agreed to marry him. Now all Percy wanted was his mother's blessing, which meant swallowing his pride and going back to Worthing.

If he had been worried about the reception he might get, he needn't have been concerned. As he strode towards Newlands Road from the station on the first Sunday in September, May saw him first. She dropped her skipping rope and ran along the road, shouting, 'Percy, Percy!'

He swept her up in the air and swung her around as they both laughed. Bea heard the commotion and came out of the door. She flung herself into her son's arms, laughing and crying at the same time. Then it was Ruby's turn, and Percy was overwhelmed. He didn't deserve this; he'd behaved very badly and had run out on everybody at a time when they'd needed him most. But, as he began to apologize, they waved his regrets away in their eagerness to get him indoors. It was only as they headed for the door together, and Percy hung back, that they noticed Rachel.

'Mum, Ruby,' said Percy, 'this is my future intended. Rachel, this is my mother and sister.'

For a second or two the three women stared at

each other in mutual surprise, then Bea held out her arms and hugged Rachel. 'I'm so pleased to meet you, my dear. Come in, come in.'

The family had invited Rex to join them for a fish-and-chip supper and he was already sitting at the table as they went inside. It was in stark contrast to the meal they'd had in the hotel some time ago, but nobody minded. They all enjoyed simply being together.

'Percy, this is Rex,' said Bea. 'Rex and I are old friends.'

Now it was Percy's turn to look surprised, but as Rex stood up to shake his hand, he quickly recovered, smiled and pumped it heartily.

'What happened to your face?' May asked Rachel.

Bea gave her daughter a nudge and hissed, 'May, be quiet.'

'It's all right,' said Rachel. 'I had an accident and cut myself.'

'Oh,' said May.

Faced with sharing what they had already bought, which would barely be enough, Jim ran down to the chip shop for two more portions, and Bea put what they had in the oven to keep warm until he came back. There was so much to catch up on. First that Percy had left the Black-shirts and, after working as a night-watchman for a week or so, was now with a firm of delivery vans. He, in turn, was surprised to hear that Bea and Rex were getting married in two weeks' time.

'Married!' cried Percy.

'Would you give me away?' Bea asked, and was rewarded by her son giving her a beaming smile and squeezing her hand.

'I'd love to, Mother.'

He discovered that Ruby was already married, and that she and Jim had started a street-photography business. 'I did write and ask you to give me away,' said Ruby, and to his shame Percy remembered the letter he'd shoved into his pocket and never opened.

'I'm so sorry I wasn't here for you, Sis,' he said, hanging his head in shame.

'You left me in the lurch,' she said. There were tears in her eyes.

'I know.'

'I had all the responsibility.'

Percy put his arm around his sister's shoulders. 'You're right, Ruby. It was unforgivable and I feel terrible about it. Please forgive me.'

Ruby sank back into his hug, remembering again the times she had been spared Nelson's slap or, on a couple of occasions, his belt because Percy took the punishment for her. He had been a good brother in the past. They had all been through some difficult times, but now it seemed that he was home for good.

She gave him a nod of forgiveness, then she and Bea listened with rapt attention while Percy told them how he and Rachel had met.

'I was afraid of him at first,' Rachel confessed. 'The Blackshirts...'

'I don't blame you,' said Ruby. 'They look quite fearsome on the newsreels.'

'Where I come from,' said Rachel, 'people disappear. They are taken to a big camp and they cannot come back home.'

'She means Hitler's concentration camp,' said Percy.

'Concentration camp?' said Ruby. 'What's that?'

'Since the beginning of last year the Nazis have been sending people to a special camp,' said Rachel. 'It's called Dachau.'

A stunned silence fell on the room. No one made any reference to her terrible scar, although they all wondered if that had anything to do with it.

Jim came back and, as Bea unwrapped the newspaper parcels, they all reached for a plate.

'I told Rachel that you were looking after a German refugee,' said Percy. 'By the way, where is John?'

'He went to live in Brighton,' said Bea.

'Shame,' Percy said to Rachel. 'Rachel is Jewish too. I would have liked her to meet him.'

As they ate, Rex told Ruby and Percy that he had loved Bea for more years than he cared to remember and that he wanted their mother to come and live at his house in Hastings. At first Bea protested that she was needed here in Worthing, but he took her hand and said, 'Sweetheart, we have already waited too many years to be together. I have a good living as a doctor, and I live in a bungalow overlooking the sea. It would be the perfect place to bring May up.'

Percy glanced at his mother and grinned. 'Sounds wonderful, Mother.'

Having finished her meal, it was May's bedtime. Percy kissed her and, as he chased her upstairs, she squealed with delight.

'I'm so pleased for you and Percy,' Bea told

448

Rachel when they were alone. 'He's a good boy. I'm sure he'll do his best to make you happy.'

Rachel smiled, but Ruby seemed far away.

Percy came back downstairs and Jim went to use the outside lav.

'There's something wrong, isn't there?' Bea whispered as she leaned towards Ruby, who was washing up the plates. 'I can see it in your face. Something is worrying you. Don't you like her?'

'She's lovely,' Ruby blushed. 'I'm really happy for Percy.' She hesitated, wanting to talk to her mother, but now that Rachel was here, how much could she say? She glanced behind her and saw that Rachel was going upstairs to join Percy and May.

'Are you upset that I'm taking your mother and sister away?' Rex interjected in a low voice. He knew he would find it hard to understand, if this was the reason for Ruby's worried expression. The arrangements they'd made would certainly give Jim and Ruby a good start in life, because it had been agreed that they could set up their home in Newlands Road and pay a peppercorn rent to her mother, to keep things legal.

'It's not that,' said Ruby.

'Is it something to do with Jim?' Bea asked. 'Are you happy?'

Ruby squeezed her mother's hand reassuringly. 'It's nothing to do with Jim and, yes, I am very happy.'

'Then what is it?'

Ruby glanced at her husband as he came back into the room.

'Ruby, I want you to know that I shall do my

best to give your mother and sister a good life,' said Rex, catching her arm lightly. 'I'm sure that whatever your concerns are, we can resolve them.'

'We said no more secrets, so what's wrong?' Bea glanced anxiously up at Rex.

'Honestly,' said Ruby, 'it's nothing to do with you and Mum, and it's nothing to do with Percy and Rachel, either. Really, I couldn't be more happy about all of you getting together.'

It was obvious that Rex was relieved, but now he seemed even more puzzled.

While everyone sat around the kitchen table, Bea had gone out to the scullery to move the washing on the clothes horse. Percy and Rachel came downstairs and Percy came to join his mother in the scullery.

'Mother, I owe you this,' he said, pushing something into her hand. 'I'm so sorry. I should have given the money to you when I sold the boat. In fact I should never have sold it in the first place. It wasn't mine to sell. He wasn't even my father.'

'You rushed off before I could explain, Son,' said Bea. 'You got the wrong end of the stick. Nelson *was* your father.'

'Then is May...? Is Rex...?'

'Rex is Ruby's father,' said Bea softly.

'Ruby's!'

While she moved things on the dryer, folding some for the ironing basket and spreading the bigger things out to dry more quickly, Bea quietly explained everything and, at the end of it, Percy looked a little sheepish. 'I've been an absolute idiot, haven't I, Mum?' he said.

'Never mind, love,' said Bea. 'You're home now.'

They re-joined the others around the kitchen table.

'Ruby,' Bea insisted, 'I want to know what's bothering you. We're all family here,' she glanced at Rachel with a small smile, 'or we soon will be. Perhaps we can help.'

Ruby shifted uncomfortably in her seat. Should she tell them what she'd confided in Albert?

'I think I can guess what it is,' said Jim. 'Am I right, love?'

She looked down and said nothing, so Jim told them what he and Ruby had discovered under the pillow in their bedroom on the night of their wedding.

'Can I see the bullet?' asked Rex.

While Jim went to fetch it, Ruby breathed a sigh of relief that Albert hadn't taken it with him.

'Is this why you asked me about the British Legion?' said Rex, rolling the bullet between his fingers.

Jim nodded. 'I didn't really believe Ruby's theory, when she told me about the others,' he said, 'but now that this has happened... Well, it puts a different light on it.'

'Others? What others?' said Percy. 'Am I missing something here?'

Between them, Jim, Bea and Ruby repeated the story once again. They told him of their suspicions about Nelson's death, and of the bullet the police found among his effects; then they told him about Linton Carver's death and the letter of confession they'd found among his things; and finally of the untimely death of George Gore.

451

'Not only that,' Bea went on, 'but Mabel Harris has a bullet too. She found it in one of Jack's pockets when he died.'

Percy listened, open-mouthed.

'The other bullets are in Granny's teapot,' said Ruby, standing up to get them. 'Mum wrote to Mrs Gore ages ago, and she's coming to Worthing for a holiday at the end of the week.'

'We plan to ask her if her husband had one too,' Bea explained.

Jim lined them up next to the bullet they'd found under the pillow.

'And, of course, the one belonging to Jack Harris,' said Bea.

'They're obviously home-made,' said Rex. 'Amateurish, crude, but clearly made by the same person, with the word *Victory* on the side.'

'Is it *Victory?*' asked Rachel, 'or is it the name Victor with a little squiggle?'

'Good Lord!' Bea exclaimed. 'It's so obvious and yet we never even thought of that.'

'Then this whole thing has to have been about the firing squad,' said Ruby. 'The men who shot Victor.'

'And you've got all the names of the men in the firing squad?' asked Rex.

'Yes,' said Bea, opening the dresser drawer. She drew in her breath. 'Oh no! It's gone!' she cried. 'Someone has taken Mabel's address book.'

Ruby helped her to look, but her mother was right. The address book was nowhere to be seen. Her stomach fell away – now she had nothing to show Albert next week. How could he possibly find Charlie Downs for them now? And supposing there were other soldiers listed within the pages: people they had all presumed were dead, but who were still alive and vulnerable?

'So let me get this straight,' said Rex. 'You think whoever put the bullet under your pillow is the same person who took the address book, and that person is instrumental in the untimely demise of at least three people, maybe four.'

'Yes,' said Ruby. Her voice was cracked and betrayed the panic rising inside her. She ought to tell them about the note threatening Jim.

He caught her hand and squeezed it as she sat back down at the table.

Rachel looked visibly distressed. 'And I thought England was a peaceful place,' she whispered to Percy.

Rex was on a roll. 'Is anybody who was part of the firing squad still around?'

'There's still Charlie Downs and Captain Blatchington,' said Ruby, her chin quivering.

'I know a Colonel Blatchington,' said Percy. 'Do you think it's the same man?'

'We thought so,' said Bea, 'and so I wrote to him, but he never answered.'

'To warn him?'

She nodded. 'And to tell him that the others were dead.'

Rex looked thoughtful. 'And their addresses were in that book?'

'Along with Linton's confession,' said Ruby anxiously.

'Which leaves us with absolutely no real physical evidence at all,' said Rex.

'We've tried to think of every single person who

was in our house on the day of our wedding,' said Jim.

'The bullet had to have been left there then,' Ruby went on. 'I only made up the bed in the morning.'

'It can't be any of our friends,' said Bea anxiously.

'Clearly, whoever it is, he's deranged,' said Jim.

'Or,' Rex corrected him, 'they could be very clever.'

'The point is,' said Jim, 'what are we going to do?'

'I think we should still try and warn Blatchington and Downs,' said Ruby.

'I'll write to Colonel Blatchington myself,' said Percy. 'I got on really well with him, and I know he thought well of me. He tried to persuade me to stay in the movement.'

'I hate to say this,' said Rex, 'but some people have already tried to point the finger of suspicion at you, Percy.'

'Me!' cried Percy, jumping to his feet and scraping the chair on the wooden floor.

'Calm down,' said Rex, looking a bit surprised at his volatile reaction. 'I'm not accusing you, I'm just saying...'

'Oh, Rex...' said Bea.

'Percy hates all kinds of violence,' said Ruby.

'Please believe me when I say I don't for one minute think you've got anything to do with these deaths,' said Rex. 'I'm just making an observation.'

'It's true that I didn't like Father,' Percy conceded, 'but I didn't have anything to do with his death.'

'Neither did I,' said Ruby stoutly, 'and I hope you aren't going to suggest that either of us had anything to do with his death.' She was more than a little peeved that her own father should suggest such a thing.

'Anyway, Percy wasn't around for Nelson's murder,' said Jim.

'I admit I left home in a huff,' said Percy, sitting back down again, 'but after I left the house, I never saw Father again.'

'What about George Gore?' said Rex. 'We were told that you were on the platform the day he died.'

'Rex,' said Bea helplessly. 'What are you saying?'

'I didn't even know George Gore,' said Percy.

'Fair enough,' said Rex apologetically. 'I don't know you, and no offence intended, but I think it was a reasonable question to ask.'

'Perhaps it's just as well that we didn't go to the police,' said Ruby sourly, 'especially if you were able to jump to the wrong conclusion so quickly.'

'I don't think they would have taken it very seriously anyway,' said Rex. 'With the best will in the world – even with the address book and the letter – all you have is circumstantial evidence. None of which would stand up in court.'

'And in the meantime,' said Jim, 'the firing squad is being picked off one by one.'

And the same person wishes you harm too, Ruby thought to herself.

'Which brings us neatly back to the real conundrum,' said Rex. 'Why on earth put a bullet in *your* bed?'

Ruby held her breath, but there was no answer to that. She glanced round the room and could see that, for everyone there, it was most unsettling. Ruby chewed the inside of her cheek. Should she tell them about seeing Albert? Now was the perfect moment.

They began to disperse. Bea had to say goodbye to Rex, because he faced a long drive back to Hastings, and Percy wanted to organize giving up his room in the attic for Rachel. He was determined to sleep on the kitchen floor.

Ruby joined in and took Rachel to her own room to get some spare bedding, while Bea and Rex said their goodbyes.

A few minutes later Ruby reappeared, saying, 'Oh, Mum, you'll never guess what.'

Rachel was looking very shaken. She was holding a piece of cloth, and tears were cascading down her cheeks.

'What did you say to her?' Percy demanded angrily as he came downstairs. He rushed to Rachel's side.

'Nothing,' Ruby protested. 'She saw John's place mat, that's all.'

'Place mat?' said Percy incredulously.

Rachel held it up. 'I recognized it at once,' she choked. 'It belonged to my sister.'

CHAPTER 41

Ruby had arranged to meet Edith during her breaktime. It was a fairly warm day, so they strolled towards the pier.

'So, how do you like married life?' Edith said, avoiding Ruby's eye.

'It's wonderful,' said Ruby.

'Really?'

Ruby smiled. 'It's not a bit like we imagined,' she said. 'You're not to think of you-know-what, but I promise you, you'll love it when you and Bernard are together.' The two friends linked arms and giggled.

'I heard about your mum's new beau,' said Edith. 'What's he like?'

'Lovely,' said Ruby.

'Where did she meet him?'

'If I tell you something,' Ruby began, 'I want you to promise you won't tell anyone else.'

'Go on,' said Edith, her eyes bright with excitement.

'Promise?' said Ruby.

'Promise,' said Edith, suddenly serious.

'Rex is my father,' said Ruby. Edith's jaw dropped. 'Yes, really. Nelson wasn't my father. Rex is.'

'Ooh, Roob,' said Edith.

They walked along Marine Parade, and, as Ruby told her the whole story, it was obvious that her friend was loving every minute. 'It's like a fairytale,' she sighed. 'So romantic.' And Ruby laughed.

They headed towards the bandstand. 'Oh, I nearly forgot,' cried Edith. 'Mrs Fosdyke is leaving.'

'Leaving?' Ruby gasped.

'They say she got the sack.'

Ruby's heart sank. Had Rex complained after all? 'Do you know where she's gone?'

'Well, she hasn't actually gone yet,' said Edith. 'She's working out her notice.'

'Then she can't have been sacked,' Ruby observed. 'If she'd been sacked, she would have gone straight away.' *Like I did,* she thought to herself.

'According to Winnie, she was asked to go,' said Edith. 'Apparently she was very rude to a guest.'

Ruby frowned, disappointment growing inside her. 'Who was it? Do you know?'

'Mrs Walter de Frece,' said Edith. 'I've never heard of her, but she used to be some sort of singer in the music halls years ago.'

'Vesta Tilly,' smiled Ruby with relief.

'The colonel has agreed to see us,' said Percy, putting the letter he'd just been reading back in the envelope. It had been waiting on the mantelpiece since it had arrived at the end of the week. 'Mosley is speaking in the pavilion on Tuesday.'

'I know,' said Ruby. 'The posters are all over town.'

'We're to be there at six on Monday – tomorrow,' Percy went on. 'Typical of the man; always considerate. He knew I'd probably be working

458

during the day.'

Ruby's reaction was one of relief. It was going to work out quite well. She would be seeing Albert again on Wednesday, so if anything new came up during the meeting with the colonel, she could tell him then.

They were alone in the kitchen at Newlands Road. Ruby was sorting photographs into their covers, labelling them clearly, ready for collection. There were a lot fewer now. Autumn was in the air and the warm days that had brought the day-trippers were all but over.

With Warwick Studios now closed, Jim hadn't been idle. He had secured a placement in Hubbard's to take a picture of every child who visited Father Christmas, and he'd persuaded a couple of local schools to let him spend half a day taking pictures of the pupils. It was a novel idea, but one that he hoped would mushroom, once the mothers began to show pictures of their children to relatives and friends.

Percy had come back for the weekend. The delivery business was doing well and he'd been able to take a couple of days away from London, because they had taken on more drivers. In the following weeks the firm was getting ready to branch out even further afield, with clients not only in the Jewish areas of London, but in the Home Counties as well, which meant Percy had plenty of work. He was becoming better off by the day, so much so that this time he had driven down to Worthing in his own car. He was here to take Rachel to Brighton, to meet Isaac. They had made contact after Bea wrote to John – as she still called him – and it had been arranged that the two of them should meet up straight away, but then John had been unwell. Now fully recovered, he was going to meet Percy and Rachel on Sunday afternoon.

Ruby turned her thoughts to getting the tea. 'Have you thought any more about finding Charlie Downs?'

'He seems to have vanished,' said Percy. 'I did as Rex suggested: I tried the British Legion and talked to a few of the old Sunny Worthing pals, but nobody seems to know anything about him.'

'Perhaps he went abroad,' Ruby suggested.

'Or died,' said Percy bleakly.

Ruby began laying the table. 'Where's Rachel gone?'

'She wanted to take a walk,' said Percy. 'She always feels cooped up after the Sabbath ends.'

'You could have gone with her.'

Percy sighed. 'Sometimes she just needs to be alone.'

Ruby squeezed her brother's shoulder. 'Poor girl.' She paused, then added, 'Has she ever told you what happened to her?'

Percy nodded. 'It's not a pretty story.' But, to Ruby's frustration, he didn't elaborate. 'It's funny being here without Mum and May.'

Ruby smiled. 'It was a lovely wedding, wasn't it?'

Bea had looked radiant. She had worn a cream-coloured plain satin sleeveless round-necked dress, which ended at the ankle. Around the shoulders it had a drape of Honiton lace, which was cinched at the waist under a wide satin waistband.

The Honiton lace then continued from the waist-band in a skirt that ended about six inches above the underdress. On her head she had a soft felt hat with a wide brim at the back, which tapered to a short brim at the front, and she carried a bouquet of creamy roses and blue delphiniums. Ruby and May had worn matching pale-blue dresses, while Rachel had worn a beautifully tailored lemon suit. Percy had never looked smarter, and Rex was resplendent in a bow tie. It seemed as if he had hoards of relatives and friends, who took over the whole of Warnes and a couple of other hotels in the town. Without exception, they were thrilled to see Rex happy at last.

'We knew he was pining for someone,' one woman told Ruby, 'but he never talked about her.'

'We thought she must have died,' her companion confided.

'He was alone for far too long,' her friend agreed. She clapped her hands in delight. 'And now he's found the love of his life again. I do so enjoy a happy ending, don't you?'

The door opened now and Rachel came in, her face flushed and her hair blown in the wind.

'Nice walk?' asked Ruby.

'I went to the pier,' she said as Percy took her coat from her and kissed her cold cheek. 'It looks as if they're building something on the end.'

'A new Southern Pavilion,' said Ruby, dishing up the potatoes. 'It caught fire last year. They've repaired the decking, but it's taken until now to decide what to do with it.'

'Dinner smells good,' Percy smiled.

They were eating fish, freshly caught and bought from Silas Reed on the beach. Ruby went to the back door and called Jim from the darkroom.

They went to Brighton on the new electric train. Rachel was very nervous, so Percy held her hand all the way. It seemed strange at first not to have a steam engine at the front of the train, with its huffing and puffing, but the ride itself was very smooth. The weather wasn't kind to them. It was a cold and wet day, but neither of them had much thought for the weather. Percy was worried that meeting her brother-in-law might be too upsetting for Rachel. She gave the outward appearance of being very tough, but Percy had seen her softer side and knew how much pain her sister's death had brought. They had made arrangements to meet at the station by the black gates.

As they alighted from the train, Percy could see John – who had now reverted to his proper name of Isaac – by the gate pier. He didn't come onto the platform to meet them, for that would have necessitated buying a platform ticket, so Rachel hurried towards him. Oblivious of Percy's presence, they stood in front of each other, overcome with emotion and unable to move. Eventually John held out his hands and Rachel put hers in his. Neither could speak.

'Let's go to the tea bar,' said Percy softly, and the pair allowed themselves to be guided to a table. He bought three teas and joined them. Rachel and Isaac spent some time trying to find the words, but eventually the memories came flooding back.

'You look so like her.'

'You haven't changed.'

When they lapsed into their native tongue, Percy could only sip his tea and hope that whatever Isaac was saying to Rachel wasn't too distressing for her.

Colonel Blatchington had left instructions that when Ruby and Percy arrived at Warnes, they were to be shown up to the Superior Suite, where he was staying. Although Ruby knew the way better than most, the porter escorted them to the lift.

Percy was still thinking about Rachel's reunion with her brother-in-law. It had been tearful and not a little painful for them both, as they remembered together her sister and nephew, his wife and child. When he was finally able to speak, Isaac had asked after Bea and Ruby, praising their kindness and telling everyone that he would be indebted to them for the rest of his life. He'd presented Percy with a hand-made pair of shoes for May and made him promise that, if they didn't fit, he would bring May over to Brighton for another pair.

The lift came and Scotty opened the doors.

'Hello,' Ruby said shyly. This was the second time she had come back to her old workplace as a guest, and each time she had found it slightly awkward meeting her old work colleagues.

Scotty smiled. 'Good evening, Miss.'

He closed them inside the lift and pulled the brass handle that operated it.

'How are you?'

'Very well, considering,' he said.

Percy and the porter had turned their backs to

face the door. When he was sure they couldn't see him, Scotty gave Ruby a friendly wink. The lift stopped, he opened the doors and they stepped out into the corridor. Mrs Fosdyke was checking behind a picture frame for dust. She inclined her head as the colonel walked by and stared stonily at Ruby as she passed her. Winnie was putting the finishing touches to a vase of flowers. She always did the big corridor displays *in situ*, as the vase, once filled with water, would be far too heavy to carry. She turned as Ruby and her brother headed for the Superior Suite, her only sign of recognition a slight nod of the head.

Colonel Blatchington was a big man. He was dressed in his BUF uniform and, as he opened the door of the Superior Suite, he snatched Percy's hand and slapped him heartily on the forearm. 'Good to see you, my boy,' he said, sneezing loudly. 'Come in, come in.'

He shook Ruby's hand politely and showed her to a seat. 'And you are?'

'My sister,' said Percy.

'Charmed, I'm sure, my dear,' said the colonel.

Ruby slid onto the high-backed chair and caressed the dark-red leather arms.

'Let me offer both of you a drink,' said the colonel, sneezing again. 'Damned flowers. Always make me sneeze.'

Percy took whiskey, and Ruby a small sherry.

Colonel Blatchington pulled out a big red handkerchief and blew his nose heartily. 'I'll have to get the blasted things taken away,' he said. He looked at Percy. 'Pity you left, old chap. You were a damned good organizer. Whole thing's going to pot without you.'

'Sorry, sir,' said Percy. 'I began to feel reservations about where we were going.'

'What d'you mean?' said the colonel, settling into another high-backed chair with a whiskey twice the size of Percy's. 'Explain yourself.'

'I hated the violence at the meetings,' said Percy.

The colonel pulled a face. 'Just troublemakers and Commies,' he said dismissively. 'Bound to make them come out of the woodwork.'

'My fiancée is Jewish,' said Percy.

'What's that got to do with anything?' the colonel boomed.

'Things are changing in the BUF,' said Percy. 'When I first joined, every person's opinion was valued and everyone was welcome. It doesn't seem to be that way any more.'

'We have to protect ourselves, dear boy,' said the colonel. 'Look what's happening in the East End. The BUF wanted to march through the streets, but it's been impossible. People from different religions – foreigners and troublemakers – have put a stop to free speech.'

'By "people from different religions" you mean the Jewish community,' said Percy.

'If the cap fits, my boy. If the cap fits.'

Ruby gave a little cough. This wasn't what they were here for.

'Sir,' said Percy, leaning forward slightly, 'with all due respect, we didn't come here to discuss the movement, or my leaving. Ruby and I came to warn you.'

'Warn me?' said the colonel, suddenly on edge.

465

'What about?'

'It's a little difficult, and we no longer have any tangible evidence,' Percy went on, 'but we are greatly concerned for your safety.'

Colonel Blatchington had a slightly bemused expression on his face. 'Go on, go on,' he said.

Ruby took up the story, beginning with Nelson's death, George Gore's accident and finally Linton Carver's murder.

'At one time we had Linton's confession,' said Percy, 'but it's been stolen.'

'Confession? What confession – and what's all this got to do with me?'

'Sir, you may remember being the CO in 1915 when a man was shot for desertion,' said Percy. 'That man was called Victor. He took off one day and smashed up his rifle.'

Colonel Blatchington suddenly paled. 'Good God! Yes, I remember that. Damned unfair, if you ask me. I would have let him go with a punishment, but a missive came through from HQ that Field Marshal Haig believed that the death sentence in such cases would serve as a deterrent to others.'

'We believe someone else is exacting retribution for his death,' said Percy. 'We cannot name that person, but we both – that is, the whole of my family – feel that you should be on your guard.'

The colonel looked thoughtful, then leaned forward and looked Percy in the eye. 'Tell me again, Bateman. I want to take this in.'

They spent another half-hour talking over what had happened. Then, looking at his watch, the colonel thanked them, saying that he had to be elsewhere. As he got up he promised Percy that he would take his concerns very seriously, and then he saw them out of the room.

Out in the corridor Winnie was packing up her things. The colonel went with them to the lift and sneezed loudly. Percy pressed the lift button.

'Come one more time to hear Mosley,' he said, getting the voluminous red handkerchief out of his pocket again and blowing his nose. 'We need dedicated people like you.'

Percy thanked him, but promised nothing. The lift was still on its way.

'I'd better get on the phone to tell them to get rid of those damned flowers,' said the colonel, having sneezed for a third time. 'Goodbye, my dear,' he said to Ruby and gave her hand a much more gentle shake. 'Nice to have met you.'

Ruby turned to face Winnie at the other end of the corridor. At the same moment her wedding florist turned round and they both inclined their heads. The lift arrived and Ruby heard the sound of opening doors.

Behind her the colonel leaned forwards and said confidentially, 'Look after them, Charles.'

Scotty saluted smartly. 'I will, sir. Thank you, sir.'

'Good man. Good man.'

Ruby stepped into the lift and turned to face Winifred Moore, who was absent-mindedly stuffing another flower into an already overfilled vase. They both started as Mrs Fosdyke came out of one of the bedrooms. Ruby glanced up at the men beside her, but the colonel and Percy were busy pumping each other's hands. As she turned back

467

to look at the two women, Ruby saw Winnie's mouth tighten. She patted her hair as she picked up her florist's bucket to go down the back stairs. In front of her and with her back to Winnie, Mrs Fosdyke watched Ruby with a dark expression.

Deeply disturbed by what she had just seen, Ruby fixed her eyes on the floor. She felt shaken and upset, and there was something about that woman that she couldn't quite put her finger on... But by the time they reached the ground floor, she knew what it was.

CHAPTER 42

'And I'm telling you, it's her.'

'You can't possibly mean it?'

Ruby could tell by the tone of his voice that Jim found it almost impossible to believe.

'You didn't see the look on her face,' Ruby insisted. 'I'd bet everything in my Post Office book it was her.'

'What – all of it?' Jim grinned. 'All two pounds three and sixpence?'

Ruby gave him a playful swipe on his arm. 'It's all I have in the world.'

'She doesn't look like a murderer,' Percy observed.

'They don't come with "Murderer" tattooed on their foreheads, you know,' said Ruby.

'Weren't you afraid that Winnie might attack the colonel with her florist's wire, while he was on his way back to his room?' said Jim with a grin.

'You have pooh-poohed this at every turn, Jim Searle,' Ruby said indignantly. 'When are you going to take me seriously? I'm telling you, she is the killer.'

Jim reached for her, but Ruby pulled away. 'I had hoped you would support me in this.'

Immediately he looked contrite. 'You're right,' he said, 'and I'm sorry, darling.'

'Maybe you *are* right,' said Percy. 'It just seems so unbelievable that a woman who looks like everybody's grandma could—'

'She certainly doesn't look like any grandma I'd ever want!' cried Ruby. She suddenly looked thoughtful and grabbed Percy's arm. 'What was she doing there?'

'Sorry,' said Percy, 'you've lost me.'

'When we went in to see Colonel Blatchington, she was hovering about in the corridor,' said Ruby. 'We were with him for at least three-quarters of an hour, and yet she was still there when we came out.'

'You mean she must have been listening through the door?' said Jim.

'Exactly,' replied Ruby. 'Do you think we should go back and tell him?'

Jim shook his head. 'I don't think that's a good idea.'

Ruby tut-tutted.

'No, listen, darling,' he protested. 'We've already told him everything we know, without having any actual physical proof. He listened out of respect for Percy, but if you voice yet another unsubstantiated accusation, the colonel might think you're a bit of a crank.'

'But we can't just leave it there!' cried Ruby. 'If something happened to him, I'd never forgive myself.'

'Let's go to the meeting and keep an eye on him,' said Percy. 'He'll be safe enough in the hotel. She's only a middle-aged woman; the colonel's a fighting man and quite able to look after himself.'

'If what I think is correct,' Ruby observed, 'she's already dispatched three other men.'

'But with them she had the element of surprise,' said Jim.

Ruby nodded dully. 'I suppose you're right,' she said.

The next day there was a real buzz in the air. All day motor vehicles were touring the streets with men carrying loudhailers encouraging people to come to the pavilion for the meeting: 'Your chance to meet the man who will bring back the "Great" in Great Britain.' 'Come and hear the country's next prime minister.' 'Meet Mosley in person – the people's choice.' Towards the end of the day the coaches arrived, lining up nose-to-tail all along Marine Parade, and an impromptu carnival atmosphere began. It was wonderful for Jim. The late-autumn sunshine drew people to the beach and he took a lot of Magic Memories snaps.

Because Bea was already living with her new husband in Hastings, Ruby had responsibility for manning the booth. She packed up at noon and went back home to develop as many pictures as possible, before returning later on, to get as many sales as she could. The light was fading by three-thirty or four o'clock, so Jim was on hand to help. It was a very busy day and they finally closed the booth at five forty-five. There was barely time to get back home with the equipment and be back before the start of the meeting in the pavilion. Ruby mashed some cooked potatoes with some leftover cabbage and fried it up to make bubble-and-squeak.

With a couple of rashers of bacon and an egg, that had to suffice for their tea. There was no time for anything else.

She wore a warm coat as they left the house, and took an old shawl to put round her shoulders, if necessary. It could get cold down by the sea in the evenings. Ruby's heart sank when she saw the crowds waiting outside. People were already standing four or five deep near the steps, and more were coming. They weren't all Mosley supporters. Some had come with home-made placards of a very different nature: *Mosley out; Say no to Hitler's lapdog;* and *No to Fascism.* Others were singing a parody, 'Poor Old Mosley's Got the Wind Up', to the tune of 'John Brown's Body'. How on earth were they going to spot the murderer amongst this lot? The people with tickets to hear Mosley speak poured into the pavilion endlessly.

The meeting was billed for seven-thirty. Ruby managed to get to the top of the steps on one side, while Jim waited at the bottom on the other side. At seven-fifteen a cheer went up. A group of thickset Blackshirts walked up the steps and positioned themselves alongside it, and before long a tall man made his way to the doors. Ruby had

471

never seen Mosley close up before; she'd only ever seen his poster. He wore a neatly trimmed moustache and had small, piercing brown eyes. At the top of the steps he turned and waved to the crowd. Colonel Blatchington hurried up the steps behind him and they all went inside.

The crowd jostled and re-formed itself. Some chanted slogans and others left, presumably for the public houses. Barnes cafe opposite was doing a roaring trade, as was the fish-and-chip shop further along the road.

Percy turned up, and Ruby came down the steps to meet him. 'Seen her yet?' he asked.

Ruby shook her head. 'Jim's waiting down there – maybe he has.'

'He says not,' said Percy. 'I'm beginning to think this is a wild goose chase, Ruby. Perhaps we've all got carried along with the spirit of adventure. I can't afford to keep taking time off work. I've worked too hard to get where I am to risk losing it.'

Ruby nodded. 'I think you might be right. If we hadn't found that bullet in our bed, none of this would be happening.'

'Shall we give up then?'

Ruby looked thoughtful. With all these big bodyguards about, nobody seemed to be in any danger anyway. Perhaps they should give up. Maybe she'd let her imagination run away with her. She was seeing Albert again tomorrow. Maybe he'd found Charlie Downs.

'Don't be too hard on yourself, Sis,' said Percy. 'You were only trying to help.'

Fuelled by meat pies and beer, the counterdemonstrators were drifting back. Before long Ruby, Jim and Percy would be wedged in and unable to get home.

'Home?' said Percy again.

'All right,' she said. 'I'm dog-tired anyway.'

She had left her shawl at the top of the railings and turned back to fetch it. All at once the doors opened and two of the Blackshirts came out and stood on either side. The sound of a fanfare came from inside the building, and she heard the roar of the faithful. Their leader was leaving. The crowd, taken completely by surprise, surged forward in a dangerous wave. An egg landed on the steps near Ruby's feet, and the angry shouts grew louder. More Blackshirts came out and formed a guard on the steps, as other leading lights of the movement came down them. These included William Joyce and Worthing's only Fascist member of the Borough Council, Councillor Charles Bentinck Budd. As yet there was no sign of Mosley or Colonel Blatchington. Ruby blinked as she saw Mrs Fosdyke standing on the steps opposite. Ruby grabbed her shawl, but now she was wedged between the railings and the frenzied mob, and the press of people made it difficult to breathe. She shouted for them to stop pushing, but her voice was lost in the volume of noise all around her.

Somebody must have hit one of the bodyguards in the back, because he suddenly turned round and threw a punch into the crowd. The woman next to Ruby was hit full in the face. Ruby heard something crack – probably her nose being broken – as the woman fell against her arm with a scream. It seemed for a minute that there was blood everywhere. As she fumbled in her bag for a handkerchief, Ruby remonstrated with the Blackshirt, but he had already turned his back on the crowd and had linked arms with his colleagues on either side of him.

More people came out of the building and the crowd surged forward again. Mosley descended the steps, flanked by the two bodyguards, who lost no time at all in pushing and shoving people out of the way. Ruby saw women and children being as roughly handled as the men. She still had her arm around the injured woman, who had pressed her handkerchief against her nose. By now the poor thing was sobbing with pain. Ruby felt something strange moving by her leg and looked down. To her horror, she saw Winifred Moore on all fours. At first she thought she must have fallen over, but then she realized that Winnie was holding an umbrella, which she had surreptitiously poked between the legs of two of the bodyguards. At the same time Ruby heard a sinister, disembodied voice saying, 'That's right, Freddie, my love. He's coming down the steps. Do it now!'

Ruby's mind was struggling to understand what was unfolding. The colonel suddenly staggered, a sudden pain making him fall – Winnie had jabbed the umbrella into his right leg with considerable force. He tumbled against the men in front of him, veering sideways as he tried to grab the rail, and taking several others down with him. Mosley was way ahead and had escaped injury, but when the momentum finally stopped, there was what seemed like a pile of bodies at the bottom of the steps. Everybody was screaming and shouting, and the guards rushed down the steps after the colonel while, on the other side of the steps, Mrs Fosdyke simply watched.

While Ruby had been helping the injured woman beside her, a man had pushed his way towards them. 'Lizzie, what happened?' Ruby explained briefly. The couple thanked her, and the man led the way through the crowd, to get her to a first-aid post. Once they'd gone, Ruby scanned the crowd for another sight of Winifred Moore. She eventually saw her further down the steps, holding onto the rail and looking rather shaken. Once again Ruby heard the same disembodied voice: 'You've done it all, my darling. Well done. It's over. Come to me, Freddie. I'm waiting.'

Freddie? That was the name Victor had called out, the moment before he died. Everyone had thought it was his brother, but now at last it dawned on Ruby: it must have been Winifred's name, and 'Freddie' was a nickname.

Ruby spun round, searching for whoever was speaking. Where was Mrs Fosdyke? The strange voice must be hers. The crowd, more subdued now, was moving away from the steps, and the cafe across the road had become the centre of attention. Some local boys were throwing tomatoes at the windows, and then Ruby heard the sound of breaking glass. In the distance she saw Mrs Fosdyke crossing the road, probably aiming for the bus stop. Ruby frowned. So that strange voice didn't come from her. Winifred Moore stumbled away in the opposite direction. Ruby heard Percy call her own name, but she was still scanning the crowd for that voice. All at once it was as if the rest of the people fell away, and she saw him. As their eyes met, she whispered out loud, 'My God, Albert Longman!'

Then it all came flooding back. That day when they'd been at High Salvington, when he'd done such a brilliant job of amusing the children. Everybody had said how clever Albert was at throwing his voice. Hadn't he made the children really believe that the furry mouse was in the wood-pile? And not only the children, but the adults too. She wondered what his connection with the firing squad could be, but there was no time for that now. Winnie was moving down the steps with a great sense of purpose, but where was she going? As she reached the bottom, she turned and Ruby felt the panic rising in her chest. She was heading for the pier. 'Come to me, Freddie...' the voice had said. Oh God ... he wanted Winnie to kill herself, didn't he? But why? Why? Calling her name, Ruby ran after her. By the time she'd turned the corner, Winifred was climbing over the locked gate leading to the half repaired pier with an agility that Ruby had never seen in a woman of her age.

'Winnie – no! Come back.'

Ruby heard more footsteps, this time behind her. A cold fear enveloped her. Albert must have followed them. The pier was hardly the place to be wandering about in the dark. The decking had been replaced, and work was under way at the sea end on a new Southern Pavilion to mirror the one on Marine Parade, but the area was loosely fenced and a large quantity of building materials was stacked there, waiting for the work to begin.

A night-watchman had been sitting huddled in his hut on the concrete surround near the gate. Obviously, hearing the sound of running, he'd come out with a mug of tea in his hands and now spotted three people heading for the building site.

'Oi,' he shouted. 'You can't go down there.'

Ruby turned for a second to shout, 'Get help. She's going to jump.'

It was pitch-black at the end of the pier, but Ruby could still make out Winifred's shape. She was leaning over the railings, looking at the sea crashing below. The pier wasn't shaking or rocking, so Ruby knew the structure itself was sound, but there was several feet of surging water underneath and, if Winnie jumped, there was little anyone could do to save her. Ruby stopped a few yards behind her.

'Winnie, wait,' she said. 'You don't need to do this.'

She turned and looked at Ruby, as if seeing her for the first time. Her expression was one of bewilderment and she put her hand to her head. Behind them Albert's footsteps slowed and stopped, and Ruby heard that same sinister voice again: 'Freddie, I'm here in the water, waiting for you.'

Winifred turned back and stared down at the heaving, inky waters below.

The hairs on Ruby's neck stood up and everything fell into place. 'Stop it, you bloody blighter,' she shouted at Albert, and turning back to Winnie she said, 'Don't listen to him, Winnie. That's not your Victor. Victor is dead.'

'Too late, Ruby,' said Albert in his normal voice.

Winnie put one hand on the rail. 'No!' cried Ruby. 'Listen to me. He's a fake. It's not real.'

Winnie hesitated, so Albert began again: 'Come, my love...'

Ruby went back and hit him on the shoulder. 'This isn't funny. Stop it, stop it.' He caught her wrists as she pounded his chest. 'You rat,' she hissed. 'I confided in you!'

She was relieved to hear the night-watchman puffing towards them, the light from his torch spilling all around them.

Caught between the two of them – the one she wanted to save and the one who was scaring her half to death – Ruby's mouth was dry and her heart was beating wildly. 'How could you do this to another human being?'

Albert suddenly bent her wrist, painfully. 'It could have all been so different,' he said menacingly next to her ear. 'If you had loved me, Ruby, I would have stopped. None of this would have happened.'

Now she was furious. 'Don't you dare blame me,' she said angrily. 'You're sick, Albert Longman. Whatever you did was your own choice. You manipulated that poor woman to murder three men. Whatever did she do to you to deserve that?'

Even in the gloom she saw Albert's expression darken. 'What did she do to me?' he said, with venom in his voice. 'She never had time for me. I'm her son, but she rejected me. All she ever wanted was *him* – Victor. So when he died, she got rid of me. What do you think of that, eh? My own mother.'

It was a shock to hear what he was saying, but Ruby was still very aware of the broken wretch who stood by the railings, waiting to end her own life. She tried to wrench her wrist away from Albert. 'That's no excuse,' she said. 'When your father died, she was most likely out of her mind with grief.'

'You should have loved me, Ruby,' he said. 'All I wanted was you.'

His head came down and he tried to kiss her. She pushed him angrily away. 'So much so that you even threatened my Jim!' she cried. 'You're despicable, and I could never love a person like you, not in a million years.'

'Come on, son,' said the night-watchman, reaching out and grabbing Albert's sleeve. 'Get away from the edge. It's not safe.'

With a roar of rage, Albert flung his arm back, sending the man sprawling. The watchman fell against a pile of scaffolding poles, which clanked together and then started to roll. As the man did his best to scramble out of the way, Albert was caught slightly off-balance, and Ruby was able to pull her wrist away and turn her attention to Winnie, who was still standing with one hand on the railings and the other on her head. Ruby grabbed Winnie's arm to pull her away, as Albert, with his back to the poles, came towards them. In that moment Ruby could tell by his face that he intended to push them both over the edge. But as the night-watchman staggered to his feet, he set another pole on the move. It hit the back of Albert's leg and he was propelled forward. Ruby and Winifred made a dive in the opposite direction, but the poles gathered velocity until Albert was pinned against the railings. The night-watchman tried to stop them, but still the poles kept coming. Finally, Albert let out an ear-piercing yell and disappeared over the edge. The weight of steel had made the ornamental mesh covering the railings give way, and they heard his body smash against one of the girders and splash into the water below. Several more poles followed him.

The night-watchman leaned over the rail helplessly. 'Good God! He's gone.'

Ruby had her arms around Winnie, who seemed disorientated and confused. They could hear more footsteps running along the pier. The night-watchman was beside himself. 'Get away,' he shouted, waving his torch. 'This is council property. You shouldn't be here. I shall lose my job. Some bloke has already gone over the edge.'

People reached out for Winifred and Ruby, and they all began to walk back along the boards. As they approached the middle of the pier Ruby heard her name being called. Thank God – it was Percy.

'You'd better come quickly, Ruby,' he said breathlessly, as he finally caught up with her. 'When all that lot fell down the steps, your Jim was underneath.'

CHAPTER 43

The new Southern Pavilion was well worth waiting for. Ruby had enjoyed the razzamatazz of the official opening and now, alongside hundreds of others, she was taking her first stroll with her mother, Rachel and May.

They reached an ice-cream kiosk part of the way down.

'Can I have an ice cream, Mummy?' May asked.

Bea reached for her handbag, but Ruby put her hand on her mother's arm. 'No, Mum. Let me, this is my treat. We'll get one in the tea room.'

They walked up the steps and into the beautiful art deco restaurant. It was busy and there was a hum of conversation as people sat chatting at the tables. At one side, behind an array of large potted ferns, there was a grand piano and a pianist played softly. Ruby looked around and spotted one table that was free. It was in a prime position, next to the bay window overlooking the place where the sea-anglers cast their rods. The 'Reserved' sign in the middle of the table beckoned. As she pulled out a chair and sat down, it was hard to believe that this was the same place where Albert Longman had gone to his watery grave less than a year ago. Despite her best intentions not to dwell on it, her thoughts went back to that dark night and all that had happened since.

Winifred Moore had been taken to hospital of

course, but thankfully she had suffered no physical damage. The damage to her mind was a lot worse, however, and it seemed that she might never be fully well again. Because of her crimes, she had been placed in a secure unit and, although she wasn't really sure she believed it, Ruby had been told that she would be well looked after. Winnie was utterly convinced that her dead husband had wanted her to dispatch the men who were responsible for his death.

'No one knew my secret name,' she would tell anyone who was willing to listen. 'As soon as he called me "Freddie", I knew it was him.'

No one knew her nickname, except a little boy who was eleven at the time of his father's death. The police traced what had happened to Albert. He had been adopted (hence the different surname), but it hadn't been a happy move. His new father was horribly strict, and this eventually fanned Albert's hatred of his mother into flame.

When he fell on the pavilion steps, Colonel Blatchington had suffered no more than a puncture wound on his leg where the umbrella went in, and a few bruises. Albert's plan had been for him to fall the length of the concrete steps, which would have resulted in serious injury. Fortunately for the colonel, he had fallen on top of other people. He was a bit shaken up, but everyone agreed it could have been a lot worse. After the Worthing incident and the riotous behaviour that followed, Mosley and his cohorts were arrested. The case went as far as Lewes Assizes, where – after clever representation by slick London lawyers – it was eventually dismissed. It was all too much for the colonel, who retired soon afterwards.

As Ruby gazed out of the window, Rachel – now married to Percy and four months pregnant – slid into the chair opposite. The waitress arrived. 'We're all having afternoon tea,' said Ruby. 'I booked it. The name is Searle.'

'Shall I bring it now?'

'Give us five minutes, dear,' said Bea. 'There are a few more to come.'

The waitress turned to go.

'When you come back,' Ruby called after her, 'can you bring an ice cream for the little girl?'

The waitress nodded and May beamed.

'I'd better take you to the toilet,' Bea told May.

'I'm coming too,' said Rachel.

Left on her own, Ruby took in the view from the window. Not only could she see the anglers, but if she turned her head slightly, the beautiful bow-window gave her a view of the coastline. The sea sparkled in the warm sunlight and people were bathing in the water. A Punch-and-Judy man had set up his booth on the beach, and children sat in front of it, patiently waiting for the show to start. She smiled to herself. How she loved this place, with the Dome cinema staring out to sea and, a little further along the coast, the magnificent Warnes Hotel, where she'd once worked.

Her thoughts drifted back to Albert Longman, and she recalled the shock and horror she'd felt when the police told her what they had found at Albert's house. He'd kept a meticulous wall chart, chronicling the demise of each of his victims. It gradually came to light that Albert had used his mother for each of the killings, with the exception of Uncle Jack Harris, whose death really was a tragic accident, thus making Winnie just as much a victim as those she had killed. In her fragile state of mind, Winnie was better than a gun or a knife to him. Her devotion to her husband had made her putty in her son's hands, and as soon as Albert spoke in that imitation voice, she became like an automaton and did whatever he wanted. It was only as Winnie patted her hair in the hotel corridor that day when Ruby had met Colonel Blatchington that she had put two and two together. As she went down in the lift, Ruby remembered the person she had thought was Percy, in the darkened street the day Nelson died. He or she was patting his or her head in exactly the same way. She also remembered that lone woman she'd seen at Nelson's funeral and realized that that person wasn't Mrs Fosdyke but Winifred Moore, the first time on her way to the boat to murder Nelson and the second time to enjoy their grief.

Ruby explained all this to the police, telling them how cleverly Albert had thrown his voice to amuse the children at High Salvington. Back then it had been a bit of fun. Who could have guessed that he was already putting his talents to a much more sinister use?

She looked around the restaurant. It was so tastefully done, and well worth the wait. Ruby loved the art deco gallery and the potted ferns dotted around the room. Her mother, her sister-in-law and May were coming back now. She smiled warmly. What a year this had been.

Jim had been in hospital for weeks, and his recovery was very slow. Both legs were broken and he'd suffered crush injuries. She remembered how she and Percy had run through the streets to get to the hospital on Lyndhurst Road that night. No chance of getting a bus or a taxi, with the rioters spilling out onto the street all around the pavilion and along Marine Parade.

When she arrived at the hospital, Ruby had waited anxiously while Jim was in theatre for an operation to fix his legs, only to be dragged away by the police to answer their questions. She'd returned the next day, exhausted, but relieved to know that her husband had survived the procedure.

The next few months were far from easy. As far as Jim's health was concerned, there was the ever-present fear of infection. The operation on his legs had been so difficult that the doctors feared he would never walk again. Jim had been devastated and had had to battle depression as well.

Her mother and May had returned to Worthing to help, and Rex had sold up his practice by the sea and come to join them. He now had a GP's practice in Heene. He had been such a wonderful support and, because Jim was related to him, it was obvious that he was getting the very best of care.

Without Jim at the helm, the photography business had to be put on hold. Now Ruby was left with the problem of how to make a living. When the doctors said Jim might never walk again, Mabel did something rather wonderful; she gave Ruby Linton's cottage, which, with a lot of hard work and plenty of help from friends and neighbours, Ruby turned into a guest house, with

Mabel as a sleeping partner. That meant she could rent out the house in Newlands Road, to generate more income.

'She's nothing if not gutsy, that girl of yours,' Mabel told Bea.

Ruby wasn't afraid of hard work and, with the guest house now up and running, she was happy. She might never get to see those places Imogen had told her about, when she'd sent her post-cards, but she wouldn't swap what she had for anything in the world.

The pianist began to play Connie Boswell's song 'Blue Moon' and Ruby found herself humming along.

Those postcards she'd received from Miss Russell were all in an old shoe box up in the loft, but she hadn't heard from her for ages. She was probably married herself now, maybe with children of her own. Ruby hoped she was happy. Life moved on, and her dear friend Edith was now only a year away from the moment when she could marry Bernard from the bacon counter. Ruby smiled to herself. He was an under-manager now, but somehow, to Ruby, he would always be 'Bernard from the bacon counter'.

She hummed a little more. The past few months had been far from easy but Ruby was luckier than most. Like the words of the song, she really had found someone to care for.

The only loose end from all the events of the past year and a half was finding Charlie Downs. Everybody hoped he was safe. And then one night Ruby had woken with a start. She suddenly remembered the lift operator at Warnes. He was

486

an old soldier. They'd always called him 'Scotty', but Ruby recalled that Colonel Blatchington had called him 'Charles'. She'd had to wait a while, until she next saw Edith, to ask her if she could find out his name, and, sure enough, Scotty's real name was Charles Downs. With Albert gone and Winifred in hospital, he was safe and sound, so Ruby decided there was no point in telling him everything. But it made her smile to think that he was there all the time, right under their noses, and they never knew.

She heard a slight commotion by the restaurant door and looked up, fearing the worst. The waitress was on her way down, but most likely they couldn't get Jim's wheelchair through the door. She rose to her feet and waved, so that they would know where the table was. Her wave died in mid-air. Rex and Percy were moving very slowly, because Jim stood between them. He had two sticks and he looked a bit wobbly, but he was walking ... walking with his head held high. Ruby drew in her breath and put her hand to her mouth.

'He's been practising for ages, so that he could do this for you,' Bea said quietly as Ruby gaped in astonishment. 'We've all been sworn to secrecy – even May.'

Her little sister looked up at Ruby, her face shining. Tears welled in Ruby's eyes. Then she heard the pianist strike up 'Happy Birthday', and every eye in the restaurant was upon her. When Jim finally stood right in front of her, everybody began to clap spontaneously.

'Bravo, Jim!' cried Rex.

'Happy birthday, darling,' said Jim, handing Bea his walking sticks. He held out a brightly coloured box. 'I hope you like your present.'

Ruby knew whatever he'd given her in the box would be lovely, but the best present in the world was seeing him walking towards her. Her blue moon had just turned to gold.

ACKNOWLEDGEMENTS

Firstly, I would like to thank Bettina Sands, who kindly checked the German text in the story. Thanks Bettina, you're a star! I should also like to thank my editors, Caroline Hogg and Victoria Hughes-Williams, for their skilful talents and, most of all, for their encouragement. The genuine stuff – not just flattery – is like gold dust to a writer, and they have been very generous. Also, I can't miss an opportunity to thank my agent, Juliet Burton. I'm running out of clichés with which to thank her, but she has helped to make this journey a truly enjoyable one.

The publishers hope that this book has given you enjoyable reading. Large Print Books are especially designed to be as easy to see and hold as possible. If you wish a complete list of our books please ask at your local library or write directly to:

Magna Large Print Books
Magna House, Long Preston,
Skipton, North Yorkshire.
BD23 4ND

This Large Print Book for the partially sighted, who cannot read normal print, is published under the auspices of

THE ULVERSCROFT FOUNDATION